OUTSTA[illegible]
MAUREEN C[illegible]

FINDING YOU/KNOWING YOU

"An absolutely wonderful contemporary romance. A delightful blend of humor and emotion, this sexy love story will definitely keep readers turning the pages."

—Kristin Hannah, author of *Distant Shores*

"The Candellano family is warm and wonderful . . . you'll get swept up in the lives and loves of these passionate and fascinating individuals."

—*Romantic Times*

"Delightful romances involving colorful and yet realistic characters make these two stories by Maureen Child a veritable feast for the eyes. The large Italian family of the Candellanos is very convincing and the characterizations are so mature and honest that the author is to be applauded for such skillful crafting and accurate portrayal . . . the heartfelt emotions leap from the pages, and the delicately blended humor and pathos render these stories memorable . . . after the exhilarating first story, readers will feel compelled to read the other one too, and neither disappoints. Maureen Child is an author to watch out for."

—*The Road to Romance*

MORE . . .

"A fresh tale of family, conflict, and love . . . the characters are endearing."

—*Old Book Barn Gazette*

"Both of these novels are engaging contemporary romances with a warm ensemble that feels like the kitchen of many readers. The story lines will hook readers because the characters seem genuine and friendly."

—Harriet's Book Review

LOVING YOU

"Maureen Child always writes a guaranteed winner, and this is no exception. Heartwarming, sexy, and impossible to put down."

—Susan Mallery, author of *Married for a Month*

ST. MARTIN'S PAPERBACKS TITLES
BY MAUREEN CHILD

Finding You

Knowing You

Loving You

SOME KIND OF WONDERFUL

MAUREEN CHILD

St. Martin's Paperbacks

SOME KIND OF WONDERFUL

ISBN: 0-312-98727-7

Printed in the United States of America

St. Martin's Paperbacks edition / January 2004

St. Martin's Paperbacks are published by St. Martin's Press, 175 Fifth Avenue, New York, NY 10010.

10 9 8 7 6 5 4 3 2 1

Chapter 1

Baby Jesus moved.

Carol Baker blinked and shook her head. "Okay, Carol. When you start seeing statues move, it's either a miracle or . . . you've got problems." She stared hard at the brightly lit, life-sized Nativity scene that filled one corner of the town square. Then she added thoughtfully, "Of course, when you start talking to yourself on top of it, that's a whole *new* set of problems."

Her Irish wolfhound, Quinn, strained at his leash, eager to continue his nightly romp through town. Carol jerked to one side in an effort to hold him back—no small task, since he tipped the scales at almost a hundred and fifty pounds. She stared harder, holding her breath as if that would help her see better.

But there was nothing.

No more movement.

No sound.

"Hold on, you big moose."

Quinn stopped and threw her a glance over his big shoulder. Cocking his head, he looked at her as if to say, "Come on, what's the holdup? There're trees to smell and bushes to pee on and I've only got so much time here."

Carol chuckled, then caught another flicker of movement from the corner of her eye. "Okay, Baby Jesus is definitely moving." Her stomach fluttered with a weird little pitch and roll. *What the hell is going on?* She looked at the huge, gray dog. "Plaster statues rarely move, just in case you didn't know, so this is truly something weird."

Quinn didn't seem to care.

That made one of them.

"So, either we go wake up Father Reilly to document a miracle, or we alert the *Enquirer*." She shifted her gaze back to the Nativity, just ten short feet away. "But either way, we really ought to get a closer look, huh?"

Everyday life was a little different when you lived in Christmas, California. Here, Carol told herself, where the Spirit of Christmas thrived 365 days a year, *all* things were possible.

Still, statues that moved on their own would be of some interest, even in Christmas.

Carol knew Christmas like the back of her hand—and she loved every square inch of it. Had from the very beginning. She'd seen the place first as a tourist, but she'd known immediately that this was the place for her. It hadn't taken her long to go back to LA, quit her job, sell her condo near the beach, and move back to the place that kept Christmas alive all year round.

In the two years she'd lived there, she'd made it a point to become a part of the town. She knew every single strand of lights, every candy cane hanging from every light pole, every favorite haunt of the tourists—who were a constant stream into town—and she knew every shop owner by their first names. She went to the city council meetings, volunteered whenever she had the chance, and hired as many local part-time workers for her own shop as she could afford.

Christmas had a sense of community, a sense of . . . *family*, that made it almost the proverbial small town. It was what people always thought a small town *should* be. A slice of life straight out of a Currier & Ives painting—minus the snow, of course. Everyone in Christmas knew everything about everybody else.

That's why she *knew* that the Nativity scene was *not* animatronic.

The plaster statues that sat, year round, in the town square didn't move. They didn't wave to the tourists who posed within the life-sized manger, draping friendly arms across Joseph's shoulders; the statues didn't shift position when they grew tired of kneeling. Didn't stretch and yawn as plaster muscles cramped from disuse. Didn't get bored with the whole "stuck in a straw-filled manger" thing and go to Tahiti on a whim. Which meant, Carol told herself, the night had just taken a sharp turn toward the Twilight Zone. She shivered, despite the lingering heat in the night.

A long strand of blond-streaked hair flew across her eyes, and she whipped it back and out of her way. She glanced around at the surrounding shadows and wondered if someone was out there now, watching her. Strange prickles of sensation crawled along her neck and down her spine. Mouth dry, she realized that this was the first time since coming to Christmas that she'd been the least bit . . . edgy.

Not scared, of course. That would be dumb. Nothing ever happened in Christmas. So what was there to be scared *of*?

Quinn whined piteously and Carol almost joined him.

Baby Jesus *had* moved.

But this was no miracle.

Well, okay, it was a miracle, but not the kind that made headlines in the tabloids or anything.

This was one of those everyday miracles that most people tended to take for granted.

An honest-to-God, real-live baby lay swaddled—she was pretty sure that was the word—in the straw-filled wooden cradle.

Stunned, Carol dropped the bright red leash and Quinn moved closer to the cradle. His big head was nearly the same size as the baby, but Carol wasn't worried. Quinn was the epitome of an Irish wolfhound. A gentle giant. And true to his nature, Quinn walked silently to the baby's side, carefully snuffled its little head, then promptly sat down beside it, as if ready to stand guard. Carol smiled, but couldn't take her eyes off the baby.

The infant squirmed, screwed up its tiny red features, and let out a mighty . . . *whimper*. Its impossibly small fists raged against the air and its little legs kicked at the pale yellow blanket wrapped around them. The baby looked pretty ticked off, and truth to tell, Carol really couldn't blame it. Not exactly a warm welcome into the world, she thought and took a step closer even as she looked around at the quiet, empty town square.

A baby didn't just crawl across the grass, toss Baby Jesus out of his bed, and climb into it himself! It had had help. But who? Who in Christmas would have abandoned a brand-new baby? And maybe more importantly, where were they now?

Another thready cry erupted from the baby and brought Carol back to the moment at hand. "What am I talking about, huh? Who left you behind doesn't matter, does it?" she half-crooned as she went down on one knee in the dewy grass. Dampness soaked into her faded Levi's, but she didn't even feel it. "You're the important one here, aren't you?" Reaching out, Carol tugged the thin yellow blanket up over the baby's narrow, naked chest and let her fingers linger there just long enough to feel its racing heartbeat.

Her heart ached. And her hands itched to hold it. But maybe she shouldn't pick it up. Maybe she should call the police or something. Damn it. A baby. Left alone. In the dark.

Quinn lowered his massive head until his hairy chin was resting on the edge of the cradle. The baby's flailing fists made contact with the dog's nose, but Quinn didn't even flinch. Instead, he sighed, deeply enough to flutter the blanket.

"Okay," she said softly, mentally dismissing thoughts of waiting around here for the police. "I know you don't know me or anything, but I'm going to pick you up now, okay?" The baby squirmed and shook its little fists and Carol scooped it up, blanket and all. Light as air, she thought, and despite the summer night, the child was shivering. She tucked the blanket it had been wrapped in more tightly around it, then held it carefully, tucking it in close to her. Smoothing her palm across its downy hair, she felt her heart twist a little. Once upon a time, she'd wanted a family. Children. But it hadn't happened, and now, holding this tiny new life close, she realized just how much she wished things had been different.

But this baby wasn't hers and she knew she had to keep her heart from getting too involved. For her own sake.

"Nothing personal, little guy . . . or girl . . . whichever," she said, staring down into milky blue eyes that studied her as if understanding every word she said. "Where's your mommy?" she whispered, tracing the tip of one finger along the baby's face. Instinctively, the infant turned its head toward her touch, opening its tiny mouth in a futile search for food. "Poor little thing," Carol said. "You're hungry, you're cold, and I'm standing here asking you questions you can't answer. It's okay. We won't talk about your mommy anymore." If babies really could understand what was happening around them, then Carol wasn't going to be the one to bad-mouth this one's mother. At least, not to its face.

Frowning, she hunched her shoulders as that tight, prickly sensation crawled up her neck again. Carol turned, letting her gaze sweep across the darkened town square. The only lights were those behind her, focused on the manger and the statues inside it.

Shadows of varying degrees of darkness surrounded her. Pale moonlight drifted down through the oaks and elms studding the border of the square and a quiet ocean breeze danced through their leaves with a rustle of movement. Park benches, lonely in the dark, waited for morning, and the tourists who would plop themselves down and drip ice cream across the glossy, green surfaces.

Up and down the main street, otherwise known as North Pole Avenue, stores were closed, sidewalks were empty, and fog lamps shone in yellow halos. The Fourth of July weekend would be starting in two days and it was as if the whole town was taking a nap to prepare. But then, Christmas wasn't exactly a hot spot of late-night entertainment anyway. The stores closed at nine and by ten, the sidewalks were rolled up and tucked away until the next morning.

"Well, except for you, huh?" Carol stroked the palm of her hand across the soft, downy dark hair atop the baby's head.

The quiet nights were just one of the reasons Carol had moved to the little seaside town in central California. Although, she thought, she wouldn't mind a little company right about now.

"But I bet you're lonelier than me, aren't you?" The baby just blinked at her.

Every other night, she and Quinn walked through the sleeping town, the big dog snuffling at every square inch of ground as though he'd never seen it before. They listened to the silence and wandered for blocks, almost never seeing another soul. In quiet houses, lamplight played behind drapes, penned-up dogs barked at Quinn's passing, and occasionally, they ran across teenagers steaming up car windows. There was peace in their nightly ritual, Carol thought. A kind of . . . magic, she supposed. Especially for someone like her, who'd grown up in the rush and noise of LA, always surrounded by too many people, having to scratch out one small corner of solitude to call her own.

But tonight, that had all changed.

Quinn leaned against her and Carol staggered with the effort to stay upright. Then bending down, she snatched up the dog's leash and talked to the baby. "We're gonna take you to see Aunt Phoebe. Aren't we, Quinn?"

Rather than taking off like a shot, as he would normally do, Quinn walked slowly, keeping time with Carol and the baby.

Jack Reilly stared long and hard at the small medical clinic at the edge of town. Like every other business in Christmas, it was decorated with tiny twinkling lights and candy-cane-red ribbon bedecked the front door. He shook his head and sighed. He'd grown up here and *still* could be surprised at the amount of *holiday cheer* the town threw at you every day.

Christmas, California, was far off the main coast road, tucked into a small dip in the hills that would have been a valley with a little more effort. But because of its location, Christmas had missed its chance to grow and sprawl into more than it was. Urban growth, like the highway, had bypassed Christmas, leaving it to find a way to survive on its own.

It had.

A couple hundred years ago, the founders had called it Billingsley, for the first man to stumble across the hills and set up a tent. But some smart guy in the twenties had come up with the idea of renaming the little town in an attempt to bring tourists in. So they'd come up with the notion of year-round Christmas. With a few changes to street signs and storefronts, they'd reinvented themselves as a place to find "magic." The plan worked.

The town thrived on tourism and clung to the familiarity of small-town life. People looking for a fun way to spend a weekend, or a place to buy ornaments and decorations, found their way to Christmas. Tourists sought it out, despite having to take a narrow, two-lane road that zigged and zagged with wild abandon along a cliff's edge.

They came in droves. As inevitable as taxes and death, the camera-toting crowd arrived daily, dragging their kids along with them. They posed for pictures outside the Reindeer Café and laughed over the street signs. Kids crawled all over the Nativity set and their parents paid to let them enter a petting zoo, where they could see Rudolph and his buddies up close and personal. Every summer, the tourists outnumbered the townies by three or four to one and, in December, their numbers were staggering. But no one complained. The tourists brought their credit cards and wallets and that kept the town going.

It was corny and old-fashioned and everything sleepy

little towns should be, he supposed. The only problem was, Jack was busily trying to forget all about the holiday that came around every December 25. Now, for at least the next few weeks, that particular date was going to be in his face, on his mind, and churning in his gut.

"Perfect." He opened the car door and stepped out into the cold, damp air. Heading across the nearly empty parking lot, he grabbed the doorknob and gave it a turn. He ducked his head as he stepped into the eerily quiet clinic. At six feet four inches, he had a habit of tucking his head in—otherwise he'd be constantly bumping it. Pausing just inside the doorway, he did a quick scan of the clinic he hadn't seen in years.

In the middle of the night, the place looked deserted, abandoned. Quiet and almost empty, it lay shadowed under the dim light of only half the overhead fluorescents. Either the clinic was saving energy, or they figured why light the place up when there weren't any patients?

Pastoral watercolors in primary-colored frames decorated the soft blue walls and the blue and gray linoleum gleamed from recent scrubbing. The front desk, manned by a nurse currently reading a magazine, was adorned with coloring-book scribbles, thumbtacked to the cream-colored beadboard.

And naturally, because this was Christmas, tinsel garlands ringed the room, draped from the ceiling to fall in festive, upside-down arches. Man. Even in the clinic, he couldn't get away from year-round Christmas.

The smell of antiseptic clung to the air and twitched at Jack's nose. He never had liked medical buildings. Logically, he knew the antiseptic was to keep things clean—but a part of him had always wondered if that strong smell wasn't some sly way to try to cover up the stench of fear and misery.

Oh, yeah, Jack thought. *He was just the guy to be out dealing with people in the middle of the night.* Shaking his head, he took another step inside and his shoes thunked heavily enough to get the nurse's attention. She looked up and her eyes brightened as soon as she saw him.

"Jack, hi."

"Tina." He nodded and crossed the floor in a few long strides. Tina Mitchell–Graves now, he reminded himself. Although her round, pregnant belly would have served as a big hint that a lot of time had passed since he'd last seen her. "I got a call at the station from Dr. Hightower about—"

"I know." Tina pointed off down the hall behind her. "She's in the back, waiting for you."

"Thanks." He started for the hall.

"So, are you back home to stay?"

He stopped briefly and shot her a quick look. "No," he said, wanting to make sure she got that little news bulletin out onto the jungle grapevine fast. "I'm only standing in for Sheriff Thompson until he's well enough to come back."

And he wouldn't have been doing *that* much if he'd been able to think of a way around it. Right now, he could be on his way to . . . anywhere would do, actually. He could be on a beach with a mai-tai . . . or in a bar with a beer. Either of which sounded better than being rousted out of bed at one in the morning. Which just went to prove his father had been right. "No good deed goes unpunished, Jack." He could practically hear the old man muttering it now, which was a hell of a job of remembering since Jack's dad had died more than ten years ago.

"That's a shame," Tina said and pushed herself up from her chair.

Jack's gaze dropped to her swollen belly and his jaw clenched. "You better sit down, Tina."

She waved off his concern. "Please. This is number three. With two kids under the age of five, who gets to sit?"

Jesus, he was getting old. Tina Mitchell had two and a half kids. Just yesterday, she'd been leading cheers while he ran for touchdowns. Shaking his head, Jack headed off down the hall, following the sound of voices drifting to him from the last examination room on the right.

"A healthy, six-pound, two-ounce baby girl," the doctor proclaimed after a thorough examination.

"And human, right?" Carol asked.

Dr. Phoebe Hightower looked over at her friend and lifted a finely arched red eyebrow. "Excuse me?"

"Hey, not such a weird question." Carol grinned at her. "On the walk over here, it—*she* was making some really strange sort of . . . *bloopy* noises."

"Define 'bloopy.' " Phoebe tucked her short, coppery hair behind her ears and looped her stethoscope around her neck. "I'm fascinated."

"You know . . ." Carol shrugged and jammed both hands briefly into her jeans pockets before pulling them out again to wave. "Noises coming from both ends. And lots of . . . *fluids*."

"Yeah, sure sign of an alien life-form."

"Hey, I'm not an idiot," Carol said. "I know babies have fluids. But you checked? No venom sacs in her cheeks? No forked, suspiciously reptilian tongue?"

Phoebe stared at her friend for a long count of five. "You've been watching the *V* marathon on the Sci-Fi channel again, haven't you?"

"Lizard babies in human suits." Carol grinned and shrugged. "Hey, you'd feel pretty silly if you missed diagnosing an alien baby, wouldn't you?"

"How embarrassing that would be."

"See? Only looking out for you, pal."

"Uh-huh. And you found her in the manger?"

"Yeah." The smile slipped from Carol's face as she stared down at the little girl, now wearing a diaper and wrapped in a nice clean blanket. She reached out one hand and tentatively stroked the tiny palm with the tip of her finger. The baby grabbed at it, and Carol felt that grip tighten around her heart.

This probably wasn't a good thing, she thought, even as she concentrated on the feel of those tiny fingers wrapped around her own. With every moment that ticked past, this baby was slipping quietly past Carol's defenses. The heck of it was, she wasn't at all sorry. Maybe she would be later, but at the moment, everything in her was busy responding to a kindred spirit.

This child, like Carol herself, had been abandoned. And who knew better than Carol what that baby would feel as it grew and had to accept the fact that she hadn't been worth keeping?

"Who could just leave her there and walk away?" Phoebe muttered and smoothed her palm over the baby's head.

"Walking away's the easy part," Carol muttered, then deliberately forced a smile. "Or so I'm told."

"Hey . . ." Phoebe winced. "I'm sorry, I just didn't think and—"

This time Carol really smiled. Her past was just that. Past. She'd moved past the hurt of never having a family. Of never having a real home to go running to when times got tough. She'd grown up in spite of everything. And she'd built her *own* home. Made her own mark. The past was just memories and memories couldn't hurt her anymore.

Still, realizing that this tiny girl would grow up with the same doubts and questions tugged at Carol. She knew how the system worked. This tiny child would be taken to a state home. She'd be laid down in one of a series of cribs. She'd cry and wait her turn for attention. She'd be fed, held and cared for, by overworked and underpaid attendants, but she wouldn't get the special time and care that *all* children were entitled to.

Her heart ached as old memories rushed into her mind along with worry for the child who was too young to defend herself against the pain that was already headed her way.

"It's okay, Phoeb," Carol said, swallowing hard. "I'm a big girl. I don't have any 'issues.' " Phoebe Hightower had been her first friend in Christmas. Heck, her first real friend anywhere. And for the past two years, she and Phoebe had bonded over Mel Gibson movies, Chocolate Brownie ice cream, and the lack of interesting men in Christmas. Well, that last part didn't count anymore, since Phoebe had stumbled across a certain sexy carpenter who had changed her opinion on dating life in a small town.

But even Phoebe didn't know everything there was to know in Carol's past. And that's just the way she liked it.

"Yeah, but still."

"Really. No biggie." She didn't want to think about the past she'd left behind a long time ago. The whole point of moving to Christmas had been to build a future and to forget the past, right? Right.

Phoebe sighed and studied Carol's eyes for a long moment before letting go of whatever she was thinking. "I have to call Social Services."

Carol's heart twinged painfully again. She looked down at the tiny baby girl and knew that she couldn't let it happen. Couldn't allow this infant to slide into the system when she was less than twenty-four hours old. She herself had far too many memories of institutional life. She'd never be able to live with herself if she simply walked away, knowing that the baby would become just another abandoned child.

Carol wanted to protect her heart. She really did. But looking at the baby, she knew she couldn't save herself by sacrificing the child.

"Do we have to?"

Phoebe just looked at her. "Yeah. It's the law. The sheriff's already been called. He'll be here any minute."

"What about if I took her?"

"Carol . . ."

"For now," she said, blurting the words out quickly as if putting hedges on her offer would make the pain less when she eventually had to give up the baby.

"Are you sure?"

Carol choked out a laugh. "No. But I can't let her go to a *home*."

Phoebe looked down at the baby, then turned her gaze back to Carol. "We'll have to clear it with Maggie . . . but I'm sure she'll approve you." She stepped to the counter and picked up the phone.

Nerves skittered inside Carol, but she fought them back. She knew what she was doing. And it was temporary, after all. She only half-listened as Phoebe talked to Maggie Reilly Cooper, the local Social Services rep. Instead, Carol watched the baby, and the baby returned that solemn stare, as if they were sizing each other up. And Carol half-wondered just what the tiny girl thought of her.

A few minutes later, the phone conversation had ended, everything was decided, and Carol's new course had been charted.

"It's official," Phoebe said.

A new rush of nerves hustled through her system. But she'd made her decision and she wouldn't change it now. "Okay, then, I guess it's just me and Lizardbaby."

Phoebe laughed and the sound seemed to echo in the small cubicle. "Honest to God—"

"Lizard baby?" A deep voice from the doorway rumbled through the room.

An instant later, Quinn did a little rumbling himself as he stood up from his post beside the examining table. The big dog's throaty growl seemed to roll on and on like thunder.

"Jesus," Jack said and took an instinctive step backward. "You brought a trained bear to the clinic?"

"Quinn . . ." The dog's rumbling stopped short and Carol looked at the man warily watching the animal. "He's my dog. He won't bite."

"Famous last words," Jack muttered and took a cautious step into the room. "Besides, he looks like he wouldn't have to bite. He could probably swallow me whole."

Carol watched him watch Quinn and she had to admit, at least privately, that she wouldn't mind taking a bite out of Jack Reilly herself.

Tall enough to qualify for mountain status, he had shoulders broad enough to balance the world and deep blue eyes that looked as though they'd seen way too much misery. By the look of it, his nose had been broken once or twice, he had a wide mouth and thick black eyebrows. His square jaw was bristled with a dark shadow of whiskers and his black hair was gleaming wet, as if he'd just stepped out of the shower when he was called to the clinic.

That thought brought up a couple of lovely images that she hadn't had nearly enough time to enjoy when he spoke again, shattering her concentration.

"You must be Dr. Hightower," he said and offered his hand.

"I am. Thanks for coming so fast." Phoebe shook his hand firmly, then nodded at Carol. "This is Carol Baker, she found the baby."

He shook her hand, too, and Carol felt a slight zap of heat as their palms brushed together. Surprised, she closed her fingers over her palm, as if to hold on to that little burst of electricity just a while longer.

"And," Phoebe was saying, "this little girl is our mysterious stranger."

Jack sidestepped around Quinn and moved in for a closer look. "Newborn?"

"No more than a few hours old," Phoebe said softly.

He shifted a look at Carol and she suddenly knew what a butterfly must feel like when it was pinned unexpectedly to a board. "You found her?"

"Yep."

"Where?"

"The manger."

"Huh?"

Carol glanced at the baby, more to break eye contact with the big man still watching her than anything else. Really, he had a penetrating gaze that could make you confess to just about anything. No wonder he became a cop.

She knew the Reilly family. Impossible to live in Christmas and not know them. Jack was the oldest, then there was Sean, a priest, then Eileen, perpetually pregnant or so it seemed, and now working on number three, then Maggie, mother of two and the local representative for Social Services, and finally, Peggy—at eighteen, the baby and family favorite. So Carol knew all about Jack Reilly, though she'd never met him before now. She knew he'd left town to join LAPD. That he'd been married and divorced. That he'd quit the big-city police force a couple of years ago—but no one outside his family seemed to know why.

He'd come back to Christmas as a favor to the ailing town sheriff. Now he was the temporary chief of their tiny department, which was why he was standing here, giving her a look that said clearly, "Talk now or down at the station."

Really, she thought. Maybe she *was* watching too much TV.

Staring up into those compelling blue eyes, Carol said, "I found her in the Nativity scene in the town square."

"And what were you doing in the town square in the middle of the night?"

Well, she didn't like the tone of *that* question. So she fired right back. "I was doing a fertility dance with my coven. Did I mention that I practice the black arts?"

"Uh-huh," he said, sarcasm dripping from his tone.

He never batted an eye. That shouldn't surprise her, though. He'd probably heard far worse in LA.

"She walks her dog every night at midnight," Phoebe said.

"He's my familiar," Carol added.

"He's a bear."

"You're really not a people person, are you?" Carol asked.

"How'd you guess?"

"Hello?" Phoebe waved both hands until she had their attention. "About the baby . . ."

"Right. I'll call Maggie. See what she wants us to do about the baby."

"I just hung up with her," Phoebe told him. "She's agreed to allow Carol to be an emergency foster parent."

Jack shifted his gaze from the doctor to the tall, brown-haired woman in the faded jeans and the too-tight white tank top emblazoned with a head shot of Santa. She straightened up as though presenting herself for formal inspection. Her eyes were the color of good scotch and her breasts were high and full, and she was just the right height for him to kiss her without getting a crick in his neck.

Not that he had any plans in *that* direction. And if he had planned on finding a woman, he'd get one just a little less crazy, thanks.

CHAPTER 2

"I really appreciate this."

Jack checked the rearview mirror and, in the dimly lit car interior, met Carol Baker's gaze. A couple of hours ago, he hadn't even met her. He'd been sound asleep and fighting his way out of a nightmare. Since meeting her, he'd been in a waking nightmare. So which one, he wondered, was worse? No contest. The sleeping nightmare was a damn sight worse than wandering the baby aisle in an all-night grocery store outside of town, with a squalling newborn, a trained bear, and a woman who wore jingle bells on her shoelaces.

But not by much.

"No problem."

"This is pretty much above and beyond the call of duty for you though, right?" she said and glanced at the infant beside her on the back seat, strapped into a car seat borrowed from Tina's minivan. "I mean," she continued, "you didn't *have* to take us baby-grocery-shopping."

"What were you gonna do, walk?" he asked and stopped at a red light just outside town. He scraped one hand across his face and wondered why his life had turned to shit. What in his karma had brought him to this low point? How had he come full circle and returned to answering the call for help in the middle of the night? Almost two years ago, he'd walked away from the force. Turned his back on the things he knew and told himself that he'd never go back again. Yet here he was—temporarily at least—back in the saddle. He couldn't get out of it. He'd already given his word. But that didn't mean he wouldn't resent being pulled back into a life he'd deliberately left behind. And it didn't mean he wouldn't walk away again—just as soon as he could.

After all, what else could he do to repent—short of dying and being reincarnated as a cockroach?

Turning his head to look at her, he stopped dead when he came nose to nose with the bear. "Jesus!"

The damn dog was sitting straight up on the passenger seat, riding shotgun with him like they were old pals. The only problem was, Jack had never been eyeball to eyeball with a dog that damn big. Brown eyes stared unblinkingly into his. Hot dog breath puffed onto his face. And he had the distinct impression the animal didn't quite trust him.

Jack knew just how he felt.

The top of the dog's head scraped the roof of the car. His big, powerful body looked cramped in the low-slung passenger seat and Jack told himself that was the problem. The dog only looked gigantic because he was sitting in a Mustang. If Jack had had a bigger car—like, say, a Greyhound bus—the dog would look normal.

"Does he have to stare at me like that?" Jack asked, never breaking eye contact with the dog.

"Like what?"

He leaned farther away from the mutt and told himself it was caution, not fear. "Like I'm a Scooby Snack."

Laughter bubbled from the back seat and the sound of

it was . . . good. He didn't want to think about why—so he added it to the already long list of things he wasn't going to think about.

"Quinn, stop scaring the sheriff."

"Who said anything about being scared?"

"I'm sure you are, but it's not manly to admit it."

"Even mountain men walked a wide path around a bear," he said tightly and ordered himself to ignore the dog still staring at him.

Scowling, he flicked her a glance, while listening to the dog, whose grumbling sounded sort of like thunder from a cloud hovering three feet over your head. In the yellow glow of the fog lamps lining the street, the blond streaks in Carol's hair shone with a golden light.

She was tall and he knew she couldn't have been too comfortable in the back seat of a Mustang. But she didn't seem to mind while sitting beside the baby. Jack could understand that. Babies tended to bring out the deepest emotions in people—good or, as he'd seen too often on the force, bad. She kept glancing at the baby, as if half-expecting it to disappear from the car seat. The whole time they'd wandered the aisles in the twenty-four-hour grocery store, she'd carried the little thing carefully—like you would a ticking time bomb. He couldn't decide if she was inexperienced with kids, worried about becoming too attached, or expecting the missing mother to come tearing into the store to reclaim her child.

That last one probably wasn't an issue. In his experience, women who abandoned their babies didn't have a change of heart and instantly become Mother Teresa. They went on about their lives, trusting that strangers would give their child what they couldn't—or *wouldn't.*

Jack couldn't quite figure Carol Baker out. Not many people would have reacted so emotionally to the situation.

Most would have taken the baby to the hospital, or called the cops and then walked away—gone back to their own lives. But Carol had not only stayed with the child, but when push came to shove, she'd agreed to take the baby in.

Why?

Even as that one single word whispered through his mind, he told himself to back off. To put aside the old instinct to pry into motivations. He wasn't a cop anymore. He'd left that world behind—along with his old life. Now was what mattered. And now he had a temporary job in the town where he'd grown up, his old room at his mother's house, a woman with Santa on her shirt in his back seat, and an abandoned baby to investigate. Not to mention the bear.

"So where do you live?" He practically growled the question and even he winced at his tone. She didn't seem to notice.

"Off North Pole, left on Jingle Bell Way."

Jack sighed.

"I heard that," she said. "What's wrong?"

"Just this town," he admitted as the light turned green and he stepped on the gas. "Christmas—everywhere you look Christmas in spring, summer, and fall." He shook his head and steered the car into a left-turn bay. "In LA, I'd always hear people complaining about how retailers started hawking Christmas earlier and earlier every year." He glanced at the blinking, electric Frosty the Snowman out in front of Elves' Hardware and choked out a laugh. "But here in la-la land, we get it day in and day out."

"I *like* Christmas," she said.

"Christmas is hard enough once a year. *All* year is a little much for anybody." Especially these days, he thought, and then instantly turned his mind away from memories he'd spent the last two years burying.

He turned left on Jingle Bell Way. "Where's your place?"

"The Victorian here on the corner."

"Naturally." He pulled up out front and parked the car at the curb. Studying her house, Jack felt another sigh building, but he squashed it. What would be the point?

The name of her shop, Christmas Carol's, was just as cutesy as any other business in town. In the dark, it was hard to tell what color the place was, but there were neatly planted gardens lining the sidewalk leading to the front steps and baskets filled with flowers hung from the eaves and dotted the length of the wraparound porch. Strings of multicolored lights outlined the edge of the roof and then twined around the porch columns. A wide, and he assumed, artificial, evergreen wreath studded with bows and ornaments decorated the front door, and electric candles had been left burning in the windows.

Jesus. She was every bit as bad as every other nut in town.

"Christmas *Carol's,*" she prompted from the back seat. "Get it?"

"Yeah," he said, turning off the engine and unbuckling his seatbelt. "I picked right up on that subtlety."

"Are you always this crabby? Or am I just special?"

He turned around to look at her and managed to avoid bumping into the dog's nose as he did. "It's the middle of the night. I've been grocery-shopping. I'm driving around with a trained bear sitting in my front seat—"

"And I appreciate it."

He kept going. "I spent an hour traipsing around a

Nativity scene looking for clues to the missing mother of an abandoned baby—"

Carol frowned at him, and quickly leaned over to cover the baby's ears with her hands. "Don't say that in front of her."

"What?"

"A-B-A-N-D-O—"

"For God's sake, it can't understand what we're saying."

Carol straightened up and glared at him. Her dog must have picked up on her sudden twist of anger because the damn thing growled again and damned if it didn't sound like another crash of rolling thunder. Jack inched backward. No point in taking chances.

"She's not an *it*. And you have no idea what she can and can't understand. People—even babies—know when they're being talked about. They know when they're loved. They know when they've been . . . A-B-A-N—oh, forget it." Quickly, carefully, she undid the straps holding the newborn into the car seat, then scooped it up into her arms, tucking the blanket around it. "Doctors tell pregnant women to talk to their bellies, right?"

A flash of memory zipped through Jack's brain and was gone again in the next heartbeat. He didn't even pause to be grateful. "Yeah. That's for the *tone* of voice to be heard."

"Then why not just hum? Why talk to them? Babies have ears. They can hear."

"Sure, but it's like me trying to understand Italian. It's just noise."

"You don't know that for sure."

"Neither do you." Jesus, had he just said that? Was he starting to sound like a third-grader? Were they about to get into a rousing chorus of "yes sir, no sir"? Or, "shut up, no you shut up"? Good God, what coming back to Christmas had brought him to. "Fine. Talk to it. Sing to it. Whatever."

Quinn whined, growled, and took a step forward. Unfortunately, that put one big paw directly on Jack's nuts. Pain exploded through his body and splintered into a fireworks show in his brain. He was pretty sure his eyes were wheeling behind closed lids. "Jesus, get off me." Groaning, he shoved at the damn dog and didn't budge it an inch. Instead, the damn thing stepped down even harder, pushing its face into Jack's and blowing hot dog breath all over him.

"Quinn, sit down."

"Not *now,*" Jack managed to choke out through clenched teeth. Breath wheezed in and out of him as he tried to scoot out from under the dog. Christ, if the dog *sat* on him, he was a dead man.

"Sorry! Quinn, no."

Now the dog was getting agitated and that's all he'd need, Jack thought. The dog gets riled and he'd have two of its paws on his nuts and then he'd be looking for a job with the Vienna Boys' Choir. With his left hand, he reached to one side, sprung the door latch, and somehow found a way to roll out from under the dog and onto the street.

Of course, he landed on a rock that jammed his right knee. So he'd have a limp. At least his nuts would recover. And at the moment, that's all he was concerned with. Kneeling on all fours on the damp street, he took several deep breaths before trusting himself to move. When he did, he swiveled his head and came eyeball to eyeball with the beast.

"You lousy, no-good son of a—"

"Not in front of the baby," Carol warned from the

back seat. "And besides, it wasn't Quinn's fault. You upset me and that upset him."

The dog was upset?

"Right." Jack choked out another groan and shook his head as his breathing evened out and the pain subsided into a dull throb he'd probably carry for the rest of his life. "You two were upset. I need a hospital, but that's not important."

"For heaven's sake, you're not bleeding."

He glanced up and caught her eye through the side window. "There are *some* things more important to a man than a slashed artery."

"Pizza and beer?"

"That, too."

She smiled. "Are you okay?"

"I'm a soprano, but I'll live."

"Not that you're exaggerating or anything."

That smile of hers was damn near lethal. He watched her face in the glow of the streetlights and almost wished he was a different man. But if he was a different man, he wouldn't be back in Christmas and he never would have met her, so no sense in that.

Climbing to his feet, he glared at the big dog as it jumped out with a lunge of movement and stood beside him. The damn thing nearly hit Jack's hip. He'd never seen a dog so big. Well, except for a Great Dane . . . but somehow, this dog even looked bigger than a Dane. Maybe it was the coarse, wiry gray hair that stood up on end all over his body. Like a punk rocker dog. Or maybe it was the deep rumblings of sound that kept roaring out around them. And maybe, he thought, pulling his foot out from under one huge paw, maybe it was just its weight.

Soon, he promised himself silently, Sheriff Thompson

would be back at the helm of Christmas where he belonged, Jack took a breath and got a grip. Hell, he'd grown up in Christmas. He could handle the place for a few more weeks. Then he'd be gone again, and from now on, he'd limit himself to weekend visits with his family. Preferably somewhere far, far away from Christmas.

He opened the back door for Carol, and she held the baby out for him to take her. He took one step forward, the dog growled, low and throaty and with a definite threat, and he stepped back, hands in the air. Glancing at the dog first, he then looked at Carol and said, "I don't think so. Your personal guardian doesn't approve."

"But—"

"You take her," he said. "I'll get the stuff from the trunk."

Carol just stared at him. She didn't think it was just because of Quinn that he'd backed off from handling the baby. For one brief second, she'd thought she saw a sheen of panic in his eyes. But that was ridiculous. He was the oldest in a family of five kids, and two of his sisters had children, so he'd had to have been around babies more than *she* had.

But, now that she thought about it, she realized, he'd kept his distance from the infant from the moment he'd stepped into Phoebe's office.

Interesting.

But not fascinating, so she scooted inelegantly out of the car, holding the baby carefully, terrified of dropping her, and then walked around the back end of the black Mustang and headed for the house. Quinn padded right behind her, his nails clicking in a comfortable pattern against the asphalt.

It was her habit to let her gaze sweep across the home she'd made in the last two years, and as always, the sight of the old Victorian filled her with a sense of . . . *belonging*. She'd carved out a space of her own in this little town. She'd planted her petunias and stock and columbine. She decorated her porch, stocked her store, and kept her Christmas lights blazing all year round.

Comfort and coziness surrounded her every time she approached the house, and tonight, those feelings were even more profound. She held a baby, close in her arms. The slight weight and subtle warmth of its body snuggled close to her felt way too good. Maybe it hadn't been such a good idea to volunteer to be the emergency foster parent.

But could she really have done anything differently? Could she, in a pitiful attempt to protect her own heart, have allowed this tiny girl to go into an anonymous nursery filled with more needy children? No. Just as she couldn't live with the fact that if she had turned her back, it would have been like the baby being abandoned twice in one night.

A fine birthday gift.

No, she'd had no choice, really. None at all. Oh, she wasn't an idiot. She knew this wouldn't last. She was a *temporary* mom. She, better than anyone, knew how the foster system worked. So she'd do her best not to get *too* attached to the baby she held so close to her heart. She'd try not to give in to the urge to resurrect long-dead fantasies she'd had about a family of her own.

She took the steps quickly but Quinn still beat her to the door. He sat down and waited while she fumbled for her key, then once the door was open, he slipped first into the house as if to assure himself that all was safe.

"We're home, little girl," she whispered and hit the light switch by the door as she stepped into the foyer. The polished wood floor gleamed. The glass covering the framed

Currier & Ives prints winked with reflected light and the pale, rose-colored walls looked soft and homey. The staircase on the right led to the upstairs apartments and the door on the left opened into her shop.

She ignored the store and started up the stairs as she heard Jack coming up the walk. "It's upstairs," she said and thought she heard him mutter, *"Naturally."*

Another hallway greeted her at the head of the stairs and she waited there for him. A long carpet runner decorated with fat, faded, yellow roses lined the narrow hall dividing the upstairs into two one-bedroom apartments. An iron wall sconce in the shape of a Christmas tree threw indistinct, watery light into the shadows.

Carol stared down at the baby in her arms and her breath caught as the infant opened her eyes and looked back at her. "Hello," Carol crooned softly. "My name's Carol and I'm going to take care of you for a while if that's okay with you."

"She's not in a position to argue, if that's what you mean," Jack said and his voice came from so close by that Carol jumped.

She shifted her gaze from the baby to the very male man standing now at the head of the stairs. Somehow, in her hallway, in the shadows, he looked even taller and . . . *crabbier* than he had at the clinic.

But Carol wasn't about to let him ruin this moment. For now, for however long it lasted, she had the baby she'd once longed for. It was a gift and she was going to make the most of it.

"You never answered me before."

"About what?" he asked and stepped onto the top step beside her, toting the plastic bags of baby supplies.

Carol tipped her head back to look up at him. "About the whole grumbling thing. Are you this way with everyone or is there something about me that brings it out in you?"

He looked at her for a long time and she tried to read what was going on behind his eyes, but he was either a master of disguise or the light just wasn't good enough. Because in those blue depths, shadows shifted and hid whatever he might be feeling.

"Look, it's been a long night," he said. "Can we just get the kid settled, then I'll go home and grab a quick hour or so of sleep."

"Fine," she said and turned away. After all, it wasn't her business if he went through life with a telephone pole up his behind. "This is my place right here." She walked up to the door on the right, painted a brilliant, cobalt blue and straightened out the little white Christmas Angel hanging on it.

He rolled his eyes, but she ignored it.

"Who lives there?" he asked, pointing to the red door across the hall.

Carol glanced at it and shrugged. "No one, yet. My last tenant moved out last month."

Jack nodded as she opened her door and let him inside.

The scent of cinnamon and apples greeted them. Strings of tiny white lights ringed the walls at ceiling level, shining like stars in the semidarkness. Overstuffed furniture was drawn together to form a small conversation area in front of a brick fireplace, which was cold now, but held the makings for a fire. Bookcases stuffed to overflowing with well-read paperbacks lined one wall and framed prints of faraway places dotted the dark red walls.

A tall bay window overlooked Jingle Bell Way and reflections of colored lights stained the wispy white curtains hanging there.

"Nice," Jack said after a long minute.

"Thanks. I like it." She led the way across the room and through an arched doorway into a kitchen that looked as though it had been last remodeled in 1940. Even the fridge was an antique.

A chrome-legged table claimed the center of the room and Jack set the bags down there as he turned in a slow circle, to get the whole image of the place. Plants. Looked like hundreds of 'em, he thought. They lined the windowsills, hung from the ceiling, decorated the worn countertops, and graced the center of the table. It was like a damn rain forest in there.

"If the world ever runs out of oxygen, I'll know where to send everybody."

She glanced around, then back at him and shrugged. "I like growing things."

Quinn stepped into the room, sat down next to Jack and glared at him.

He sighed. "Your dog have something against me?"

"He's very protective."

"I'm sensing that." He shot a look at the dog. Quinn never blinked. "Look, if you're set—"

"Oh, I'm sorry. Of course you want to get back to your mom's house."

He winced.

"Problem?"

"No." But the thought of going to his mom's—when he knew without a doubt that his sister Maggie, after hearing about the abandoned baby and putting Carol temporarily in charge, had no doubt called their mother to share the news—was a little daunting. His mom would be sitting in the living room, waiting for him to fill her in on every damn detail and he'd probably never get back to sleep.

Instantly, memories of his mother waiting up for him to get home from his dates rose up in his mind. Weird how many years had passed and some things didn't change.

No man over twenty-five should live with his mother, Jack thought. Even temporarily.

He pushed thoughts of Mom and the coming interrogation out of his head for the time being. "So do you need any more help with anything before I go?"

She looked at him, then at the baby, then back at him. "I just have one question."

"What's that?"

Her dark brown eyes went wide and he caught a flicker of panic darting across their surfaces as she asked, "What do I do now?"

Journal entry

I did it.

I had the baby and nobody knows.

I put her in the manger and then hid in the bushes until Carol and her dog came. I knew they'd come. They always walk around at night and they always go through the square.

Carol took the baby, just like I knew she would.

And now I'm alone again.

What do I do now?

CHAPTER 3

It took more than an hour to get the baby settled down. Once she was fed and changed and tucked into bed, she dropped right off to sleep, blissfully unaware of just how shaky her world was at the moment.

"A drawer," Carol murmured, looking at the tiny baby asleep in the center of her lingerie drawer. True, the drawer was no longer in her dresser, and she'd lined it with a soft blanket for padding and then tucked a pillowcase tightly over the blanket to make do as a sheet . . . but it was still a drawer.

Quinn sat down beside the makeshift cradle and kept watch over the sleeping baby, completely ignoring the two people talking behind him.

"Good temporary crib," Jack said, moving up behind her in the dim light. "Solid, high sides to keep her contained—"

"Contained?" Carol looked up at him as he stared down at the baby with all the emotion a man would give a slide under a microscope. "She's not in a dog run."

He shifted a glance at her. "All I'm saying is, the drawer will do."

"For now," Carol said and couldn't resist reaching out

to straighten the soft terry towel she'd used as a blanket to cover the baby. "But then, this is probably only for now anyway, right? I mean, the mother will probably turn up and then—" She looked up at him again. "Then what? Would they give the baby back to her?"

"I don't know," he said. "It would depend on a lot of things. There'll be an investigation. And she may not be found. Seems like she went to a lot of trouble to leave the baby and disappear."

"We shouldn't be talking in front of her," Carol muttered and stepped out of her bedroom, back into the living room.

"It's not like she's listening and taking notes," Jack countered.

"She can hear," Carol said, but didn't really want to get back into that argument again. What was the point? He'd never admit she was right, anyway.

Her eyes widened as she took in the changes in her apartment. A few hours ago, the place had been, as always, tidy. A place for everything and everything in its place. Good God, how often had she had *that* little phrase drummed into her head as a kid?

The women in charge at the group home where she'd grown up had insisted on organization being the key to good living. Of course, when you were running a home for a dozen or more kids and were forced to work around a revolving door that spit kids in and out of the system with dizzying speed, organization was your only defense.

And Carol had learned her lessons so well, being neat had simply become part of her nature.

Until tonight. Now, she had a true mess on her hands. Bags of baby supplies littered the room. Disposable diapers were stacked on one end of the couch and cans of formula and brand-new baby bottles were lined up on the coffee table like soldiers awaiting orders. A few tiny undershirts that she'd spotted on the baby aisle at the grocery store were lying on the table along with powder, shampoo, diaper-rash ointment, and a few other things she'd simply grabbed and thrown into her shopping cart.

Who would have guessed that babies required so much . . . *equipment*?

Oh, yeah, she was perfect for this job.

She picked up one of the undershirts and blankly studied it for a long second or two. So tiny. So incredibly small. And the baby who would wear it was so helpless. Unable to defend herself against a well-meaning-but-completely-out-of-her-depth adult.

From the corner of her eye, she saw Jack heading for the front door and a small curl of panic blossomed in her chest. "You're leaving?"

"You're quick," he said. "Gotta give you that."

She ignored the sarcasm. "You could stay a while."

"Gonna miss me?"

"You're crabby, but at least you know your way around a baby."

"The oldest of five picks up a few things."

And children who'd grown up in foster care knew exactly squat, Carol thought. The babies who'd drifted in and out of the group home had never stayed long enough for any of the older kids to connect with them. After all, *everyone* wanted to adopt a baby. Carol pushed old memories aside and tried bribery. "I can make you some breakfast or something . . ."

One corner of his mouth tipped up briefly. "I don't think so. If I hurry—and can avoid getting sucked into a Reilly family interrogation—I should be able to get a good . . ." He checked his watch. "Fifteen, twenty minutes of sleep before sunup." He opened the door, stepped into the hall, and paused, looking at the closed door across from him.

Carol stopped just short of walking right into him. God, he was leaving. Okay, he wasn't friendly. Or charming. Or particularly nice. But he was another grown-up, and right now she was beginning to feel just a little too much *alone.* Maybe she hadn't given this idea enough thought. Maybe she'd just reacted emotionally to the thought of that tiny girl being tossed into the system. Maybe, she thought finally, Lizardbaby would have been better off with someone who knew what the hell they were doing.

"Basically," she said, "with the baby, I mean, I feed one end and change the other one."

"Yeah." He glanced at her and that brief look from those ice blue eyes shot straight to her already ragged nerve endings and gave them a good shake. "Just don't confuse the ends and you'll be fine."

"Great. You're a regular Dr. Spock."

"Live long and prosper."

"*Doctor* Spock, not *Mister* Spock." Ordinarily, she might have enjoyed knowing that Jack Reilly, despite his crabbiness, obviously enjoyed sci-fi. But at the moment, she was too intent on trying to keep him there.

"Whatever." He slid his gaze from hers, took a single long step across the hall, grabbed the doorknob of the empty apartment and opened the door.

Surprised, Carol followed him. "What're you doing?"

"Looking." He walked into the furnished room and hit the light switch.

"At what?"

"Peace."

"Huh?" Behind her, she heard the click of Quinn's nails

as he came out to join them. The big dog leaned against her side and Carol automatically slapped one hand to the doorjamb to hold herself—and Quinn—upright.

She watched as Jack moved through the empty living room and kept one ear tuned to her own apartment, just in case the baby woke up.

"You need a tenant?" Jack asked, glancing back at her over his shoulder.

She stared at him, but he was already moving farther into the room, letting his gaze slide across every square inch of the place. Carol did the same thing. It wasn't quite as decked out as her own apartment, but she thought it looked cozy.

Dark, hunter green walls with cherrywood crown molding made for a traditional-looking room. Sort of an Early American gentleman's-study effect. Twin overstuffed chairs huddled in front of the brick fireplace and there were a couple of throw rugs to warm up the polished oak floors. A table or two, a matching pair of Craftsman-style lamps throwing puddles of light across the room, and dozens of books crammed into custom-made bookcases completed the place. The bay window had the same view of Jingle Bell Way as her apartment, and the colored lights lining the outside of the house tossed blurred splashes of color against the glass.

Her last tenant, Sandy Davis, had stayed a year, then moved on, and Carol was looking forward to finding someone new to rent the place. It was nice having a friendly face so close by.

But she sure wouldn't consider Jack Reilly a "friendly" face. Gorgeous, yes. Friendly, no. One long stare out of those icy blue eyes of his and he had her babbling even more than normal. Which probably wasn't a good thing. "The apartment's for rent, but—"

"Good." He cut her off before she could come up with a good reason that he shouldn't have the apartment.

"You know," she said, talking to his back as he stalked through the hall to take a quick look at the bedroom. She knew what he saw. A bed, a dresser, and two nightstands plunked into a long, narrow room painted the same hunter green. A moment or two later, he came back through the hall, then marched across the room into the kitchen. "It's not all that peaceful here."

Quinn followed him, his nails clicking against the floor, his low grumble of discontent rolling through the room.

The kitchen light flashed on, spilling a shaft of bright light into the shadows.

"Hey, watch it, you big moose," Jack muttered.

"Quinn—" She called the dog, but since he didn't respond, he was apparently more interested in keeping an eye on Jack. Carol could hardly blame the dog. She'd been watching the man all night, herself.

"You're sitting on my foot," Jack complained.

Carol smiled briefly, imagining the man and dog glaring at each other. But then she realized that was just one more reason why this wouldn't work.

"The shop's downstairs," she called out, hoping to dissuade him. "People coming and going all the time and—"

He was opening cupboards, probably not even listening to her. Stubborn, she thought. And rude. This was *her* place, after all.

"Did you know the cupboard door under your sink comes off?"

She winced. She'd been meaning to get to that. "Yes."

"I can fix it."

"So can I," she said. She just hadn't gotten around to it

yet. "Look, I don't know if this is such a good idea." Hmm. Handsome crankypants living within spitting distance of her? No. She didn't think so. One cowardly voice in a corner of her mind, of course, argued that hey, a guy who knew a little something about babies would be a handy thing to have around. But a more rational voice shouted the little coward down by reminding Carol that any man who could stir her up with a glance would be a dangerous one to keep too close.

"I wouldn't be here long," he called out. "Is there a coffeepot in here?"

"Of course there's a coffeepot. Wouldn't be a furnished apartment without the means to make coffee, would it?"

"Good."

He flipped off the kitchen light and walked back into the living room, Quinn just behind him. Jack stopped a foot or two away from her. "I'll take it."

Quinn sat down.

Jack sighed and pulled his foot out from under the dog.

She glared up at him. "I didn't say you could have it."

"Why can't I?"

"Because . . ." Come on, Carol, she told herself, *think*.

His gaze steadied on her and Carol wanted to shift position nervously. So she didn't.

"You need a tenant," Jack said bluntly. "I need to get out of my mom's house for the time I'm in town before she drives me nuts. It'll work. For both of us."

Carol blew out a breath. He was standing so close, she could practically feel the heat from his body ripple off him in waves. His jaw was tight, his eyes narrowed and grim, and he stood, feet braced wide apart, arms folded over his broad chest, like a man set for a fight.

Not exactly the image of a congenial tenant.

"Look, Chief or Captain or—"

"Just Reilly'll do."

She arched one eyebrow. "One name. Like Cher?"

His lips tightened into a grim slash across his face.

"Fine," she said. "Reilly. I don't even *know* you."

Now one of his black eyebrows lifted briefly. "Is that a prerequisite for renting your apartment?"

"It'd help."

"You know my family."

True. And the Reillys were a nice family. She shot him a look. Well, most of them were.

"I even *like* your family."

He gave her a grim smile. "You don't have to like me and I don't have to like you," he said through gritted teeth. "I'm looking for a place. You need a tenant."

"Not this bad, I don't."

He unfolded his arms, exhaled in a rush of frustration, then shoved one hand through his hair. "I'm quiet, I'll pay you in advance, and you won't even have to know I'm here."

Oh, she'd know. It'd be impossible to *not* know. Heck, he took up half the hallway just standing there. Seeing him every day. Hearing him every night. The apartments were so close, they'd be living in each other's pockets.

On the other hand, she thought, it was just temporary. And he had been nice—grudgingly—tonight. He'd helped her out. The least she could do was return the favor. Especially since it would be good to have someone close by who knew a little something about infants.

Abruptly, she nodded. "The rent's eight hundred a month."

"Deal."

She held out one hand to shake on it.

Quinn's rumbling growl filled the hall.

Jack enfolded her hand in his.

Heat slammed into her and Carol almost felt every one of her nerve endings standing straight up to sing the "Hallelujah Chorus."

Oh, this was so not a good idea.

Mary Alice Reilly plopped down in a chair and watched her son throw his clothes into a bag. She knew her children. And even grown, they were still and always would be her children. Her gaze slid from Jack to the room where he'd grown up. His baseball trophies still lined the shelf that circled the room just below the ceiling. Posters of now retired athletes decorated the sky blue walls and the white curtains she'd made herself still fluttered in the breeze at the windows. It hardly seemed possible that so many years had gone by. If she closed her eyes, she could still see Jack, tall, gangly, with a shock of black hair continually falling into his eyes. Her firstborn and the one most like his father.

Stubborn.

Though, if she were to be honest, he'd gotten a little of his hardheadedness from her, too. She lifted one hand to smooth her graying red hair and told herself to be patient. Of all five of her kids, Jack had always been the hardest one of them to get to open up. When he closed up, you couldn't get anything out of him with a crowbar.

But that had never stopped her from trying.

And she'd never been known for her patience.

"I don't understand why you have to leave."

"I'm not leaving," Jack told her and tossed shirts into his duffel bag from across the room. "I'm moving."

"Leaving, moving." She waved a hand. "What's the difference?"

"Distance," he muttered and pitched some socks after the shirts. "I'll still be in town until Sheriff Thompson recovers."

"But you don't want to be."

He stopped, laid both hands on top of the dresser that had been his for the first eighteen years of his life, and slowly turned his head to look at her. Her knowing blue eyes stared back at him and Jack remembered that he'd never been able to fool her. Even when he was a kid, she'd been able to spot a lie at a hundred paces. "I said I'd do it. I'm going to."

"Then you'll leave again."

"Yeah." He shifted his gaze back to the pitifully few garments left in his drawer. He was traveling light these days.

"How far?"

"Huh?"

"I asked," she repeated, "how far? How far will you have to run to get away from yourself?"

"Let it go, Mom."

"That's not gonna happen," she said calmly and pushed up out of the chair. At fifty-five, she was as trim as she'd always been and moved just as quickly. In a few brisk steps, she was standing beside him, staring up into his eyes, silently daring him to look away. "It wasn't your fault, Jack. When are you going to see that?"

Jack sighed. This was why he had to move out.

His mother's understanding and concern were just too damn hard to take. She loved him, so she wasn't willing to see the truth. The truth that Jack lived with every damn day.

That it had all been his fault.

And he didn't deserve redemption.

"What's the deal?"

They both turned to face Peggy, standing in the open doorway. At eighteen, she was the last of the Reilly kids and the only one still living at home. Her short red hair peaked in jagged points around an elfin face with a dusting of gold freckles across her nose and cheeks. Short and slim, she looked just like he imagined fairies or pixies would. Born when Jack was a senior in high school, their father had called Peggy his little bonus—unexpected, but more than welcome. It had been a little embarrassing at the time for Jack to be forced to accept the fact that his parents were actually still having sex. But from the moment she was born, he'd been wrapped around her finger.

That didn't mean he wanted to talk to her at the moment, though. "Beat it, brat."

"Wow." Peggy grinned up at him, slapping one hand to her chest. "Be still, my heart."

"Go away, Peggy, your brother and I are talking."

"On second thought," Jack told his sister, "stay."

Peggy slipped into the room, flopped onto his bed, then rolled onto her stomach, swinging both legs in the air. "Is this the great escape?" she asked, reaching for the duffel bag and peeking inside.

Their mother sighed and narrowed her eyes. "Aren't you supposed to be at the hotel?"

"Eileen's covering for me," Peggy said.

"Eileen should be at home lying down," Mary Alice countered, thinking of her third child, very pregnant with *her* third child. "That baby's due any day."

Peggy grinned. "How tough is it to pick up the phone and say, 'Ho-Ho-Hotel, how can I help you?' "

Jack groaned. The hotel. He'd put in his time at the family-owned business. Surrounded by Christmas trees, stockings hung by the fireplace, and year-round carolers. He didn't blame Peggy a bit for sneaking out.

"So what's going on with this baby thing?" the girl asked, propping her chin in her cupped hands. "Everybody in town's talking about it, but nobody knows anything."

Jack wasn't eager to discuss the baby, but it beat the hell out of the talk his mother was determined to have. "Not much to report," he said and carried two pairs of jeans to the duffel. Smacking Peggy's hand aside, he shoved them into the bag, then headed back to the dresser. "Somebody abandoned a newborn girl last night."

"Just awful," Mary Alice muttered. "When Maggie called to tell me that you and that nice Carol Baker were taking care of the poor little thing, I could hardly believe it. Why, things like that don't happen in Christmas."

"God, Mom," Peggy said, rolling onto her side to prop her head on one hand. "Don't you watch the news? Stuff like that happens everywhere."

"Listen to the world traveler," her mother said.

Jack ignored the bickering. In the Reilly household, if you weren't arguing, you weren't talking. "Peggy, have you noticed any pregnant women around town?"

"You mean besides Eileen?" She grinned again and he found himself answering that smile. Impossible not to. Another good reason for getting out of the house.

"Yeah, since Eileen's still cooking hers."

"Nope."

"What about the girls at school?" Mary Alice asked, frowning. "Wasn't there something a few months ago about Lyssa Devon . . . ?"

Peggy pushed up to kneel on the mattress and rolled her eyes dramatically enough to send them cartwheeling right out of her head. "God, Mom. That was mono. Lyssa had mono. Not a baby. Something like that I would have noticed."

"So none of your girlfriends have been putting on weight the last few months?" Jack asked.

Peggy sniffed and lifted her chin. "If they were, I wouldn't rat them out. But they're not. I mean, please. We're not stupid. We have to go to all of those health classes and listen to all the lectures about AIDS and STDs and stuff. And how condoms are the eighth wonder of the world and no one should leave home without one."

"Condoms don't always work, you know," Mary Alice pointed out.

"I know," Peggy said, interrupting the lecture she'd already heard dozens of times. "Don't worry, Mom. I'm not doing anything. And when I do, I'll be careful. I mean I wouldn't let some high school sleazoid touch me anyway and besides—"

"Okay, now you can shut up," Jack said. It was one thing to know that his parents had had sex. It was something else again to think about his little sister rolling around in the back seat of some fast-talking teenager's car.

"Geezzz," Peggy complained, scooting off the bed and slouching toward the door. "You guys asked the questions, remember?"

"Go to the hotel," her mother called as Peggy slipped into the hallway. "Send Eileen home to rest."

"Yeah, yeah." The resigned voice floated back to them from the end of the hall. "It *is* summer vacation, you know."

Jack, sensing his mother was about to jump back

into their previous conversation, took advantage of her momentary distraction. Zipping up the duffel, he slung the strap over his shoulder and headed for the door himself. "See you later, Mom."

"Sunday dinner. Here."

"Right."

Once her kids were gone and the old house had settled into quiet again, Mary Alice glanced around her son's old room and sighed. The years went by too quickly, that was the trouble. By the time you figured out that the times you were living were the best, they were over and nothing more remained than a few blurry snapshots and a handful of memories.

Frowning, she remembered the flash of old pain in Jack's eyes and wished she knew a way to combat it. Why was it, she wondered, that the older your kids got, the harder it was to see them hurt?

When they were little, a kiss and a Band-Aid would do the trick.

But as scraped knees gave way to broken hearts and troubled souls, it was so much harder to find the words to help.

Chapter 4

Carol saw him arrive.

Hard to miss him, really. He parked his Mustang in front of the shop, climbed out, and sunlight hit him like a spotlight aimed at an actor on stage. His too-long black hair ruffled in a breeze and a shadow of whisker stubble darkened his jaw. He looked up and down the street, then slowly swiveled his head to stare at the house. For one brief, weird instant, Carol was sure that his gaze, hidden behind his dark glasses, had locked with hers. And in that split second, she wished she'd taken the time to put on some makeup this morning. But really, she'd figured that dealing with the baby and staying awake to help customers was the best she could hope for. Makeup was just *way* out of the realm of possibilities for the day. Heck, she'd been lucky to find her hairbrush and a minute and a half to use it.

But her racing thoughts ended abruptly a second later, when he reached into the car and grabbed what looked like an old army duffel bag. He was serious, then. He really was moving in. A scowl on his face, he headed for the front door with the slow, measured gait of a man walking to the gallows. Gee, he seemed real happy about the prospect, too.

Her own, tall, black-haired, blue-eyed ray of sunshine.

"Sure," she said, glancing at the baby, lying in her drawer atop the counter, "this is gonna work out fine. Mr. Charm. I can see it now. We'll share late-night coffees. Have picnics in the backyard." Carol laughed to herself, but couldn't quite squash the flash of pure female interest that rose up in her as she watched him move.

So tall. His legs looked impossibly long in worn, faded jeans. His running shoes were battered and the dark red short-sleeved shirt he wore emphasized the width of his shoulders. His black hair gleamed in the morning sunlight and the frown on his face deepened with every step that brought him closer to the front porch.

Carol's stomach jittered, but she hid it well when he took a sharp left after entering the building and pushed open the door to the shop. Bells on the door jangled a welcome that was clearly lost on him.

"Look who's here, Liz," she said, smiling briefly at the sleeping baby. "It's Sir Charm-a-lot."

"Cute." He grimaced, but at least his features showed some kind of animation. She'd begun to think his face was frozen into that scowl.

"I try."

He pulled off his sunglasses and reached into his shirt pocket. "Here's the rent check. One month. In advance."

Quinn stood up behind the counter and his low, deep-throated rumble rolled out into the room.

Jack shot the dog a quick look as he handed the check over. She took it, her gaze landing on the upper left-hand corner. Plain, gray paper. Boring. No designs. No funky little sayings or artwork. Nothing to tell her anything about his personality. Plus, he'd drawn lines through his address. Apparently, he'd left LA behind him permanently. He'd made it clear that he could hardly wait to get out of Christmas, so where, she wondered, was he actually headed? Then she wondered if even he knew the answer to that question.

Tapping the check against her fingertips, she asked, "Do you have any ID?"

"Trying for cute again, huh?"

"I've been told I'm *very* cute," she assured him.

"Uh-huh. By your coven, no doubt."

"Well, sure. If you can't count on your own coven to support you . . ."

He leaned one hand on the counter. "Maybe you don't remember, lady, but I'm working on about twenty minutes' sleep here."

"Yeah, me too." Carol'd been working on caffeine and nerves all morning. But she wasn't snarling at people. A damn shame that a man as amazing-looking as he was had such a sucky personality. "But I'm not taking it out on you."

His mouth twitched. "You're obviously a much better human being than I am. Congratulations. Can I have the key?"

She sighed, hit a button on her antique cash register, and when the drawer slid out, she snatched up a key from the till. Slamming the drawer shut again, she handed him the key. "You're really going to have to work on those people skills."

"I'll make a note." He took the key from her, his fingertips scraping along her palm.

She snatched her hand back as if it had been burned, and stuffed it into the pocket of her short denim skirt. But tucking her hand away didn't get rid of the sizzle still humming through her skin. When it had happened at the clinic, she'd told herself she was just tired. Imagining things.

Now that that little flash of heat when he touched her had happened again, she figured the safest way to deal with it was to ignore it. Forcing a laugh, she talked to the baby, but aimed her comments at the tall man watching her. "There you go, Liz. You were right. If he's taking notes, he *can* read and write."

"You're a laugh a minute, aren't you?"

"You laughed? And I missed it?" she countered, studying the scowl seemingly etched into his features.

"Never mind." He picked up his bag, then stopped. Turning his head, he looked at her. "Liz? You named the baby Elizabeth?"

"Nah." Reaching over, Carol covered the baby's ears and whispered, "Liz—you remember. It's short for Lizardbaby."

"Oh, for—"

"Hey, you never know."

"Crazy," he muttered, heading for the door. "This whole town is crazy. Always has been. Always will be."

"Yeah?" she answered, raising her voice as he moved farther away. "If everyone around you is a loon and you're the only one sane . . . maybe *you're* the crazy one."

He stopped at the door and, over his shoulder, shot her a long look through shadow-filled eyes. "That's been said before."

Then the bells bounced and clanged as he pushed through the door and went upstairs.

Quinn settled down for another nap as soon as Jack left.

Crazy, huh? Well, better crazy than boring. Better crazy than lonely. Better crazy than . . . Carol shook her head and dismissed thoughts of the surly sheriff with the amazing, haunted eyes. Instead, she shifted a look at the baby, now wide awake and watching her. "Well, hi, Liz . . ." She scooped the tiny infant into her arms and held her carefully, gently.

She was getting better at this, she thought. She'd only been in charge of the baby for a few hours, but already, she felt almost . . . competent. "Poor baby," she whispered and instinctively swayed with a gentle, side-to-side motion. "You really got the short stick, didn't you? But don't worry, okay? Until they find you a mom and dad, I'll take care of you." Carol ran the tip of one finger along the baby's soft, full cheek and smiled when she turned into Carol's finger, expecting lunch. "They will find you parents, you know. You're a baby. Babies always get adopted."

Her mind drifted back, whether she wanted it to or not. Carol was ten when her parents died in a car wreck on the 405 freeway. There hadn't been any other family, so she was named a ward of the court and sent to the county home for kids. Distinct memories still lived in her mind. She could recall with perfect clarity the terror cringing inside her when she walked up those steps for the first time. She remembered kids freezing in place when the door opened and she stepped inside. Whatever game they'd been playing was forgotten as they checked out the latest addition to the already crowded house.

Before she'd lost her family, she'd had her own room and a backyard and a dog. And then almost instantly, she'd been just one more girl in a house full of kids, with no privacy, no backyard, and the knowledge that her dog had been sent to the pound.

Those first few months in the home, she'd spent most of her time crying for what she'd lost. But eventually, she smiled again and learned to hope again and even dream about having a family again. Carol remembered wearing her best dress, smiling at prospective parents when they stopped in at the home. She remembered desperately trying to look smaller and *younger* than she actually was. Everyone knew that once you hit a certain age, adoption was not a part of your future. So for that first year, she'd slumped her shoulders and crouched and smiled, and when none of that worked, she'd pretended not to care when she was overlooked again and again.

The year she was eleven, she tried to fit in at the different foster homes she'd been placed in, but temporary children didn't seem to fit anywhere and soon she and the system had stopped trying. The year she turned twelve, she was back at the group home and there she'd stayed until her eighteenth birthday, when the state had said, "Happy birthday, Carol. Now get out."

She patted the baby and let herself remember the fear of standing on her own two feet at eighteen. No one to lean on. No one to count on. But she'd found a way. Her grades had won her a scholarship and she'd finished college with a degree in business and the vow to build herself the life she'd always wanted.

"I did it, too," Carol murmured, letting her gaze drop to the tiny baby in her arms. "I got a job, earned good money, and saved it. Then I bought this place." She ran one finger along the baby's cheek. "So don't worry. Things'll work out for you, too."

The baby's fists raged at the air, as though she were already trying to claw her way out of the situation.

Carol leaned over and kissed that tiny, sweet-smelling forehead and inhaled the scent of baby shampoo on her fine, dark hair. "I'll try to do a really good job of taking care of you, Liz. But I can't love you." Her fingertip gently traced that rosebud of a mouth. "So, just don't do anything really cute, okay?"

The baby opened milky blue eyes wider and stared at her. Carol sighed. Maybe crankypants was right. Maybe she was crazy. Thinking she could take care of this baby and not forge a connection—when her heart was already melting.

The baby cooed and waved its tiny fists in the air again, as if demanding attention. "You're already cute, aren't you? So basically, I'm already in deep shit."

Jack stood at the window of his new apartment and thought about the landlady. From the moment he'd stepped into her shop, he'd felt it. An awareness of Carol Foster that he didn't like and didn't want. Apparently, though, he didn't have much to say about what his body responded to.

She'd looked . . . too damn good, standing there, watching him out of whiskey-colored eyes. The blond streaks in her hair shone like gold and her skin was the color of warm honey and probably tasted just as good, dammit. She looked so at home, standing in the middle of what looked like an explosion of Christmas goodies. Crystal and pewter and porcelain and wood all competed for shelf space in a shop that was at once both cluttered and somehow neat and orderly. Just like in her apartment, the scent of cinnamon and apples flavored the air, making the place seem welcoming, despite the reminders of a holiday he'd just as soon forget.

But when Carol's mouth had twitched into a smile, he'd forgotten everything but her. Annoying woman. Hell, the whole situation was annoying.

Being back in town was enough to make him crazy

even while stirring a hornet's nest of some pretty good memories. Jack sipped at his coffee and remembered. He'd left home right after college. He'd always known that he wouldn't stay in Christmas. It just hadn't been big enough for him. It had felt too confining to a man who'd always wanted adventure. Well, he thought, he'd had the adventure and it hadn't been all it was cracked up to be.

In LA, he'd become a cop and found what he'd thought was a great life. He'd had everything he'd ever wanted, planned on. Everything had rolled his way. Until one night, when everything in his life shattered.

More memories stirred and images rose up in his mind before he could quash them. In seconds, the comfortable little apartment in Christmas faded away and Jack was back in the dark.

He could almost feel the cold drip of rain sliding down the collar of his shirt to roll along his spine. If he let himself, he'd hear the wind whistling past the drunks and homeless crouched inside their cardboard mansions, trying to escape the pounding rain that eroded their homes. His fingers curled into a fist as if he could still grip the police-issue revolver he used to carry. He squinted into the sunlight and instead saw neon-shattered darkness. He could almost smell the stink of garbage that had littered the alley the night his world blew up.

But almost wasn't good enough. Coming up out of the past like a drowning man striking for the surface, he pushed the memories down into the dark hole that used to be his heart. Cold filled him and he shivered, taking another swallow of coffee he hoped was hot enough to ease the chills away. But this cold had been with him for two long years and he had a feeling he'd never really be warm again.

He glanced down and grimaced tightly to see his hand shaking. What the hell kind of cop was he that memories could shake him to the bone like that? "No kind," he muttered, fisting that hand helplessly.

As the images faded, he told himself the knot in his stomach would unwind. Eventually.

But his world would still be shattered.

Nothing could change that.

He took another swallow and let the too hot liquid scald his throat like a penance.

Now he was back in Christmas. And he was still Catholic enough to believe that this was some kind of just punishment. A sort of Purgatory—a home for those not quite ready for Hell.

Not ready for prime-time sinning.

He snorted a choked-off laugh and slapped one hand on the wall beside the tall bay window to stare out at the street below. Since moving to LA, he'd only come back home for brief visits with the family. He'd never planned on moving back here. But plans had a way of falling apart on a man when he wasn't paying attention.

"Not for long, though." He took another gulp of the coffee that was strong enough to leap out of the cup and jump down his throat on its own.

Maybe it was fate dragging his sorry ass back to Christmas. If he'd never answered the phone that day his mother had called asking him to step in for Sheriff Thompson, he wouldn't be standing here now, talking to himself. But he knew more than most that you couldn't go back. You couldn't change what had already happened. If you could . . . things might have been different.

Now that he was here, though, there was no way out of this mess. He'd given his word and though his "honor" was a little ragged around the edges these days, it was all he had left. The best he could hope for was that Sheriff Thompson recovered in time to reclaim his job and save Jack's sanity.

Staring out the window of his new apartment, he watched a group of teenage girls start up the walk toward the shop. In the summer light, they looked impossibly young and carefree. Their giggles floated up to him like bubbles on the breeze. He spotted Peggy in the bunch and that was enough to convince him to do without the nap he'd been planning on and go back to the office. His baby sister had learned at the master's—their mother's—knee. And he knew without a doubt that given half a chance, Peggy would be in here, giving him a pep talk or yelling at him or in general being a pain in the ass. Well, he didn't need another pain. He'd just moved in across the hall from one.

Setting the coffee cup down on the windowsill, he walked across the room, grabbed his keys, and shot down the stairs.

When the bells over the door clanged again, Carol looked up, though she needn't have bothered. She'd heard the girls long before the door opened. Their bright laughter and eager chatter shattered the quiet in the store and drowned out the soft music playing on the stereo behind the counter.

"Morning," Carol called out.

Two of the girls simply headed straight for the counter Carol liked to think of as her bread and butter. Though the shop specialized in "An Old-fashioned Christmas," with one-of-a-kind, handcrafted gifts and ornaments, she also carried little specialty items like lipsticks, eye shadows, and nail polishes: Just the thing to keep the town's teenagers coming back in a steady, loyal stream.

But apparently, at least three of her customers were more interested in little Liz than in OPI polish today.

"Wow, is this the baby?" Lacey Reynolds asked and leaned in for a better look at Liz, sleeping in the crook of Carol's arm. Lacey's soft, blond hair swung over her cheek and her blue eyes lit up with interest as she tugged the hem of her oversized sweatshirt down over her belly.

"Dork," Peggy Reilly said with a laugh and shoved the other girl. "Of course it's the baby."

A flicker of movement caught Carol's eye and she glanced to one side in time to see Jack, ducking his head as he left. He looked like a man trying to escape and a part of her wondered just what it was he was running from. And why he hadn't bothered to say hello to his little sister. Then she shrugged her thoughts away and turned her attention back to the girls.

Lacey grinned, and tugged at her sweatshirt again. Always overweight, the girl had been diligent about Weight Watchers for the last several months or so, and though she was thinner now than she used to be, she was still self-conscious enough to wear clothing two sizes too big for her.

"It's so little." Donna Flynn pushed her dark hair back from her face, then stuck her hands in the pockets of her shorts as if half-afraid someone might ask her to touch the infant.

"Most of us are when we're brand-new," Carol said, smiling.

"Yeah, but you never really think about it until you see one up close and personal," Peggy said and leaned in to watch Carol lay the baby into the carrier sitting atop the counter. "I mean, my sisters have kids and all, but who pays attention, you know? Is my brother here? I mean, he lives here now, right?"

"Yes, he does. But I think I saw him leave," Carol said and to herself added, *Running like ghosts were chasing him.*

"Bummer," Peggy said.

"How is your sister Eileen?" Carol asked, keeping one eye on the girls over by the lipstick counter. They were all good kids, but temptation was a strong motivator and she'd hate to have to be on the phone to their mothers complaining about shoplifting.

"Crabby," Peggy said shortly.

Must run in the family, Carol thought, remembering the scowl on Jack's face and his shuttered eyes.

"Somebody just left the baby in the manger?" Lacey asked quietly, reaching out one finger to stroke the child's closed fist. Then she lifted her soft blue gaze to Carol. "Everybody's talking about how you and Quinn found her last night."

At the mention of his name, Quinn pushed himself to his feet and walked around the counter to lean against Lacey in welcome. Lacey worked part-time in Carol's store during the summer and the girl was one of Quinn's favorite people.

"Hi, sweetie," the girl said, running one hand over the dog's big head.

"Word about the baby traveled fast," Carol said.

"Are you kidding?" Peggy grinned and looked from Lacey to Donna before shifting her gaze back to Carol. "Every mother in town is having 'the talk' with their daughters. Like we've never heard of sex before. And hello? The baby's here already. A little too late for the sex-ed campaign, you know?"

Donna groaned and moved along the counter, studying the silver earrings hanging from a rack near the cash register. "My mother's off the deep end. Started asking if I know anyone who was fat and suddenly got thinner."

Lacey grimaced and folded her arms over her chest.

Peggy noticed and jabbed her with an elbow to the ribs. "Oh, chill out, Lace. You've been *losing* weight, not putting it on. Nobody thinks it was *you*."

"Totally," Donna said, nodding until her hair jumped around her face. *"Parents."* She shook her head as if completely dumbfounded by the stupidity of adults.

"Really," Peggy chimed in as she flipped through a stack of brochures announcing the Fourth of July celebration. "Like we wouldn't notice somebody pregnant. What, are we complete morons?"

"I know," Lacey added as she rubbed Quinn's head. "It's not like you could hide something like that. I mean, Vicki Chambers was getting fat for a while."

"Yeah," Peggy said, picking up one of the flyers to fold and jam into her shorts pocket. "Now the PTA's probably going to drag out the whips and chains to interrogate all the fat girls."

Carol sighed inwardly. She could understand how the mothers in town would be a little frantic. And even why the girls were so dismissive. But the simple truth was, *someone* had had a baby.

And that someone had walked away from it in the middle of the night. But try as she might, Carol couldn't think of a single local girl who could have given birth. Anyone suspiciously pregnant would have been the talk of the town for months. And the only chubby girls Carol knew of had been steadily dropping weight for the last several months—ever since a Weight Watchers office had opened up on the edge of town.

Heck, her Alien Baby theory made more sense than thinking a high school girl could cover up a pregnancy in a small town. So, if it wasn't a local girl . . . then it had to be someone passing through. And Carol wondered if the woman would keep on going—or if already she was turning around and coming back to claim her baby.

Her heart clenched at the thought. And she had to remind herself that she was *not* getting attached to Liz. She absolutely was not.

Right.

Then she thought about Jack Reilly and the determined glint in his eyes. He might not *want* to be the town cop, but anybody with half a brain could see he *was* a cop clean down to the bone.

"I bet *we* could figure out who the mom is," Peggy said.

"You think?" Lacey frowned and rubbed Quinn's head.

"*We* know the girls in town better than our parents do," Peggy insisted, getting a decided gleam in her eye at the thought of playing detective.

"Maybe you should let your brother handle this," Carol suggested.

But Peggy wasn't listening. In fact, Carol could almost see the wheels turning behind her pretty eyes.

"Carol," one of the other girls called out from across the store, "did you get the new pearl polish in yet?"

She gave Peggy another wary look, then turned back to business. "Yes, it's in the back room." She glanced at Lacey. "Would you mind getting it for me? I don't want to leave the baby."

"Sure." Lacey slipped behind the counter and through the door to the storage room.

Donna and Peggy wandered off, exploring the shop, laughing with their friends. Which left Carol plenty of time to indulge her thoughts. Unfortunately, most of those thoughts went straight to the tall, dark, and cranky man who'd just run for the hills.

Maggie Reilly Cooper trusted her instincts. She was a good judge of character and, more often than not, went with her gut instincts when making a decision.

Which was how Carol Baker had become temporary foster mother to a newborn baby girl. It wasn't always easy to find emergency foster families. And since Carol had offered to help out in a pinch, Maggie would have been crazy to turn her down.

"There are a few forms to fill out," she said and drew a sheaf of papers from her briefcase. Setting them on the kitchen table, she slid them over to Carol to read and sign.

While she waited, Maggie indulged herself and scooped the baby up out of her drawer bed. Her youngest was in kindergarten now and every once in a while she got that old urge for another baby. Which she promptly stomped out. Babies were fun, but it was even better when the little curtain climbers could pour themselves a cup of juice when they were thirsty. Still, "She's a cutie, isn't she?"

"She really is."

"How are you getting along with her? Any trouble?"

"Oh, you mean except for the part where I don't know much about babies?"

Maggie laughed and rocked the sleeping infant. "You'll learn. We all do."

"You said you were looking for a more permanent situation for Liz. Any luck yet?"

"Nope." Maggie sighed and smiled at the baby. "You're

it, Carol. There's no one else to take her right now. So, if you're still okay with it . . ."

Carol straightened up. "Sure. I'll keep her. At least until you find a permanent home for her."

"First," Maggie said with a sigh, "we have to try to find the mother." It went against the grain, she thought. The calm, rational part of her mind knew that any number of things could combine to make a woman desperate enough to abandon her own child—and then regret the action later. But the emotional, lead-with-your-heart part of her wanted to say, "No. Give your baby up and you don't get it back." Because, really, what was to keep the mother from changing her mind again? Abandoning the child again? Or worse, neglecting it or abusing it?

Thoughts of her own two kids roared through her and the protective instincts of a mother lion charged to the front of her brain. She'd do anything for her own kids, so it was damn hard to understand a mother able to simply walk away from her child.

"What are the chances of finding her?" Carol asked, signing first one form and then the next.

"Slim to none, unless she wants to be found," Maggie admitted. Laying the baby down again, she picked up her can of soda and took a long drink. "Let's face it. Christmas is a little town. If someone around here were pregnant and then suddenly not, we'd notice."

"True . . ."

"Secrets have a shelf life of about twenty-four hours around here," Maggie said. "More than likely, the mother was staying in a motel near here, dropped the baby off, and kept on going."

"What does your brother say?"

"Which one?" Maggie asked, with a laugh. "Sean's at the rectory, fielding frantic phone calls from parents, wanting to know how to talk to their kids about this." She sighed. "And Jack doesn't say much about anything these days. At least not to me."

He'd changed so much in the last couple of years, he didn't even seem like the same brother she'd always known. And she wasn't the only one worried. "But he's working on it. Talking to people. Asking questions." Maggie tipped her head to one side. "I hear he's your new tenant."

"Another temporary situation," Carol assured her.

"How is he so far?"

"Crabby," Carol answered before she thought about it. Then she winced. After all, not only was Maggie Reilly Cooper Jack's sister, but a representative of Social Services. Carol really couldn't afford to piss her off. Not if she wanted to keep little Liz around.

But Maggie laughed. Blue eyes flashing, she shook her head, swinging her dark red hair back from her face. "Yeah, he is crabby. More so now than he used to be, too. But he's a good guy underneath all the crap." Then her features softened. "Just wish we could convince him of that. He's had a bad couple of years . . ." She bit her bottom lip and let her words trail off, sentence unfinished.

Carol wondered what Maggie was leaving unsaid, but didn't ask. After all, she'd never been a part of a family, but she knew how they worked. They circled the wagons, protecting their own from outsiders. You didn't have to be on the inside to know it existed, she thought. Whatever secrets Jack had would remain secret unless he spilled them. And Carol really couldn't see that happening, so she'd just have to learn to live with her curiosity.

Dammit.

"Okay," Maggie announced as she checked over the

papers before stuffing them back into her brown leather satchel. "That'll do it." She stood up, swinging the bag's strap over her shoulder, then stopped just as she took a step toward the door. "You know, if you want, I could get Jack to stop by my place and pick up my kids' old crib."

Glancing down at the drawer, Carol nodded. "You bet, if you're sure you don't need it."

"Trust me on this," Maggie said, heading for the door, "I'm never going to need it again." She grabbed the doorknob, gave it a turn, and grinned at Carol. "Congratulations. You are now the proud foster mother of a bouncing baby girl."

Carol smiled and thought about how her life had come full circle. As a child, in one lonely year, she'd had a series of foster homes herself, bouncing from one place to the next, always hoping for permanence. Always hoping to find the one place where she could belong. Where she could stay.

Now, *she* was the foster parent.

And it wasn't permanent this time, either.

Carol's heart ached a little as she stared down at little Liz, so tiny, so beautiful.

Still, she had the baby for now. She would enjoy it. She would relish every minute, and then when it was time, she would let little Liz go. Because keeping her would mean loving her. And she couldn't do that. Couldn't love and lose.

Not again.

CHAPTER 5

Journal Entry:

Do babies remember?

Does she lay in her little bed and wonder where I went? Does she think I'm coming back to get her? Or is she glad I'm gone? Does she miss me?

I miss her.

I didn't think I would.

God. What kind of mom just leaves her baby all alone?

Will she think I didn't love her?

I do.

I really do.

But love's just not enough.

Summer heat baked through the trees on the cliff edge, sizzled on the sand below, and glinted off the surface of the ocean like light dazzling off the edge of a knife. The air shimmered, like it was trying to build a mirage. Peggy Reilly tipped her sunglasses down to get a better look at it. But an optical illusion really didn't compare with the guy stepping out of the waves, shaking his head, sending water droplets flying from his long blond hair.

She sighed a little in pure appreciation. Seriously, JT Hawkins had really been working out. His excellent abs were totally dreamworthy.

The day was perfect. Her shift at the hotel was over until tomorrow, summer crowds dotted the beach, and the scent of coconut oil drifted in the hot, still air. Perfect.

Especially while she had such a great view of JT.

"Hello? Earth to Peggy."

Peggy sighed again, pushed her glasses back up the bridge of her nose, and without taking her gaze off JT, said, "Huh?"

"Clever." Lacey tossed a bottle of suntan lotion at her and grinned when Peggy yelped. Once she had her friend's attention, she said, "We were talking about tomorrow?"

"What?" Peggy reluctantly gave up the JT stare-fest and swiveled her head to face her friends. Donna and Lacey were looking at her like she was nuts. "Tomorrow what?"

"The Fourth?" Donna said in a tone that implied the word, "duh."

"The party?" Lacey prompted.

"Oh . . ." Peggy nodded, lay back in her sand chair, and let her gaze slide back to where JT and his friends were laughing and throwing a football around. Naturally, they were only doing it so the girls on the beach would watch and admire—so who was she to deprive them and ruin the grand plan of the universe? "You really think the party's going to come off now?"

"Why not?" Donna wanted to know.

"Baby alert," Peggy muttered and slathered on another

layer of SPF 30. Hey, redheads didn't tan—they boiled. "Every parent in town is going crazy over this abandoned baby."

"Not just the parents," Lacey said, her gaze drifting over the people scattered over the sand. "Everybody's talking about the baby."

"Well, yeah," Donna said. "I mean, *I'd* like to know who the mom is."

Peggy thought about it for a long minute, following Lacey's gaze to sweep across the beach. She'd grown up in Christmas, just like Lacey and Donna. They knew all the same people, had been in school with them for like . . . *ever*. So how could somebody sneak a pregnancy past any of them? "Maybe we could figure out who she is."

Lacey snorted. "Yeah? How?"

"I don't know." Peggy shrugged and smiled. "But we're all nosy, right? We can at least *try* to think of who it might be."

"Could be fun." Donna opened her eyes and glanced at them. "Like a detective novel or something."

"Maybe," Lacey said, sitting back in her chair and tipping her face up to the sun. "I mean, how hard can it be?"

"Exactly." Peggy smiled to herself and tossed the tube of sunblock to her towel.

Lacey tugged her too big T-shirt a little farther down over her bathing suit. She'd lost a lot of weight over the last few months, but she was still a little self-conscious about her body. "But before we turn all Sherlock Holmesy, what about the party?"

"I say we party." Donna stretched out on her towel, holding her arms out from her sides like she was about to be nailed to a cross. "We're good to go."

Peggy wanted to think so. Since graduating from high school the month before, the senior class of—as the students fondly referred to it—Bah Humbug High had been planning a celebration. One last blowout together before their small class was split up and everyone went on to college and jobs, most of them leaving Christmas behind. A party that they'd been planning for the last two months. One that Peggy'd really hate to miss. But now, with the baby thing and her mom on Teen Patrol and her brother Jack the temporary police chief . . . things didn't look so good.

"We *are* going, right?" Lacey asked.

Peggy looked at her friends and smiled. Lacey and Donna were really gung ho for this party. In the last few months, they'd been on serious diets and for the first time in, like, ever they both were looking pretty darn good. Be a shame to waste it, right?

And this summer was really their class's last chance to be together. Not to mention the fact that the senior-class party was a Christmas tradition. Plus, once they were all off at college, nothing would ever really be the same again. They'd come home on vacation, sure, but everything else would be . . . different. Besides, she thought, it's a party. What could go wrong?

"Damn straight," Peggy said and tipped her face up to the sun. "A party's just what we need."

Liz had been fed.

Her diapers had been changed.

She'd burped like a champ.

And she was *still* screaming.

Something was definitely wrong.

Quinn whined and whimpered in sympathy. His cries rose and fell in tandem with the baby as though they'd arranged a concert in harmony.

This was one concert, though, Carol would have gladly missed.

"Quinn," she said tightly, "you are *not* helping." But the big dog only paced in time with her, his intermittent cries keeping a rhythm as his nails clicked against the floor.

Shadows filled the room. From outside the windows, the glow of the Christmas lights sparkled like jewel-toned stars. Wind rattled the windowpanes and a flickering light flashed from the muted television as space aliens battled the valiant defenders of Earth. Ordinarily, Carol would have been on the couch, with a bowl of popcorn, cheering the good guys on. Tonight, though, she was fighting a battle all her own.

Carol jiggled the baby gently and patted her diapered behind and swayed and hummed and, as a last resort, tried singing. But even *she* couldn't relax when she was singing, so she stopped that pretty damn quick.

Liz's cries continued, as if she were an opera singer trapped in a time loop, stuck singing the same aria over and over again.

She was really out of ideas.

The baby's face was now beet red and that couldn't be a good thing, right? Couldn't babies have strokes or something? And if not Liz, Carol was pretty sure *she* was close to a stroke.

"Oh, I so suck at this," she whispered, her words getting lost in the storm of Liz's screech. Shaking her head, Carol reminded herself just how many times over the years that she'd dreamed of this. Of having a child, building a family. Who knew that she had, apparently, no talent for child care?

Carol glanced at her phone, sitting silent and useless on an end table beside the overstuffed floral-fabric couch. She couldn't call Phoebe—the one person she would ordinarily turn to in a crisis of this magnitude—because Phoebe had deserted her in her hour of need. Instead of being in Carol's apartment watching the *Stargate* marathon on the sci-fi channel and eating buckets of popcorn, Phoebe was out having sex. Yes, *sex*.

Carol's back teeth ground together. Whether the flash of emotion that shot through her body and was gone again in an instant was self-pity or envy didn't really matter. The point was, Phoebe had thrown her best friend over for a chance at mind-boggling sex with a gorgeous carpenter.

Some people, Carol thought, had absolutely no loyalty.

Although, she really couldn't blame Phoebe any. Cash Hunter, the carpenter in question, filled out his Levi's in such a way, he could melt the resistance of a nun—much less that of an overworked doctor.

Sadly, it had been so long since Carol had had sex herself, she was pretty sure she wouldn't remember what to do if the opportunity presented itself. Which she really didn't have to worry about, since the chances of that opportunity popping up were slim to none. Especially at the moment. A screaming newborn was a better birth control device than a condom.

"Come on, Liz," she murmured, softly stroking the baby's stiffened spine, "give me a break here, okay? I'm doing the best I can." And her best was apparently pretty pitiful. Carol's ears rang with the echo of the baby's screams and her heart ached for the poor little thing. Something was obviously wrong and Carol obviously had no idea how to fix it.

Nothing like a baby to make you feel completely inadequate.

Lizardbaby had her own issues and seemed, Carol

thought as the headache behind her eyes cranked up another notch, able to go without breathing for exceptionally long periods of time. The baby's wails went on as one, long howl, unbroken by gasps for air.

The Alien Baby thing flitted through her mind again, but she let go again almost instantly. Carol was just too damn tired to play the game.

"It's okay, sweetie, honest." If her voice sounded a little strained, she was hoping the baby wouldn't notice. "You're safe. You're warm and dry and . . . *really* cranky." She blew out a breath that ruffled the fringe of bangs over her forehead and did nothing to ease the frustration simmering inside.

Quinn sat down in front of her and his big head nearly reached her waist. He looked up at her, watching, clearly offering silent doggie support.

Carol hardly noticed.

Cranky.

That one word echoed over and over again in her brain until it finally rang a bell.

Maybe you had to *fight* cranky *with* cranky.

And she had the veritable *king* of cranky living right across the hall.

But was she desperate enough to go to him for help? Was she really willing to swallow what was left of her pride and admit that she couldn't handle a six-pound shrieking baby?

Another screech sounded in her ear and rattled through her brain.

Yes, she thought. Yes, she was willing to ask for help. She was willing to barter or bribe to get it.

So there was nothing else to do.

She had to admit defeat.

Hey, if Mr. Charm was going to live across the hall,

she might as well get some use out of him. And if it wasn't exactly the kind of use Phoebe was even now getting out of the carpenter, well, no one but Carol had to know she felt any twinge of regret.

Starting across the room, she barely heard Quinn's nails clicking, first loudly, then muffled, as he raced across bare wood and throw rugs, keeping pace with her.

"It's okay, Quinn. We're good. We're just calling in the cavalry."

She grabbed the doorknob, threw the door open, and . . . ducked—just in time to avoid Jack's knuckles, raised to knock.

Quinn growled, a low rumble of sound that almost overwhelmed the baby's cries.

Almost.

"I was just coming to see you."

Jack's gaze shot first to Quinn, then slammed back up to Carol's. "What the hell are you doing to that baby?" he demanded at the same time she spoke.

"Doing?" Carol repeated, hearing her voice climb to a note it had never reached before. Swaying and jiggling and rubbing, she glared up at him. "Well, clearly, I'm abusing her viciously. Can't you tell by how pleased I look?"

He rolled his eyes.

Wow, Carol thought. Animation. But before she had time to be thoroughly stunned, he ducked his head, stepped into her apartment, and scooped the wailing infant right out of her arms.

Silence dropped on the room.

Absolute silence.

It was eerie.

Carol yawned widely, trying to pop her ears, sure for one brief, terrifying second that she'd gone deaf. But a heartbeat later, she was reassured by the sniffling sound the baby made as she stared up adoringly at Jack Reilly.

"You little traitor," Carol muttered. One look into those big blue eyes of Jack Reilly's and little Liz had curled up and cooed. Irritating as hell. Especially irritating because damned if she didn't want to do the same thing.

Jack held Liz cradled in one strong arm and he swayed gently from side to side, like a man who knew what he was doing. His eyebrows lifted as he inclined his head toward Carol, as if accepting a standing ovation for a role well played.

"How did you do that?" she demanded, silently figuring that if she'd done all of her pacing in a straight line, she'd probably have made it to Utah by now. But despite her every effort she hadn't been able to do in hours what Jack had done in seconds. "Come on, spill the secret. How?"

"Charisma."

Carol choked out a laugh.

"The evidence is in front of you." His lips twitched into what might have been a smile if he'd tried just a bit harder.

No doubt just as well he hadn't, Carol assured herself, since that one, brief glimpse of a not-quite smile, had done some interesting things to her blood pressure. Wow. She must be even more tired than she'd thought.

He stared at her for a long minute or two and the look in his eyes softened as one corner of his mouth lifted slightly. "What?"

"You know," she said, before she could stop herself, "you're pretty cute when you're not frowning at the world."

Instantly, the scowl she was becoming so familiar

with was back in place. "And," he said, "you're not at all annoying until you open your mouth."

"You know, remarks like that will *not* get you a cup of coffee and a piece of cake."

He stilled. "You have cake?"

Ah, Carol, she told herself, you can really snag the men. Just bring on the baked goods and they're putty in your hands. "Chocolate."

"Sold."

"On one condition."

"I have to listen to you?"

"That, too," she admitted, then added as she leaned in and watched Liz's eyes slowly, inexorably close, "But the main one is, you have to put Liz to bed and make sure she stays asleep."

"Hmm. Listen to her scream or you talk? Quite the dilemma."

"Don't toy with me, Reilly. You're looking at a woman on the edge."

One dark eyebrow lifted again and Carol had to remind herself that he hadn't come to sweep her off her feet and into a passionate embrace. A shame, really. But in the long run, probably just as well.

"You get the cake. I'll take care of the baby," he said after a long second or two.

"I'm on it."

She turned and left him and Jack's gaze just naturally dropped to the curve of her truly excellent butt. The hem of her denim shorts was frayed and a few long, white threads fell against her tanned thighs as she walked into the kitchen. Her T-shirt was short and Jack caught tantalizing, mouth-watering glimpses of her sleekly tanned back as she moved with a grace that was smooth and easy and, he thought, all too intriguing.

She hit the light switch and he blinked against the sudden brightness.

Jack had had no intention of sticking around Carol Baker's place. One, it was the middle of the night and, two, he didn't think it was a smart move to spend too much time with a woman he'd already noticed smelled like springtime. Now that he was noticing her thighs and the narrow span of her waist, there was even more reason for him to head for the hills.

Women like her were complications, and when a man's life was as seriously screwed as his was, one more complication just wasn't something he should be looking for.

Deliberately, then, he looked away from the bright light of the kitchen and retreated to the shadows. His apartment was laid out exactly like hers, so he went toward the short hall and took a quick right into her bedroom. He saw the crib his sister Maggie had loaned her, set up on the far side of Carol's bed, and headed for it.

A slash of moonlight speared through the window, illuminating the darkness enough that he didn't trip over the quilt rack Carol kept at the foot of her bed. Or stumble into the little stool sitting in front of an old-fashioned dressing table and mirror. In the pale wash of light, he noticed the framed landscapes on the wall, the antique quilt covering the queen-sized bed, and the Tiffany-style shade on the bedside lamp. Her closet doors were open and he saw that her clothes were as organized as her shop. There was a lot of *stuff* in the room, but somehow, it didn't look messy. Everything was neat and tidy and . . . cozy.

Unlike his own place across the hall, which was . . . serviceable. But then, his place wasn't a *home,* was it? He wasn't surrounding himself with memories and scraps of his past, as Carol so obviously was. In fact, he was doing everything he could to completely forget about his past.

Which would be a hell of a lot easier if he could just get through a whole night without dreaming about it. Like most other nights, that recurring nightmare had had him up and pacing his apartment like a caged animal. He walked because he couldn't sit still under the onslaught of images racing through his brain. He stayed awake because in sleep, came pain. And he was here, in Carol's apartment, because dealing with a screaming infant was still better than being left alone in the past.

The baby squirmed in his grasp, and with that gentle movement, she dragged him back to the matter at hand. Just for a second or two, he stared down at the baby and smiled. Her dark hair was just a dark wispy promise and her tiny mouth puckered and worked like she was sucking on a bottle. Her long, dark eyelashes brushed her cheeks and her little chin wobbled as her mouth worked.

"You're a cutie, aren't you?" he whispered, running his finger along her cheek. "You ought to take it easy on Baker, though," he said, one corner of his mouth tipping up. "She's doing her best."

The baby yawned hugely and Jack grinned. "Apparently, I'm boring you."

He'd always had a gift with babies. They just seemed to like him for some reason. When his little sister Peggy was born, no one in the house could make her stop crying—except Jack. His father had called it the magic touch.

Magic touch.

Yeah, like Midas in reverse, Jack thought. One touch from him and his world turned to shit. Shaking his head, he reached over the bars of the crib and laid the baby down on the freshly ironed sheets.

"Liz," he whispered as he drew up the soft blanket to cover her. *Lizardbaby*. Shaking his head, he asked himself, What kind of woman comes up with something like that? He chuckled softly, amused in spite of himself. Carol Baker was different. Intriguing.

But even as he thought it, he told himself it wasn't that he was thinking about Carol, so much as he was trying *not* to think about himself.

Christ, he'd been thinking about nothing but himself and his own problems for the last two years. Even *he'd* had enough of him.

Carol stood in the open doorway and watched him as he studied the baby. The slant of moonlight defined his silhouette as he leaned in to cover Liz with a blanket and something inside her shifted at his tenderness. What was it about the image of a strong man with a baby that could stab at a woman's heart?

"Is she asleep?"

He turned, and even though his face was in shadow, she felt the power of his gaze lock onto her. The night seemed suddenly darker and more intimate. Moonlight shimmered behind him. She heard him breathing, felt the tension radiating from him in waves of heat that reached for her from across the room. Her insides jumped and her pulse raced. A swirl of something dark and hot and needy opened up deep within her and Carol swallowed hard.

"Yeah," he said after several long heartbeats of time passed.

"Good," Carol whispered, squeezing the single word through a throat tight enough to strangle her. "Thanks."

He nodded and she wished she could see his features, read his eyes. Then she might know if he was feeling the same, surprising sense of . . . expectation that was spiraling through her. And if she could, she asked herself, what then?

Walking toward her slowly, he stepped out of the patch of moonlight and drew close enough that the light from the kitchen illuminated his features. She saw his eyes and felt a nudge of sympathy for the shadows she glimpsed in their depths. What had brought him back home to Christmas? To a place he clearly didn't want to be? Was it just to help out the sheriff, as he kept insisting? Or was there more to it than even he knew?

He stopped just short of the doorway, an arm's reach from her, and Carol held her breath. The quiet of the room settled between them and she could almost hear her own heart beating. Not a good thing, she told herself as her mouth dried up and her throat closed.

His shoulders looked impossibly broad and the brush of whiskers on his jaw made him look even more dangerous than she knew he was. Oh, not dangerous in the sense of her actually being afraid of him.

But definitely very dangerous to her nice, calm world.

She'd built a life for herself here in Christmas. She'd carved out a spot for herself here. It was everything she'd ever wanted.

A home of her own.

A place to belong. Stability. Comfort.

Ordinary.

People always turned their noses up at the word "ordinary." But Carol liked it. She much preferred it to words like "risky," or even "exciting." Growing up, she'd dreamed of a place like this. She'd clung to the fantasy images of home and hearth to get her through the loneliness. And now that she'd finally found what she'd been chasing all her life, Carol wasn't ready to lose it. Not by falling for a pair of icy blue eyes with too much past and not enough future in them.

CHAPTER 6

"The cake was worth it," Jack said and forked up the last bite.

"Your mom does great things with chocolate." Carol scraped the remaining frosting off her plate, then licked her fork clean. Who needed manners when chocolate was involved?

"She always did," Jack admitted, then leaned back in his chair, cupping a mug of coffee between his palms. "We always had plenty of desserts around the house."

"Must have been nice."

"Oh, yeah." He smiled and shook his head. "I was eight before I realized that not *all* cookies were broken."

"What?"

"Mom brought home the desserts she couldn't sell. Lopsided cakes, broken reindeer cookies . . ." Smiling, he remembered those good times and felt a tendril of warmth snake through his soul. "She used to say that's why she'd had five kids. So there'd be enough of us to eat her mistakes."

"You've got a great family."

"Yeah, I do."

The Reillys were always there. Always behind him.

Always ready to support him even when he didn't want it. Even when he didn't deserve it. They were a solid unit, surrounding him with love and concern. Which was, sometimes, damn hard to take.

His gaze shifted to Carol. The corners of the kitchen were dark. Only the light directly over the small table shone brightly, spotlighting the two of them. With the hanging plants surrounding them and the soft music drifting through the radio on the counter, it felt . . . *cozy* sitting here with her. And he hadn't felt cozy in a long time.

Her eyes looked soft and dreamy. Her mouth curved in a small smile that seemed to hit him as hard as a well-thrown punch.

"How about you?" he asked, his voice hushed, to match the quiet solitude of the moment. "Where's your family?"

She inhaled slowly, then reached down and stroked the big dog that was never far from her side. "He's right here."

"The *dog*?"

"Careful," she warned. "He's sensitive."

"Got it." God knew, he didn't want to insult a dog that stared at him as if Jack were a walking steak dinner. But he wasn't finished asking questions. "No family at all?"

"Nope." She forced a smile, but he could see by the shift of emotion in her eyes that the smile had cost her. "My parents died in a car accident when I was ten."

"That's hard."

"Yes, it was."

"No brothers or sisters?"

"Nope. Only child."

The sorrow in her tone prodded him to try to make her smile. "An only child. I used to dream about that when I was a kid."

"Trust me," she said, one corner of her mouth lifting briefly, "it's not that great."

"Maybe not," he conceded and thought about it for a long minute. Actually, he couldn't imagine a life without his mother, his bossy sisters, or his brother. Alone might be good once in a while, but family had their points, too.

"With no family, it must have been tough losing your folks that young."

She lifted one shoulder in a shrug he didn't believe for a minute. "It would have been tough at any age."

"True. So, you went to Social Services."

"Yep." She lifted her chin in defiance of whatever sympathy he might offer her. "Bounced through a few foster homes, then ended up in the group home until I was eighteen."

And he understood clearly why she'd volunteered to take little Liz in. "So you didn't want Liz going to the county home."

"No," she said and lifted her cup of coffee for a steadying sip. In the overhead light, her eyes flashed. "I just couldn't let that happen."

A smart-ass mouth and a tender heart, Jack thought and found her an intriguing combination. Too damned intriguing.

A change in subject seemed like the best idea. Out of the blue, he asked, "Wasn't there an actress named Carol Baker?"

"Yeah." Carol smiled. "I'm not her."

"I noticed."

"Really?" She grinned, and this time the lingering sadness in her eyes faded away completely. "Notice anything else?"

That was the problem, he thought. He noticed too damn much about her. The way she smiled. The light in her eyes. Her voice, her laugh, the way she moved. He didn't want to notice, dammit. And sitting here in the dimly lit room with her wasn't helping anything.

"Yeah," he said, pushing himself to his feet. "I noticed it's late and I'm tired." He stared down at her for a long minute, then turned and headed for the front door before he could give in to the impulse to stay. "Thanks for the cake."

The main street was blocked off for the parade and the crowds were already staking out slices of sidewalk with lawn chairs and coolers. American flags whipped in the ocean breeze and the scent of hot dogs rolled down the street with all the subtlety of a tank.

Locals and tourists mingled in a strangely orderly mob as they waited for the beginning of the parade. Kids clutched balloons as tightly as their parents clutched them. Teenagers wandered through the crowd feigning boredom while scoping out the mob of people, looking for their friends.

Traffic was blocked off, the merchants were doing a booming business, and the carnival at the edge of town was cranked up and in high gear. Just another Fourth of July in Christmas.

Jack walked to the wide window of the sheriff's office and looked out at the milling crowd beyond the glass. The sun blasted down out of a picture-perfect sky, warning of the heat still to come. By late afternoon, there would be cases of sunstroke, sunburn, and a few drunks looking for a place to sleep it off. The cop in him prepared for the day. The man in him remembered other Fourths, when he'd happily joined the legion of people celebrating.

His eyes narrowed as he scanned the crowd, picking out familiar faces. Davis Holloway was already sprawled in the bed of his ancient Chevy truck, a cooler full of beer beside him. His grandchildren scrambled in and out of the truck, just as Jack and Davis's sons used to do. Edna Folger, her silver hair shellacked into submission, sat under her purple and white striped umbrella, a thermos of iced tea at her feet.

Others kept moving, shifting, like dancers maneuvering around a crowded floor. And Jack's gaze kept pace, as he studied them all. If he was looking for one particular face in the throng of people, he wouldn't admit it—not even to himself.

Though he couldn't stop looking.

Shop doors were thrown open in silent invitation. Neighbors smiled, or stopped to gossip. From down the street came the garbled notes of the high school band tuning up. From the air-conditioned comfort of the sheriff's office, Jack was as separate from it all as he would have been if he were still in LA.

And damn it, he wished it were different.

The office door flew open, slamming into the wall behind it, letting in a blast of heat along with a shaft of noise, bright and edgy. Jack turned his head and smiled.

"Swear to God," his brother Sean muttered as he slipped in the door and closed it quickly after him. "Being around those kids makes a man grateful for vows of celibacy."

Jack turned and headed back to the desk at the far side of the room. Sean Reilly, at thirty-four, was just a year younger than Jack and they could almost have passed for twins. Sean's black hair was a little shorter, his nose hadn't been broken once in Pop Warner Football, and usually, he had a soul-deep patience that shone from his eyes.

Sean was an Irish Catholic mother's pride and joy. He'd entered the seminary straight out of college, where his grades and aptitude for languages had earned him a spot to study and be trained at the Vatican. Now, after his ordination, he was, at least temporarily, assigned to his home parish in Christmas.

Didn't seem to matter how far away you strayed, Jack thought idly, eventually, all roads led not to Rome but to Christmas.

"No shit, Jack, those kids are terrors."

"Is that any way for a priest to talk?" Jack asked with a choked-off laugh as he noticed the wild gleam in his brother's eyes.

"That's not the priest talking," Sean assured him, "it's the uncle." He stalked across the room, grabbed the coffeepot and a heavy white mug, and helped himself. Once he'd gulped down half of it, he sighed and looked at Jack again. "Maggie's kids are future thugs. I can see it."

Jack shook his head and sat down behind the desk, propping his elbows on its cluttered surface. "Granted, Mike's a little wild, but Patrick?"

"Patrick's a born follower." Disgusted, Sean shook his head and scraped one hand across the back of his neck. His gray T-shirt was stamped PROPERTY OF THE VATICAN and his jeans were worn and faded. "Trust me on this. Mike'll plan their way into San Quentin one day."

"What, no faith?"

"In those two?" Clutching his coffee cup, he headed for the chair in front of the wide, paper-strewn desk and dropped into it. "Mike's eight years old and I caught him in the sacristy, stealing unconsecrated hosts to play tiddlywinks." He leaned back in his chair. "Hell, who knew kids still played tiddlywinks?"

Jack hid a smile. "Hey, they weren't consecrated."

Sean lifted one black eyebrow.

"And," Jack continued, "I remember some kid breaking into the sacramental wine and—"

"I was twelve," Sean reminded him hotly. "And Dad made sure I didn't sit down comfortably again until I was nearly thirteen."

"So criminal tendencies run in the family?" Jack asked, then thought of something else. "Hey, maybe this means Mike'll become a priest, too."

Sean shuddered. "God help us all."

A short, sharp bark of laughter shot from Jack's throat. Damn, it felt good to laugh again, however briefly. "What'd you do to the kid?"

Sean gave him an evil grin. "He's at the church now, polishing pews."

"You're a hard man."

"That's why I make the big bucks."

Jack snorted. "What'd Maggie say?"

"Do I look like an informer to you?" Sean asked, insulted that his brother would think he'd rat on his nephew. The kid might be a budding criminal, but there were "guy" rules to keep in mind.

Jack nodded. "You letting him out in time for the parade?"

"Yeah." Sean smiled. "Told him I'd take him and Patrick to the carnival."

Propping his sneakered feet on one corner of the desk, Sean cradled his coffee on his chest and studied his older brother. There were too many shadows in his eyes these days. But that was to be expected, he supposed. It was at least a good sign that he'd come home. Even if it was only to do a favor for Ed Thompson. "How's the sheriff coming along?"

"Recuperating," Jack muttered, staring down into his own coffee as if looking for the key to the universe. "Not as fast as I'd like. His doctors say it'll be another two to three weeks."

"You say that like you just got a life sentence."

Jack lifted his gaze and narrowed it meaningfully. "Don't start with me, Sean."

"I didn't say anything." *Yet,* Sean added silently. He'd been talking to Jack off and on for the better part of two years now and it had been like trying to punch his way through a brick wall with a stapler. But he wasn't about to give up. He'd be damned before he let Jack piss his life away.

Especially over something that wasn't his fault and couldn't be changed. But that was so like Jack. All his life, he'd been the one to take on burdens that others would drop. Jack was the "responsible" one. He was the one Mom had turned to when their father died. He had a ready ear to listen to anyone else's problems, but he kept his own troubles locked away inside him.

The strong silent type, Sean thought now. But even *strong* men had a breaking point.

"Don't you have somewhere to be?" Jack asked.

"Not yet, Sheriff." He smiled to himself as his brother winced at the temporary title. "You're looking the part today, with the uniform shirt and all."

"Gotta have a police presence with this kind of crowd in town."

"Uh-huh." Sean swung his feet to the floor, set his coffee cup down on the desk, and leaned his forearms on his thighs. "Why don't you admit that you love it?"

"Sean . . ."

"You're a cop, Jack. A good one. And you miss it." Frustration bubbled inside him. "Dammit, you know you do."

Jack pushed to his feet and glared down at him. "I told you not to start, Sean."

"I'm not starting," he said, leaning back in the chair again. "I'm *continuing*. There's a difference."

"I don't need you to save my soul, thanks."

"Somebody has to."

"Maybe it's too late."

Sean stood up and looked his brother dead in the eye. Since only a half-inch separated them in height, that was no problem. For two years, Jack had punished himself—and his family—by staying away. He'd turned inward, and lost sight of what was because of what had been. But now that Jack was back in Christmas and forced to stay a while, Sean was going to take advantage of the situation. "In my line of work, it's never too late."

"In mine, it often is. Forget it, Father Sean."

Sean held up both hands and hunched his shoulders. "Fine, fine. I can take a hint."

"Yeah?" Jack smirked. "Since when?"

"Nice." Sean backed off. For now. No reason to try to get everything said in one day. He had plenty of time to get through to Jack. And God knew, he'd need every minute of it. But for the moment, he changed the subject. "Anything new on the abandoned baby?"

Jack's gaze narrowed in suspicion, as if he were trying to decide whether or not to trust the abrupt shift in conversation. But a second or two later, he grabbed at it like a drowning man snatching at a rope tossed into a churning sea. "No, nothing." He shook his head and sat down again. "I've been looking into it. Put Slater and Hoover on it, too."

Sean nodded. Ken Slater and Bob Hoover were only part-time deputies, but apparently Jack was calling out all the help he could wrangle.

"Henry down at the Silent Night Motel says there was a pregnant woman staying at his place for a week or so," Jack said, fatigue staining his voice. "She paid her bill in advance though, so he didn't see her at checkout time. Couldn't say if she was substantially thinner or anything."

"The ladies at the church are talking about nothing else," Sean admitted. In fact, the whole town was concentrating on the mysterious appearance of the newborn. Suspicions were high and rumors were flying faster than Eddie Horton's fastball. "And Mom's right at the top of the gossip chain."

"Big surprise."

"Well, she's worried about Peggy."

"Peggy?" Jack just stared at him. "Little sis weighs about a hundred pounds. Plus, she wears those skimpy, stomach-baring shirts all the time. No way that baby was hers."

"Yeah," Sean said wryly, "even Mom can figure that out. But our dear mother's still having trouble knowing that Maggie and Eileen have sex. She doesn't want to think about her baby girl being of an age where—"

"Yeah," Jack said quickly, holding up one hand to cut him off. "Neither do I."

"The point is," Sean said, enjoying the irony that the only one of them who *couldn't* have sex was the one person willing to discuss it. "Something unusual happened here; something no one can understand. And it's making everybody a little tense."

"I know." Jack briskly scraped both hands over his face. "I keep getting calls with 'helpful' tips. So-and-so lost weight. So-and-so left town and suddenly came back. I even had someone call yesterday to remind me that Jennifer Stephens is just back from her semester in Europe and didn't I think I should be checking her out? Jesus, you'd think the whole town had suddenly joined the FBI."

Sean frowned thoughtfully. Jennifer. Eighteen. In Peggy's class. Hard to imagine a teenager having a baby and nobody knowing about it. Especially around *here*. Slowly, he shook his head. "An abandoned baby is big news."

"In LA, it would hardly have rated a small column on the back page of the paper."

"As you're so fond of pointing out, this is *not* LA."

Jack sighed and pushed his fingers through his hair in frustration. "Because it's not, we should have an easier time finding the mother. But it doesn't look like we're going to. We'll keep looking, of course, but—"

"Probably won't have any luck."

"No. The important thing is, the baby's fine."

"That's something we can be grateful for," Sean murmured. "At least the mother cared enough to leave the child where it would be found."

"Wouldn't have been found until morning if Carol and her damn bear weren't out prowling."

Sean looked at his brother as both of them thought about that for a minute.

"Coincidence?" Sean asked.

"Pretty lucky coincidence, wouldn't you say?"

"Under most circumstances, yes." Sean's gaze dropped to the surface of his coffee as he thought about the citizens of Christmas and tried to imagine *any* of them abandoning a child. He just couldn't do it. Lifting his gaze to Jack again, he shook his head. "It had to be a lucky break, that's all."

Silence stretched out for a moment or two before Jack agreed. "It's summer. Even a damp, cool night wouldn't have been enough exposure to kill the baby. More than likely, the mother was just driving through town and stopped long enough to drop off her little bundle. Figuring the baby would be discovered first thing in the morning. Mother of the year is long gone by now."

"Which leaves the baby where?"

"Right now, with my landlord."

"Ah, yes." Sean smiled again and wiggled both eyebrows. "Carol Baker. Pretty."

"If you like the type."

He snorted. "You mean tall, tanned blondes with big brown eyes? Yeah, it's a tough type to like."

"Aren't you a priest?" Jack muttered and stood up.

"Yeah, but I'm not dead," Sean reminded him. "Or blind."

"Butt out, Sean."

Struck a nerve, Sean thought, pleased that at last, Jack was taking an interest in *something*. It had been too long since he'd allowed himself to care. Too long since he'd started shutting people out of his life because his wife had turned out to be a lying bitch. But even as that thought crossed his mind, Sean inwardly winced. In his line of work, he really wasn't supposed to pass judgment. But as he'd told Jack, he was neither dead nor blind.

He felt like celebrating, though. This was the first sign of life Sean had seen in his brother in nearly two years. If a pretty blond and a newborn baby could make this much of an impact on him in a few days . . . just imagine what might be accomplished in the next few weeks.

"Is she coming to the parade?" Sean asked.

"Carol?"

"No, *Mom*."

Jack scowled at him. "Probably. Maybe. I don't know," he grumbled. "How the hell should I know what she's doing?"

Sean smiled into his coffee cup. This was getting better and better. "Why don't you ask her to join the family for a picnic and fireworks?"

"Because we're not going steady, I'm not taking her to the damn prom, and there is no malt shop in town," Jack sneered. "Christ, Sean, back off, will you?"

"Feeling a little testy, are we?"

Jack walked around the edge of his desk and headed for the door. "Feeling like pushing your luck, aren't you?"

"Onward Christian Soldiers."

"Very funny."

"Thanks," Sean said, standing up and turning to face him. "Now how about you come by the rectory tomorrow night? Father Duffy's out of town for a week. We could grill some steaks, have a couple beers—"

"No, thanks."

"Why not?"

"I know you mean well, Sean," Jack said, "but what's that old saying about the road to hell being paved with good intentions?"

"I'm a priest, remember? I don't do hell."

Jack looked at him for a long minute. Maybe not, he thought, but cops did hell all the time. Even *ex*-cops. "Yeah, well, I don't need a confessor. And if I did, it wouldn't be my little brother."

He stopped at the door and looked over his shoulder at him when Sean said, "Who do you need, Jack?"

"Nobody," he said tightly. "Not anymore."

"Who're you lookin' for?"

"Hmm?" Carol's gaze swept the crowded carnival grounds for what had to be the hundredth time in the last hour. "Looking?"

Phoebe laughed, shook her head, and slapped Carol on the shoulder. "That's just pitiful."

Carol swiveled her head around and lifted one eyebrow. "Excuse me?"

Phoebe's lips twisted into a sniffy pout. "Play dumb all you want, but I know a 'searching gaze' when I see one."

Smiling, she said, "Shut up, Phoeb."

"Oooh. Well, I guess *that'll* show me."

Her friend's smile assured her that the subject hadn't been dropped. But then, why would it be? She could hardly convince Phoebe that she wasn't looking for Jack, when even *she* didn't believe herself. Carol gave it up and glanced down at the stroller where Lizardbaby was snoozing through all of the commotion surrounding them. Strange, the kid wouldn't close her eyes in a quiet room. But give her crowds, screaming kids, and piped-in circus music and she was down for the count.

And Liz had slept through a lot. Dozens of people had stopped them on their stroll through town to admire the baby and to make silly noises at her. They'd had plenty to say to Carol, too. About what a good person she was to take in a foundling. About what kind of creep the mother must have been to walk away from her own child. It was all Carol could do to stand there and listen.

She didn't want Liz to hear any of it, that was for sure. But she smiled politely and resisted the urge to check people for germs before letting them stick their sweaty faces into the stroller.

Her heart flipped as she stared down at the tiny baby asleep in the shade of the stroller's cheerfully striped awning. She didn't deserve any of the accolades people were heaping on her. She hadn't taken the baby because she wanted to do a "good thing." She'd taken Liz in because she couldn't bear the thought of the baby getting lost beneath a mountain of paperwork and well-meaning strangers.

She certainly hadn't planned on loving Liz, though. She'd done her best to protect her heart against a child that would, eventually, be taken from her by Social Services and placed for adoption.

But the simple truth was, trying *not* to love a baby was like trying to empty the ocean with a sieve.

What she could do about it now, she had no idea. Carol steered the stroller around a couple of deep ruts in the grassy field. She smiled at Thelma Jackson and stepped a little faster, to avoid having to stop and let the baby be admired again.

"You realize," Phoebe said, leaning in to grin at her, "I'm not dropping the subject. I'm just giving you enough time to come up with a better lie than 'huh'?"

Carol laughed shortly and let a sigh slide from her throat. Phoebe wouldn't give up until she'd found a way to make Carol admit what she was thinking. So she gave in early to avoid the hassle. "Fine. I was *sort of* looking for Jack."

"Sort of?" Phoebe said on a hoot of laughter. "Honey, if you'd been looking any harder you would have been in a point position like a Labrador."

"Oh, thanks. That's attractive."

"I call 'em like I see 'em." Phoebe shook her coppery hair back from her face, then tilted that face to the sun. "God, it feels good to be outside on a day like this."

Good. A shift of subject. "Crowds, heat, blistering sun. What's not to like?"

Phoebe shot her a sidelong glance. "I hear the unmistakable sound of a tense woman. A woman who needs to get laid."

"You know, Phoebe," Carol said with a shake of her head, "sex is really not a cure-all."

"Obviously, you just haven't had the right 'prescription,' yet."

"And you have?" She shot her friend a look and watched as a self-satisfied smile curved her mouth. "Okay, stupid question."

"True," Phoebe said and gave a tiny shiver along with a short sigh that told Carol she was remembering having her latest prescription filled. "Cash is . . . amazing. Mind-altering. Soul-awakening . . . what else?"

"Never mind. That's enough."

"Okay, now that's a bad sign," Phoebe told her. "When you don't even want to *hear* about great sex, it's been too long."

"Will you stop talking about it in front of the baby?"

"She's asleep," Phoebe pointed out.

Carol rolled her eyes.

"God, honey, in the two years I've known you, you've gotten 'lucky,' and I use the term *extremely* loosely in this situation, exactly once."

Carol winced as eight-month-old images raced through her brain. Images Phoebe had dredged up. Ben Higgins wouldn't exactly take up much space in her memory book. If she had one. She'd dated poor Ben for nearly a month before the fateful night. He was safe and boring and, she'd thought at the time, better than staying home watching TV.

Oh, that last night had been a disaster—starting with the two of them going out to dinner with his mother and ending with a *way* too brief roll in the hay. Poor Ben. He'd finished almost before they started, then spent twenty minutes apologizing. Nope. Not a happy night for either of them.

Still, she managed to suppress a shudder as she said, "I'm not looking for a relationship."

Her friend snorted and took a big bite of her grape Sno-Kone, pausing a moment to lick the purple juice from her bottom lip. "Honey, who said anything about a relationship? I'm not talking about Mr. Right, here. Mr. Wrong would do for the moment. I'd just like to see you find a *man*. Even temporarily. Hell, even for one night."

"Gee, thanks, Mom." Laughter colored Carol's tone. Phoebe meant well, but then, every woman who was getting regular sex from a guy who looked like carpenter Cash meant well.

"I'm just saying," Phoebe went on as if uninterrupted, "a little sex clears out the cobwebs."

"Uh-huh, but I'm a little busy at the moment," Carol said, nodding toward the still-sleeping baby. Quinn brushed his heavy body against hers as if to remind her that he too was there. Automatically, she dropped a hand to his broad back.

"And the baby's great," Phoebe said, smiling at Liz as she said it. "I'm glad you've got her. But there's more out there for you than one tiny baby."

"Phoebe—"

"You're interested in Jack, right?"

"Interested?" she echoed and thought about it for a minute or two. "Fascinated" might be a better word.

"Intrigued," even. It's the shadows, she thought. The shadows in his eyes. They pulled her in even when she knew it was stupid. Women always made the mistake of thinking they could change a man. Or help him. Or whatever. Well, she'd made that mistake once.

A person was going to make mistakes, that was a given. But a *smart* person didn't make the *same* ones.

"Never mind," Phoebe said with a small laugh. "You don't have to admit it. That little stream of drool says it all."

"What?" Carol lifted a hand and swiped at her dry chin, then shot her friend a dirty look. "Very funny."

"Hey," Phoebe said and tossed her Sno-Kone wrapper into a nearby trash can. "A medical professional *and* a comedienne. I live to serve."

"Uh-huh." Pleased that Phoebe was letting go of the "get Carol laid" campaign, temporarily at least, she changed the subject entirely. "And how'd you manage to get the holiday off from the clinic?"

"Bribery," Phoebe said. "I promised Dr. Phillips that I'd work the next four weekends in exchange."

"Ouch."

Phoebe lifted her face to the sun again. "Worth every hour." Then she glanced at her watch and said, "Hey, let's head back. The parade's about to start and one of my patients is doing a baton twirl in front of the band."

"Who?"

"Lucy Chambers."

"Lucy?" she asked, frowning as the image of the tall freshman rolled through her mind. "Doesn't she have a broken leg?"

"Yep." Phoebe grinned, dropped an arm over Carol's shoulders, and said, "She's in a walking cast, but there's nothing wrong with her twirling arm."

Carol turned the stroller around and moved along with the crowd, drifting back toward North Pole Avenue. She kept one hand on Quinn's broad back, threading her fingers through his wiry gray hair, to keep him close in the crowd. Not that he'd ever willingly leave the baby's side, she thought. The big dog had become a canine nanny of sorts. He stood guard over the sleeping infant day and night, and when he did sleep, it was beside her crib. Carol smiled to herself. It was hopeless, she thought. Both she and her dog were already in love with the baby.

If she had to give Lizardbaby up, it was going to kill her.

Journal Entry

They're looking for me.

Everyone's talking and speculating.

The sheriff is asking lots of questions and even the kids in town are looking at each other and wondering. I feel like everybody's watching me, but I know they're not. They wouldn't believe that I'm the baby's mother.

It's even hard for me *to believe it.*

But my heart's so empty, it must be true.

Chapter 7

Fire rained from the sky in brilliant flashes of blue and green and gold. The echo of color disappeared against the backdrop of the black, star-dusted sky. Interlocking circles made of blazing red and brilliant yellow decorated the night briefly, then sparkled into oblivion. Trailing flashes of light blinked wildly, then burned into ash long before they could drop into the black sea below.

The crowd oohed and aahed. Kids darted across the sand, running with sparklers despite the shouted warnings from their mothers. Couples cuddled beneath quilts, their heads tipped back to enjoy the spectacle. Families gathered, generations coming together, however briefly, to share the magic in the night.

And Carol, Mary Alice Reilly thought, was sitting on the corner of the blanket, looking as though she felt like an interloper. She sighed a little, because she'd hoped that after two years in Christmas, Carol would have begun to feel more relaxed when invited to join the family. But she was a sweet girl and Mary Alice would keep trying.

Turning her head slightly, she looked at her gathered family and smiled. Maggie and Eileen and their husbands and kids crowded together. Peggy was off with her friends. Father Sean held six-year-old Patrick on his lap and tickled the boy every time another blast of light rocketed into the sky. And Carol kept glancing at the baby asleep in her stroller as if expecting the child to disappear.

"How're you doing with the baby, honey?" She practically had to shout the question to be heard over the crowd and the thunderous sound of the fireworks.

"Good," Carol said, with a glance into the stroller. She stifled a yawn and Mary Alice smiled knowingly.

"Not getting much sleep, though, are you?"

"Not a lot," the younger woman admitted with a half-laugh.

"Tell you what." Mary Alice leaned in closer, stealing a glimpse of the tiny newborn sleeping peacefully through the riotous night. "Why not let me take her home for the night and—"

"Oh, I couldn't . . ."

Waving a hand in dismissal, Mary Alice said, "Trust me, I've got all the stuff she'll need. And besides, with Eileen due to pop again any minute, I could use a refresher course on newborns." The poor girl looked like she was ready to drop, anyway. Mary Alice well remembered a time when she would have been willing to do just about anything for one night's uninterrupted sleep.

Carol reached for the baby's foot and smoothed her fingertips across the tiny, bootie-covered toes. "I don't know . . ."

The matter was settled then, as far as Mary Alice was concerned. Eager now, she pulled the stroller closer to her and fought the urge to scoop the sleeping baby into her arms. "Don't you worry about a thing," she said, giving Carol's hand an absent pat. "She'll be fine with me and you can come and get her first thing in the morning, if you want."

"Well . . ."

"You might as well cave now," Sean said from his post nearby. "Mom's itching to get a hold of that baby."

Carol glanced at the man who looked so much like his brother. In the flickering light of the fireworks, Sean's eyes gleamed a pale blue and made her remember the icy shadows in Jack's eyes. Both men held an undeniable appeal—but even if Sean hadn't been a priest, Carol knew she'd still be more attracted to Jack. Sean's smile was open, unguarded, and his eyes weren't haunted.

So what did it say about her, that she was drawn to the brother with trouble stamped all over his face?

Journal entry—

I saw the baby again today.

Carol smiles at her all the time and I think I saw the baby smile back. Can babies that tiny really smile?

She's beautiful, and so small. But she's not mine anymore.

It's the Fourth of July. Independence Day. My independence, too. I'm not a mom. I'm just me again. I did the right thing. I know I did.

But I wish I could touch her again.

I didn't think I'd miss her so much.

The finale crashed into the sky with a series of ear-splitting roars and eye-searing colors. And once it had twinkled itself into blackness, the crowd moved as one.

Tired people packed up baskets and coolers and sleeping kids and headed for the parking lot and the town beyond.

Voices rose and fell with the same steady regularity of the ocean waves rushing to and racing from shore. There was a sameness to it, a comforting normalcy that reached into Jack's heart and eased it a little. It had been too long since he'd felt a part of something like this. He hadn't realized how much he'd missed it.

He heard her approach long before he saw her. It was the bells, he told himself. The jingling on her tennis shoes. It was like belling a cat. He always knew when she was close by. Although, he admitted silently, he'd probably be aware of her even without the early-warning system.

When he spotted Carol and her guard bear weaving their way through the crowd, a flicker of something warm and wonderful sparked inside him. His heart quickened and he felt the rush of blood in his veins. What was it about her? How did she continually sneak her way into his thoughts? Under his defenses?

Carol Foster was a dangerous woman. Even more so because she didn't know how dangerous she was. So she kept right on doing whatever the hell it was that kept getting to him. And for some damn reason, he couldn't seem to stay away from her.

Her blond-streaked hair was windblown and wild, as if a man had spent hours raking his hands through it. He curled his fingers into his palms to keep from doing just that. Instead, his gaze raked over her. From the top of her head and her slightly sunburned nose, down her skimpy tank top with the elf on it, across her denim shorts and along the length of her tanned, smooth legs. Something low inside him crouched and growled in a hunger he hadn't known in way too long. If he had any sense at all, he'd turn his back and head the other way.

He started toward her before he could talk himself out of it.

"Where's the baby?" he asked, when he stopped directly in her path.

"Whoa." She stopped short to avoid crashing into him. Then tipping her head back, she met his gaze, one corner of her mouth quirked slightly. "Is this an official investigation?"

Fine. He'd asked the question a little more harshly than he'd planned to. But it was hard to talk when there was a knot of need lodged in his throat. A need he didn't want to think about, much less admit to.

Jack nodded absently to the people passing by him. "No. Just curious." He glanced down at the dog watching him through suspicious eyes. "Hi to you, too."

Quinn murmured his opinion in a low growl.

Carol's hand dropped to the big dog's head and the animal leaned into her while she smiled. A truly great smile, Jack thought as the full force of it hit him hard. There was warmth in that curve of her mouth and the same warmth shone just as brightly from the depths of her dark brown eyes. Even in the dimly lit dark, it was as though a light clicked on behind her eyes and Jack wanted to bask in the heat she offered; he wanted, suddenly fiercely, to stand in the light with her, despite knowing that he belonged in the darkness.

"Quinn's just protective," she said unnecessarily as the big dog's upper lip curled back on a rumble that erupted from his broad chest.

Warily, he kept an eye on the oversized hound. "Quinn just wants to eat me."

Her mouth twitched again. "Not really. Chew on you for a while, maybe."

"Well, that makes me feel better," he said and lifted his gaze from his nemesis to Carol. "You gonna tell me where the baby is?"

"She was kidnapped."

His body stiffened. His gaze narrowed. His heart thudded to a stop and his breath caught in his chest. Every cell in his body went on red alert. *"What?"*

"Hey," she said, reaching out to lay one hand on his forearm. "Just a joke, Sheriff."

Heat shot from her hand up his arm with the effect of a stray lightning bolt. His breath slid from his lungs slowly, like air escaping a leaky balloon. Stupid. Of course she was kidding. If anything had really happened to Liz, Carol wouldn't be standing here quietly driving him insane. He kept his gaze locked with hers and tried not to feel the sizzle of her hand on his flesh. Her skin was soft, her hand small, and yet her touch seemed to go bone deep.

God, he wanted to be warm again. He wanted to feel the heat of her against him.

Scraping one hand across his face, he took a step back, letting her hand fall from his arm. "Sure it was a joke. Sorry. Long day."

"Yeah," she said, still watching him as if expecting him to explode any minute. "It was."

Someone slammed a cooler into his right knee and Jack moved to one side. Though what good that would do when the crowd surrounded them on both sides like the parted Red Sea, he didn't know. But he was in no hurry to move on. No hurry to stop talking. Which was weird, since he couldn't remember a time in the last two years when he was actively seeking conversation.

She swayed slightly as the crowd surged around her, as if she were caught in a riptide and fighting for her balance. "Liz is with your mom."

"*My* mom?"

"Uh-huh." Carol jerked a thumb over her shoulder. "Liz fell asleep and, well, I almost did too," she admitted on a soft laugh. "Right in the middle of the pounding noise and fireworks. Started falling asleep sitting up."

His gaze ran over her, head to toe and back to her eyes again. Eyes he couldn't seem to look away from. Eyes he didn't want to stop staring into.

"Anyway," she said, clearing her throat and shifting position under his solemn stare. "Your mom noticed and offered to take Liz home for the night. Let me get some sleep."

"Sounds like her," he admitted. Nothing his mother liked better than a baby in the house. Maggie and Eileen had done their best to keep Mom happy on the grandchildren front. But she hadn't stopped hoping that Jack would come through for her, too. She wanted more little Reillys running around and she wouldn't be getting them from Sean. But, Jack thought, with a small twist of pain at the bottom of his heart, she didn't have much chance of getting any out of him, either. Not anymore.

"So you're free," he said tightly.

"Yeah."

He dragged his gaze from her mouth and idly watched faces stream past him. "You want to catch a cup of coffee or something?"

She looked as surprised by the suggestion as he felt. Hell, he didn't even know where the words had come from. All he knew for sure was that he hadn't stopped thinking about her since their late-night coffee and cake the night before. He kept seeing her, in the bright light of the kitchen, surrounded by wildly overgrown houseplants. He heard her laughter, he saw her eyes. Even sleeping, her image chased him, which was, he silently admitted, a damn sight better than the dreams that usually haunted his sleep. But the point here was . . . what was the point again?

Oh, yeah. He didn't want to be alone. He was so damn tired of alone.

"Sure," she said after a long minute or two of studying his features as if waiting for his head to do a 360-degree spin. "Where? Reindeer Café?"

He shook his head. Not in the mood to deal with his family—and he'd surely run into them at their restaurant. "Come back to the office with me?" he suggested. "Gotta close up, anyway."

"Okay."

He turned and she fell into step beside him. Naturally, Quinn kept his big body between them—like a living, breathing, old-fashioned bundling board. And a part of Jack was grateful. Keeping Carol at a distance was getting harder. Best for all of them if the bear continued to stand guard.

Over the rumblings of the crowd, he heard the jingle bells she wore on her shoelaces again. Music danced along with her at every step. Cheerful. Bright. And, he'd thought only a day or two ago, *annoying*. He heard that tinkle of sound at all hours of the day and night. It burrowed through her apartment door, across the hall, and into the silence of his own apartment. Refusing to be ignored or silenced, the tinkle of bells continually reminded him just how close she was. Just how . . . alive she was.

And just how silent his world had become.

Hell, it hadn't always been like this. He remembered

a time when he'd rushed at life like an adventure waiting to be discovered. He'd had a wife and a baby on the way. He'd had a job he loved and a partner he'd trusted.

Until he'd lost it all in one rainy night.

"They did a great job on the fireworks this year, didn't they?"

"What?" He glanced at Carol and stepped out of the way of an old woman pushing through the crowd, using her umbrella like a cattle prod. "Yeah. The Dooleys always run a good show."

"I know."

"Right." Stupid. Of course she knew. She'd dug herself so deeply into Christmas, she was more connected here now than he was.

Not that he wanted connections anymore.

Not that he missed them.

Carol glanced up at him and noticed his jaw twitching spasmodically. Gritting his teeth? Well, wasn't that nice? If he was that miserable about going for coffee with her, why had he offered?

And more importantly, *why* had she agreed?

Wasn't it enough that he lived directly across the hall from her? That she could hear him moving around in his apartment? That whenever she heard the roar of the shower in his place she was imagining him wet and naked?

Okay, back up.

Get a grip.

And for heaven's sake, stop listening to Phoebe extol the virtues of good, healthy, uncomplicated sex.

But that was the key word, right? Uncomplicated. There was absolutely nothing uncomplicated about Jack Reilly. The man walked around under his own personal rain cloud. He snarled louder than Quinn if anyone came too close and kept whatever he was thinking and feeling buried so deep under layers of crabass that she couldn't tell from one minute to the next what he was going to say.

Like the coffee invite, for instance.

Where had that come from?

No. Her life was fine as it was. She had the added bonus of Liz now . . . temporarily, at least. She didn't need this. Didn't need to start caring about someone else. She didn't want to risk it. Her emotions were swinging wildly from one extreme to the other. Her brain raced with too many thoughts to slow down and count.

Tired, she thought. She was just too damn tired to be dealing with any of this. Carol swiped her hair back from her face and realized that she was also way too tired to be trusted with him. Phoebe's suggestions kept rattling around in her brain.

Sex.

With Jack.

Not a good idea.

Wasn't she teetering dangerously close to her breaking point already? Hadn't she allowed Liz into her heart, despite her best attempts at protecting herself? Did she really need to start caring about Jack? A man who had made it painfully obvious that he wasn't interested?

No. She didn't.

Best thing to do then, she decided, was to back out of this coffee thing and go home. Alone.

"You know," she started.

"I was thinking," he said, practically at the same moment.

"You first," she said.

"Not important. Go."

She blew out a breath, stepped around an overflowing trash can, then came back to walk beside him and Quinn again. "Okay, I was just going to say that maybe coffee isn't such a good idea."

He looked down at her briefly before shifting his gaze ahead again. "Yeah. Funny, so was I."

She stared at him for a long minute. Her steps slowed a bit, and he matched his stride to hers. The rest of the crowd surged past them until there were just a few stragglers on the beach behind them.

"Well, then," Carol said, trying to remind herself that this was a good thing.

"It's nothing personal," he said tightly and she looked up in time to see that jaw muscle twitch again.

"Sure," she said, "I can see that. It's not personal. It's not me you don't want to have coffee with. It's anybody. Or is it just the coffee you don't want?"

Anger warred with disappointment inside her and neither feeling made sense. Hadn't she already decided to not get involved? Hadn't she only a minute or two ago told herself that Jack was a bad thing for her equilibrium?

Yeah. But, it was one thing to back out of something because you felt it was the right thing to do. It was another thing entirely to have a guy jump back and away from you like a vampire dodging a well-aimed crucifix.

Phoebe was off with Cash Hunter again, enjoying every last minute of her day off. And Carol was going home to watch a *Twilight Zone* marathon and eat popcorn with Quinn. Sure, life was fair.

Jack stopped dead.

Carol walked past him, then stopped and looked back at him. "What now?" she demanded, just a little more hotly than she'd planned. "You want me to walk on a different beach?"

He scraped a hand across his face, turned his gaze on her, and studied her for a long minute or two. A cold, crisp wind danced in off the ocean and lifted her hair with icy fingers. Now that the people were gone, Carol heard the soft hush of waves sliding in to shore more clearly. The scent of gunpowder still clung to the air, but the only sparklers in the sky now were the glittering stars.

"You're not part of my plan," he muttered, pinning her with a gaze that was sharp enough to draw blood.

"Excuse me?"

"You. My plan. Never the twain shall meet."

One eyebrow lifted. She set her hands on her hips and stared at him, baffled.

"Don't give me those big brown eyes, either," he snapped.

She shook her head and tapped the heel of her hand against her temple. "Huh?"

"Oh, please." He snorted, scowled at her, then slid a glance around them, making sure they were alone. "You know what you're doing."

"Walking, you mean?" she asked. "Yeah, I do it often. Almost every day now for years."

"Cute."

"You sure spend an awful lot of time telling me how cute I am for a man who doesn't want to have coffee with me."

"You didn't want to have coffee, either."

"Not the point."

"Right. The point is, the plan."

"Ah, yes." She nodded sagely, having no idea at all what the hell he was talking about now. "The *plan*."

His tan uniform shirt was wrinkled and stained with God knew what after spending a long day dealing with a town full of people. His black hair was ruffled by the same wind dancing around them, his blue eyes shone in the dim light, and his really terrific-looking mouth was twisted into its perpetual scowl.

Damn it.

He looked really good.

"I'm only in town for a few weeks," he snapped. "Then I'm outta here. I'm not getting involved with a woman who jingles when she walks and wears felt elves on her tank tops."

Carol glanced down at the front of her shirt. Winky the Elf was damn cute, she thought and she wouldn't let Jack ruin the fun she got out of wearing her Christmas-themed clothes.

"Well, who asked you to get involved?" she demanded, taking a step closer to him and jutting her chin up to a fighting tilt. "I don't remember saying anything at all like, 'Hello, big boy.' "

He frowned at her. "I'm just saying—"

"Oh, you've already said plenty, trust me."

"I'm trying to do you a favor, here."

"Gee, thanks."

"You don't know anything about me," he said, his voice hitting a low, deep note that scraped along her spine and settled somewhere south of the pit of her stomach.

She would *not* be affected. She would *not* give in to the simmering attraction bubbling between them. "I know your brother and sisters got all the charm in your family."

"I'm not trying to be charming."

"Well, congrats," she snapped. "You're doing a hell of a job."

"I'm just saying—" He broke off, glanced up at the blackness overhead, then shifted his gaze to her again.

"Me being here. It's temporary. That's all. I didn't want you to—"

"What? Plan a wedding? Book the church?" She took another step closer and poked him in the chest with her index finger. "You're amazing. You really are. I give you a cup of coffee and a piece of cake to thank you for helping me out last night and you're worried I'm looking for a wedding dress?"

"Nobody said anything about a wedding."

"You did."

His eyes widened. "You *are* nuts."

"No, I'm just standing in awe."

"Apparently not stunned into silence, though," he muttered.

"So what exactly *is* your plan, Mr. Wonderful?" She lifted a hand. "Not that I'm trying to find my way into it, just color me curious."

"My plan is to get out of here."

There was such deep longing in his voice, she almost ached for him.

"Why do you hate this place so much?" she asked, her voice softer now, more confused than angry.

"It's not hate," he said, looking out toward the edge of town where multicolored lights twinkled and shone in the darkness with tiny splotches of primary colors. "It was a good place to grow up—naturally every kid in town thinks it's corny as hell, but the people are good." His voice softened a little and Carol tried not to hear the sigh behind his words. "Couldn't hate this place even if I tried. But being surrounded by Christmas can make you a little crazy." He looked pointedly at her tank top.

"What?"

"Nothing," he muttered. "Hell, you fit right in here, don't you?"

"You mean, do I like it here? Yes."

"Yeah." He laughed shortly. "You didn't play on a high school football team that was known all over the county by its nickname: Santa's Little Helpers."

"Oh, yeah, there's a hardship. Growing up in Christmas."

He snorted. "Hey, when you're a teenager, you want to live in a cool place—not the Capital of Corny."

"Poor you."

He shot her a look from the corner of his eye.

Disgusted, Carol shook her head. "You grew up in a great little town with a family and friends. Hard to feel sorry for you."

His gaze narrowed. "I didn't ask for your sympathy."

He shifted his feet in the sand, spread his legs wide, and folded his arms across his chest. Heck, Carol thought, it was practically textbook body language. Closing himself off, shutting her out.

"Didn't you?"

His jaw went tight and his voice even tighter. It was as if each word were snapped off deep in his throat and then hurled at her. "You don't know anything about me."

"Back atcha."

He inhaled sharply and nodded. "You're right. I don't."

"And don't want to."

"Right again."

"Fine. We'll leave it at that then, Reilly."

Something flashed across his eyes and she thought it might have been relief. Well, what the hell was she supposed to make of *that*?

Last night, they'd had cake together, whispering in her kitchen, keeping their voices pitched low so they wouldn't wake up Liz. They'd talked about the baby and how much out of her depth Carol was. They'd been almost . . . friendly.

They'd shared *chocolate,* for God's sake. That meant something.

"You know," she snapped, giving in to the urge to say everything she was thinking. "Your attitude stinks."

"*My* attitude?" he echoed, giving another quick glance around at the emptying beach.

"I'm not the one who asked for a date and then canceled it in the next breath."

He drew his head back and stared down at her. "Who said anything about a date?"

"You did."

"I said *coffee.*"

"That's a date," she argued.

"No it's not, it's coffee."

"Why do I scare you so much?" she blurted, watching his eyes in the darkness, trying to read the emotions behind the shutters he kept constantly in place. Her heartbeat raced and she knew she should leave it alone. But she just couldn't do it.

He sighed, reached out to her and tipped her chin up with the tips of his fingers.

Heat washed through her with that slight, almost tender touch. But the chill in his eyes dissipated the heat quickly enough.

When he let his hand fall to his side again, she could almost convince herself that heat had never been there. But the wild thump of her heart told her differently.

He shook his head. "You don't get it, Carol. *I* should scare *you.*"

"You don't," she said, her voice a soft hush of sound that was swept away by the wind. How could he scare her? The pain inside him wasn't being directed outward—no, he was only hurting himself.

He narrowed his gaze and said tightly, "*That's* why we're not having coffee."

She blew out a breath. If she had any sense at all, she'd listen to his warning. But she couldn't make herself turn away from his eyes. From the steady ache in them. From the shutters locked so firmly over whatever he was feeling.

Whatever she might have said, though, was lost as his radio crackled. Scowling again, he pulled it free of his belt. "What is it?"

"Got a complaint from the Silent Night Motel." Ken Slater's voice punctuated the night with sharp clarity and even Carol heard the tinge of humor in the man's tone. "Seems the senior class is having the annual orgy."

"Oh, Christ." Jack wiped a hand across his mouth, shot Carol a look, then muttered, "I'm on my way."

The radio clicked into silence again and Carol looked up at him. "Annual orgy?"

Jack sighed, already moving. He'd hoped that they'd already had the big party. Or that maybe the senior class would wait until he was gone again to roll out the beer kegs. But he should have known better. "Every year," he grumbled, "the seniors have one last blowout. A huge party that always gets a little out of control."

And every year, the local cops were called on to break it up. Why this rite of passage hadn't died out years ago, he didn't know. All he knew for sure was that he *really* didn't want to have to deal with a bunch of drunk teenagers tonight. Especially since, he told himself with another sigh, his little sister was no doubt right in the thick of things.

"Tonight's the night, huh?" She hurried her steps to keep up with his long-legged stride.

Moonlight splashed across the ground, outlining the discarded papers and soda cans that had been left behind by the crowd. But Jack hardly saw them. He was remembering *his* senior party. How the beer had flowed like a river. How couples had split off from the group. How Sheriff Thompson had been stuck dealing with weepy girls, not to mention their parents.

It was going to be a long night.

Jack stopped suddenly and looked at Carol. If he had a woman along with him, *she* could handle the girls. "Yeah. And no way do I want to have to deal with the girls in this crowd alone. Feel like being the female assistant?"

She only thought about it a minute. He saw moonlight dance off the surface of her dark eyes and watched in fascination as a small smile curved her lips.

"Do I get a badge?"

Chapter 8

At the edge of town, the Silent Night Motel sat far back from the highway among a grove of stately oaks, like a shining beacon to tacky.

On the roof, Santa clung to what was left of his sleigh. And the five and a half reindeer still attached to the sled tipped drunkenly to one side of the roof, which was missing too many shingles. The neon *gh* in the motel's sign had burned out, leaving the remaining letters to lovingly spell out *SILENT NIT*.

The city fathers had been trying to clean up the old motel for years. But Henry Beevis, the owner, was eighty years old and didn't give a good damn if the town didn't like his place. In fact, Jack had long thought that Henry really enjoyed being the one piece of poison ivy in a town full of mistletoe.

Jack parked his squad car in front of the registration lobby and shut off the engine. Jesus, he hadn't been to the motel since his own senior-year bash. And it hadn't changed a bit since then. Henry hadn't even invested in a new coat of paint. Instead, the old fart just slapped different-colored patches over worn areas, giving the motel the appearance of having multicolored measles. The gravel drive and parking lot sprouted weeds every few feet and the drapes over most of the windows were threadbare, giving anyone who passed by a free peepshow.

"In a weird sort of way," Jack muttered, "finding out this place is still a dump is kind of comforting."

"Yeah," Carol whispered, leaning forward to take it all in. "As long as you don't have to actually *sleep* in one of those rooms."

"Not without an inoculation and a flea collar," Jack assured her.

His gaze swept the parking lot and landed on the area in front of the two end units. Cars were parked in a wicked jigsaw puzzle of varying sizes and shapes. Kids milled around outside, wrestling, making out, or dancing in the moonlight. Even with the car windows rolled up, Jack heard the party, rolling into high gear.

Music blared from the last two units of the single-story motel, and blasted through the open doors of a big black truck parked beneath one of the oaks. Lamplight spilled from the open doorways of the rooms and the undraped windows into the parking lot. Teenagers, a veritable *sea* of them, drifted from the rooms to outside and back again. Laughter rang out over the roar of the music, and in one corner of the lot, a fight was just starting as two boys, surrounded by their friends, prepared to beat the shit out of each other.

"Wow," Carol murmured from the seat beside him.

"That about says it all." He glanced at her, her face illuminated by the dashboard lights. "I'm guessing your senior-class party was different?"

She swiveled her head to look at him. "Didn't have one."

He frowned. "Everybody has a senior-class party."

"Okay," she said, "technically, there *was* a grad night. A cruise in the harbor, dinner and dancing. I didn't go. Couldn't afford to buy the ticket."

She shrugged and he told himself not to notice how the straps of her flimsy tank top slid lower off her shoulders with the movement. Just like he'd been telling himself since she got into the car with him that he couldn't smell the faint scent of coconut suntan lotion she'd rubbed into her skin.

He blocked that image and tried to imagine her young, alone, and too broke to go to a party that her whole senior class had probably talked about for weeks. Sympathy rose up inside him like the incoming tide, but he pushed it back down. She might have needed his sympathy when she was a girl. She didn't need it now. And wouldn't thank him for it.

"Well, lucky you. You're about to find out what you missed." He blew out a breath, and did his best to uncoil whatever it was inside him that was twisted into a knot threatening to strangle him. But he had a feeling that as long as she was within reaching distance, that knot wouldn't be easing any.

He shouldn't have brought her. He knew that. But dammit, teenage girls at a party would respond better to a woman than they would to him. Plus, he had no doubt at all that his little sister was in the middle of that would-be orgy. And no way was he going to walk in and find Peggy in some teenage groper's hot little hands.

Just went to show how different being a cop—*temporarily*—in Christmas was, to being on the force in LA. He couldn't imagine any situation in which he'd have taken a civilian along with him on a call in the city. But here, he was grateful to have her.

Of course, he thought, as Quinn jutted his big head

from the back seat to breathe hotly across Jack's cheek, he could have done without the company of the dog.

Deputy Ken Slater pulled in alongside Jack's car and rolled down his window. So did Jack.

"Looks like a good one this year." Ken grinned and looked years younger than his actual thirty.

"Loud, anyway," Jack agreed. "You stop by the desk, tell Henry we'll clear everyone out."

"Right."

"Then come back and you can help call parents."

The other man frowned, but nodded. "I hate that part."

He climbed out of his car and headed for the office, while Jack turned to Carol. "You sure you're up for this?" he asked, figuring it was only fair to give her a shot at changing her mind. Though he hoped to God she didn't.

"Ten-four." She gave him a half-assed salute as she smiled at him.

"Cute, Carol," he said, watching that smile and thinking she was *way* more than cute. "Real cute."

They got out of the car, leaving the bear locked inside with the windows down, and headed for party central. The few kids who noticed them didn't even try to make a break for it, which only proved they'd had too much to drink. Didn't even know when the party was over.

The gravel beneath their feet scratched and bristled with every step, competing with the noise of the stereo blasting out of the truck's open windows. Shaking his head, Jack, feeling as old as dirt, reached in past the steering wheel and turned the key off. Instantly, the noise level was cut in half. Only the music from inside one hotel room provided the atmosphere now and *that* he could shout over.

But before he could say anything, the complaints started firing.

"Hey!"

"Put on the tunes, man!"

"What's the deal?" A kid with long brown hair, a beer in his hand and a sneer on his face, tilted his head back to glare at Jack.

"Party's over." Jack took the kid's beer and emptied it into the gravel. Then shaking his head again, he grabbed the boy's upper arm and motioned Carol to his side.

A couple of girls squealed and made a dash for the motel room.

"You separate out the girls," Jack said, already moving for the door while dragging the reluctant boy along with him. "I'll take care of the guys."

"Dude," the boy said, "you're gonna pay for that brew."

They both ignored him.

Carol shot a glance at the milling crowd within the first room. "What do you want me to do?"

"Collect car keys, pass out Kleenex to the criers, and look out for the pukers." The kid in his grasp tried to make a belated break for it and Jack grunted as he tightened his grip, then frowned when the kid started hurling. Shaking his head, he added, "Then we start calling moms and dads."

"Roger." She snapped him another salute and Jack laughed shortly.

Even the kid puking beside him couldn't quite ruin the sensation that laugh had triggered inside him. Damn, it was good. Good to feel. Good to laugh. Almost as good as it was just watching Carol Baker walk.

At that thought, he mentally reined himself back in

and glanced at the kid wobbling unsteadily beside him. "You think you're sick now? Wait'll tomorrow, hotshot."

Two hours later, the last kid had been picked up and the last threat of "Wait till we get you home" had been delivered.

Carol looked around at the mess left behind by the crowd of kids and was fervently glad she wouldn't have to be on the clean-up crew. The motel rooms were trashed, which, she supposed, was bound to happen when you shoved fifty or sixty teenagers into two small rooms. But they'd pay for it tomorrow. By cleaning and repairing and working through hangovers that would surely be hideous.

Sitting in Jack's squad car, she watched him as he walked the perimeter, checking out the few remaining cars in the lot for kids who might have managed to hide out. Tall and muscular, his black hair shone in the moonlight, and the muscles in his chest and back shifted and moved beneath that uniform shirt as if performing for her benefit. And she was enjoying the show.

But it wasn't just his looks, she thought, remembering how easily he'd handled angry parents, sick kids, and crying girls. He might think he was an *ex*-cop. But the truth was, he'd never be *ex*. Helping people was in his bones. Knowing the right thing to say and the right thing to do was second nature to him. She'd seen Ken Slater turn to Jack a half-dozen times during the last two hours, for advice or help. She doubted Jack even realized himself just how good he was at the job he claimed he didn't want.

"You're not lis-ning."

The slurred voice from the back seat made Carol turn.

Jack's little sister Peggy, working on a few beers too many, swayed in her seat as if trying to balance on a high wire. The girl's blue eyes were bleary and her face looked a little green in the dim light. Carol figured the girl was soon going to be paying for her share of the party. As would Lacey, she thought, remembering how the girl had stumbled into Deputy Slater's car for the ride home. Sighing, Carol figured that her part-time clerk would be calling in sick for work tomorrow.

"You're right. I wasn't listening." She turned back to watching Jack move around the parking lot and only tuned half an ear to what Peggy was complaining about.

Peggy threw both hands wide and let them fall to her lap dramatically. "*Nobody* lissens."

Carol sighed. Probably be easier to just hear the girl out than to try to ignore the drunken rambling.

"Okay, I'm listening now. What do you want to say?"

"Quinn, get down." Peggy pushed the big dog's head out of her face. "Hones', Carol. Was jus' a li'l beer." She held her index finger and thumb up, measuring just an inch or so.

"And you're only a little underage."

Peggy's mouth twisted and she pushed her hair back from her face, then blinked as if she couldn't remember what she was doing. "Jack didn't haf'a be so mean about it."

"He didn't call your mom," Carol pointed out, with a quick look into the back seat.

"He's gonna tell 'er, though." She scooted forward on the seat and laid her forearms on the back of the front seat. Leaning in close, she blinked, tried to focus, then said softly, "You could ask him not to."

"What?" Carol turned her head again, came eyeball to eyeball with Peggy, took a whiff of cheap-beer breath and pulled back a little. The girl's eyes were practically wheeling in her head as she leaned even farther in and kept talking.

Putting one finger to her lips, she grinned and stage-whispered, "Won't tell Mom if you ask him not to."

"(A) I wouldn't ask him," Carol said with a half-smile, as she watched Peggy try to focus on her face and fail miserably. "And (B) you're wrong."

"Man." Peggy flopped back into the seat again, all ninety pounds of her, slumping bonelessly against the vinyl in a wild drape of despair. Wrapping her arms around Quinn's neck, the girl said, "He so totally goes for you."

Carol just stared at her. "Huh? Who?"

"Jack."

Oh, yeah. Jack was so fond of her he'd backpedaled his way out of a cup of coffee. Feel the devotion. "Peggy . . ."

"I'm serious," the girl said on a huffed-out sigh. "Can tell when he looks at you."

Carol shifted in her seat to get a better look at the completely drunk young girl behind her. "Tell what?"

Peggy snorted a laugh, then dropped one hand to her stomach. "Oooh. I don't feel so good." She frowned, swallowed hard, then said, "Please. Like you didn't notice."

The girl was drunk, eighteen, and looking for a way out of trouble. Hoping a little flattery would buy her some time and maybe an inroad with her brother. Carol kept telling herself all of those things, but somehow, she didn't really care. "Notice what?"

The girl sighed again and ruffled the few stray curls that had drifted across her forehead as she nestled closer to Quinn. She patted the big dog with a heavy hand and Quinn only winced and took it. "He looks at you like—like—" She took a breath and exhaled dramatically when she found what she was looking for. "Like Quinn looks at dinner. You know, all hungry and stuff."

Hungry?

Carol's throat tightened and her insides jumped. Heat, liquid, tight heat roiled through her body and settled low enough to make her want to shift in her seat again. Ridiculous, she told herself, to believe anything a girl with too much beer in her had to say. But a part of her really wanted to believe.

Unfortunately, the part that wanted to believe was a lot louder than the more rational half of her brain. She twisted back around in her seat, as Peggy snuggled up to the long-suffering Quinn, and focused her gaze on Jack as he took long strides into the lobby of the motel. Through the wide windows, she watched him shake hands with Henry Beevis and placate him when the bald, skinny old man started flapping his hands and shouting.

Then Jack turned suddenly and it felt as though his gaze slammed into her. Even from a distance, even with the glass and a cold, summer night between them, she felt the heat of that stare sink right into her bones. Ripples of sensation swirled through her and Carol found herself really hoping that Peggy was right.

"Thanks for your help," Jack said as they stood in the hallway separating their apartments.

The Christmas-tree sconce threw scattered light into the hallway, banishing the darkness but conjuring shadows.

"It was sort of fun, in a weird kind of way."

"Fun? Calling angry parents to come and pick up their drunk teenagers?" He leaned against the wall and looked at her. Damned if she didn't look way too good at two in the morning. She'd helped, too. Kept the female hysterics to a minimum and smoothed out a few rough edges with parents. She'd handled Peggy and helped him deal with his furious mother when they dropped the girl off at the Ho-Ho-Hotel. She'd kept her sense of humor through the whole damn thing and, even now, she was still smiling.

Her soft, blond-streaked hair fell on either side of her face and her brown eyes looked even deeper, richer than usual in the pale hall light. His gaze fixed on her mouth, and as he watched, she licked her lips and set a fire blazing inside him.

It had been too long, he told himself. Too long since he'd been with a woman. That was the only reason she was getting to him. It wasn't her laugh. It wasn't the weird sci-fi fixation that had her quoting old movies all the time and naming a newborn Lizardbaby. It wasn't her gentleness with little Liz or the easy way she had with his kid sister.

This was just lust, pure and simple.

And what man wouldn't be churning for a taste of her? Those long, tanned legs of hers looked tempting, and all too clearly, he could imagine them wrapped around his waist, pulling his body deeper, into hers. He stifled a groan as he shifted his gaze from her legs, then only made things worse as he noticed that beneath the little elf on her tank top, her nipples pushed at the soft fabric of the shirt.

Jack's hands itched to touch them.

"Okay," she admitted, leaning back against her own side of the hall. "It wasn't fun for them. But I've never been a cop before."

"You're still not."

"Not officially . . ."

"Not any way at all."

"Whatever." She waved one hand as she grinned at him. "It was still . . . interesting."

"Yeah, watching teenagers throw up beer is always a good time."

"I'm not talking about the kids," she said, watching him through eyes dark enough to lose himself in. "I'm talking about watching you."

He snorted.

"I mean it. You're good at it," she said softly. "Being a cop, I mean."

One eyebrow lifted as he shook his head. "*Ex*-cop."

"No." She pushed away from the wall and took a step closer.

In the narrow hallway, that put her about a breath away from him. His breath staggered in his lungs as he fought to concentrate on what she was saying—not how good she smelled.

"You can quit the force, but you're still a cop."

"Only temporarily," he reminded her.

"Nothing temporary about it. No matter what you think. It's in your bones," she said. "It's who you are."

Her gaze locked with his.

He couldn't have looked away if his life depended on it. And just for one wild flash of time, he thought it might. But life wasn't that fragile. Not even his.

"You can walk away from your job," she said, "but not from who you are."

"You're wrong." She had to be wrong. Otherwise, what was left to him?

"No I'm not. Watching you tonight, I learned a lot about you. Maybe more than you wanted me to know."

"Carol . . ."

"You're good with people, even when you don't want to be," she said and reached up to stroke her fingertips along his jaw.

Jack closed his eyes and hissed in a breath through clenched teeth. Her touch inflamed him, setting a match to the kindling that had been stacked inside him for days. If she didn't stop pretty damn fast, they were both going to get burned.

"You're fair," she said, her fingertips still smoothing against his skin, "but firm. You didn't let the boys fast-talk their way out of trouble and you didn't even give Peggy a break."

His sister, he thought. Good. Good. Focus on his sister and he'd be able to ignore what Carol was doing to him with a simple touch. "Peggy's gonna have enough trouble tomorrow from Mom. She didn't need it from me, too."

"See? Firm. Fair."

The slide of her fingers against his flesh pushed any thoughts of his sister right out of his head. Actually, her touch made thinking impossible at all.

He caught her hand in his and squeezed until he was almost afraid her slender bones would snap under the pressure. He eased up a bit, but didn't let her go. He had to keep her from touching him. Had to keep her from reaching the shadows deep within. "You don't know what you're doing here," he warned. Hell, she needed a warning. She needed to get the hell away from him before they both did something she'd regret.

And she would regret it if she let him too close. Jack knew it. Eventually, she'd see that there was nothing left in him that was worth her time.

"I know exactly what I'm doing," she said softly, ignoring Quinn's low rumble of disapproval. "I'm trying to get you into bed, Sheriff."

His body reared up and roared. His blood screaming, his heart racing, he looked down at her and remembered the first thing he'd thought of when he met her. That she was just the right height to kiss without getting a crick in his neck. And God, all he wanted now was to taste her. To devour her. To lose himself in her until even his own memories couldn't touch him. But he couldn't find peace himself at the cost of hers.

Mouth dry, palms damp, he kept a fierce grip on her hand and told himself to back off. To get a grip on the raging need pumping through him. "Don't."

"Too late," she said and stepped even closer.

One more half-step and her breasts would be pressed against his chest. He'd feel the hard, pebbled tips of her nipples burning into his flesh. He'd feel the length of her slim, tanned legs sliding along his. Her mouth . . . "Dammit, Carol, back off."

She blinked up at him and in the lamplight he saw emotions darting across the surface of her eyes. Fast, though. Too fast to identify. Too fast for him to keep up, even if he'd been trying harder.

Gritting his teeth, he tried again to warn her off. "You keep looking at me through those big, wide eyes and I'm gonna do something you'll be sorry for later."

"If you do what I want you to do, why would I be sorry?"

His grip on her hand tightened, then slipped to her wrist. He felt her pulse skipping wildly and knew her heartbeat ran in tandem with his own.

"You don't know me," he ground out.

"I know enough."

"Not nearly enough," he assured her.

"Then show me the rest," she said, leaning into him and tipping her face up to his.

Dammit, he wasn't made of steel.

He wanted to drown in the warmth of her eyes. Lose himself in her touch. He wanted to feel again. With *her*.

He dropped her hand, snaked one arm around her waist, and pulled her tightly to him. Dipping his head, he took her mouth as he'd been dreaming of doing. Parting her lips with his tongue, he swept into her warmth and swallowed her gasp. Her arms reached up and entwined around his neck. He felt her fingers run through his hair and her short, neat nails scrape against his scalp.

Every nerve ending in his body came to life as if waiting for just this moment. She made him feel alive. His heart thundered in his ears and he held her tighter, closer, as if needing to feel her heartbeat to keep his own going.

Need.

It drove him.

Sang inside him.

And pushed him to claim what she'd so foolishly offered.

Carol held on and let the world tilt around her.

Skyrockets went off behind her closed eyes and were bright enough, colorful enough, to make the night's fireworks look like a child's sparkler in comparison. His arms came around her, holding her so tight she could hardly breathe. And she didn't care. Didn't care about anything but his mouth on hers, his breath sliding into her lungs, his hands on her body.

In one corner of her mind, she heard Quinn whimper and knew she'd have to let him into the apartment. But she didn't want to tear her mouth from Jack's for even that long. He tasted her, delving deep, and she met his driving quest with an eagerness that rocked them both.

She'd never known this kind of raging desire. Never experienced the wild, roller-coaster ride Jack had set her on. His mouth, his hands. He touched her and her body pleaded for more.

Then he broke the kiss and buried his face in the curve of her neck. His mouth drifted across her skin and Carol shivered, feeling the ripple of desire shake through her like the circles in still water after a pebble's been tossed in.

She heard a whimper and was surprised to note it had come from her. She hadn't known she could feel such a wildness inside her. Hadn't known she could want so desperately. Need so much.

When his arms tightened more firmly around her middle, she sagged into him, giving herself up to the sensations coursing through her.

So she nearly fell over when he very quickly, very forcefully, lifted her off her feet and set her back and away from him.

"That's it, Baker. That's enough."

"Huh?" She blinked and tried to catch her breath. The world was still spinning around her. Unfortunately, she'd been kicked off the whirlwind. She swayed unsteadily, so she locked her knees to stay upright. "What do you mean, that's it? What's it?"

He reached up and shoved both hands along the sides of his head before lifting his hands high and letting them fall again. "This. That's as far as this goes."

The world wasn't spinning anymore but her mind was a little numb and her body was still simmering with the flames he'd stoked inside her. "Says you?"

"Since I'm the only one with a working brain at the moment, yeah."

There was an insult in there, she thought numbly, and

as soon as her brain kicked back into gear, she'd sort it out and let him have it. For now, she settled for, "Are you crazy?"

He choked out a harsh laugh that stained the air and sounded painful. "Probably," he admitted, broad chest heaving as he worked for air.

The sizzle in her blood died off to a faint echo of what it had been a minute or two ago. Carol missed the heat. Missed the hunger raging inside her. Missed the feel of his arms around her, dammit. She wanted it back.

All of it.

Wanted to feel that wild rush into oblivion. Wanted to be held close to him where she could feel his heartbeat racing and know that she was the cause.

But judging by the look in his pale blue eyes, that wasn't going to happen. At least, not anytime soon. So she gathered up what was left of her dignity and clutched it tightly to her. "Okay, then. Fine. Back out of coffee. Back out of sex . . ."

"Baker—"

She held up a hand. If he apologized, she was pretty sure she'd have to kill him. "Don't say it," she warned.

"If you're thinking I'm sorry," he ground out, "you're wrong. I'm not sorry. And that's the point."

She sighed and pushed one hand through her hair. "What are you talking about?"

One hand shot out and grabbed the back of her neck, his strong fingers digging into her skin as though he were trying to brand her with his touch. Dragging her close again, his gaze raked over her features before finally meeting hers. "I'm not sorry," he muttered thickly. "That's the point. I wanted you and I took you."

"Wrong, big shot," she snapped, glaring up at him. "*We* wanted. *We* took."

"You're still not getting it," he said, shoving one hand through her hair and tangling his fingers in it. "If we did this, *you'd* be the sorry one."

She stared up into his eyes and saw that for once, the shutters keeping her and everyone else out were gone. She read desire, need—and regret—in his eyes before he let her go again and took a step closer to his own front door. She felt the trembling start low in her body and then spread until every nerve in her body felt as though it was exposed to the air chilling the hall between them. She inhaled slowly, deeply, then released the breath on a long sigh.

Carol swallowed the disappointment, the frustration, boiling inside her as she grabbed hold of her doorknob and gave it a turn. Quinn darted through the partially opened door and went inside the apartment, his nails clicking jubilantly against the floorboards. But Carol didn't go in. Instead, she looked over her shoulder at Jack, still standing there watching her through pale blue eyes that would be haunting her dreams.

"You know what I'm sorry for, Reilly?"

He shoved both fisted hands into his pockets and braced himself like a fighter waiting for a sucker punch. "What?"

"I'm sorry you stopped."

He opened his mouth.

She held up one hand to keep him silent so she could finish what she wanted to say. "You're not trying to scare me off, Jack," she said, keeping her gaze locked with his. "You're trying to scare *yourself* off." Taking one step into the apartment, she turned and faced him head-on. "Is it working?"

She didn't let him answer. She just closed the door, shutting him out.

Jack stood there watching it as if he could see through the wood to the room and the woman beyond. The woman who touched things inside him he'd thought long dead and buried. The woman who made him wish he was a better man.

As he listened to the soft tinkle of the bells on her shoes, he muttered, "No, it's not working. Not working at all."

CHAPTER 9

A few days later, the senior-class bash was becoming legend and life had slipped back into what passed for normal in Christmas. Tourists crowded the streets, merchants rang up heavy sales, and everyone but the kids tried to hide from the suffocating heat of summer.

Lacey looked out through the front windows of Christmas Carol's and watched some of her friends head for the beach. She sighed a little, wishing she was going with them. But her part-time job was letting her sock away money that would give her some spending cash when she left for college at the end of summer.

"Just two more months," she whispered, needing to hear the words said aloud. Soon, she'd be living in a dorm at Long Beach State. She'd be on her own for the first time in her life. Going to college on a scholarship she'd worked her ass off to win.

But for now . . . her gaze swept the familiar street baking in the sun in front of her. A curl of worry spiraled through the pit of her stomach, but she fought it down. She'd waited for this chance all her life. A chance to get away from the familiar. From the town where everyone knew her—and her mother—and to build a life different from the one everyone expected her to have.

"Lacey?"

Carol's voice cut into her thoughts and she forced a smile as she turned around to face her boss. "Yeah?"

"Everything okay?"

"Sure." She plastered a smile on her face as she met Carol's interested gaze. "I uh, just finished stocking the Santa coasters and the angel bells."

"Good, thanks." She set the baby carrier on the counter and leaned in to smooth one hand over the top of the baby's head. She slanted an interested look at Lacey. "No problems at home because of the party?"

Lacey flushed, and dipped her head to hide the color she knew was racing into her cheeks. This was why she had to get away. People knew too much here. What they didn't already know, they found a way to discover. And being the daughter of the town drunk just meant that Lacey got way more than her share of nosy questions. Not that Carol was being nosy, she thought quickly. No, her boss was different. Nicer about it. But still, Carol knew. And her knowing made Lacey uneasy.

"Mom was okay about it," Lacey said with a shrug she hoped would be enough to make Carol stop asking questions. "We had a talk."

It had been brief.

Lacey'd walked in the front door and stepped into a dark room illuminated only by the flickering light of the muted television set.

Just like most nights, her mom had come home from work, plopped herself in front of the old-movie channel, and drunk herself to sleep. It hadn't always been like this. Her mother hadn't always been such a sad and lonely woman. Before her husband died, Deb Reynolds had been . . . different. Everything had been different then, Lacey thought, remembering the laughter that used to fill the house. But that was a long time ago and a lot of tequila had floated under the bridge since then.

Her mother, snoring lightly on the couch, woke long enough to ask, "Lacey? That you?"

"It's just me, Mom." Lacey dropped her purse onto the table behind the sofa and walked across the room to turn off the TV. Flashing black-and-white images disappeared. Moonlight drifted in through the chink in the living room drapes and bathed the room in a flattering glow. Sadly, Lacey stared down at her mom for a long minute, then picked up a crocheted afghan. Draping it across her mother, she turned for her own room.

"Honey?"

Her mother's whisper hushed into the silence.

Lacey stopped and looked back. Pain skittered through her. Pain and disappointment and a tired pity that tore at her. "It's okay, Mom," she said, her voice pitched low. "Just go back to sleep."

"Did you have fun, honey?"

Lacey leaned back against the wall, closed her eyes and pretended, just for a minute, that her mom's voice wasn't slurred. Just for a minute, she imagined that her mom was sober and wide awake and furious that her daughter had been at a party broken up by the police. Even being in trouble would be better than being overlooked.

But reality tripped back into her mind and destroyed her fantasies. Reality was always just a blink away and she'd stopped playing pretend when she was a kid. "Yeah, Mom, the party was fun."

"Good. Thass good."

Lacey's eyes squeezed briefly shut as the memory of

that night ended. Then taking a deep breath, she hunched her shoulders in defense against Carol's concerned gaze. She didn't want to talk about it. Didn't want to think about it anymore. Wasn't it enough that she had to live it—knowing that everyone in town knew just what her home life was and felt sorry for her?

She'd had more sympathy in her life than anyone should have to experience. And as much as she liked Carol, Lacey just didn't want any more of it. One more kind word or sympathetic glance and she might choke.

"If you're sure you're okay—"

"I am," she said firmly and pasted another smile on her face—this one bright enough to irritate a blind man. "Everything's cool. Really." Couldn't be any cooler, right? Most of her friends had been grounded—but Lacey was still flying free.

"Okay, then," Carol said, smiling. "We got that shipment of candles yesterday. Would you mind setting them out on the shelves near the front window?"

"Sure." Grateful for the escape, Lacey headed for the storeroom and glanced at the baby as she passed. "She's sleeping again?"

Carol laughed and her eyes got all sparkly. "She's a champ at sleeping. At least, during the day. But then, what else would she be doing at the ripe old age of a week?"

"Six days, isn't it?"

"Yeah." Carol stopped, thought about it for a minute, then nodded. "I guess it is." She turned and smoothed one fingertip over the baby's chin. "Just six days, Liz. You're still a spring chicken, right?"

Lacey watched her boss coo and make stupid baby noises for a few minutes, and felt a little weird. She'd never seen anyone talk to a baby so much. Carol was always joking around and having conversations with Liz like the baby understood what was going on. She told her stories or fairy tales and then would cover her ears if she didn't want Liz listening. Like the baby knew one sound from another or something. Weird.

"So, you want the candles in the window?"

Carol looked at her briefly, the smile for the baby still on her face. "*Close* to the window. Not in it. In the window, the sun would melt them, despite the glass tint."

"Right." Lacey started for the storeroom and stopped when Carol spoke up again.

"Lacey? You sure everything's okay at home?"

Home? A cold fist squeezed her heart and Lacey breathed slowly, deeply, to dissipate the ice. "Sure. Why wouldn't it be?"

"No reason." Carol's voice was soft, as were her eyes.

Pity was a hard thing to choke down. She should know, she'd been strangling on it since she was old enough to understand that not everyone's mom spent most of their time on the couch with a beer in her hand.

Carol meant well. Lacey figured they *all* meant well. But that didn't make it any easier to accept.

"I'm gonna go get the candles unpacked." Before her boss could start asking more questions Lacey didn't want to answer, she ducked into the storage room and took a breath as soon as the door closed behind her. Her gaze swept the neatly stacked boxes of new merchandise and the shelves where stock had already been unpacked and sorted. There was order here. It was soothing, she thought, to be able to step into this room and find everything the way it was the day before and the day before that. Here, things stayed where she put them and belonged where they stayed.

Unlike home.

Funny, she thought, that word should bring up different feelings. It should make her feel warm, she guessed, as she slit open the strapping tape on the box closest to the door. Peggy and Donna were always complaining about home, but they didn't really mean it, she knew. Sometimes, she was convinced they were only bitching about their moms so Lacey wouldn't feel so bad about her own. But that was dumb, since she knew Mrs. Reilly and Mrs. Flynn and neither one of them was like her mom. Not even close.

A small twist of guilt nagged at her.

Sighing, she tore the cardboard flaps open, then pulled out the Styrofoam peanuts, dropping them neatly in the trash can set aside for that purpose. As she went about the familiar task, her brain wandered.

Carol seemed happy with the baby. And she seemed like she was getting a little better at the whole "mother" thing. As that thought presented itself, Lacey wondered if that was how it was supposed to work, learning and getting better at the mom thing as you went along. And maybe if it was something you had to learn—you could forget it, too.

Her own mother wouldn't exactly get an A+ on the mom meter. Which was, she told herself firmly, the main reason she was never going to have kids.

Jack drank the coffee, forcing it down his throat. Christ, what was it about cop-house coffee? Every department seemed to be outfitted with the one coffeemaker that could turn perfectly acceptable coffee beans into a liquid more like sludge than a beverage. Hell, this stuff, after sitting on the burner for four hours, was almost thick enough to chew.

Still, he took another drink and let the caffeine hit him hard. Maybe if he could get some sleep, he wouldn't need the artificial kick in the ass. But since every time he closed his eyes, he was assaulted by either a nightmare or the torment of Carol's tempting mouth, sleep wasn't really an option.

The last few days had dragged by. He'd dodged Carol whenever he could, but it didn't matter if he could see her or not. He heard her and her damn bells. He swore he could smell her—that hint of coconut that seemed to cling to her skin. And his brain kept reminding him how she tasted, how she felt, pressed against him. Not to mention his body screaming at him with annoying regularity to give in and take what she'd offered.

So far, his brain was still one up on his body, his bruised heart, but who the hell knew how long that'd last?

He leaned back in his desk chair—Sheriff Thompson's desk chair, he mentally corrected—and stared out the window at North Pole Avenue. Summer tourists clogged the sidewalks and the parking slots along the curbs. Sunlight baked the town under a heavy summer hand and the blue sky didn't offer a single cloud to tone it down.

Deputy Slater was out answering a call about a home run slammed through the plate-glass window at Mrs. Claus's Bookstore and Deputy Hoover was off fishing. Not a hell of a lot to take care of in Christmas.

Small-town life puttered along, pleased with itself. Merchants did business, kids hit the beach, and cops—or ex-cops—sat and wondered what the hell they were doing there.

When the phone on his desk rang, Jack snatched at it, grateful for a distraction. "Sheriff's office."

"Jack?" the voice on the other end of the line asked. "That you?"

His features stiffened and a block of ice formed in his gut. He knew that voice well. A blast from his past. "Yeah, Lieutenant."

"I don't believe it."

Lieutenant Hal Jacobson, LAPD. Jack's superior up until two years ago, and a friend who'd tried like hell to keep him on the force. "How'd you find me?"

"I'm a detective, remember?"

"Yeah." Jack scraped one hand across his face, leaned his elbows on the desktop, and stared blankly at the wall opposite him. "What's up?"

"You mean besides me wanting you to come back to work?"

"Not gonna happen."

"I can still get you back in. With your grade and seniority. But I won't be able to offer it much longer."

"Didn't ask you to offer at all."

"You're one stubborn son of a bitch, you know that?"

"That's been said before." He squinted at the corkboard on the far wall and idly counted the colorful push-pins tacking up notices.

"No shit."

"What do you want, Hal?"

The other man sighed and Jack could see him clearly in his mind's eye. Sprawled in his chair, his habitual navy blue tie loosened at the collar of his rumpled white shirt, his black suit jacket hanging over the back of his chair. There'd be a pot of cold coffee on the corner of his desk and an empty ashtray right beside it. Hal had quit smoking four years ago, but he hung on to the ashtray to remind him, he often said, of the "good old days."

"What I want is you back at work," Hal said tightly. "Where you belong."

"Wrong question," Jack admitted, telling himself he'd opened that door. Now he could shut it. "Why are you calling?"

"The suit."

"What?"

"The lawsuit the family brought against the city? It's done. Settled."

Jack's fist tightened around the phone receiver and his gaze locked on a dark red pushpin as if holding that gaze meant his life.

"You still there?"

"Yeah." He would always still be there. In that alley. Rain pounding on him. Gunshots echoing like thunder, rolling out around him. He would forever feel the kick of his weapon in his hand. Hear the screams of pain. Smell the scent of death.

Always.

Forever.

There.

On the other end of the line, his old friend blustered, "Dammit, Jack, this was never your fault."

"Fault doesn't matter, does it?" Jack forced the words through gritted teeth. "I walked away. They didn't."

"You should be punished for living?"

Who said he was living? Oh, he'd survived. He was still breathing. Still waking up every morning to face another day. But was he alive? Not the way he had been in the hours before that last shift had ended.

So was surviving enough?

"Fine. Be a martyr." Hal's voice was resigned, disgusted. "I've got your shit all boxed up, taking up space in the locker room. You never collected it."

"Don't want it." That life was in the past. Everything

he'd left behind in his desk, the bureau, in his locker, belonged to that life and had no part in what was left of this one.

"Too goddamn bad," Hal muttered. "I'm sending it out. If you don't tell me where to send it, I'll send it to the damn sheriff's office. That address I can get on my own."

Jack closed his eyes, rubbed them with the tips of his fingers, hoping to ease the ache that had settled there. It didn't help. "No. don't send it here." All he needed was for Ken Slater or Hoover to see a package from LAPD. That would open up questions he didn't want to hear and feed the gossip chain that kept Christmas turning. He couldn't have it sent to his mother's house, because Christ knew he didn't need that kind of grief, either.

Quickly, he gave Hal Carol's address. "I should be there another few weeks, anyway."

"Fine." Hal paused. "I'll get it out today. And Jack . . ."

"What?"

The other man sighed, no doubt sensing that he was talking to a brick wall. "Never mind." Then he hung up.

Jack took a breath and very carefully set the receiver back in its cradle—severing his last ties with LAPD.

The Reindeer Café was everything it should be.

White plastic icicles hung from the edges of the roof and an enormous evergreen wreath decorated the etched-glass front door. Red ribbon encircled the white pillars lining the wide front porch, looking like giant candy canes and lacy snowflakes dotted the surfaces of the gleaming windows.

Inside, to the left of the front door, was the lobby of

the Ho-Ho-Hotel, a quiet, cozy setup, with overstuffed sofas drawn up in front of a now empty stone hearth. Brightly colored braided rugs decorated the polished oak floor and vases of red and white carnations sat atop three of the tables.

To the right of the entrance was the Reindeer Café. Red vinyl booths lined the wall in front of the wall of windows and small, square wooden tables filled the rest of the room. Old-fashioned chrome and red vinyl seats lined the polished wood counter, and a glass case beside the cash register displayed the cakes and cookies the restaurant was known for.

A handful of customers were sprinkled around the room, most of them senior citizens, snapping up the "early bird" dinner specials. The aromas coming from the kitchen made Carol's mouth water and she was glad that Maggie had asked to meet here, in her family's restaurant.

Mary Alice Reilly, her daughter Peggy, and two other waitresses manned the counters and tables while two cooks worked in the kitchen. Carol lifted a hand in a wave, then headed for one of the booths. As she slid across the red vinyl, she set the baby carrier on the table in front of her.

It only took a second or two for Mary Alice to come out from behind the counter and hurry over. A clean white dishtowel tossed over her left shoulder, she stopped beside Carol, laid one hand on her shoulder, and leaned in for a closer look at Liz.

"What a doll baby," she murmured.

"She really is," Carol said, her own gaze fixed on Liz's milky blue eyes. In just under a week, Liz had become . . . vital. Carol'd tried to hold back. Tried to keep an emotional distance. But it was just impossible.

Liz had sneaked into Carol's heart and now she was there to stay.

Which meant it was going to tear that heart in two when the county finally took Liz away and placed her in a permanent foster home. A small, stabbing ache poked at her, like a too sharp needle.

"I can't believe how much she's grown in just a week."

"Six days." Just six little days, Carol told herself and nothing in her life would ever be the same. Which made her wonder about why Maggie had wanted this meeting. Was the county going to take the baby today? Had a foster family already been found?

Her stomach fisted and suddenly the delicious aromas filling the restaurant weren't quite so pleasant. She swallowed hard against the slick, oily feeling in her gut and told herself that there was no point in worrying. Not until she'd seen Maggie. Heard what she had to say.

Oh, God.

Had they found the baby's mother?

No. Jack would have told her. Wouldn't he?

A headache burst into life behind her eyes and Carol reached up to rub her forehead.

"You don't mind if I hold her, do you?" Mary Alice said as she scooped the baby up in experienced hands.

"No, of course not."

"Oh, there's just something about a little one, isn't there?" she said as she slipped right into a dip-and-sway motion that had Liz cooing.

"She's amazing," Carol said softly.

Mary Alice tore her gaze from the baby and shifted it to Carol. She tilted her head to one side as if studying a particularly stubborn problem. "You're still not sleeping much, are you?"

Carol sighed. "Clearly, the cosmetics I use are overpriced."

"Nonsense." Mary Alice smiled down at the baby. "You look lovely. Its just that one mother can see the sleepiness in another."

Carol's heart skittered and her already unsteady stomach did a slow dip. "But I'm not her—"

"To all intents and purposes you are," the older woman said, cutting her off. "The woman who's up in the middle of the night mixing formula and changing diapers is the mommy."

Mommy.

Pleasure and fear tangled up inside her and did their best to keep her from breathing.

"You ought to let me keep her again," Mary Alice was saying. "Go home. Take a nap. Get some rest. Pick her up tomorrow."

Carol's gaze locked on the baby. If she was going to lose the baby, then she wanted every hour with her that she could get. "It's tempting, but—"

"Hi, Mom!"

Both of them turned around to watch as Maggie rushed up to them. Hair windblown, sunglasses tucked into the open collar of her plain white shirt, belted khaki slacks, and slip-on loafers, Maggie looked like a harassed professional. Which she was.

She stopped next to her mother long enough to plant a quick kiss on the older woman's cheek. "Hi, Mom," she said, then, "What a day." She dropped onto the bench seat opposite Carol. "Hi," she said, grinning. "Want anything?"

"Iced tea," Carol said.

"A woman after my own heart." Maggie looked across

the restaurant at her little sister. "Peggy. If you love me, iced tea. Large. Make it two."

"And if I don't?" Peggy called back, laughing.

"Iced tea. Large." Maggie lifted one dark red eyebrow. "Smart-ass," she whispered.

"Margaret . . ."

Carol grinned. She'd never had a family of her own, but she knew a mother's tone when she heard one. Obviously, so did Maggie.

"Right." She shrugged, dumped her briefcase on the seat beside her, and flipped the small brass latches. Lifting the lid of the leather case, she reached in, pulled out a manila folder, and then shut the case and laid the file on the table. "Uh, Mom," she said, looking up at the woman still cooing at the baby. "Take a walk, okay?"

"Excuse me?" Mary Alice glanced at her daughter.

Maggie winced and smiled. "I've got to talk business with Carol and—"

"Oh, of course." The older woman beamed at her daughter. "Carol, if you don't mind, I'll just take little Liz with me back to the kitchen. You just let me know when you're ready to leave—or if you want to take me up on my offer."

Carol watched them go, then slowly turned her head to look at Maggie. Her eyes were bluer than Jack's, darker, more open somehow. Her deep red hair was cut in a wedge that shifted gracefully with her every movement, then slipped back into place. Maggie's smile was friendly, but her eyes were now wary, so Carol braced herself.

"Offer?" Maggie asked.

"Your mom wants to keep Liz overnight again."

"Nothing Mom loves more than babies," Maggie said, then asked, "How're you getting along with the baby?" Before she could answer, Peggy delivered two super-sized iced teas in frosty, thick glasses. Maggie smiled her thanks, then shifted her gaze back to Carol.

Once Peggy left, Carol stalled by unwrapping her straw and poking it into her tea. "Fine. Everything's . . . fine."

"Good."

"Is there a problem?" Never ask, she told herself, a little too late to bite the words back. Never open the door to a problem. Wait until trouble kicks the door down. Don't go out to meet it. But it was too late now. Whatever was coming had already been invited.

"No."

Carol's stomach unfisted.

"Not really."

The fist tightened again.

"What's that mean?"

Maggie took a long swig of her tea, sighed as if she'd just seen heaven, then leaned back against the vinyl seat. Tipping her head to one side, she studied Carol for a long minute before saying, "A bed's opened up in the children's home."

"Oh."

The home. She remembered what the home had been like. Even as a kid, it had seemed . . . cold. Empty, though the halls had been crowded with kids who had nowhere else to be. No one to want them. No one to care. She'd seen the baby room. Two rows of cribs where babies of all ages slept and spent their days waiting for attention from too few workers with not enough time.

As an adult, she could look back and see that they'd all done their best. There just had never been enough hands. Or enough money. Or enough attention.

Now, when she thought of the baby room, with the

cribs lined up side by side, she thought that they'd looked like small, individual jail cells. And the tiny inmates were lost in a system that simply couldn't cope.

"You only signed on as an emergency foster parent, Carol," Maggie was saying.

"I know." Because she hadn't wanted to care. Hadn't wanted to fall in love with the baby she was now nuts about. Emergency foster situations never lasted long. She should know that better than most. There was a revolving door on the children's welfare system, and most kids got seasick from swinging in and out of helplessness with dizzying speed. But somehow, Carol'd thought she'd have more than a week.

"We can take her into the home tonight." Maggie's voice was soft, sympathetic. Her eyes shone in the last dying rays of the sun as it slanted through the windows and lay across the manila file like a sign from heaven. "In another week or two, we'll have her in with a permanent foster family."

There it was.

Little Lizardbaby would be gone. Carol wouldn't even be a blip in the tiny girl's memory, but she knew darn well she'd carry Liz in her heart forever. Oh, God. Her stomach twisted and reached up with icy fingers to give her heart a squeeze, too. Was this what a heart attack felt like?

"Or . . ."

Carol's gaze snapped to Maggie's. "Or?"

Maggie leaned her elbows on the tabletop and linked her fingers together. "I was wondering if you might be interested in being the baby's permanent foster mother."

"Me?" Carol fell back against the seat.

"Why not you?" Maggie smiled slowly, one corner of her mouth lifting.

She inhaled sharply, deeply. Her stomach settled and her thudding heartbeat eased into a steady, even rhythm. She hadn't even considered it because she hadn't wanted to care. But now that she did care, could she walk away from this chance to love and be loved?

No way.

This was a gift.

She could *keep* Liz.

She wouldn't have to be alone ever again.

From somewhere in the kitchen, Liz sent out a wail that sounded impressive enough for a baby twice her size. And Carol grinned as she turned from the sound to face Maggie. "I think Liz is trying to tell me something. And I vote with her. Where do I sign up?"

CHAPTER 10

With Liz gone, the apartment felt . . . *lonely*. Carol smiled to herself. Strange how quickly you could get used to something. She'd lived on her own ever since leaving the foster care system. Never had a roommate. Hadn't wanted to share the *space* it had taken her years to find.

Now, though, she shared her life with a tiny girl who seemed to fill up every corner of the world. And with Liz spending the night at the Reillys', the silence in the apartment was nearly deafening.

The bottle of chardonnay was half-empty when Carol heard Jack come home. Funny. A week ago, she hadn't known him. Beyond his belonging to a family of people she considered friends, she hadn't known anything about Jack Reilly. Now, he belonged here. He'd become a part of her life as surely as little Liz had. Surreptitiously, he'd slipped into the fabric of her world and made himself a part of the whole.

Now, the sound of his footsteps on the stairs rattled through her and set off tiny explosions of anticipation in her blood.

Ordinarily, those thoughts would have sent her scrambling for time to consider the ramifications. To think about just what she was letting herself in for. But tonight, she was only glad to hear him.

He moved quickly up the stairs and along the faded floral carpet runner in the hall. His steps didn't slow. He didn't pause in front of her door. Instead, he went quickly to his. As he had been for the last few days. He was trying to avoid her. Had done a damn good job of it, too. Because she'd allowed it. Allowed him to back away from those few moments of incredible connection they'd shared with a kiss that had rocked her to her toes.

She'd figured that he'd needed a little time to adjust to whatever was happening between them, so she'd steered clear of him. She'd been willing to let him lock himself up in his apartment. To reinforce the wall that he kept between himself and a world he was determined to stay apart from. A wall that would keep that kiss from ever repeating itself.

Until tonight.

Tonight, the wall came down. Well, maybe not all the way down, she admitted. But she'd certainly ram a hole through it. Because tonight, she wanted to celebrate. She didn't want to be alone. She needed someone to talk to before she burst. And since Phoebe was working at the clinic, *guess who* was the lucky winner?

Carol hurried across the room, Quinn hot on her heels. His nails clicked cheerfully against the wood floor and Carol did a quick, unsteady dance and dip to the music dripping from her stereo as she slid up to the door. Grabbing the old-fashioned cut-glass knob, she gave it a twist and yanked the door open in time to see Jack ducking into his own apartment.

"Freeze!"

He did.

Carol grinned to herself as he slanted a look at her over his shoulder.

"Hey." A curl of pleasure unwound inside her. Who said watching TV wasn't educational? "What do you know? That worked really well. I've never actually said it before and—"

"Why now?" he asked, one eyebrow lifting in a high arch as he watched her.

She met that eyebrow lift with one of her own. Although she didn't have the one-brow lift down like he did, so both of hers went up, which really didn't have the same effect at all. But Carol absolutely refused to let that cranky tone of his bring her down. She'd expected the snarls and the shutters in his eyes and had surprised him anyway.

She wouldn't back off now. "No way," she said, shaking her head and holding up one hand like a crossing guard protecting her charges. "You're not going to ruin this for me."

"I'm not doing a damn thing, Baker. Just going into my place."

"Nope. Not tonight." She reached out to grab his forearm. Her fingers held on and tightened when she felt him flex the muscles lying just beneath his warm skin. Ribbons of something really delicious spooled throughout her body. She swallowed hard. "No locking yourself up tonight, mister."

"You're drunk."

"Not yet."

"Your eyes are rolling."

She grinned at him. "Well, that explains a lot." Huffing a breath in and then out again, she squinted up at him. "You only have the one set of eyes, right?"

"Last time I looked."

"Okay good." She'd eat a little something before having more wine, she decided. But she *would* have more wine. And she wasn't going to whoop it up alone. "Come on in."

He shot a look through her open apartment door and then lowered his gaze to take in the less-than-welcoming stare Quinn was giving him. "No thanks."

"Come on, Reilly." She didn't put a plea in her voice, but she couldn't keep it out of her eyes. "Give me a break. Come in and have a drink with me."

He blew out a breath, turned and stared down at her. There was no welcome in his eyes, but he hadn't shaken her hand off, so Carol took that as a good sign.

"Why?" he demanded.

"To celebrate."

"What?"

She frowned at him. "Jesus, you're a good time, you know it?"

One corner of his mouth tipped up briefly, then flattened again a heartbeat later, just before she had enough time to enjoy it.

"What's going on?"

Carol smiled again. "That's what I'm trying to tell you, so come on."

She dragged at him, and when he reached back and closed his apartment door before letting her pull him after her, she counted it as a victory. But just to be sure, she didn't let go of him until they were inside her apartment and she'd closed the door behind him.

A classic-rock channel on the radio pumped in a clash of sound that, even with the volume turned low, refused to be ignored. The Beach Boys sang about good vibrations and Carol did a quick little sidestep along with the steady beat. Then she grinned and reached out to snag up the bottle of wine and a glass off the coffee table.

Filling one for him, then topping off her own, she handed Jack one of the etched crystal glasses. While he held it, his gaze still on hers, she lifted her glass, clinked it to his, and grinned at the musical ping of crystal meeting crystal.

"To me," she crowed as she took a drink, then swallowed and frowned when he didn't mirror her action.

"Hello?" she said. "This is a toast. You're supposed to drink to me, too."

"Do I get to know why?" he asked, that corner of his mouth twitching again.

Seriously, she thought as her heart did a fast trip and hammer, if he ever really gave her a flat-out grin, it'd probably knock her on her ass. He was more potent than the wine.

"Why?" she repeated, then said, "Oh!" She laughed and reached out for him, laying one hand on his forearm again. He just felt . . . good. Why not touch? she thought. Why not feel *everything*? Tonight of all nights? "That's right. Haven't told you yet. I'll tell you and then we'll try that toast thing again. It's about Liz."

"The baby?" His gaze narrowed as he shifted a quick, calculating glance around the room. "Where is she?" he asked as his gaze slid back to her. "You lose her again?"

"She's at your mom's." Carol tipped her head to one side and stared up at him. And it was *way* up, she thought absently. Really tall, Jack Reilly. Really tall and really gorgeous and really . . . cranky. But that was okay. She was sort of getting used to the crabbiness. To the glowering expression and the coolness of his eyes.

And she knew it was because every once in a while, he let that guard down. His lips fought to smile. The shutters in his eyes creaked open just far enough to show her the warmth waiting inside him. And those small tastes of what he was really like were enough to intrigue her beyond reason.

She took another sip of wine and let the cold, slightly fruity liquid slide down her throat and turn to ice in her stomach. It didn't do a thing toward cooling her off. And really, did she want it to?

"Your mom is really the greatest, you know? I mean, she's so nice and everything and—"

"Yeah," he agreed tightly. "She's great. So what about the baby?"

"Oh, yeah." Her fingers curled tightly around his arm and she swore she felt his muscles quiver under her touch. She gave him a squeeze, then let him go long enough to turn, take three steps toward the stereo, then quickly come back again. Quinn walked with her, his big body ranged alongside her like some overpriced bodyguard. When she stopped again, though, the dog had had enough and lay down in front of the couch, where he could keep a wary eye on both of them.

"It's the best," Carol said. "Just the best. I mean, I didn't think this would happen. Didn't really want to let myself think this would happen, you know?"

She frowned as she tried to make sense of her own jumbled thoughts, crowding together in her mind, each jockeying for position. And as her brain worked, she tried to explain. To him. To herself.

"Because, really," she said, scooping one hand back and through her hair, pushing it away from her face. "If you just let yourself feel, sometimes things get all screwed up in your head and then your heart gets all twisted and before you know it . . . *pow,* you get slammed. And you can't figure out what you did to get pounded into the ground." She shook her head now as memories raced in to fill the gaps between her thoughts. Images of other times when she'd trusted, when she'd taken a chance—only to be emotionally pummeled by whatever fate was willing to take a hand. She blew out a breath, let her smile come flooding back, and told herself that this time it would be different. "But then it happened, so I figured, why not?"

She took another sip of wine, reached down to the tray of food on the table and snatched up a pretzel. Taking a bite, she chewed as she talked, waving her glass in dramatic circles that sloshed the pale, almond-colored wine to the very brim of the glass and over. "I mean, when you get the chance, you shouldn't just look away, right? Maybe there's a reason—a purpose—and if you don't grab the opportunity, maybe you'll be really sorry and spend the rest of your life wondering if you were an idiot for not grabbing what you could when you could." She took a breath, tipped her head back, and stared up at him. "You know what I mean?"

He met her gaze and she read the confusion there. "Not a clue."

"Huh?"

"You haven't told me what's going on."

She inhaled sharply, told herself that she'd had enough wine for the moment, and looked up at him. Her gaze moved over his face. From the thick black eyebrows to the pale, icy blue eyes, to the slightly imperfect nose and the growing shadow of beard on his jaw. A lock or two of his black hair fell across his forehead and she had the weirdest urge to reach up and push it back. To run her fingers through his hair and then smooth it down with her palms. She wanted . . . "You really are amazing-looking."

His gaze narrowed.

"Even when you do that—your cop face—you just . . . wow."

"Carol—"

"I've been thinking about that kiss," she said as bubbles drifted through her bloodstream, popping, expanding, reproducing. "A lot. Have you?"

"No."

"Liar."

His jaw twitched and she was willing to bet he was gritting his teeth. Which meant she was getting to him as much as he was to her. Some consolation, she supposed.

"Okay," she said suddenly. "We'll let that go for now."

"Thanks."

She held up a hand again. "But we'll get back to it."

"Oh, no doubt."

Carol grinned and felt the smile slide right down inside her. She couldn't help it. She held the warmth of it to her tightly and told herself that *this* time, it would be different. *This* time, she wasn't going to be slammed. Or hurt. Or devastated. *This* time, taking a chance would pay off.

She took a long gulp of her wine, swallowed, then blurted, "I'm gonna be Lizardbaby's permanent foster mother."

There. She'd said it. Out loud.

And it sounded . . . wonderful.

She waited for a reaction.

What she got was a frown.

"Thought you only wanted the baby for a while," he said. "Thought you didn't want it to be permanent."

She nodded and her hair swung forward, hanging over her left eye until she shook it back. "That's what I said, sure. Because, well." She scowled, too, then admitted, "I was sort of afraid, you know, that if I loved her too much, I'd lose her and then it would hurt too much, but then I already love her—too late there—and when Maggie was talking to me about this . . . it occurred to me that love is a gift."

He snorted a laugh and stared down at the wine he'd yet to taste. "A gift."

"Yeah. It's like what Christmas morning must feel like to a kid," she said. "You know, coming downstairs, seeing a tree all lit up, with wrapped packages underneath it. Maybe snow falling outside the window and a fire in the fireplace and inside it's all cozy and warm." She sipped at her wine again. "That kind of gift."

He was watching her again and she shifted position slightly as his steady gaze started making her a little uneasy. "What do you mean, 'what it *must* be like for a kid at Christmas'?"

"Whoops." Carol leaned over, set her wineglass down on the coffee table, and paused long enough to give Quinn's wiry head a pat. "That sort of slipped out, huh?" She shook her head. "No biggie. I just, I don't remember many mornings like that, so I'm guessing it would be pretty great."

"There's a story there," he muttered.

"Not much of one," she said with a slightly tipsy shrug. "Sad little story—but hardly on a Dickensian scale. The people at the home did their best, I guess."

"Right." He was watching her again and his blue eyes were darker, softer.

"Anyway," she continued, her voice lifting, "I'm just saying that if love is a gift, then not taking it is almost . . . rude."

"Not taking it is safer."

"But less fun."

Jack stared down into her soft, whiskey-colored eyes

and wondered about her even more than he had before. He had his own secrets, God knew. And now he'd discovered a few shadowy places in the one woman he wouldn't have expected to be carrying them.

She didn't talk about her childhood much, but he knew that it had been a far cry from his. He'd had everything, she'd had nothing. And yet . . . which of them was the happier human being? Which of them carried the darker shadows? Which of them hid from life rather than going out to look for it?

And why the hell did he care?

His grip on the wineglass tightened until he was almost sure the fragile crystal would shatter in his hand. Lifting it, he took a long swallow of the chilled wine and wished it were Irish whiskey. He could use the fire right now, to ease away the chill dancing in his blood, in his heart.

She was watching him and he felt the heat of her gaze and was tempted to use *her* fire to warm himself. To ease the chill in his bones. But going down that path was something that would only make a complicated mess into a tangle of threads that might never come undone again.

"Love's not a gift," he blurted, forcing himself to meet her eyes. "Love's a bill. Due and payable."

"Huh?"

He sighed and took another long drink, grateful now for the wine she'd poured him. "People love you," he murmured, "you owe them. 'I love you, so don't make me worry. I love you, so don't hurt me. I love you so—' " He broke off, biting the words back, and took another tack altogether. "Take the Reillys. Sean's saying masses for me, my mom's lighting candles, my sisters are whispering about me and stop when I come in a room. They're worried, so they're handing me a bill."

"You're wrong."

"Am I?"

"They only want to help. To make you feel better. To—"

"They can't." He could only look into those eyes for so long without folding. Without giving in to his own need to dive into them and lose himself. So he turned away. Turned his back on her and walked across the room to stare out the front window at the night beyond the glass. He set his wineglass down on the window ledge and leaned into the wall beside the window. "I didn't ask them to help. No one can."

"That's the thing with families, or so I'm told. You don't *have* to ask."

"It would have been easier," he told himself, his voice just a hush above the Beatles complaining about an eight-day week, "if I'd never come back. I shouldn't have come back."

"Jack, what's wrong?"

"Never mind." His gaze focused on the flower beds lining her front walk. In the moonlight, they looked black-and-white, torn from an old movie set. Light and shadow. As colorless as he felt. As his life had been for the last two years. Until Carol. Until the baby. "Let it go, Baker."

"You keep telling everyone to let it go," she said, and he heard her crossing the room to stand behind him.

No tinkling bells tonight, though, he mused. She was barefoot. He'd noticed her long, tanned legs, denim shorts frayed at the hem, dark pink polish on her toes. He noticed everything about her, dammit. Her scent reached out for him, grabbing him by the throat, demanding he take it into himself. Coconut and springtime, he thought. A hint of some kind of floral scent mingled with the coconut in her lotion that drove him insane and kept intruding on the dark thoughts that wanted precedence in his mind.

"What is it that makes you so unhappy here?" she asked, her voice softly rising above the music's steady beat.

He didn't turn around. Didn't dare. She was too close and his nerves were on edge.

"Its not being *here,*" he said, shaking his head as he lifted his gaze to the nearly full moon staring back at him from a black sky. He placed one hand on the cool glass. On the opposite side of the window, the multicolored Christmas lights shone. Just out of his reach. As so much was beyond his reach, now. "I've always loved this place. This town." Damn, it had been a long time since he'd admitted that. "Oh, we made fun of it, growing up, but . . . it's home. I just don't belong here anymore." And by damn, that was a hard thing for him to accept. A harder thing to live with. That the one place you craved to be was the one place you couldn't go back to. "I don't belong with my family. With these people."

"Why?"

She touched him.

A simple, light touch on his shoulder. He felt the weight of her small hand on his body and wanted more. Wanted to feel her skin on his. Wanted to lose himself in the laughter and warmth she promised. Wanted it so badly, he could have begged for it.

But he didn't.

Instead, he told her why she should back away. As far away as he kept his family and the friends he'd grown up with. Turning away from the pale, ivory light of the moon, he faced her, staring down into whiskey eyes that shone up at him with more emotion than he could handle. Grabbing her shoulders, he held on tightly, his fingers digging into her bare arms. "Because I don't deserve it. I don't deserve this place. And if I stay here too long, they'll know it and they won't want me here anyway."

"Of course you *deserve* to be with your family."

"There's things about me you don't know, Baker. And they're not pretty."

"Ugly enough to keep you from your family?"

"I think so." He waited for her to pull out of his fierce grip. To take a step back from him that would put worlds between them. But she didn't do any of that and he shouldn't have been surprised. Carol Baker never reacted the way he expected her to. Maybe that was part of why he was so damn fascinated by her.

"You're crazy," she said after what seemed like an eternity of moments.

He laughed shortly and let her go, wincing only slightly when he saw that he'd left the imprint of his hands on her arms. He curled his fingers into fists by his sides and tried to laugh about it. "Yeah? That's what I keep saying about *you*."

She shrugged and the little reindeer decorating her red tank top shifted and moved over her breasts. Jack blew out a shaky breath.

"Takes one to know one?"

"Maybe," he agreed and took a shallow breath. Couldn't risk inhaling her scent, having it cling to him as he went back to his own apartment for another long night of sleeplessness.

But she wasn't going to let him go yet. He saw it in her eyes even before she reached up to cup his face between her palms. Heat speared through him, going deep, seeking out all the dark, cold places inside him, leaving Jack shaken and hungry for more.

"Your family doesn't think you *owe* them, Jack."

"You're not letting this go, are you?"

She shook her head. "No."

He reached up and took hold of her wrists, but didn't pull her hands away from his face. Didn't think he'd be able to bear it if she stopped touching him. God, he wanted her. More than anything, he wanted her.

"You're too drunk for this," he said, knowing he had to give her this one chance to back out. To change her mind.

"No I'm not," she said, going up on her toes. Just before her mouth brushed over his, she said, "I'm just drunk enough."

CHAPTER 11

Jack grabbed her and yanked her close, pulling her body tightly to his. "Be sure," he muttered thickly.

She looked up at him and her whiskey-colored eyes swam with desire and hunger and fed the flames already scorching his insides.

"I'm sure," she said, lifting one hand to smooth his hair back from his face, skim her fingertips along his cheek. "Oh, boy, am I sure."

He drew a long, unsteady breath, then indulged himself by taking one moment to etch her features into his brain. Beautiful. Soft. Yet he knew there was steel inside her, too. And that crazy mingling of vulnerability and strength touched him like nothing else ever had. Made him wish he was the man he used to be. Made him wish he could hold on to her and keep her tightly to him. To claim her.

She was the one bright spot in two years of shadows. And dammit, he *wanted* her. Needed her. Everything about this woman got to him like no one else ever had. And for tonight . . . she was his. "Good. Because later, I won't be sorry."

He couldn't regret this. He needed it too much.

Needed to be with her more than he'd ever imagined.

Her lips curved and his gaze dropped to that luscious mouth.

"Who asked you to be?"

He kissed her smile away.

No niceties. No slow warm-ups.

Just need.

Pure, but not simple.

There was absolutely nothing simple about Carol Baker. He'd known it the minute they met. When she'd smiled up at him and fought his bad temper with good humor. He'd known it watching her deal with a baby she hadn't expected, even while protecting her own heart.

As she should be protecting herself from him.

He needed her. Dammit, he needed her as much as he needed air in his lungs. And he knew if he didn't have her in the next few minutes, the lack of her would kill him.

One hand at the back of her head, his fingers speared through the soft fall of blond-streaked hair, threading through the smooth strands and holding her in place. Silky tendrils of blond and brown danced across his skin like a whisper of wind, sighing in off the ocean, tantalizing him with the barest of touches.

He couldn't taste enough of her. He deepened the kiss, taking what he needed, giving what he could. And mentally said to hell with consequences. He'd said he wouldn't be sorry later—but one small, still rational corner of his mind knew there would be regrets. But that was for later. Much later. Now was all that mattered. All he could think about.

They'd been headed toward this moment since that first meeting in the clinic. When she'd turned her face up to his and challenged him with a smile. He'd felt the danger even then. And he hadn't steered clear. Hadn't been able to keep from wishing things were different. Hadn't been able to stem the tide of need that washed up inside him every time he heard the damn bells she consistently wore.

He groaned tightly, fisting one hand in the back of her tank top as if afraid she might try to steal away from him. He couldn't let her. In that wild, raging moment of time, she was the only thing holding him centered on the planet. Her heat. Her strength, her incredible mouth.

His tongue swept past her lips, devouring all she had to offer, taking her warmth and stealing it, burying it deep within him, where the cold waited to again lay claim to his soul. With Carol in his arms, the cold was held at bay—and he could almost remember what it had felt like to be alive. Really alive.

He claimed her, mouths mating, tongues dancing, breath mingling. She sighed into him and he felt her surrender as she pressed her body to his. The hard, rigid tips of her nipples burned against his chest and still it wasn't enough. Not even close. He wanted, needed, to feel her naked. Flesh to flesh. Body to body.

Heartbeat to heartbeat.

Brain racing, body burning, he claimed her, staked out a territory he'd only begun to see as his. And before that thought had time to worry him, she opened to him, welcoming him in.

That small, lonely voice in the corner of his mind thought to warn her. To tell her to back off and throw his ass out of her apartment while she still could. He was no good for her. No good for anyone. But dammit, it had been so long. He couldn't give her up, he thought, as sensations washed over him like high tide reclaiming the dry shoreline. His senses were on overload and he wanted more.

He held her closer, pressing her body to his, and couldn't feel enough of her. She groaned again and tore her mouth from his, gasping for air, her lungs heaving for it. He dropped his head to the curve of her neck and tasted her skin, soft, sweet. Her scent filled him, imprinting itself on his mind, and he knew he'd never be completely free of the memory of her.

"God, you taste good," he murmured against her neck.

She shivered in his grasp and tipped her head to one side, giving him access, offering herself. She swept her hands up to his shoulders and her fingers curled into the fabric of his shirt. He felt the imprint of her fingers as clearly as though she held a match on each one of her fingertips.

She moved against him, rubbing her body along his, stoking the flames within until they licked at his soul and threatened to engulf him. He'd never known anything like it. Never experienced this incredible urgency. She was all. She was everything. And right now . . . she was *his*.

He stared down at her for one long minute, indulging himself in the shine of her eyes. Her breath came fast and hard, her lips were swollen, puffy, and even more tempting than usual. As he bent his head to kiss her again, she went up on her toes to meet him.

It was a brief, soul-shattering, brush of mouth to mouth and left him even more staggered than before.

"Jack . . ." She sighed his name and something inside him shifted with the fierce strength of an 8.5 earthquake.

He didn't want to feel it. Didn't want to acknowledge that there was more here than bodies moving against each other. It was easier—so much easier—to tell himself that it was only sex.

Chemistry.

Hell, hormones.

But even he couldn't believe that—so he buried the truth in a dark, quiet corner of his heart and fought to keep it there.

"I need to touch you," he whispered, voice tight, throat strangling with the need roaring up to snatch at him.

"Me, too," she said and swallowed hard. "Need to be touched. Need you to touch me. Now."

His hands dropped to the hem of her shirt and pushed up and under it, scraping along her rib cage up to the firm, soft mounds of her breasts. A groan sounded from his chest as his hands cupped her, his thumbs and fore-fingers tweaking her nipples, pulling, teasing, rubbing.

She sighed and leaned into him, pressing her body more firmly into his touch, silently demanding more. Demanding that he feed the fire he'd built inside her.

"So good," he muttered and thought it would be great if he could just take time enough to yank the shirt up and over her head. But he couldn't stop touching her long enough to do it. Couldn't bring himself to lose the plea-sure of her body in his hands.

His gaze clouded, his brain short-circuited, and his breath stopped hard in his lungs when Carol shifted in his grasp. Reaching down, she grabbed at her shirt and pulled it off herself.

Carol couldn't breathe.

There didn't seem to be enough air in the room. She kept trying, but it was as though the oxygen in the room had thickened and she couldn't pull enough into her lungs. Her brain was dazzled and her gaze was a little gray at the edges, but she saw all she needed to see.

The shutters in his eyes had lifted. Just enough to give her a glimpse of the man beyond them. She saw hunger—raw and powerful—in his gaze. And she saw tenderness that seemed to surprise him. She saw the rapid pulse beat at the base of his throat and heard his ragged breaths as he too fought for air.

Then she shifted her gaze, looking down at his big, strong hands cupped over her breasts. His fingers, long, tanned, spread over her much paler flesh, and as he stroked her nipples again, she shivered with a tremor that raced along her bloodstream and settled low in her belly. Breath staggered from her lungs and she hoped desperately she'd be able to draw another, because she didn't want to miss a thing.

His hands moved on her body, stroking, smoothing, and she watched, as if hypnotized. She couldn't tear her gaze from the sight of him touching her. An ache pooled in her center and throbbed to the beat of her heart. A curl of something warm and liquid rolled through her, spiraling out to every corner of her body. Tiny tentacles of need reached out for places inside her she'd thought couldn't be touched. And once there, that need ripened until it rose, screaming, to her brain.

"Jack—don't stop," she managed to say and couldn't figure out how she'd managed to squeeze those few words past the knot lodged in her throat.

"Not a chance," he assured her. His voice was a low, almost dangerous rumble of sound and it set off a whole new set of explosions deep inside her.

His thumbs and forefingers continued to work her nipples and she felt the deep, drawing sensation all the way to the soles of her feet. She struggled for air and then thought, *Screw it*. Breathing was overrated anyway.

Lifting both hands, she covered his and held him to her while he stroked her breasts. She felt each shift of his fingers, went with him as he moved his hands up and down her body, linked her fingers with his and felt her own flesh as if for the first time.

From somewhere behind her, she heard Quinn whining softly and she fought to focus. "It's all right, Quinn," she murmured and gasped as Jack bent his head to briefly take first one nipple, then the other, into his mouth. "Oh, *God,*" she said on a sigh. "It's *so* all right."

The big dog wasn't convinced though and stood up to lean against her, putting his solid weight into pressing her up against Jack. With her abdomen flush against his, she felt his body, thick and hard, and her own went up in flames in response.

Oh, man.

"That's it," Jack muttered.

"It?" she repeated, babbling now. Eyes wide, she stared up at him, horrified, babbling. "What do you mean, that's it? You can't leave me like this."

"And I can't do what I want to do to you in front of your trained bear." He looked over her shoulder at the animal and glared at him. Then bending, he scooped her up into his arms, lifted her off the floor, and stalked across the room to the hallway.

Quinn's nails clicked along right behind him and Carol shot the big dog a look over Jack's shoulder. She should probably feel guilty about this, she thought. But she didn't. It wasn't every day some gorgeous man picked her up and carried her off to be ravished. Ravished. God, what a good word. She swallowed hard. "Go lay down, Quinn."

Jack stepped into her bedroom, kicked the door closed behind him, and then walked to her bed. Dropping her onto the mattress, he stared down at her while he ripped his shirt off and tossed it to the floor. He rummaged in his wallet, came up with a condom and gripped it in one tight fist.

"Always prepared?" she asked, a smile in her voice despite the tension rippling through her body.

"Hell, it's so old it might not work."

"I'll risk it."

In seconds, he'd stripped but hardly gave Carol a moment to enjoy the view before he was leaning over her.

"Get outta those clothes, Baker," he muttered, his fingers working at the button of her denim shorts.

"Oh, yeah," she whispered brokenly as she did her best to help him with a zipper that wouldn't give. "Right there with ya, buddy."

The damn thing stuck, but Jack didn't let that stop him. Grabbing hold of the two edges of her shorts, he broke the zipper, ripped the shorts and her ivory lace panties down and off her legs, and tossed them onto the floor beside his jeans. "I'll buy you a new pair."

"No problem," she said, already reaching for him as he tore open the condom foil and sheathed himself.

The antique quilt beneath her felt cool and soft against her skin. Moonlight speared through the gap in the curtains and a whisper of an ocean breeze sneaked beneath the partially open window.

He climbed onto the bed, scraping his palms up along her legs as he moved. That pale wash of light from the moon outside splayed across his broad chest and sculpted him in a silvery glow that stole what was left of Carol's breath. He was tanned and fit and strong and just looking at him was enough to curl her toes.

Then as he touched her, his fingers spearing into the damp heat waiting for him, she bucked, her hips coming off the bed, her feet planting themselves firm on the mattress. Her hands fisted in the quilt and hung on for dear life. It had been so long, she felt her body hum into action at top speed. In seconds, she was near a peak she suddenly didn't want to rush to. She wanted to enjoy this, dammit. She didn't want it to be over before it began.

But she didn't seem to be able to stop herself.

"Jack!"

He touched her deeper, faster. Thumb stroking over the sensitive nub of her sex until the world spun behind her closed eyes and all she could do was hang on to the bed beneath her.

"Enjoy," he whispered. "Take it."

"I want—" She swallowed thickly, tossed her head from side to side, and lifted her hips into his hand. "I want to feel you—"

"You will," he promised, that deep voice humming in the air around her like a drone of bees.

"It's coming—" She couldn't stop it. Couldn't hold it back. It was too much. Too hard. Too fast. Too deep. She rode the crest as it lifted her higher and higher. Her hips rocked, her breath staggered in time with a ragged heartbeat, and then he plunged two fingers inside her and she knew she couldn't wait. Couldn't hold it back. And she gave in to the shimmering glory of it, crying out his name as the world splintered into colorful shards and crashed down around her.

"Oh, God," she whispered as the last of the tremors raced through her.

"Again," he whispered and dipped his fingers deeper inside her, stroking her body with smooth strokes designed to send her up in flames one more time.

"I can't—" Oh, she wanted to. Wanted it more than anything, but as he touched her deeply, intimately, she thought she just might shatter. But even as she considered it, she thought it would be a hell of a way to go.

"Jack—"

"Right here, Baker," he muttered thickly and slid up the length of her, rubbing his hard body along hers until new, brighter, starbursts of sensation splintered behind her eyes.

She rocked her hips and opened her legs wider, wanting to feel him again. Need began its slow, deliberate build and she discovered that she *could* go again. And more than that, she *needed* to go again. But she wanted to feel more than his fingers inside her. She wanted him to fill her. To slide into her body and complete it. To ease the budding ache within and begin a new fire that would erupt around them both.

Jack couldn't touch her deeply enough. Having her unravel at his touch had unnerved him. Feeling her body fist and tremble around his hand, he'd given himself up to the pleasure of watching her dissolve. Of seeing her eyes go wide and glassy. Of hearing her breath choke from her lungs. Of feeling her body tremble.

His heartbeat thundered in his ears. The world had narrowed to this one bed. This one woman. This one moment.

Her damp heat called to him. He needed her now even more than he had before. He wanted to bury himself inside her and ride the wave of satisfaction with her this time. And then he wanted to do it all again. And again. Watching the soft brown of her eyes shine and dazzle with pleasure and need, he felt an invisible fist squeeze his heart. There was more here. More than he would ever be able to claim, and that knowledge nibbled at his mind even as his body demanded his full attention.

First one finger, then two, he dipped within her, reveling in the soft, damp heat that surrounded him. This was what he'd craved. This was what he'd needed so desperately.

This woman.

This night.

She opened wider for him and he glanced down to where his hand met heaven, and everything in him yearned for more. Pulse beats of urgency thundered through his head. He couldn't wait. Couldn't last another minute without being a part of her.

She was a siren's song. She was everything that had been missing from his life. And for this one moment in time, he would have it all.

He moved to position himself between her thighs and she lifted her hips in welcome. Opening her arms to him, she looked up into his eyes and held his gaze while he pushed his body into hers. One long thrust and he was buried so deeply within her, he thought wildly that he might never find his way out again. And he wondered if he would ever want to.

Her body took him in, surrounding him, holding him. She lifted her legs and locked them around his hips, keeping him tightly within until all he could feel was her. All he could see were her eyes.

He groaned and rocked against her. Her head tipped back into the bed as she arched into him, taking him deeper, more fully into her body. Her arms wrapped around him, holding him close as he moved within her. He set the rhythm and she followed eagerly, her movements mirroring his in a dance that felt as old as time and as new as dawn.

"Jack," she whispered, one hand sliding around to cup his cheek, push his hair back from his face. Short, sharp breaths exploded from her lungs as he rocked her hard, harder. "Jack, it's so good . . . so . . . right . . ."

"Let go," he murmured, watching her eyes, needing

to see pleasure shimmer there when she slipped over the edge.

"No," she shook her head, licked her lips. "This time with you. Wait for you."

"Together, then," he whispered and took her hand, linking his fingers with hers.

She squeezed his hand.

He squeezed back.

Gazes locked. Emotions seared.

And in moments, still linked together, they tumbled over the precipice.

"Okay," Carol said faintly a few minutes later. "Can I just say . . . *wow*?"

"That about covers it." He snorted a choked-off laugh and she groaned slightly. "Sorry. Too heavy."

"No." She caught him, wrapping her arms around him when he would have moved to one side of her. She wanted him here. Still buried deep inside her. Still causing shimmers of sensation to bubble through her body. Carol sighed, closed her eyes and wiggled her hips, enjoying the flash of feeling that darted from her center straight up through the top of her head. "Don't move yet," she told him. "I like it."

"Yeah," he admitted, levering himself up on one elbow to look down at her. "It's not bad."

Both of her eyebrows lifted. "Not bad? Just 'not bad'? That's like saying, 'Chocolate tastes okay.' Or 'Led Zeppelin was a pretty good band.' "

One corner of his mouth twitched and her stomach did a fast pitch and roll.

"Stones were better."

"Agreed."

He lifted one eyebrow. "You agree with me on something?"

"Bound to happen sooner or later."

His lips twitched again.

"You've got a great mouth," she whispered suddenly and shifted one hand to draw the tip of one finger across his lips.

He bent his head to nibble at her bottom lip. "I'm kind of fond of yours, too."

Quick, sharp jolts of electricity staggered through her veins. She felt his body stir inside her. Seems they were both more than ready to go again. At least, the spirit was willing. But she had a feeling that if they tried that again in the next minute or two, they'd kill each other. "Oh, man . . ."

"Yeah." Slowly, then, he rolled to one side, and lay like a dead man on the quilt beside her, eyes staring glassily at the ceiling.

Without his warm, solid weight atop her, Carol felt the chill of the night air dance across her body, raising gooseflesh and sending a shiver rolling along her spine. She wanted to do it all again. She wanted to slow down next time and enjoy the whole process. There'd been such an urgency this time, it had been all explosions and fireworks. Now she wanted to try it slow and deliberate and lingering.

But Jack wasn't even touching her now. It was as if the explosion of desire had shattered him and sent him sprawling to the other side of the universe.

The moon drifting through the curtains sent lacy patterns of light splashing across the walls and ceiling. From the living room, classic rock thumped a steady beat that almost sounded like a heartbeat.

She inhaled sharply, deeply, and wanted to just go on enjoying the soft glow spreading through her body. Unfortunately, her lover . . . she hugged that word to her for a minute or two . . . had different plans. Now that the passion was spent, he was going to be sprinting for the door. She'd known he would. Had expected it, even. That didn't mean she had to like it.

Dammit. But she could already feel Jack distancing himself as he sat up and reached to the floor for his clothes.

He froze. "Shit."

"What?" She blinked and tried to focus on the snarling look on his face as he glanced over his shoulder at her.

"Condom broke."

Her heart gave an odd little thump. "Well, that can't be good."

"Ya think?" He stood up, snatching his pants up from the floor and stepping into them.

Ramifications rattled through her. She wasn't an idiot. But she also wasn't going to ruin what had been a terrific little bout of sex by worrying about something that *might* happen.

"Are you healthy?" she asked.

"Yes." The word was bitten off.

"Me, too."

"And that's it?"

"Well, I could have you shot, but that seems a little harsh."

"This isn't a joke, dammit."

"It's not the end of the world, either," she snapped, and mentally said goodbye to the lovely little glow she'd enjoyed so briefly.

"Yeah, how does getting pregnant strike you?"

"Also not apocalypticlike," she said tightly, meeting

his steely blue gaze and giving him back as good as she could.

"That's not even a damn word."

"It is if I want it to be." She sat up, pushed her hair back from her face, and met him glare for glare. Stark naked and completely comfortable with it, she folded her arms over her chest. "I wasn't exactly planning on getting pregnant," she said, "but if it happens—which it won't—I'll handle it."

Shaking his head, he stared at her as though she had just sprouted wings. "I knew this was a mistake."

"Hey, I didn't hold a gun to your head or anything."

"Doesn't matter," he said, picking up his sneakers. "Look. I'm—"

"You said you wouldn't be sorry later," she reminded him, cutting him off quickly. She so didn't want what was left of her good cheer to disappear in a burst of wanting to bash him over the head with something heavy.

He inhaled sharply and let it out on a slide of frustration. "Yeah, I did."

Carol scooted off the edge of the bed and walked to him. She watched him watch her, his gaze drifting over the length of her before lifting again to meet hers.

"Jack," she said softly, lifting both hands to cup his face. "You don't have to be careful of me. I can look out for myself. I've been doing it for a long time."

His jaw twitched and she knew he was gritting his teeth again. The shutters she was so used to seeing in his eyes were back again and she couldn't help wondering what secrets lay behind them. What pain haunted him.

"I don't want to hurt you."

"I know that."

He lifted one hand to her cheek, touched her briefly, then let that hand drop to his side again. "But I probably will."

Then he turned, opened the door, and pushed past the waiting Quinn to leave the room. It wasn't until she'd heard her own apartment door open and close after him that she sat back down on the bed and whispered, "Yeah. You probably will."

CHAPTER 12

Jack caught up the rebound, took three running strides, then jumped, slamming the basketball through the hoop. He landed flat-footed on the rectory driveway, then bent over, bracing his hands on his knees as he swiveled a look at his brother. "That's two games out of three. You buy dinner."

Afternoon sun sizzled from a cloudless blue sky, slanting a bronze light over everything. Not a single breeze stirred the steaming air and the asphalt beneath his feet felt soft and mushy, as if the heat were melting it. He wouldn't have been surprised. Hottest day of the year so far and to Jack it felt as though the fires of hell were reaching up through the ground to singe him. Only right, he thought, briefly remembering how he'd stormed out of Carol's apartment the night before.

Damn, he'd really screwed things up royally.

He'd hurt her and he wasn't sure how to fix it. He kept seeing her eyes. Awake, asleep, didn't seem to matter. She haunted him and he wondered what the hell to do about it.

He glanced at his brother. Sean was dripping in sweat, too, and Jack figured hell couldn't reach a priest, so maybe it was just summer and not fiery retribution.

Sean whipped his damp hair back out of his eyes, then wiped his sweaty face with his forearm. "Let's go three out of five."

"Christ," Jack said as he drew a long, deep breath of hot air into his lungs. "Don't you know when to quit?"

Sean grinned. "Name me one Reilly who's a quitter."

Jack stiffened slightly.

"Besides you," Sean added.

"Low blow, Sean." Man, the last thing he needed at the moment was a lecture from his younger brother. Anger chewed at his insides, but to be honest, he wasn't mad at Sean. Just himself. No surprise there.

Striding across the driveway, he snatched his T-shirt off the grass and used it to wipe the streaming sweat from his bare chest. "If you're gonna start talking to me, I'm going home."

"Wait up, wait up," Sean said, as Jack started walking down the driveway. "Sorry. Cheap shot."

Jack stopped. Quitter. It wasn't a name he liked to think fit him. Never in his life had he walked away from a battle. Until two years ago.

But that hadn't been a fight he could win.

He'd gone in losing.

Turning around, he looked at his brother. Sean stood in the middle of the driveway, staring at him hard enough to see into his soul. To see things Jack didn't particularly want looked at.

Reaching up, Sean shoved both hands through his hair, then let them drop to his sides again. "You can't blame me for trying."

"Yeah, I can."

Nodding, Sean tore off his dark green T-shirt and wiped his face before tossing it into a heap at the side of the driveway. Then he braced his feet, lifted both fists, and threw a couple of short, sharp jabs. "Okay then, come on. Let's go a few rounds. Make you feel better."

Despite himself, Jack smiled briefly. "I think it's a sin to beat the crap out of a priest."

Sean snorted a laugh. "Probably. If you could pull it off. Who says you can?"

"Me." Jack shook his head as he started back up the drive. Sean shifted position, keeping his fists up and ready and a wary eye on Jack.

Jack walked past him, and headed for the old ice chest sitting in the grass beneath an ancient oak tree. The air in the shade was at least ten degrees cooler and he sighed with the relief of it. His head was pounding, his skin still sizzling, and there was an ache around the heart he'd thought had shriveled up and died two years ago.

Sighing, he flipped up the red lid on the cooler, reached inside and pulled two bottles of beer free of the half-melted ice. Frigid water clung to his hand as he scraped it across his face before turning. He held one of the bottles out toward Sean like a peace offering.

Sean kept his fists ready and suspicion in his eyes. "Is that a real offer?" he asked. "Or a trap to get me close enough to pound on?"

"It's a beer, Sean." Jack sighed. Hell, if he tried to take a swing at a family member every time they stuck their noses into his life—he'd be a human windmill. "Just a beer."

"Okay, then." Sean's long legs carried him into the shade in just a few strides. He snatched the bottle from Jack, twisted off the top and took a long, satisfying swig. After a long minute or two, he slanted a look at

Jack again. "Want to tell me what's got that dark cloud you live under even blacker than usual?"

Jack spread his arms wide. "Does this look like a confessional to you?"

"How would you know?" Sean countered. "Been a hell of a long time since *you* were in a church."

Jack took a long drink himself and let the icy brew spread a chill throughout his body. He welcomed the cold. Hell, he was more used to the cold than warmth anymore anyway. So what if he'd gotten close to real heat the night before? So what if he'd indulged himself and pretended, if only for a while, that he was *entitled* to it? So what if he'd allowed himself to believe for a moment that he'd paid his penance?

"As long as you keep saying masses for me," Jack said, taking another sip, "I'm covered." He dropped to the cool, soft grass and stretched out, the bottle of beer cradled on his abdomen.

Sean sat down close to him and studied the heat shimmering in waves above the driveway. He'd thought to get Jack talking. But he should have known better. His brother was, if nothing else, closemouthed. Always had been. Had to pry his troubles out of him with a crowbar. Or, Sean considered briefly, a two-by-four upside the head.

Of course, that wasn't very priestly, either. So instead, he took another shot at the "confession was good for the soul" thing. "What's going on, Jack? And why won't you talk to me?"

He didn't even open his eyes, but his mouth tightened into a grim slash across his face. "Can't you just be my brother? Do you have to be my priest all the damn time?"

"I *am* being your brother, idiot." And damn, it hurt

to see his older brother torn up like this. Two years he'd suffered, punishing himself for surviving something he couldn't have changed. "How much longer, do you figure?"

Jack turned his head and opened one eye to stare at him. "How much longer for what?"

"Until your sentence is complete."

His eye closed again, as did the rest of his features.

But Sean wasn't a Reilly for nothing. He'd never give up. Not as long as there was a chance to help Jack find what he'd lost. "You were your own judge and jury, Jack," he said, his voice quiet, but filled with determination. "I figure you know the sentence handed down better than anyone."

"If I promise to go to mass on Sunday, will you let this go?"

"Tempting," Sean admitted. "But no."

Jack sat up, gripping his beer tightly. Sunlight filtered through the oak leaves and laid dappled shadows on his face. Even after all this time, his eyes were still shadowed and he clung to the nightmare like a dying man holding on to his last hope.

"People died that night, Sean."

"Yeah, Jack." Sean reached for him, squeezed his brother's forearm. "*Two* people. Not three. You didn't die, too."

"Yeah I did," Jack muttered. "I just didn't have the sense to lie down."

Journal entry:

People are still looking for me.

It's weird, but every once in a while, I want to just stand out on North Pole Avenue and shout, "It's me. I'm the one you're looking for. I'm the one who gave away her baby."

But nobody would believe me.

Nobody's even thought for a minute that I might be the one.

But I am.

I'm the one who walked away from the one person who would have loved me.

Christmas Carol's bustled with chattering tourists. Voices rose and fell with a constant roar of sound that successfully drowned out the Christmas music drifting through the stereo speakers. While their wives picked up and put down Carol's entire inventory, bored husbands kept tired eyes on children. Most of them had probably come into the store to escape the outside heat, Carol knew. But a little air-conditioning could convince at least a few of them to open their wallets.

She shifted a look at the teenage goody counter and smiled at the girls clustered there. Even on her day off, Lacey ended up in the store, Carol thought, smiling. Of course, in Christmas, there weren't that many places for teenagers to hang out. Lacey, Peggy, and a few of their friends giggled and gossiped as they examined the new nail polish and lipsticks that had just been stocked. Still smiling, she turned her gaze on the baby, enthroned in her carrier, propped on the counter.

"You're gonna be a giggler, too, aren't you?" Carol asked, stroking the baby's soft cheek with a fingertip. Liz waved her tiny fists, screwed up her delicate little mouth, and gave a mighty . . . yawn.

Hers, Carol thought. The baby was *hers*. This bundle of love was here to stay. Permanently. And in a few months, she'd apply to adopt Liz officially. Then they'd be a real family. A family that no one and nothing could pull apart. The family she used to dream about.

Of course, in this reality there wouldn't be a handsome daddy coming home from work to kiss his wife and play with his kids. Instantly, an image of Jack blossomed in her brain and Carol fought back a sigh. The night before, they'd connected, in more ways than just physically—though that part had been awesome.

And then he'd retreated behind the wall he kept built around himself. A wall so high, Carol had no idea how to scale it. Or even if she should.

That was the hardest part to admit. She just didn't know if she should keep trying to reach a man who was so bound and determined to keep her out.

"What do you think, Liz?" she whispered, as the bells over the door clanged to announce yet another visitor to the shop.

Looking up, Carol smiled at her UPS man. "Hi, Tony."

"Hey." He nodded and balanced a large box on his hip as he handed her the electronic pad. "Got a package for somebody named . . ." He checked the label. "Jack Reilly. He your new tenant?"

"Yeah, but he's not here."

"Doesn't matter. I'm way behind today. Hit a traffic pileup on 101. You sign for it and I'm outta here."

"You got it," she said and scribbled her name on the Etch A Sketch–like space provided. He dropped the box on the counter next to the baby.

"See you, Carol," he called out as he headed for the door again.

"Right. See you next trip." But she wasn't watching Tony. Instead, she looked at the box. The return address read, "Detective Hal Jacobson, LAPD." Curious, she tucked the box below the counter, then tried to forget about it while she faced a customer buying an entire set of hand-carved wooden angel ornaments.

Journal entry:

The baby smiled at me today.

And it felt . . . weird.

Almost like she knows who I am or something. But she can't. She's just a baby. And besides, nobody knows the truth.

Carol's going to be her foster mother for real, now. That means she gets to keep the baby forever. But that's good. I left the baby in the square so Carol would find her. I wanted Carol to have the baby because I knew she'd love her.

I'm happy.

Really.

"Somebody got lucky."

Carol's eyebrows lifted. "It *shows*?"

"Only to those who love you," Phoebe assured her as she threw open her front door and stood back so Carol could step inside her house. "So, details."

Carol set the baby carrier down on the coffee table, then reached down and undid the straps holding Liz safely inside. Lifting the tiny girl into her arms, Carol turned to look at her friend, already plopping down on one of the two red floral couches in the big room.

"It was . . ." She fished for an appropriate word and just couldn't find one. Nothing was big enough. Complex enough. *Great* enough. She blew out a breath. "Really good."

"Well, that was nice. And annoyingly vague." Phoebe

brushed her red hair back from her face, propped one elbow on the arm of the couch and studied her. "This wasn't just sex for you, was it?"

Carol frowned at her friend. For heaven's sake, was she really that transparent? "Are you giving up medicine for fortune-telling or something?"

Phoebe grinned and shook her head. "It doesn't take a gypsy to see what's in your eyes, Carol," she said. "God, you're glowing like a nuclear reactor."

"Swell. Now I'm a nuclear accident."

"Hand over the baby and tell me what's going on."

Carol bent down and slipped Liz into Phoebe's waiting arms. Then she turned and started walking in circles around the living room.

She'd been in Phoebe's house so many times, it was as comfortable as her own place. Her gaze moved idly across the oversized furniture, the Tiffany lamps, and the polished oak floor. There were medical books stacked on the coffee table and thrillers and romances tucked into the bookshelves. An army of pewter and crystal fairies danced along the mantel over the fireplace and the wooden blinds at the windows were thrown open, allowing sunlight to slant into the prisms hanging there, throwing pale, wavering rainbows around the room.

"I didn't mean to do this, you know," Carol said, not sure if she was speaking to Phoebe or herself.

"Fall in love, you mean?"

Carol whirled around and stared at her friend. "I haven't. Not yet. Not completely. Probably. I'm pretty sure."

Phoebe shook her head and cuddled the baby close, running one unpolished fingernail along her tiny cheek. "Face it, Carol. You're sunk."

She sighed and let herself drop over the back of the sofa onto the cushions. "I am. It's pitiful."

Phoebe laughed gently. "No, not pitiful. Just you."

"What's that supposed to mean?"

Her friend sighed and lifted her gaze from the baby to Carol. "You're just not the casual-affair kind of woman, Carol. Face it. You're the home and hearth and kids and dogs type."

"And you're not?"

Phoebe winced a little.

Carol saw it and said quickly, "I'm so sorry, Phoebe. I wasn't even thinking."

"It's okay. Long time ago." Not in her heart, of course. There, it was always yesterday. The day she'd gotten a phone call telling her that her husband and son had been killed in a traffic accident. But in reality, it had been five long, lonely years.

"I'm really sorry, Phoeb."

She smiled at her friend and eased old pain into the locked room in the bottom of her heart, where she usually kept it. "Relax, Carol. I'm good." She inhaled sharply and forced a smile she hoped didn't look as brittle as it felt. "My point here was . . . I had my white picket fence, the family, and the dog. I'm not looking for that again."

Carol looked at her for a long time and Phoebe hoped dearly that her friend would just let this go, because she really didn't want to stare at her own past anymore. Thankfully, Carol seemed to sense that.

"Just call you Footloose Phoebe?" she asked, smiling.

"That's right." She blew out a breath and nodded to herself. "Love 'em and Leave 'em Phoebe. That's me. But you're different, Carol."

She smirked. "Whether I am or not isn't really

important. The thing is, I'm falling for the wrong guy again. And I can't seem to stop myself."

"Maybe you shouldn't."

"Huh?"

"I mean it, Carol." Phoebe glanced down at the sleeping baby and felt her uterus contract in regret. "If Jack is what you want, maybe you should go for it."

"And forget about what happened the last time?"

"You were a kid."

"I was twenty-two."

"Exactly."

"I loved him." Carol stared at the ceiling. "I really did, you know? And he let me build up all these fantasies about us and having a family and how good it would all be. He never said a word. Never told me that he didn't want what I did. Never told me about—" She stopped, as if she'd changed her mind abruptly about what she'd been about to say. Then in a heartbeat, she started up again. "Never told me that he was sleeping with the bimbo down the hall from his place. I almost *married* him, Phoebe."

Phoebe watched her with sympathetic eyes and felt a really strong urge to go and hunt down the little bastard who'd hurt Carol, just to punch his lights out. " 'Almost' is the key word in that sentence, honey."

"Yeah, I know." Carol shot her a look. "But I was wrong about him, Phoebe. So *way* wrong, it's amazing. If I didn't see what a jerk he was . . . how can I be sure I'm seeing the real Jack?"

Phoebe sighed. "Your ex was a total creep and he hurt you. But that doesn't mean Jack will, too."

"He keeps warning me off of him," Carol admitted. "Even last night, I could see it in his eyes, that he wanted me to say no. To turn away. But I couldn't. Didn't *want* to."

"See?" Phoebe said, delighted when the baby opened her big blue eyes and stared up at her. "The jerk didn't try to warn you off. He just sucked you into his orbit, chewed on you for a while, then sent you spinning off into space. Jack's already trying to keep you from getting hurt. Which means, at the heart of him, he's a nicer guy."

"Maybe you're right," Carol said as she sat up. "And speaking of nice guys . . . how's your favorite carpenter?"

Phoebe's smile slipped just a little. "Ah, Cash has moved on."

"Really?"

"Yep." Phoebe knew she'd miss Cash's company, but her heart wasn't wounded and that's how she liked it. She wouldn't get so involved with a man that losing him would kill her. Not again. "He finished my new closet, then packed up his little tool belt and stole off into the night. Well, okay, not night. Late afternoon. But you get the picture."

"I'm sorry?"

"Don't be," Phoebe assured her as she stood up, still cuddling little Liz close to her chest. "Cash was . . . well, amazing, really. But we both knew it wasn't a permanent thing. Want to see my new shoe and purse rack?"

"You bet."

"Afterward, we'll nuke our popcorn and watch the movie." She glanced over her shoulder at Carol. "Which one did you rent?"

"*Star Wars.*"

Phoebe sighed. "Han Solo and popcorn. Does it get any better than that?"

Remembering the night before, Carol thought, oh, yeah. It got way better than popcorn and a great movie.

But on the other hand, Han Solo couldn't reach into her chest, pull out her heart, and stomp on it.

Now, could he?

Carol got home late.

Liz was sound asleep and didn't even stir when Carol gently lifted her from the infant carrier to the crib. Standing over the baby, she tucked a soft, pale yellow blanket around her, then smoothed the palm of her hand over the baby's wispy cap of dark hair.

"We're home," she said, her voice a whisper as soft as the moonlight trailing through the window to lay in silver squares along the floor and the end of her bed. Smiling to herself, Carol turned on the baby monitor, picked up the receiver, and then looked down at Quinn, already curling up in sentry position beside the crib.

Her heart twisted and she bent down to stroke the big dog's head. He pushed into her hand and Carol obligingly scratched behind his ears. "Take good care of our girl, okay?"

He huffed out a breath, then dropped his head to his paws, prepared to drift into doggie dreams of giant biscuits and wide-open meadows.

Still smiling, Carol left the bedroom door open and walked into the living room. For some reason, she was antsy. Didn't really feel like going to sleep, but couldn't find anything to occupy her enough that she couldn't think. Even during the movie, her mind had kept sidling back to the night before. And when Han Solo couldn't keep your brain busy, you were in bad shape.

Jack, she thought, giving in to her mind's insistence on thinking of him.

She hadn't even seen him today.

Between working and then the movie with Phoebe, she'd hardly been home. But remembering the look on his face when he left her bed the night before, she had the distinct impression that even if she'd been hanging around outside his front door, he would have walked right past her. Back to avoidance.

Walking through the shadow-filled living room, she stopped at the wide front window and stared down at the dark street below. Why did she feel so . . . unsettled? Stupid question, she told herself. It was him. It was all Jack.

Her body was still thrumming in memory of his touch. And fires that hadn't burned inside her in years were now nearing flash point. Resting her forehead on the cool glass windowpane, she closed her eyes and remembered it all. Every touch. Every sigh. Every rocketing sensation that had splintered through her body and left her eager for more.

Blowing out a breath, she opened her eyes and turned from the window to walk the confines of the room. Her steps were slow, measured, as steady as her heartbeat, which really wasn't all that steady at the moment. God, she missed those midnight walks with Quinn.

She'd had time then to wander through the darkness and let her mind drift. But she couldn't be taking Liz out in the damp night air, so the walks were history now.

Holding on to the baby monitor, she came around the corner of the sofa and spotted the box. She'd forgotten all about it earlier. And now . . . she checked the antique pendulum clock hanging on the wall above the television set—it was midnight—too late to take it to him.

But she could set it outside his door so he'd find it in the morning. Hooking the monitor receiver onto the pocket of her shorts, Carol bent down and picked up the big box and was grateful that despite its size, it wasn't heavy. Opening her own door, she stepped across the hall and set the box down again.

Then she straightened up and laid one hand on Jack's door as if she could sense what was going on inside. Dumb. And even while she told herself to go back to her own apartment, she was leaning closer to his door, listening. If she heard a TV or a radio, she'd just knock on the door and give him the box tonight. If she didn't . . . she'd just have to talk to him tomorrow, she thought.

And that's when she heard it.

Jack's voice.

Shouting.

Chapter 13

Carol didn't even think about it.

She simply reacted.

Racing back across the narrow hall, she reached inside her door for the keys she'd dropped onto the white hall table along the wall. Snatching them up, she went back to Jack's door, fumbled briefly to find the right key, then used it, opened the door, and stepped inside.

Silence dropped on her and for a moment or two, she almost believed that she hadn't heard Jack's shout. He was probably sleeping and wouldn't thank her for crashing into his place and making herself at home.

She glanced around the room and wasn't surprised that it looked the same as it had the day she'd rented it to him. There were no personal items lying around. No pictures on the walls, no magazines on the tables—not even a stray coffee cup. It looked . . . and *felt* empty.

But then, he was a master at keeping himself separate from everything and everyone. And as she glanced around the living room, she realized that he'd even cut *himself* out of his life.

"Drop it!"

Her heart jolted. She whipped her head around and looked at the closed door to Jack's bedroom. His voice sounded . . . desperate.

"Will!" he shouted. "No!"

Her heart jolted. Was he being attacked? Carol went on instinct again. She grabbed up a nearby lamp and hefted it high in her right hand, ready to use it as a weapon if she had to. Running across the room to the bedroom door, she grabbed the knob, gave it a turn, and pushed the door open. Stepping inside, she came up short as she realized that Jack wasn't under attack.

He was asleep.

Carol's heart pounded in her chest and she had to fight to even out her breathing. All prepared for a fight, she paused in the open doorway to give the adrenaline still pumping through her bloodstream a chance to fizzle out.

Moonlight danced across the bed where Jack lay tangled in the sheets. Sweat beaded on his bare chest and his features were screwed up into a mask of frustration and pain. His hands fisted in the sheets as his legs thrashed like a drowning man trying to kick his way to the surface of the water.

She set the lamp she still held down onto the table beside the door. Then, rushing to the side of the bed, Carol leaned over and looked down at him. He wasn't under attack by an intruder. This was Jack's own mind turning on him. He was tortured, fighting his way through a nightmare that was so vicious it even gave *her* cold chills.

She reached for him, laying one hand on his bare shoulder. His skin was damp with sweat and cold despite the warmth of the room. She felt the tension in his bunched muscles as he battled whatever demons were chasing him through sleep. Her heart ached for him even as her stomach pitched with worry. "Jack . . . Jack, wake up."

"No!" The word charged from his throat in a frantic cry. Then he came up swinging. Sitting straight up, eyes wild and still focused on the images clouding his mind, he grabbed her. Throwing her across the mattress, he pounced, straddling her, pinning her shoulders to the bed and glaring down at her as though she were the guardian to the gates of hell.

"Jack!" Carol's breath heaved in and out of her lungs as she stared up into the eyes of a stranger. Wide and glassy, those pale blue eyes didn't even see her. Carol knew that to him, she was just another part of the dream that he was still fighting free of. His jaw tight, his mouth a thin slash of fury, he hissed in air through gritted teeth as his hands tightened on her upper arms.

Backlit by the moonlight, his silhouette was dark and huge. Sitting on her abdomen, his weight pressed her down into the mattress, and Carol realized that she was *way* out of her depth. But still, she wasn't scared. Not of him. Never of him. "Jack," she said softly, as soon as she got her breath back. "It's me. Carol."

His grip on her shoulders loosened slightly, but he made no move to get off her.

"It was a nightmare, Jack," she said, her voice softer now, soothing, as she tried to ease him down from whatever visions were still clinging to the edges of his mind. As she watched, breath caught, his eyes cleared, slowly losing that wild, almost feral gleam.

"Carol?" He shook his head. "What the hell . . . ?"

"I heard you shouting—"

"Dammit." He let her go and sat back, still straddling her hips.

"I had to make sure you were all right."

"I'm fine." His voice sounded like a tightly strung wire close to snapping.

"Yeah, I can see that."

"You shouldn't have come in here," he said and eased off and away from her. He rolled to one side, then slipped off the edge of the bed in one smooth action. It was only then she noticed he was naked.

He grabbed his jeans off a nearby chair and tugged them on, keeping his back to her as if he couldn't bear to look at her—or for her to look at him. But naturally, she couldn't take her gaze off him. Carol sat up on the mattress, pushed her hair back and out of her eyes, and told herself to breathe. Just breathe. Not an easy order to follow when Jack turned around again to face her. Chest bare, his jeans unbuttoned at the waist, he braced his feet wide apart and faced her with his chin up as if daring her to take a punch at it.

Moonlight slanted over his skin and spotlighted him like an actor on a stage. His broad, muscled chest looked as though it had been carved in marble by a master sculptor. And even in the dim light, she saw the shadows in his eyes. Felt the chill of his ghosts still haunting the room.

"I scared you."

"Surprised me," she corrected, needing to let him know she hadn't been scared. Worried about him. Concerned. Startled, when he flung her over his body onto the mattress. But not scared.

He reached up and shoved both hands along the sides of his skull as though trying to keep his head from bursting. When he let his hands fall to his sides again, he just stared at her. A long, heavy sigh slid from his lungs as he hunched his shoulders and looked at her steadily. "Did I hurt you?"

Carol's heart twisted. Was there anything harder to see than a strong man brought to his knees? Guilt shimmered in the air between them, but she wouldn't let him suffer over this. Whatever else was happening here, he was trying to keep his private demons from touching her. She wouldn't add to the misery stamped on his features, so she resisted rubbing her upper arms where bruises were probably already blooming in the shape of his fingerprints. "No. You didn't."

"Thank God." He scraped one hand across his face, as if trying to wipe away the memory of the last few minutes. Then he inhaled wearily and folded his arms across his chest. "Go home, Baker."

"Jack—"

"I mean it. Get out."

Oh, he meant it. She could see that in every furious line of his body. Tension shimmered off him in thick, dark waves that reached out long tentacles to tug at Carol's heart. How could she walk away from him when he was so alone already, it tore at her?

"Not a chance." It might have been the smart thing to do, but she could feel his pain from across the room and couldn't pretend she didn't. No matter how much easier it might have been. "You were having a nightmare."

He snorted a laugh that sounded like sandpaper on a chalkboard and turned away from her, staring out the window at the dark beyond the glass. "Yeah, you could say that."

"Who's Will?"

He snapped her a hard look over his shoulder. "What'd I say?"

"You warned him to get down," she said, scooting to the edge of the bed and then off of it. Standing up, she walked through the patch of moonlight to stand beside him. She laid a hand on his forearm and felt him flinch. But he didn't pull away. Maybe he needed the contact too much to pull back, even though that was clearly what he wanted to do.

"Who's Will?"

"Doesn't matter."

"You were shouting at him in your sleep." She tightened her grip on his arm when she felt the muscles beneath her hand clench. Tipping her head back, she tried to look into his eyes, but he kept his gaze on the window in front of him and the night beyond. His eyes narrowed, his brows drew together, and she knew he was seeing it all again. The images from his dream were still with him. Still hurting him. "It matters."

He closed his eyes briefly. "Leave it alone, for crissake."

She couldn't. Wouldn't. This was as close as she'd come to discovering the reasons for the shutters in his eyes. For the secrecy. For the emotional distance that radiated around him like a circle of barbed wire, keeping out trespassers. "Because leaving it alone's done you so much good, right?"

He slanted her a quelling look from the corner of his eye. "What the hell do you know about it?"

It was going to take a lot more than a replay of his snarling and sniping to keep her from trying to reach him. That growl of a voice of his had become a part of her everyday world. She knew it as well as she knew the deep-throated rumblings from Quinn. And she knew that neither of them were as dangerous as they liked to think.

Carol stepped out in front of him, forcing him to look at her instead of the night that had him so damn fascinated. When he finally met her gaze she steeled herself against the echo of pain she read in those icy blue depths. Pulling off a bandage—especially an *old* one—hurt. But pulling it off quickly was bound to ease the pain in the long run. He'd been tugging at the edges for too long. It was time for a quick yank.

"What do I know?" she asked, challenging him. "I know that you're making your family nuts with worry." She poked him in the chest with the tip of her index finger and had the satisfaction of seeing him scowl in response. "I know that you're miserable. That you avoid coming home—the one place *most* people run to when they're hurt or in trouble. But not you. You lock yourself away and turn into a crab-ass to keep everyone at a distance. And when you *do* come home"—she poked him again for good measure—"you act like being here is a punishment. I want to know why."

"And I should tell you because . . . ?"

"Because I'm Switzerland," she said, reaching up to smooth his hair back from his face. He flinched again, pulling away from her touch, but when she followed his movement, he gave it up and allowed the tenderness. "I don't have a stake in your life, Jack. I'm not family. I'm—"

One eyebrow lifted and a small, almost wistful twist of his lips gave her heart a little jab.

"Yeah?" he asked. "You're what, exactly, Baker?"

"An innocent bystander?" she offered.

His eyes went cold and dark again as he said, "Haven't you heard? It's always the innocent bystanders that get the shaft."

"I'll take my chances." She wouldn't let go of this. Old wounds were tearing at his soul. And she had to at least *try* to help.

He sighed and fatigue seemed to fall on him like a

shroud. His body slumped, shoulders drooping. His eyes closed, then opened again so that he could look at her. "Go home. Take care of the baby."

"Got her covered," Carol said and unhooked the baby monitor from her pocket. She set it down on the table beside her, turned up the volume, and then looked at him. "Spill it, Reilly. Who knows, maybe it'll make you feel better."

Jack stared down at her and wished he could share in that lollipop-and-roses outlook. But he knew damn well that talking about a nightmare only made it more real. Gave it definition. Gave it life beyond the dream world where he'd fought to keep his own personal demons locked away. If he let them out now, there'd be no shoving them back into the shadows.

They'd be here.

In the room with him.

With Carol.

And what, he wondered, would she say if she found out about him? Would she still give him that wide-eyed look that turned his insides into a churning mass of need and confusion? Would she still be so damn willing to look on the bright side, when she found out his best friend was dead because of *him*?

Hell. If the truth chased her off, then maybe that was what he should do. He'd tried to stay away from her for all the good it had done him. Maybe if he could prove to her that he was a son of a bitch, she'd catch on and stay away.

And if she did?

Well, it would be no more than he deserved, though God knows, he'd miss her. Miss arguing with her. Miss hearing about her weird devotion to science fiction movies. Miss seeing her with Liz.

Just *miss* her, dammit.

His eyes felt gritty and his throat as dry as an August night. His heart still thundered in his ears and felt as though it was about to jump out of his chest. And it wasn't just the aftereffects of the dream, this time. No, this was a whole new set of variables.

Because this time, Carol had been there. Carol had seen him at his worst. Hell, he'd thrown her onto the damn bed and held her down like she was a street punk. Groaning internally, Jack scraped his palms over his face and wished to hell he could wipe away *that* memory. But he wouldn't be able to. It would stay with him. It would become just one more brick to add to the wall surrounding him.

Her scent nudged at him . . . making him remember other things, sweeter things. Like the feel of her in his arms, where she fit against his body like the last piece in a complicated jigsaw puzzle. Like the soft sigh of her breath on his neck. Like the warm, welcoming heat of her body when she'd brought him in from the cold.

And maybe because of that night, the night when he'd found peace—for a while—he owed her the truth.

He stared down into her eyes, and even in the moonlight, he saw the golden shine of them and wished— "Fine," he said sharply, forcing the words past an ever drier throat. "You want to know what's going on. I'll tell you."

He tore his gaze from hers, because he couldn't look into that warmth and say what he had to say. Better to stare out at the cold, black night. At least *it* was familiar.

"It was nearly two years ago. Christmas Eve."

She sucked in a breath and held it.

"I can almost hear the rain, even now." His voice went soft, hazy, as memory took him, pulled him deep into the nightmare he normally fought to stay clear of. "Pounding, driving rain. Water slamming into the street, splashing against the windshield in waves.

"I had the graveyard shift. Couldn't get out of it. My wife was pissed about it, wanted me to call in sick. Said we had to talk." He choked out a laugh that felt like tiny knives digging at his throat. "Told her I couldn't, that we'd talk in the morning. But she talked anyway." God, he could see her, standing in the small living room, hands clasped at her waist, fingers locked and squeezing until the knuckles were white. He swallowed, but his mouth was dry, so it did no good.

"She told me she was pregnant. I remember grabbing her, swinging her around, proud. Happy. Then I noticed she wasn't celebrating."

He felt Carol's hand on his arm again and was grateful for it. But he didn't stop. Didn't think he could, now that he was finally saying it all out loud. It was as if the long-bottled-up words were chasing each other in the effort to be said. They came in a rush. Even the hardest of them.

"She told me the baby wasn't mine."

"Jack . . ."

"Said it was Will's." His back teeth ground together, but he kept talking. "My partner. My best friend." Betrayal sparked inside him, as fresh and bitter as it had been two years before. The sharp slap of it hit him hard, nearly doubled him over with the memory of how he'd lost everything that mattered to him in one black night.

"Oh, God, Jack." Her fingers tightened on his arm and Jack shifted his mind from the pain. He concentrated on her touch. On that anchor to help him through the rest of the nightmare. He was a blind man, stumbling through a minefield and trusting his life to the strength of the one slim rope he could cling to.

"She said she was leaving me and that she couldn't lie to me anymore." He blew out a breath and shook his head. "I don't know why she suddenly couldn't manage it. She'd been lying to me for months with no trouble at all." Jack reached up and viciously rubbed the back of his neck, short fingernails digging into his own skin, diversifying the pain scrambling through him. "I couldn't even look at her," he admitted. "I was sick. Body. Heart. So I left and went to work. With Will. Every time I looked at him, I saw him and Kim, tangled up together, naked."

A long, shuddering sigh slipped from between his lips. "God, I wanted to hit him. I wanted to smash in the smiling, lying face I'd known and trusted for years."

A soft sigh of sound erupted from the baby monitor and he quieted, listening to the tiny snuffles echoing from the radio. Then Quinn rumbled out a dog version of a lullaby and the baby quieted again.

"Go on," Carol said, and he heard the strained thinness of her voice and wondered what she was thinking. If she was feeling pity for him. Hell, of course she was. But that was because she didn't know it all yet. Hadn't heard the worst of it. When she did, everything would change. And in one night, he'd lose everything again.

Only this time, he'd be losing the promise of something that might have been. And maybe that was worse than what he'd lost before. Maybe.

"Will knew something was wrong," Jack said, sliding back into the images rolling through his brain with the grace of a freight train. "But I didn't say anything. What the hell was I supposed to say to him?" he demanded of no one in particular. " 'Hey, congratulations. I hear you and my wife are having a kid. You must be so proud.'?"

"Jesus, Jack—"

He shook his head and narrowed his gaze on the blackness outside the window. The dark that was even now threatening to swallow him whole. "We went through most of the shift without a problem, then we got a call. A homicide." His throat squeezed shut and he wished desperately for a drink. But alcohol wouldn't help. Christ knew he'd tried to drown himself in vats of Irish whiskey for months after that night. But he'd only surface hours later with a hangover and even more crippling pain. So he'd given it up and tried to live with the pain.

"We pulled into an alley behind a strip mall in east LA. Streetlights were out. But that didn't mean anything. Kids were always breaking the lights with rocks . . . or bullets. Our headlights bounced off the rain like a laser, blinding. And the storm kept raging. Water roaring like a river down that alley and pounding off the windshield like it was coming out of an upended bucket. Couldn't see a damn thing."

He squinted, trying in memory to see what he hadn't seen that night. But the images were still blurry, indistinct, and nothing could change what had happened. "Will got out of the car first. Don't know why. Just worked out that way. He headed for the back of the building, where our phone caller had said the body was. Even in the rain, that alley smelled like a cesspool. Rotting garbage and Christ knows what else." He shook his head as the stench filled his nostrils.

Not even the scent of Carol's perfume of springtime and coconut was enough to dislodge that memory. "I was a step or two behind him. Still so damn mad at him, I could hardly stand the sight of him. My brain kept giving me images of Will and my wife. In my bed. Couldn't shake 'em." His fists tightened helplessly at his sides. There'd been nothing to hit then and there was nothing now. And God, he wanted to hit something. To pound on *something* until his hands were bloody.

"It didn't feel right. Couldn't see a damn thing, but the alley didn't feel right. Will didn't notice. His rhythm was off. He was wondering what the hell was wrong with me, so he wasn't paying attention to what was happening. I knew it. I could see it in him." He inhaled sharply, deeply, and blew it out again in a rush.

"The first gunshot came out of nowhere. Went wild, slammed into the building behind me, splintering the brick into little pellets of stone that snapped around the alley like bees. Will stopped. He just . . . stopped."

Shaking his head now, he saw it all again in his mind's eye and still couldn't understand why his friend hadn't dropped into a crouch—gone for cover. Something. "He just stood there, looking at me like he was confused about what was happening. I shouted at him to get down, but the muzzle flash sparked like lightning at the same time and it was too late. Will got hit."

Carol didn't speak and he was grateful. Instead, she moved in closer to him and wrapped her arms around his middle and simply hung on, tipping her head back to stare up at him. He shifted his gaze from the night to her eyes and told himself to not look away, because at the moment, the only light in the world was right there. In those pale brown eyes shining up at him. "He staggered into the damn Dumpster and trash rolled out of it and rained down on him when he dropped."

He took a breath. "I couldn't get to him because the damn shooter was still firing. The shots were going wild, though. Hitting Will must have been pure luck, 'cause this guy's aim was shitty. I was behind the car. He couldn't get a clear shot at me."

Reaching for Carol, he grabbed her face between his hands, kept his gaze locked on hers and said, "I watched for the muzzle flash. And when I saw it again, I fired off three rounds. There was a scream." A scream that still rippled through his head and brought goose bumps to his flesh every damn night. "And then the whimpering started. Like from a kicked puppy or something. Soft cries, nearly buried under the sound of the rain pummeling down around me. I couldn't go to Will. Not yet. Had to make sure the shooter was out of the picture first."

"Of course you did."

He didn't want her understanding. Couldn't take it because she hadn't heard all of it yet. Didn't know the worst of it. Couldn't grasp the depth of the nightmare. Not yet.

"I found the shooter. Huddled in a doorway, curled up in a tight ball. He'd dropped the gun and was holding his stomach, like he could push all of the blood back inside. But it was running red into the rain, and his hands were too small anyway."

Silently, she tightened her grip on his waist.

"He looked up at me and the rain fell on his face, splashing against his eyes, and he said, 'It hurts. Make it stop hurting.'" Jack's eyes swam and his vision was as blurred as it had been that night. "He was *ten,* Carol. A little kid, who should have been at home watching cartoons or something and instead he was lying in a stinking alley, bleeding to death. He was trying to earn his way into a gang by killing a cop."

"Oh, my God."

He rushed on, letting the words fly now in his race to

get it finished before she pulled away from him. Before he could read the censure in her eyes.

Before he lost his nerve.

"I called for the paramedics, secured the gun, and went to check on Will. But it was too late. He was dead. Eyes wide open and staring up at the rain, he just lay there, dead in the garbage. And I wanted to scream at him to get up so I could beat the shit out of him for stealing my wife. My family. But he was dead so there was nothing to do. Nothing I could do."

"Jack . . ."

"That's not all, dammit." He grabbed her upper arms and squeezed as if afraid she'd try to make a run for it. To get out before she could be sucked even further into the nightmare his life had become. "You wanted to hear it, so hear it." He sucked in air like a man who couldn't get enough into his lungs. "I got a *commendation* for shooting the kid. For facing bodily harm in defense of a fellow officer. I killed a ten-year-old boy and they gave me a fucking medal for it."

Even the words tasted foul in his mouth. It didn't matter that there hadn't been a choice. Didn't seem to matter that the shooting had been called justifiable. None of that took the sting out of his heart, his soul. A boy was dead and Jack wasn't.

And as soon as he'd looked down on that boy, he'd known he couldn't walk into a dark alley again. Known he couldn't take the chance of killing another child. Yet leaving the force had destroyed what was left of his life.

"You did what you had to do."

"That's what I tell myself. If I didn't believe that, at least in my head, I wouldn't be able to live with myself." Now that the words were out, he felt almost lighter. As if by purging the blackness inside, he'd allowed a small sliver of light to penetrate the corners of his soul. And like a freshly cleaned wound, the ache throbbing inside him was sharper, brighter than it had been when it was simply festering.

"Believe it, Jack," Carol said, her voice a soft hush of steel.

"I want to," he admitted. "*Need* to." He sucked in another gulp of air and let it slide from his lungs an instant later. "My wife left me on Christmas morning. To this day, she's convinced I *let* Will die. That somehow I didn't protect him as I normally would have because of what she'd told me before shift."

"That's ridiculous."

"Is it?" he asked quietly, staring down into pale brown eyes that held more light than he'd known in two years. "God help me, I don't know anymore."

Chapter 14

"All I *do* know is that I don't belong here anymore."

Carol's heart twisted. "What do you mean?"

"This place. This town. I don't deserve to be here. Not anymore. And it's too hard to pretend I do." He pointed at the window and said, "The worst night of my life happened on Christmas Eve. Here, I'm surrounded by it. Reminded of it everywhere I go. It's a constant punishment." Then he stopped, and swiveled his head to look at her.

The Christmas lights on the other side of the glass threw multicolored shadows into a shifting dance across his taut features. His eyes were in shadow, but every line in his body screamed with the pain he'd been carrying for two long years.

"On second thought," he said softly, "maybe I *do* belong here. Maybe this is the perfect place for me. My own little purgatory." He scraped one hand across his face again in a frustrated gesture that tugged at Carol's heart even while she steamed over it.

"The only problem is," he said, more to himself than to her, "the longer I stay, the harder it is on my family. And I can't be with them. Not after what I did. Staying here only drags them into it, too, and *they* don't deserve that." Then he focused his gaze on her. "Neither do you."

Carol's brain raced.

Her heart ached for him, but she could see in his features that he wasn't looking for sympathy. He just wanted her to run. To turn her back and walk out on him—as his bitch of a wife had, she thought. As his partner had.

He *expected* her to leave.

And maybe it would have been easier on him if she did.

But Carol had no intention of walking away from him. If anything, she wanted to hold him tighter, closer. To somehow ease the pain that was tearing at him.

He reached down and plucked her arms from his middle and took a step back.

It was only a foot or two of space separating them, but it might as well have been miles. She looked up into his eyes and saw that the shutters were firmly in place again. Shutting her out. Shutting himself *in.*

Well, he'd taken one step. He'd opened the door to his past and now it was simply too late to close it again.

"You can't be serious," she blurted and, after the words were out, thought perhaps she might have handled that a little better.

"You think I'm making this up?"

"No." She shook her head and took a step toward him, but he moved too, keeping that buffer between them. "I *mean,* you can't really believe that you *allowed* Will to die. Purposely."

He lifted both hands and rubbed the heels of his palms against his eyes. When his hands dropped to his sides again, his shoulders slumped as if he were standing beneath a burden too heavy for any man to carry. "I don't know anymore. I just don't know."

"Well, I do," she snapped and figured that kindness wasn't what he needed right now. He needed brutal honesty. He needed a kick in the ass. He needed a slap upside the head with a two-by-four. Unfortunately, she was unarmed, so she used her only weapon at hand—her mouth, and the fact that she wasn't afraid to say what he *didn't* want to hear. "You didn't stand there and *allow* someone to *kill* your partner."

"Carol—"

"No. This is bull, Jack." She stepped in close again and this time when he tried to shift away from her, the backs of his knees hit the bed and he was caught. She pushed her advantage. Stepping up close to him, she actually felt the chill that held him in its grasp snaking out to ensnare her, too.

She ignored the cold though and fought past it with the heat of her own outrage. "You were mad and you had a right to be."

"Yeah, but—"

"You were hurt." Carol cut him off, waving a hand to keep him quiet. "Betrayed by the people you trusted the most."

He sucked in air, swallowed hard, and tipped his chin up to a fighting tilt. Unwilling—unable—to accept sympathy. Fine. She wasn't offering any.

"When your *wife*"—she sneered that word and his eyes flickered, letting her know he'd caught the disgust in her tone—"told you she'd cheated on you—*lied* to you—*deceived* you . . . that she'd been sleeping with your partner—"

"Jesus, Baker—"

His eyes went wide with surprise, or shock, she wasn't sure which. But she wouldn't apologize. She couldn't say enough bad things about any woman who would do that to a man like Jack. "When she made her grand confession, did you at least tell her what you thought of her?"

"I was a little shell-shocked." He straightened up and shot her a glare that should have fried the ends of her hair. Still, she kept right on, throwing words at him so fast, he didn't have a chance to close them off.

"Not surprising," she snapped, absolutely disgusted with the woman she hoped she'd never meet. Carol kept muttering to herself as she took a step away from him.

He relaxed a little as she moved off, then straightened up and tensed again when she turned around and came right back.

"Jesus," he muttered.

"That . . . *bitch* had the nerve to look you dead in the eye and tell you *that* when she knew you had to go out there onto the streets with Will?" Carol reached up and grabbed handfuls of her own hair and gave it a yank. The resulting pain at least was better than the ache settled in her heart. Then she let go of her hair and shook a finger in his face. "On Christmas Eve, yet. When she knew that you'd be locked in a car for eight solid hours with the man she'd screwed you over with? *That's* when she decides to tell the truth?"

A short, sharp sound shot from his throat, and under other circumstances, Carol might have thought it was a bark of laughter. But that couldn't be. Not while she was reaming him. Not while she was so furious on his behalf she could hardly see straight.

"And when you came under fire—" She snapped the question out. "Did you run? Did you leave Will lying there in the rain while you saved yourself?"

"No, but—"

"No," she repeated hotly. "The man you thought was

your friend—the man who'd slept with your wife—was lying there hurt and you did what you could to save him."

"Yeah, but—"

"Did you know the shooter was a child?" she demanded, slapping one hand in the middle of his chest.

"No." He frowned, remembering again, and she wanted to drag him out of the past bodily and force him to stay here. In the present. With her.

"It was dark," he said. "Raining. I saw the muzzle flash—"

"And fired back."

"Yeah."

"Did you have any other choice?"

"Not if I wanted to live."

"Did you want to live?" she asked, her voice dropping a notch or two. This was the big question, she told herself. This was what she had to know. What he had to decide. And if she'd asked the question fast enough, he'd answer it from the gut.

"I didn't want to die," he said with a growl of menace that ordinarily might have been enough to have her backing off a bit. Giving him a little space. But not now. Not when they'd come this far already.

"Not the same," she said quickly, her gaze locked with his, demanding he see her. Silently, her gaze demanded more. Demanded the truth. "Did you want to *live*?"

"Yes."

Good answer.

"Then why aren't you?"

She went up on her toes, threw her arms around his neck, and hung on as if half-expecting him to pluck her off and toss her aside. He did neither.

His gaze never left her face. He studied her features

as if trying like hell to make out a foreign language. His gaze moved over her face, her mouth, her eyes, and settled there. "I'm breathing, aren't I?"

"There's more to living than simply breathing, Jack."

"And I'm supposed to just forget that kid?" he muttered thickly. "Forget what happened in that alley?"

She watched the pulse beat at the base of his throat and felt the thundering pounding of his heart against her own.

"No," she said, her voice softer now, "being who you are, you couldn't, even if you tried." She scooped one hand around to cup his cheek and felt his jaw twitch beneath her palm. "But you might try remembering that the child you killed was *trying* to kill *you*." She shifted her hold on him then, and tightened her grip on him, sliding one hand up to thread through his thick, black hair.

"And Jack, if all you're doing is breathing . . . then the boy *did* kill you. You might as well have stayed in that alley."

"You don't get it," he said, staring down into her eyes. "Every time I close my eyes, I see it all again. It plays out, just like it did that night, and I try to change it. Try to make it different. And I know it's a dream and still I think, maybe this time. Maybe *this* time, it'll be different."

"But it never is."

"No."

"And how long are you going to punish yourself for surviving?"

One corner of his mouth lifted into a reluctant smile. "Now you sound like Sean."

"Smart man." Carol smiled up at him. "I knew I liked him."

"Sure. He's smart 'cause he agrees with you."

"Right." She kept that smile on her face, even when her insides trembled. Even when she wondered if he was going to step back and away again. If he was going to turn his back on her and tell her to mind her own business. Because if he did, she was going to fight him.

"And I should, too."

She nodded. "In a perfect world."

"World's never been perfect."

"True."

"But some nights," he said softly as his gaze moved over her features like a caress, "are closer than others."

His gaze never left her eyes. She felt the heat of them, the strength in them, pouring into her as she came close, angling her head for a kiss.

"I'm not the man you want me to be," he said, as her mouth stopped just a breath away from his.

"Maybe not," she conceded, knowing that this step she was about to take was a dangerous one. For both of them. "But you are the man I want."

He sucked in air and rocked back on his heels as if her words had delivered a blow he hadn't been expecting and wasn't quite sure how to deal with. His hands opened on her back and he splayed his fingers against her spine, and even through the thin material of her dark blue tank top, she felt his touch slide right down to her bones.

He bent his head to kiss her, then stopped. Hesitated. "The baby—"

In the midst of the heat swamping them both, he could put the brakes on long enough to worry about the baby. Her heart swelled with emotions thick and rich. He didn't see what kind of man he was—but she did. And for now, that was enough.

She glanced at the baby monitor on the nearby table.

"We'll hear her," Carol said and slanted her mouth over his, putting Liz and everything else out of her mind. The baby was safe and just a soft cry away. But for now, Jack needed her more. As much as she needed him.

His mouth came down on hers with a fierceness she'd never known before and Carol held on for that fast slide into oblivion that she knew was headed her way.

He grabbed her and held her close, lifting her feet clean off the floor in a wild attempt to hold her tighter, more firmly to him. His arms came around her waist, her rib cage, and squeezed tightly enough that she could barely draw a breath. She hardly noticed. Carol wanted him close. Hard against her. Wanted to feel him come out of the shadows and back into the world he'd lost two years before.

Her blood still pumped hot and furious at the woman who'd cheated on him. The friend who'd betrayed him. And for the dead child who'd lost so much that losing his life hadn't seem like too high a price to pay just to belong.

But her mind couldn't keep up with the sensations coursing through her body, so Carol stopped trying to think. Stopped trying to make sense of the tangle of Jack's life and instead simply gave herself up to the need to be here. Now. With him.

Her heart ached at his hungry tenderness. Despite the anger still rippling through him, he held her with care. Took her mouth, her breath, her heart, with an innate gentleness that drew her to him despite her own best intentions.

She'd felt it coming for days. Probably from that first moment when he'd looked at her in Phoebe's office. It had been inevitable. And impossible. And more beautiful than she'd ever imagined.

She was in love with a man who was so caught up in the past that he couldn't see a future.

He tipped her back onto the bed, and Carol fell willingly, taking him down with her. The mattress beneath them bounced with their landing, then seemed to curve up around them, cradling them together atop the quilted comforter.

Burying his face in the curve of her neck, inhaling her scent, losing himself in the feel of her, Jack let himself dissolve in the sensations he'd only found with her. He dragged his hands through her thick hair and tangled his fingers in the soft strands. And a corner of his mind whispered a warning—that he was as tangled in her life as his hands were in her hair. But he didn't care. Didn't care about anything save the next kiss. The next stroking caress. The next soft sigh and whispered moans.

She was all.

She was so much more than he'd ever thought to find again.

She tipped her head back and he followed the sleek line of her long, almost elegant throat with his lips, his tongue. Tasting her, defining her, needing to know every inch of her body. Needing to become a part of a woman so much a mixture of warmth and humor and stubborn determination.

Carol Baker was so many women rolled into one. She got into his head, wormed her way into his heart, and was well on her way to invading his soul.

His hands moved over her body and he thought that he would know the feel of her anywhere. They'd only been together once and yet she seemed to have been branded into his memory. He touched and she shifted beneath him. She sighed and his heart lifted. She moaned gently and everything in him went still and tight. He wanted her.

More than he'd ever wanted anything or anyone in his life.

And the wanting was killing him because he knew, at the core of him, he couldn't have her.

Levering up on one elbow, he stared down into those golden eyes that shone with such a warm light, he felt the glow of them down to the bottom of his soul. He felt the first tremors of something almost magical rock him and knew that he was walking a fine line. This woman had slipped too far past his defenses already. Soon, he knew, he'd never get her completely out of his system, even if he tried.

In the moonlit room with the crackle of a baby monitor the only sound, he knew he'd found something special. He only wished he hadn't found it too late.

"Jack?" She smoothed one hand over his cheek. "What is it?"

He deliberately cleared his mind. He didn't want to think. He only wanted to feel. God, it had been so long since he'd felt anything like the alluring ease she brought to him.

"Nothing," he lied and slipped one hand beneath the flimsy fabric of her tank top to cup her breast. His thumb dusted across her hardened nipple and a trembling sigh slipped from between her lips. He smiled. "It's nothing that won't hold until tomorrow."

"Good." She licked dry lips. "Because I really don't want you to stop."

"No worries there."

"Except," she whispered as she arched into his touch and sucked in a ragged breath. "You broke your last condom."

He smiled. "Smart-ass. Always a smart-ass." His hand

slipped down along her rib cage, across her abdomen, and beneath the waistband of her soft cotton drawstring shorts. From there, it was just a fast slide toward heaven. He cupped her and she moaned through gritted teeth. He touched the damp heat of her, felt himself drowning and entranced, let himself be drawn under. "I bought more," he admitted. "God help me, I was hoping for this and bought more."

"Smart man." She lifted her hips into his hand.

"Sometimes." This wasn't smart. He knew that. He also knew if he didn't have her in the next few minutes, he'd die from the emptiness crouched inside him.

"Then stop talking and kiss me." She grabbed his face between her palms and drew his head down to hers. Tongues tangled in a wild dance of breathless anticipation. Blood roared, hearts pounded, and bodies ached.

Seconds flew past as they each tore the clothes from the other. Feeding the hunger roaring through them, they gave and took. Bodies brushed together in a sinuous dance that pushed them higher and higher, toward the goal that lurked just beyond their reach.

The air in the room seemed heated almost beyond the point of easy breathing. But the muffled sounds of skin meeting skin and hungry sighs were more than enough to sustain them.

Hunger roared up inside Carol. Fiercer, more demanding than before. She needed to show him, to let him see that she wanted him, all of him. She kissed his throat, his chest, she moved until she could reach more of his skin, running her fingers across his flat nipples until he trembled and she felt the rush of raw, sexual power fill her. She could do this. She could bring this strong man to a quivering peak. And she reveled in the knowledge, wanting to do more, feel more.

"Let me have you," she whispered, her voice muffled against his sweat-dampened chest.

"Ah, God, Carol," he murmured, "you *do* have me."

"More," she said, her voice a breathy hush in the still room. "I want more."

Carol pushed him over onto his back, and kept her gaze locked with his as she straddled him. His hands moved up to caress her breasts as she stroked her own palms up and down that finely sculpted chest until she knew every inch of him. Until she felt as though his body had been burned into the tips of her fingers.

"I want you now," he muttered thickly and she heard the need grating in his voice.

"Now," she agreed, but didn't shift with him, as he tried to roll her onto her back. "But *my* way," she said, rising up onto her knees.

"You're gonna kill me." He swallowed hard, keeping his gaze locked with hers.

She saw sparks of something hot and delicious flash in his eyes and Carol felt her own body quicken in response. He touched her. Touched her so deeply, she was sure she'd never be the same.

"Not until I'm through with you," she promised with a wicked smile that slammed into him hard.

His hands at her waist clenched spasmodically as she tortured him slowly by fanning the flames within. As she slowly lowered herself, taking him into her body, he groaned and clenched his teeth, straining to hold on. Dammit, he felt like a horny teenager, about to explode way too soon just from the damn thrill of her body accepting his.

Then she moved on him, languidly at first, her body sliding up and down on his with an almost liquid ease that enthralled and tortured him and pushed him closer to the ragged edge of control.

She lifted her arms high, as if reaching for the ceiling, and her body, illuminated by the moonlight, seemed to glow with an inner fire that sizzled the air in the room until Jack could hardly draw a breath. She rocked her hips, taking him in deeper and then shifting, twisting as she rode him, increasing the pressure, doubling the intense pleasure bursting inside. Her body held his tightly, surrounding him with the kind of warmth he'd thought long lost to him.

Jack stared up at her, silhouetted in the moonlight, her breasts dusted with a silvery light that almost seemed to sparkle over her. She tipped her head back and sighed, her body still moving, writhing, still shaking him to his core.

All he could do was hold on. Yet he had to touch her. To reach down and stroke the heart of her, where their bodies joined. He felt her body kick in response and as the first trembling ripples of completion raced through her, he gave himself up to the glory of her and poured all he was, all he'd ever hoped to be, into her depths, knowing, believing, she wanted it all.

Minutes, hours, *eternities* later, Carol lay in the curve of his arm and relished the tingling sensation still shimmering inside her. She stroked one hand lazily across his chest and felt him tremble.

"You *are* trying to kill me," he murmured, "aren't you?"

She smiled against his heated flesh. "I told you. Not until I'm done with you."

He caught her hand in his and held it, his fingers closing over hers. "If you're not done yet, you're gonna have to give me a minute or two."

Carol tipped her head back to look up at him. "I can do that."

He stared down at her and something deep and dark flashed across his eyes. "You keep looking at me like that, and it's not going to take very long."

"Promises, promises," she teased.

"Now, *that's* a challenge." He rolled over, pulling her under him, letting her take his weight so that he could feel the sweet brush of her nipples against his chest. Her heartbeat pounded hard and beat in tandem with his own. He bent his head, kissed her, nipping at her bottom lip, feasting on it.

She trembled, lifted her hands to encircle his neck and—

Liz's soft, whimpering cry drifted from the baby monitor and over that gentle sound came Quinn's low-throated response. This time though, the baby wouldn't be soothed by her nanny-dog. The now plaintive wail built slowly until it speared through the room, demanding attention.

Carol smiled up at him.

Jack nodded, kissed her again because he needed to, then rolled over, freeing her. "Guess that's our cue that the party's over."

"Yeah." She sat up, pushed her hair back from her face, then looked over her shoulder at him. "Come with me."

He just looked at her. "What?"

"Don't be here alone," she said, stroking one fingertip along the middle of his chest, sending lightninglike bolts of expectation darting through his system. "Don't make me be alone."

"Carol—"

"Sleep with me, Jack. Hold me."

She leaned over him even as the baby's cries erupted in earnest and Quinn's high-pitched whine joined in for a concert in beleaguered harmony.

"Come home with me tonight."

He wanted to. God, he wanted to leave this empty apartment, if only for the night. He wanted to hold her as she slept and keep her warmth as a shield against the cold that would slide back into his heart the moment he fell asleep. Staring up into those eyes that had now shifted to the baby monitor with a stab of guilt shining in their depths.

She had to go.

He had to be with her.

It was simple then, wasn't it?

"I'll come," he said and felt the smile in her eyes slam home in him.

"Good." She kissed him, hard. Quick. Then grinned as she jumped off the bed and grabbed up her clothes. Clutching them to her chest, she snatched up the baby monitor and headed for the door. "Don't be long," she called out, then disappeared in a rush of movement that he would always associate with Carol.

Jack pushed off the bed, and grabbed his jeans from the chair where he'd tossed them hours ago. Tugging them on, he headed out right after her, eager now to be away from the shadow-filled room that felt so much emptier with her gone.

He stepped into the hall and instantly noticed the box sitting on the carpet runner outside his door. Addressed to him. Carol must have been bringing it over when she heard him in the throes of that nightmare.

His heart felt suddenly heavy in his chest and he

slapped one hand to the ache. He didn't have to look at the return-address label to know it was from Hal. He felt it as surely as if what was inside that box had reached out with bony fingers to give him a shake.

Gritting his teeth, Jack shoved at the box with his foot, pushing it along the floor and over the threshold into his apartment. He didn't want to think about what might be inside. That part of his life was over, as he'd told Hal. Whatever flotsam had been left behind, he sure as hell didn't need.

Through narrowed eyes, he stared at the damn thing, half-expecting the flaps on the box to fly open and everything tucked within to jump out at him.

From Carol's apartment came the sound of the baby, still crying, and Carol's soft, soothing voice, calming her, reassuring Liz that she was safe. Loved.

Jack knew where he belonged—in the dark. The shadows. But he also knew where he yearned to be. He shot a look through Carol's open door and instantly felt the welcome of the light-filled rooms spear out to draw him in.

He wouldn't go back to the shadows—those memories—again tonight. Tonight, he would be with Carol. Shoving the box into his empty apartment, he temporarily closed the door on his past and stepped into the present.

Chapter 15

A week later, July had dragged Christmas along behind it, hammering at the town with hot, sweaty fists, just to keep it in line. Tourists came and went, kids admitted to summer boredom, and aggravated parents lit candles to the school gods.

Situation normal.

Carol kept one eye on the customers milling around her shop and the other on Liz, happy as a little princess in her carrier on the counter. The baby was staying awake now, for longer periods of time. She smiled a lot and followed movement with a shift of those milky blue eyes. She enjoyed having Quinn close, taking comfort from the big dog's loud, steady breathing and the occasional whine. Liz was becoming a little person, with a personality all her own. Carol smiled, grateful for the front row seat to watch it all as it happened.

Having Liz perched on the counter at the shop every day made work even more fun for Carol than it had been before. People chatted easier when a tiny baby was there to spark conversations. Without even trying, Liz made people smile, she made them stop long enough to pause and admire the miracle of life.

And absolutely everyone who came into the store—from the customers to the UPS man—had to make silly noises at her. The man in the corner, Carol thought now, sliding him a quick look as he inspected the hand-carved stocking hangers, had even snapped a picture or two, calling Liz the cutest little elf he'd ever seen.

Darn it, she *did* look cute, Carol thought, smiling at the baby, dressed in her little reindeer-decorated jumpsuit. What had she done with herself before Liz? And how could she ever have thought she could get through her life without children in it?

Laying one hand gently atop the sleeping baby's tummy, Carol felt the rapid, steady beat of a tiny heart and knew that her world would never be the same. And it wasn't just Liz. It was Jack.

For the last week, he'd spent more nights in her bed than in his own. Habit had become routine and routine had become second nature. They laughed and talked and made love, and every day she thought she saw him opening himself more to the possibilities around him.

But there were still shadows in his eyes that hadn't lifted. Pain she couldn't touch and a part of him she couldn't reach. And she ached for him. She'd taken that terrifying first step with both Liz *and* Jack. She'd let them into her world and the two of them had taken it over.

Without them . . . she couldn't even imagine the emptiness in her heart, the silence in her life.

Maybe she was just pumping her balloon up so high that when it popped she would make a lovely spatter on the ground far beneath her. But dammit, she'd had little enough in her life to lift a balloon toward. Shouldn't she appreciate it while she had it? Shouldn't she get all the joy out of life she could?

Liz jumped in her sleep, her tiny body jerking in the carrier and Carol dragged her thoughts away from her own swirl of emotions and soothed the baby with a whispered hush. What did babies dream? she wondered. Did they still remember heaven? Did they dream of games yet to play? Knees yet to skin? Hearts yet to break? "Don't worry, sweetie," she murmured, "I won't let anything hurt you." She leaned over and dropped a soft kiss on the baby's forehead, then reached down to pet and soothe an anxious Quinn.

Still smiling, Carol looked into the dog's big brown eyes. "You're in love with her, too, aren't you?"

The big dog whined, but didn't move from his position directly beneath the baby seat. Clearly, he took his responsibilities as self-appointed nanny seriously.

"Now if only you and Jack could call a truce," she muttered with a shake of her head.

"Miss—" An impatient voice sounded out from the corner where angels of all sizes and shapes were perched, hung, and stacked to best advantage. "How much is the little glass angel with the crooked halo?"

Before she could answer, an older woman at the opposite side of the store spoke up. "If you wouldn't mind, I'd like to take a closer look at this music box. The one with the dancing snowman."

Carol looked from one end of the store to the other, then, sighing, scooped Liz out of her carrier and cradled her close. People had been in and out all day. Friends, customers, and just a few slipping into the air-conditioned building long enough to build up a resistance to the heat. Business was good, so she shouldn't complain. But she sure could have used Lacey's help today. Going first to the angel woman, she flashed a smile, and mentally rang up sales.

Journal entry:

I saw her again today. The baby. Liz. I wouldn't have named her Liz, but it seems to suit her.

Carol is so excited because she gets to keep Liz for good, now. She says because the mother wasn't found, Liz has become a ward of the court. Sounds official. But just because I didn't tell anybody about the baby, that doesn't mean I'm not still her mother.

You can't change that.

No one can.

I'll always be her real mother.

I want to be her mother.

And Liz should know that.

"Can you believe it's almost time to pack?" Peggy pushed her sunglasses higher up her nose and shot a quick look at Lacey. "I mean, we'll have to be there in August and that's just next month."

"Weird, huh?" Lacey asked and reached for her Diet Coke. It was warm and flat, the ice having melted an hour ago. But neither one of them wanted to give up their prime slice of beach for a long walk to the deli for a refill. "I can't imagine not living in Christmas."

"*I* can," Peggy said with dramatic relish. She leaned over the edge of her sand chair and gripped Lacey's forearm. "Think about it, Lace. You and me. In a dorm at Long Beach State." She lifted her dark glasses and wiggled her eyebrows. "*Hours* away from any watchful eyes. It's gonna be *so* great."

"Yeah," Lacey said, fighting back the twist of nervousness nibbling at the bottom of her stomach. She fiddled with her straw, moving it up and down through the plastic lid on her drink until it screeched like a demon.

Peggy looked at everything like an adventure about to happen. Lacey envied that ability and figured it was probably more fun than having your stomach swarm with butterflies every time you tried something new.

"It will," she said, determined to believe it.

This was everything Lacey had worked and studied for. A chance to go to college somewhere new. Where no one knew her. Where no one would care where she was from—only who she *was*. She could reinvent herself, be whoever she wanted to be.

The only trouble with that plan was, she wasn't entirely sure just who that someone was.

The sun scorched the sand and the tourists intent on getting a tan they could brag about when they went home. Most of the locals skipped the beach on weekends rather than fight for chair and blanket space. But time was short, as Peggy said, and every chance they got, the girls headed for the beach like bees to flowers.

It was all so familiar and sort of comforting, Lacey thought, letting her gaze sweep the shore and the ocean just beyond. Kids raced in and out of the water, chasing and then running from the incoming tide with squeals of pleasure that echoed in the still air. From not too far off, a radio blasted some head-banger rock, and the lifeguard in his tower scoped out the waves, looking for someone to rescue.

Summer in Christmas.

Nothing ever changed here. But it all felt different anyway. Maybe because she was starting to say goodbye to it, if that made any sense.

"I bet we'll be roommates," Peggy was saying, drawing Lacey's attention back to the conversation. "And if we're not, we could maybe switch with the people we are rooming with so we can be together."

"That'd be good." Peggy Reilly wasn't afraid of anything. Since fourth grade, the tiny redhead had been leading the parade, with Lacey more than happy to follow along after. They made a good team. Peggy was crazy enough to ensure they had fun and Lacey was nervous enough to make sure they were safe.

But on her first foray out into the big, wide world, Lacey would just as soon have the brave and stalwart Peggy as a roommate. Adventure was one thing, but comfort was nothing to be sneezed at.

"I'm telling you, Lace," Peggy said, tipping her head back briefly to feel the sun on her face. "I'm ready for school. It'll be a vacation. Ever since my sister Eileen had her baby, the Reillys have been working me to death."

"Oh, shut up, you're just as nuts about the baby as the rest of them."

"Sure," Peggy said with a grin and a wink. "But honest to God, they're all rushing over to help Eileen and they're dumping the other kids on *me*. 'Don't want the new baby to catch a cold,' " she mimicked with a sigh. "So I'm the designated baby-sitter, and let me tell you, that Mike?" She shook her head. "He's a little pain in the ass."

"I like him."

"Me, too," Peggy said and shrugged a bit. "But he's not nearly sneaky enough to get away with all the stuff he tries to pull."

Lacey felt another twinge of envy for Peggy's big, loud family. She might complain, but there was nothing she liked better than to be in the middle of a shouting match with her sisters, her brothers, and all of the assorted nieces and nephews.

"And speaking of babies," Peggy said with a sigh, "Jack says they're no closer to finding the mother of little Liz."

"Where's he been looking?"

"Everywhere," Peggy said. "He told Sean that he'd called in favors up and down the coast, checking on hospitals and clinics, looking for a woman who'd recently given birth. Nothing."

"I asked a friend of mine over at Chandler High," Lacey said, remembering the conversation she'd had just last week. "Anna says that nobody at her school's been getting fatter and then suddenly losing weight. So I don't know where else to look."

"I know." Peggy pushed her hair back from her face and squinted into the sunlight. A small, evil smile curved her lips as she admitted, "I was kind of hoping Jennifer Stephens would turn out to be the mom . . . you know, Miss Rich Bitch goes to Europe for a semester?"

Lacey nodded, enjoying the image. "That would have been good."

"But she's so bony, no way did *she* have a baby recently."

Lacey tugged her sweatshirt down over the tops of her shorts. Not that she was self-conscious or anything; after all, she'd lost a lot of weight in the last few months. But still . . . thinking about Jennifer's size six body was enough to make anybody a little less than confident.

"Anyway," Peggy said, shaking her hair back from her face, "leaving my fascinating family and abandoned babies out of the conversation . . . Sophomore year, I'm thinking we should get an off-campus apartment." She slurped at her own Coke until the straw noisily sucked air. "Can you just see us? Down in Long Beach, just us? *So* great." She laughed to herself. "Just think. No big brothers sticking their noses in. No more cleaning hotel rooms or scrubbing the restaurant kitchen. No more working at Carol's for you. We can get jobs down on the pier or something. Be at the beach every day, far from anybody who knows us. Just you, me, and a campus full of new and interesting guys."

Peggy made it sound as wonderful as they'd always planned it would be. The two of them had been waiting for this chance for what felt like forever.

And now it was almost here.

Away from home. From family. From everything familiar. It's what she'd always wanted, Lacey thought as Peggy kept talking, expanding on her plans until they took on the size and scope of an invasion. Lacey hardly heard her anymore.

Nerves rattled around inside her and woke up the butterfly brigade napping in her stomach. Instantly, they swarmed, fluttering wings and flying in formation until she had to swallow hard or lose her Coke, right there on the beach.

Everything would be all right, she told herself firmly and slapped one hand to her stomach, trying to ease those butterflies into going back to sleep.

Ed Thompson stretched back in his recliner and settled his butt into the cavern he'd dug out in the soft, worn leather. Nothing like a man's own chair for comfort.

He looked up at Jack Reilly and told himself that the young fella needed to learn a little something about relaxing. Looked as tightly strung as Ed's wife Wanda.

And nobody was as tense as Wanda. Except that she *had* been unwinding some these past couple of weeks.

"How's everything down in town?" Ed prompted, getting down to the business of the visit.

"Fine. Normal." Jack moved around the den, scanning framed photos and certificates hanging on the wall and then idly thumbing through fishing magazines stacked on the coffee table.

"No problems?" Ed narrowed his gaze on the younger man.

Jack snorted. "Cheryl Stephens filed a complaint. Says people are spreading rumors that her girl Jen is the mother of that baby."

Ed shook his head and huffed out a disgusted breath. "Abandoned babies in Christmas. Never thought I'd see it." He sucked in a gulp of air and blew it out again in a rush. Then he picked up the TV remote to have something to do with his hands. "But Cheryl's spitting into the wind. Can't stop a rumor with a complaint. Just adds fuel to it. Folks figure she's got something to hide, they'll just dig deeper. Nothing people like better than to talk about somebody who isn't them."

"What I said," Jack admitted and sat down on the arm of the red and blue plaid couch. "It's not Jen, anyway. The girl was in school in Paris. I checked. Talk will die down eventually."

"When something juicier comes along."

"True." Jack held his baseball cap between his hands and turned it incessantly, front to back, front to back. "Elves' Hardware had a break-in," he said conversationally.

"A burglary?" Ed came halfway out of his chair before Jack grinned at him.

"Tommy Henderson forgot his car keys when he closed up and then broke the window in the back door to get 'em. Old man Saugus nearly had a heart attack when that burglar alarm went off." Then he winced as if just remembering that Ed's heart attack was what had brought Jack back to town in the first place.

Ed waved a brawny hand at him. "My heart's fine. Just a little angina they called it. No need to walk soft around me."

"Then you'll be coming back soon?"

Now, was that disappointment or eagerness in the boy's eyes? Ed wondered. The flash of emotion had come and gone so quickly, he hadn't been able to identify it in time to recognize it. "Wanted to talk to you about that."

Something new flashed in Jack's eyes and this emotion Ed spotted instantly. Suspicion.

"What?"

"Wanda and me have been talking about getting one of those RVs and hitting the road."

"Huh?"

"I'm gonna retire, Jack." Hell, it didn't even hurt to say the word out loud anymore. It had stuck in his throat up until a week ago. As if admitting he was retirement age was saying he was too damn old. But a few afternoons in bed with Wanda had proven to both of them that there was fire in the old goat yet.

And dammit, he didn't want to waste what time he had left sitting behind a desk, riding herd on tourists and parking citations. "It's time," he said shortly, figuring Jack didn't need to hear his reasons. "And I want you to take the job permanent."

Jack shot to his feet as if someone had lit a rocket under his ass.

Ed talked fast. "I already spoke to the city council, they're all for it. Ken's a good deputy, but he hasn't got the patience or the experience to deal with the townies or the tourists. And Hoover . . . hell, he'd as soon fish as sleep."

"No."

"Don't say no yet, dammit." Ed pushed himself more upright and glared at the younger man. Hard to have a good argument when you were practically stretched out lying down. "I've known you since you were a boy. All you ever wanted to be was a police officer. You were a damn good one too, Jack."

" 'Were' being the operative word."

"Bullshit." Ed slammed one closed fist down on the arm of the recliner. He knew the story. Was one of the few people in town who did. Probably just him and the Reillys. But when he'd offered this temporary job to Jack, he'd done it with all the information he could gather. He'd called LAPD and gotten the inside scoop from Jack's lieutenant. And the rage he'd felt on Jack's behalf hadn't settled yet. The boy had taken a hard hit that long-ago night, that was for sure. But you couldn't build your life around the events of one single night.

"That was a mess down there, no mistake," Ed said shortly. "But you did what you had to do and you've got nothing to be ashamed of."

"I'm not staying," Jack insisted. "I can't."

"Can't or won't. Only you know the truth." Ed shoved his recliner back a notch, settling back into the comfortable sling of leather and sprung coils. "You think about it. You've got a little time yet."

"How long?" The question came through gritted teeth.

"I'm not officially retired for another two weeks, so I'm holding you to our deal," Ed warned, shaking his remote control at Jack. He scowled at the damn thing, then dropped it into his lap. "You agreed to take over for me and that's what you'll do."

"Two weeks."

"That's right," Ed said tightly, knowing Jack would never go back on his word. "And you do some thinking, Jack. This town needs you."

"Just get better, okay?" Jack muttered, not even replying to that last statement.

"I will. And so should *you,*" Ed said.

But Jack was already headed for the hallway that would lead him to the front door.

"This town needs you, Jack," Ed called after him, "and you need this town, you damn hardheaded—"

He was gone.

Ed flopped back in the recliner and told himself he should have tried for more finesse. But there were times for smooth-talking and there were times to just say the truth flat-out. And dammit, it was past time somebody told Jack Reilly to stop paying for someone else's crime.

"Is Jack gone?" Wanda said as she stepped into the room wearing her new blue satin floor-length robe.

"Yeah, the obstinate, stubborn, foolish—" Ed's eyes widened as Wanda pulled open the edges of that slinky robe to display smooth skin and—Ed's breath caught hard in his chest—black stockings and a matching black bra and panties.

She walked toward him, a slow, secretive smile on her face, and Ed felt his heart jump in his chest.

"Who said retirement was boring?" he muttered as his wife of forty years cuddled in on his lap, took the remote control and turned off the TV.

Jack stepped outside, closing the Thompsons' front door behind him. He sucked in a long, deep breath and felt the hot, still punch of summer hit him hard. Up here on the hillside, there was no ocean breeze to take the sting out of the heat. Even if there had been, though, it wouldn't have helped. He felt as if he couldn't breathe. Couldn't draw enough air into his lungs to get his body to move, his mind to think.

Permanent.

Hell.

He scooped his hair back from his forehead, then settled his cap on his head, pulling the brim down low, to shield his eyes from the glare of the sun. He stared down the hill toward Christmas and told himself he'd walked into this with his eyes open. Doing a friend a favor. Well, no good deed goes unpunished.

It felt as though steel jaws were snapping closed around his ankles. He was trapped. By family. By friends. By good old Ed. By Carol.

He'd come home temporarily and all of a sudden it was as if he was in a labyrinth and couldn't find the way out. Didn't even know if there *was* a way out. Or if he should try to find it.

Down there, in the town, life moved on pretty much as it did every day. Nothing really changed in Christmas. The only thing that really changed were the people living in it. God knew, he'd changed. This had been his home. And now, Christmas was like an old suit. He wasn't sure it still fit, and even if it did, he didn't know if it would look good on him anymore.

"Permanent," he muttered, and if there was a flicker of excitement . . . eagerness in him for the word, he ignored it. He hadn't come back here to stay. He couldn't stay. Could he? No. He hunched his shoulders as if ducking a responsibility he no longer wanted. He stalked toward the 4Runner with the gold star and the word "SHERIFF" on the doors. Opening the driver's side, he climbed in, turned the key, and hit the AC. Cold air slapped at him and he turned his face directly into the vent. Hell, he needed all the help he could get, to cool off before facing the town again.

Carol stopped at the grocery store after closing the shop for the day. With sunset, most of the heat had slipped away, and the sky was a burst of rose and peach that dipped down into the ocean at the horizon.

Two kids on skateboards whizzed past her, the steel wheels on their boards roaring like lions loose on the street. She left Quinn outside the market, and carrying Liz, stepped inside. She only had a few things to pick up, so she walked straight toward the aisle with the baby food, grabbed a can of formula, then walked to the last aisle for a package of spaghetti.

"You hungry, sweetie?" Carol crooned as Liz began to shift and twist in her arms. "Almost dinnertime, it's okay."

Muzak drifted from the overhead speakers and a fluorescent light over the meat department flickered wildly in time with the beat. The scent of freshly baked bread wafted from the bakery and mingled with a bank of fresh flowers waiting to be bought and carried home.

Striding down the aisle, Carol hesitated as Mary Alice Reilly turned a corner and stopped directly in front of her.

"Carol!" she said, pleasure coloring her tone as a bright smile wreathed her face. "What a nice surprise."

"Hello, Mrs. Reilly," Carol said, tightening her grip on the small red plastic basket she held in her right hand. "Congratulations. I hear you're a grandma again."

"At last," Mary Alice said with a quick grin. "I thought

Eileen was just going to carry this one for the rest of her life."

"Mom and baby are doing well?"

"Great," Mary Alice said. "That little girl is just the sweetest thing—" She reached out and trailed a fingertip along Liz's left arm. "Of course, not nearly as pretty as *this* one."

"Oh, of course," Carol said laughing. "And you'll say the same thing to Eileen, won't you?"

"I will, and stand by it. No baby's as pretty as the one you're holding at the moment." The older woman cocked her head and looked at her for a long minute. "This baby's been good for you, Carol. As good as you've been for Jack."

"What?"

"He doesn't know it yet, but I think he's happier than he's been in a long time." She reached out and gave Carol's arm a fond pat. "And I think it has a lot to do with you."

A flicker of something warm and lovely darted through Carol's stomach and disappeared again. "Mrs. Reilly—"

"Mary Alice, honey. Call me Mary Alice."

"Thanks," Carol said quickly and took a step around the other woman's cart. "But you should know that—"

The older woman shook her head and interrupted her neatly. "I know all I need to know," she said, smiling. "And now, I've got to finish up here so I can feed Peggy, then get over to Eileen's house." She started walking, then paused and looked back over her shoulder. "You say hello to Jack for me."

"Okay, I will." Carol watched her go until she rounded the end of the aisle and moved out of sight. Then she dropped her gaze to Liz. "I think his mom likes me."

Smiling to herself, she headed for the checkout counter, then stopped, remembering she needed tampons. "Rats. Okay, Liz, one more thing, and then we're outta here."

She hurried to the last aisle and while she walked she started thinking, mentally counting. Her steps slowed as she realized that she should have started her period days ago. "No," she muttered, as if needing to hear the word aloud. "I couldn't be."

But she remembered that first night with Jack. The broken condom. And she wondered.

Standing in front of the tower of tampons, she let her gaze slide to one side, where it landed on a row of home pregnancy tests. Hand shaking, she reached for the closest pink and white box and dropped it into her basket.

CHAPTER 16

Word of Carol's purchase rippled through town like circles on the surface of a lake after a pebble was tossed in. Susie Cooper, the cashier, had immediately called her mother, the beauty operator, who had told Edna Halstead, her customer, who had then called her bingo team and they'd spread the word as fast as they could dial the phones.

This was the juicy piece of gossip Cheryl Stephens had been hoping for. Her daughter was old news. No one was talking about the abandoned baby anymore. They were all too focused on Carol's pregnancy.

By the time Carol reached her apartment, half the town knew about the test she had purchased and the other half were being told.

When the phone rang at the sheriff's station, Jack snatched it up. "Sheriff."

"Are you going to marry her?"

"What?" He knew the voice. He just couldn't believe the question. He pulled the receiver away from his ear and looked at it before slapping it to his head again. "Who is this?"

"It's your mother and that was a simple question."

"My mother's not crazy, so you must be a stranger," he said tightly. "Goodbye."

"Don't you hang up this phone, Jack Reilly," she said in a tone that could still send shivers down his spine. "I want an answer to my question."

His jaw clenched and his fist tightened around the phone. How the hell could she even ask him that? She knew exactly what had happened the last time he'd been married. He'd turned out to be the first divorce—*ever*—in the Reilly family. Not something he was looking to repeat. "You want an answer? Here it is. I'm not getting married."

"So you're going to leave your child without a father?"

"Child?" Cold dropped into the pit of his stomach. "What child?"

"Carol's pregnant."

Air rushed from his lungs. The room tilted and he gripped the arm of the chair to keep from being tossed to the floor. Carol? Pregnant? Instantly, his mind darted back. Back to that first time. When that ancient condom he'd used had broken. He'd managed to forget about that. Told himself that it would be all right. That one time wouldn't make that big a difference. And to be honest, Carol hadn't been worried about it, so he hadn't seen a need for him to say any rosaries over the situation.

Pregnant? He slumped back in his chair and wiped one hand across his face. "She told you?" She'd told his *mother* and not him? Stunned, he felt a pang of hurt ripple through him because Carol hadn't said anything to him. Then worry and confusion crowded behind the twinge of disappointment and demanded their turn at recognition. He didn't even know yet how he felt about a possible baby. "Why the hell would she tell *you* and not me?"

"Of course she didn't tell me," his mother snapped, clearly at the end of her patience. "I heard about it from Tessa Baker. She got it from her daughter who works at the beauty shop with Ellie. She heard from her mother who called her after Susie's mom told her. Susie sold her—Carol—the pregnancy test."

Now his head was spinning. Christ. Had he really forgotten how things worked in a small town? Hadn't he and Ed just been talking about the gossips and how they'd be looking for something new to chew on? Looked like they had it. "Good to know the spy network's still up and running."

"This is no time for jokes, Jack Reilly."

"Trust me, I'm not laughing." He swallowed hard as he fought to come to grips with the idea of Carol pregnant with his kid. This changed everything. While his mother ranted, Jack's brain raced.

He saw his plans to get out of town go up in smoke. How the hell could he leave Christmas and walk out on his own child? How could he live with himself, knowing he'd turned his back on his own?

Then other feelings reared up inside him and squashed him flat. Once before, he'd listened as a woman told him she was pregnant. And before he could even react to the news, she'd informed him that the child wasn't his. A yawning blackness opened up inside him as Jack felt the rage of that moment, the disappointment and disgust roar through him, as fresh in memory as if it had been yesterday.

But then another image was layered over that painful one. And he saw Carol, as clearly as if she were standing in front of him. He saw how she was with Liz. Holding her. Loving her. As she would love a child of his. And something inside him yearned to be there. To be a part of it. Even while one cowardly corner of his mind was looking for a way out.

He had to talk to Carol.

"Mom?"

She kept talking, a runaway train of advice and threats and pleas.

"Mom!"

She stopped. "What?" One word, snarled as only a loving mother could.

"I've gotta go." He hung up before she could get started again. Then he stood up and headed for the front door. Snatching his cap off the wooden peg on the wall, he dragged it on, stepped out into sunset, and closed the door behind him.

Lacey knocked on Carol's apartment door and waited, twisting her fingers together as the butterflies in her stomach swirled in agitation. Ever since she heard about Carol buying the pregnancy test, she'd known she had to come here. Had to do something. But that didn't make it any easier.

Carol threw the door open and stood there smiling, Liz cradled in the curve of her left arm. Quinn instantly surged forward, pressing his huge head beneath Lacey's right hand in welcome. Her fingers moved through his thick, wiry hair and she held on, trying to soothe the jitters hopping through her system. Now that she was here, she didn't know what to say. How to say it.

Earlier today, everything was still good. Sort of. She and Peggy had been talking about college again. Making plans again. Plans that now wouldn't be coming true. A twist of disappointment snapped free inside her, but she tried to ignore it. Maybe it just wasn't meant to be, she thought. College? For Lacey Reynolds? Daughter of the town drunk?

Her stomach lurched and nausea rolled through it, climbing up her throat, choking her. Carol was the only one in the whole town—except for Peggy—who'd ever thought Lacey could go places. Carol had believed in her. And now, she was going to hate her.

"Lacey." Carol smiled, but questions filled her eyes. "What're you doing here?" Concern was layered over the surprise as her smile faded. "Is everything all right?"

"Yeah." *No. Nothing* was all right. And maybe it never would be again. She was so scared. Fear was alive and thumping to the beat of her heart. She'd been thinking and thinking all afternoon and she knew what she had to do. She just wasn't sure how to do it. "Can I, um, talk to you for a minute?"

"Sure, honey." Carol stepped back and said, "Come on in."

Lacey's gaze swept the room, littered now with baby stuff. Bibs and blankets and stacks of clean laundry. Tiny shirts with even tinier snaps that looked like doll clothes. There were two boxes of disposable diapers in one corner and the TV was on—an episode of *The X-Files*, a hum of noise in the background.

"I was just finishing up feeding Liz," Carol said and sat down on the couch, picking up the baby bottle off the table in front of her.

Lacey watched as the baby opened her mouth and shook her little head until she got a good grab on the rubber nipple. Carol laughed and looked up at Lacey. "She's a good eater. Probably be ordering a hamburger by next week."

Lacey smiled, but it trembled on her face. This was right, she told herself. Being scared was natural. She'd been scared before. But she had to do this. For her. For Liz.

"Carol . . ."

Her gaze narrowed. "There *is* something wrong, isn't there?"

She wanted to cry. Wanted to tell Carol how she was sorry to let her down. How she'd meant to go to college, just like she and Carol always talked about, but that boy had been so nice. And he'd really *liked* her. He'd said she was beautiful. Nobody had ever told her that before, and then when he left, Lacey had figured no one would ever have to know about those nights they'd been together.

Until she discovered she was pregnant.

But it wasn't the time to tell Carol all of that. The only thing that mattered now was what she had to do. What she'd *come* here to do. And to say.

Lacey took a deep breath, steeled herself, and blurted out the truth. "Liz is *my* baby, Carol. *I* left her in the manger so you'd find her. You and Quinn." Her words came faster now, tumbling from her mouth in a mad dash to be said. "I didn't want to leave her, but I had to." Lacey heard the tears in her own voice. Her throat tightened and her vision blurred. Still, she saw Carol stand up slowly. Liz kept eating, her short breaths sounding loud in the stunned silence.

Carol looked as though all the breath had left her body. "Lacey—"

"I'm sorry, Carol, I know you really love her, but I do, too," Lacey said, her heart twisting with a sudden, sharp pain that seemed to shimmer through her and grow as it spread. Cold. She was so cold. "I didn't know what to do before. But I do now. I have to take care of Liz myself."

Carol's vision narrowed to a pinpoint. She stared at

Lacey and saw a terrified girl, bravely trying to do what she thought was best. But at the same time, she saw in Lacey's eyes the end of her own dreams. Liz was a warm, slight weight in her arms. The small sounds she made as she drank her bottle had become as familiar to Carol as her own heartbeat. Her life—her world—revolved around the baby.

And now she was going to lose her?

Then a calm, clear, rational voice in her mind screamed, *Why should you believe her? Anyone could claim to be the baby's mother.*

True. But at the same time, she realized that there was no reason for Lacey to be doing this. No purpose in trying to lie about it when one visit to Phoebe for an examination would prove or disprove the lie. And why would the girl suddenly decide to pretend to be the mother who'd abandoned her child?

Lacey wasn't the kind of kid who did things for attention. Quite the opposite. She kept as low a profile as possible because of her mother's reputation. A part of Carol couldn't believe that the girl she'd known for two years was standing in front of her making these claims.

It didn't make sense. None of this made sense. But one look in Lacey's eyes told her that the girl was speaking the truth. The hard, cold, bitter truth that meant Carol was going to lose Liz.

Her arms tightened instinctively around Liz. "Lacey, *why?* Why didn't you tell me before? Why did you leave her in the first place?"

The girl swiped tears from her cheeks with the backs of her hands. "I was scared. I couldn't tell my mom. I couldn't tell anybody. You would have been so disappointed in me." Her face crumpled and she fought a battle with her trembling bottom lip and lost it. "I didn't think I'd get pregnant. I didn't—" She blew out a breath and shook her head.

"How, though?" Carol's words slipped out, and when she saw Lacey's gaze sharpen, she shook her head. "I don't mean how did you *get* pregnant. But how did you hide it? From everyone? From *me*?" *And why hadn't she noticed? How had a teenage girl hidden her pregnancy so completely that Carol had never noticed?*

Lacey sniffled and ran one hand under her nose before swiping tears from her cheeks. A short, harsh laugh shot from her throat. "It wasn't hard. Nobody looks too close at a fat girl."

"Oh, Lacey . . ."

"I went on Weight Watchers and I was really good about it, too, so even though the baby was getting bigger, I *lost* weight. And with the sweatshirts and everything . . ." She shrugged, then wrapped her arms around her chest and held on. "Nobody noticed anything different. I was still just fat Lacey."

God. For months, the girl had kept her secret. She'd hidden in plain sight.

"And then when I had her, I thought about you and how you and Quinn are always walking through the square at night and I knew you'd find her and take good care of her."

The baby hiccuped and Lacey jumped, then moved away, pacing quickly around the room in jerky steps, waving her hands as she talked. She choked out a laugh that sounded to Carol as though it were drowning in banked-up tears. The girl rubbed her face with her fingertips. "I had the baby and I put her out in the manger 'cause I knew she'd be better off with you. You didn't have anybody, so I knew you'd love her like she should be."

She whirled around and faced Carol, eyes glistening. "But now *you're* pregnant."

The accusation fired across the room like a bullet and hit its mark. Carol swayed in place, eyes wide, breath caught somewhere behind the knot in her throat. "What?"

Lacey struggled for air, too, as if firing that bullet had been as difficult as being hit with it. But she swallowed hard and snapped, "You won't want Liz now. You'll have your own baby. So I want mine back."

"Lacey—" Carol took a step and stopped. This was all happening so fast. Everything felt so out of control. So crazed. She couldn't make sense of it. Any of it. "Pregnant? I'm not—how did you—" She closed her eyes, sighed heavily, and almost groaned.

The pregnancy test she bought at the grocery store.

Idiot. She should have gone to Phoebe for the stupid test. Then no one would know what she suspected. Then Lacey wouldn't be standing here reclaiming Liz and shaking the foundation of her world.

"I'm not," Carol said quickly, then backtracked. "I mean, I don't even know if I am or not. I haven't taken the test and—"

"But you might be."

"And I might not," Carol said quietly, somehow keeping from screaming. "But either way, it wouldn't change anything. I love Liz, Lacey."

The girl looked at her through blue eyes swimming in tears that overflowed into tiny rivers that streamed unheeded down her cheeks. "I know, but I do, too." She slapped one hand to her chest as if trying to keep her heart from bursting. "I watch you with her, watch her laugh and smile and see you kiss her and I think it should be *me*. She should love *me*." Lacey hugged herself tightly and choked back a sob tearing at her throat. "*I'm* her mom. She should know, Carol. She should know that I love her, right?"

"God, Lacey . . ." Carol's heart ached like a bad tooth. The girl's misery was real and blistering the air in the room. But pain swamped Carol, too, dragging at her, smothering her in hot, throbbing waves of agony that peaked and valleyed and peaked again.

This was love, she thought. This was the risk. This was the price.

"You're going to college," Carol said, reminding the girl of her plans. Of her dreams. She didn't hear the desperation in her own voice because she was too focused on Lacey's.

"I can go later," she said breathlessly, and her expression was stubborn, determined. "I can go part-time. I can get a job and study, too."

The walls of her fantasy palace crumbled. "Lacey, why? I'll take good care of Liz. You know I will. You can still have your dreams. All of them."

Lacey shook her head, bit down hard on her bottom lip, and stepped in close to Carol. Reaching out, she scooped Liz out of Carol's arms and into her own. She stared down into her daughter's face and smiled through her tears. "It doesn't matter. College isn't that important."

Carol wanted to snatch Liz from Lacey's arms. Wanted to turn back time twenty minutes—an hour. Back to when everything was good. Back to when she and Liz were still a *family*. How could she do it? How could she hand this child over to another child? And how could she allow Liz to be taken away simply on this girl's say-so? She couldn't. Maybe it was reaching for straws. Maybe she was fooling herself. But she had to be sure.

"Lacey . . ." The girl looked at her. "I can't just hand her over to you like this. Liz is in the system now. We'll have to contact Maggie Cooper."

Lacey paled, but lifted her chin and nodded. "Okay."

"And Maggie will want proof that you're Liz's mother." *As do I,* Carol thought wildly, but didn't say.

Lacey's blue eyes widened in surprise. "I wouldn't lie to you."

"If what you're saying is true," Carol pointed out in a low, hurt-filled voice, "you've already lied to me. And everyone else in town. For nine months."

Lacey bit her bottom lip and looked from Carol to the baby in her arms again. Without shifting her gaze, she said simply, "What do you want me to do?"

Go home, Carol thought wildly. She wanted the girl to go home. Then go to college. To leave Carol's house and put everything back the way it had been a few minutes ago. But that wasn't going to happen and a cold, hard voice inside her whispered that she should have been prepared for the pain. Should have been expecting it.

But she hadn't.

She'd stopped protecting her heart.

She'd allowed herself to love and now she had to pay.

Inhaling sharply, Carol walked to the phone and picked it up. "I'll call Maggie. Have her meet us at the clinic. Phoebe can examine you." She stopped and looked at Lacey. "Have you seen a doctor since Liz was born?"

The girl shook her head.

"Oh, Lacey . . ." Carol sighed and punched in the numbers. *Children having children.* As she listened to the phone ring, Carol clung to this one last hope like the survivor of a boating accident clinging to a battered life preserver. The hope that Phoebe would examine the girl and tell her that Lacey hadn't recently given birth. But in her heart, Carol knew that wouldn't happen. She already knew that her brief stay in her own little slice of heaven was over.

An hour later, they were back from the clinic and the three of them stood locked in awkward silence in Carol's living room. Emptiness yawned inside Carol and she wanted to crawl into the blackness creeping through her. But there were still goodbyes to be said.

Quinn's low, muted whining reached through the pain clawing at her and Carol dropped one hand to his big head. She wound her fingers through his hair and held on, anchoring herself to a world that kept rocking around her.

Maggie clutched her briefcase in both hands and her eyes, so much like Jack's, swam with sympathy and understanding. Throughout the last hour and a half, Maggie had been the rock to Carol's reed buffeted by a rising tide. Clearly, she was as reluctant as Carol to give Liz over to her mother. But in courts, a parent's rights took precedence.

"I'm sorry," Lacey whispered, never taking her gaze from the baby staring up at her. "I'm sorry, Carol, but I have to have her. I just *have* to."

Tears filled Carol's throat. "I know. I know, Lacey." *She didn't know. Didn't want to know. She wanted the baby she loved.* She tightened her grip on Quinn and hoped the big dog was strong enough to hold them both up.

"Lacey," Maggie said softly, "why don't you take the baby and go down to my car? I'll be right there."

"Okay," the girl said, and headed for the door.

Carol swayed again, felt another sharp hit to her heart as the child she loved so much was swept from her life. Her breath staggered, her eyes filled, blurring the room, which was beginning to spin. Lacey opened the door and Carol came out of the trance holding her in place. "Wait."

Lacey looked back at her, eyes wary.

But there was nothing Carol could do to stop the girl. To stop this from happening. To reclaim the happiness that had been hers just a couple of hours ago. Phoebe's examination proved that Lacey had indeed given birth recently. Maggie had made the decision to, temporarily at least, return the baby to her birth mother. There was no hope to cling to. There were no second chances. In her heart, she knew Lacey was Liz's mother and no amount of pleading with God at this late date was going to change that. Instead of focusing on the pain whipping through her insides, Carol thought of Liz. Her needs. Her comfort.

Ignoring the pity in Maggie's eyes, Carol grabbed the wildly flowered diaper bag, and carried it across the room, walking like a zombie. "You forgot this." She slung the bag up over Lacey's shoulder, then took one heartbreaking moment to smooth her palm over the top of Liz's head.

Sucking in a gulp of air, Carol buried another sharp stab of pain and forced words past a throat too tight for air to pass through. "She wakes up about two and she's hungry again."

"I'll feed her."

"Sometimes," Carol said, as tears slid from her eyes to trail unheeded along her cheeks, "she likes music. Soft music."

Lacey lifted her teary gaze to Carol's. "I'll remember."

Brown eyes locked with blue. Carol nodded slowly,

brokenly, as if her body couldn't quite recall how to respond to her brain's commands. She bit down hard on her bottom lip and didn't cry out when Lacey took Liz and slipped through the door.

As the girl's steps echoed along the hall and down the stairs, Carol locked her knees in a desperate effort to remain standing.

"I'm so sorry, Carol." Maggie laid one hand on Carol's arm.

"I know."

"I want you to know," Maggie said and waited for Carol to look at her. "Lacey will have the support of the agency. She won't be completely on her own in this."

Carol nodded and didn't bother trying to form words.

"And I'll be handling her case personally," Maggie continued. "I'll make sure Liz is safe and well cared for. You don't have to worry about that."

Another nod.

Her throat closed up tight.

Banked tears burned her eyes.

Her lungs heaved unsuccessfully for air.

"I'm *so* sorry, Carol." Maggie's voice, as gentle as a cloud, settled over her, but it was no comfort.

There was no comfort for her in this.

Her heart had broken into jagged little shards slicing at her chest—and it was going to *stay* broken.

Finally, Maggie stepped past Carol, moved into the hall, and quietly closed the door.

Silence crashed down on her.

Quinn whined and butted his head against the backs of her legs. That was all it took.

Carol crumpled, dropping to the floor bonelessly. Pain erupted from the emptiness inside her and geysered from her soul. A long, low moan tore from her throat and echoed through the apartment that was too big without Liz in it—and too small to hold the agony tearing Carol's heart apart.

Chapter 17

Conversations dried up the minute Jack came close. Hidden smiles or the occasional wink had him hunching his shoulders. He *felt* stares boring into his back as he walked along North Pole Avenue; his family had called his cell phone so many times, he'd finally just shut it off. He didn't want to talk to anyone about this. Not yet. Not until he'd had a chance to come to grips with the whole thing himself.

Shouldn't take more than a year or two.

He hated being talked about. His shoulders hunched in self-defense as he drove through town. He'd used his own car rather than the sheriff's vehicle, hoping to avoid too much attention. Hadn't worked. Small-town citizens knew *everyone's* car. Damn, he hated this. Christ knew, he'd lived through being the subject of enough gossip after that Christmas Eve in LA.

His chest felt tight, like some unseen fist was squeezing his lungs shut. He was a little light-headed, too, but was willing to put that down to the lack of air.

He never should have come back to Christmas. That's where this all started. He should have listened to his instincts and stayed the hell away. Now, because he hadn't, the shit he'd landed in just kept getting deeper.

He needed more time to think, dammit. Though why he thought that might help, he didn't know. He'd been thinking for hours and *still* hadn't found a way out of this.

Bottom line, it came down to the kind of man you were raised to be.

And damn it, a Reilly didn't walk out on his responsibilities. Like it or not, there was only one answer to this situation.

God help them all.

Jack had stalled as long as he could. He'd walked around town, down to the beach, and then driven up into the hills, losing himself in the cool green of the trees that promised a respite from the summer heat. Now, the stars were out and Christmas was closing its doors and folding up its sidewalks for the night.

He parked his car in front of Carol's place and climbed out. A stray breeze dancing in off the ocean fluttered past him, lifting the ends of his hair and teasing the back of his neck with damp, icy fingers. He looked up at the windows on the second floor.

His own apartment was dark—it looked abandoned. Light seeped from behind the curtains at Carol's place. Not as bright as usual, though, he thought, narrowing his gaze as he studied it. No one moved behind the sheer fabric at the windows. There was no soft echo of classic rock drifting through the partially opened windows and—an even bigger sign—there was no flickering light cast by the TV. She didn't have the television on and he knew there was a *V* marathon on tonight. Smiling to himself, he remembered that she'd circled it in red on her calendar.

The first whisper of concern drifted through him and

he told himself he was being ridiculous. So what? She wasn't watching TV. *Lots* of people made it through the night without ever once turning the TV on.

Not Carol, though, his brain taunted. Not on a night when she would ordinarily be front-row center on the couch with a bowl of popcorn on her lap.

Frowning, he started for the front door, and just as he did, one of the deep shadows on the porch moved. Jack stiffened, froze in place, then relaxed as Quinn pushed himself to his feet and stood at the head of the short flight of steps. The dog's silhouette was huge and the low rumble of thunder blossoming from his wide chest reminded him of *The Hound of the Baskervilles*.

"You want to chew on me a while?" Jack muttered, headed for the porch now with quick strides. "Get in line."

Quinn didn't move out of his way. The big dog stood his ground, keeping his gaze fixed on Jack's like some sort of canine hypnotist.

"Perfect," Jack muttered, meeting that stare with a glare of his own. "Look, you don't like me, I don't like you. We'll call it a draw, okay?"

The dog took a step closer and whined.

A spidery feeling crawled across the back of Jack's neck. Quinn didn't usually come whining to him. Growling, yes. Snarling, sure. But whining? No.

Jack glanced around at the darkened porch, then back to the front door and the house beyond. If Quinn was out here, where the hell was Carol? She and the damn bear were practically attached at the hip. She wouldn't let him just wander around on his own.

That uneasy sensation skittered from the back of his neck, all the way down his spine and back up again. Something was wrong. He felt it.

He *knew* it.

Reaching out, he laid one hand on the big dog's massive head. Quinn leaned into him for one brief moment, then took the steps down in a tangle of long, powerful legs. When the dog hit the sidewalk, he stopped and turned to face Jack.

"What?" Jack just stared at him. For crissake, was he supposed to be a doggie mind reader now? "Is Timmy in the well?" he muttered, feeling like an idiot.

Quinn only whined again, walked close and butted his head against Jack's legs before taking another step or two down the sidewalk.

In the glow of the streetlights, Quinn looked massive, and dangerous as hell. His dark eyes stared up at Jack, and for a single heartbeat, Jack thought he could almost *hear* the dog asking for help. "Damn. Timmy really *is* down a well, huh?"

Worry erupted in the pit of his stomach and then spun crazily. Something was definitely up. And his heart staggered as his cop's brain took over and drew graphic images of just how many things could be wrong. Just how badly Carol could be hurt.

He didn't want the images. Didn't want them staining his mind so that the possibilities would always be there. But there was no dislodging them now. Just as there was no way to stop the quickening sense of fear that began a wild gallop through his bloodstream. He could fight it with practiced calm. With logic. With the need to be focused. But he couldn't defeat it.

He could only endure as fear escalated to dread.

He came down the last two steps and stood beside the now practically quivering dog. Quinn obviously needed to be moving. Jack knew just how the animal felt. Every muscle in his body was tensed and poised for action.

"Okay, then," Jack said, giving the dog's big head a quick stroke. "Don't just stand there. Take me to Carol."

As if shot off a coiled spring, Quinn took off in a ground-eating lope. The animal's long, powerful legs raced down the sidewalk, splashing through one pool of lamplight into the next. Jack wasn't far behind him. He didn't have four legs, but at six foot five, he had *long* legs, and he wouldn't allow Quinn to outdistance him.

The night air smelled of summer. The damp sting of salt air swept past him, picking up an old echo of charcoal barbecues. Jack hardly noticed. The only sound he heard was the sharp slap of his tennis shoes against the sidewalk and his own heart thundering in his chest. He came across a kid's forgotten tricycle in the middle of the sidewalk and hurdled it like an Olympic sprinter, never slowing down. Quinn took a corner, then darted across North Pole Avenue.

The shops were darkened, just a few splashes of brightly colored neon glowing in the night. Deserted, there were no cars or tourists hustling up and down the street—there was only stillness. Except for the click of Quinn's nails against the pavement and the steady beat of Jack's running steps.

His breath puffed in front of him in short bursts. His gaze narrowed, sweeping the streets, the sidewalks, and then focusing on the dog, his one link to Carol.

"Where the hell are we going?" he muttered, but didn't pause to think about it. To wonder. All he focused on was keeping up with the dog flying along the ground like an oversized salt-and-pepper bullet, headed for the town square.

Oak trees lined the square in a tidy row, with low-growing, flowering bushes interspersed between their gnarled trunks. The scent of flowers, roses and others he couldn't identify, was heavy, clinging to the wide patch of manicured grass that sat in the center of town. Quinn slowed down, gave a muffled *woof* that sounded as deep as a cannon shot.

Jack was right behind him. He stopped suddenly as he came out of the line of trees and his tennis shoes slid on the damp grass.

Across the square from him, Carol sat in the shadows on a bench near the well-lit Nativity set. Instantly, the tight band around his chest loosened and Jack drew his first easy breath since starting the late-night sprint through town. She was okay. His heart slowed down, and his brain clicked off the graphic images of mayhem and violence it had been playing on a continuous loop.

He wanted to swallow hard enough to dislodge his heart from his throat, but his mouth was dry. Thinking of Carol hurt or in danger had terrified him. Seeing her now, perfectly safe, irrationally infuriated him. What the hell was she doing sitting out here in the middle of the night? Letting that damn bear run around town terrifying him into imagining all sorts of hideous things?

Why the hell wasn't she at home?

Silently, he watched as Quinn trotted up close to the woman, then plopped his butt down right in front of her. Carol didn't move. Didn't reach out a hand toward the dog she loved. Hardly looked as though she'd noticed he was there. Anger fizzled into black worry that settled like an icy ball at the bottom of Jack's stomach.

Something was definitely wrong.

And he was pretty sure he knew what it was. Obviously, the thought of being pregnant with his kid wasn't sitting any easier with her than it had with him. Naturally, the next emotion on the food chain was guilt. It bit Jack hard, tearing a chunk off his soul and chewing on it long enough to make him shift his stance uneasily. What the hell could he say to her? *Sorry I screwed with your life?*

Shit.

Quinn turned his big head and stared across the distance at Jack as if to say, *What's the holdup? I brought you here. Do I have to do everything?*

As his charging heart settled into a regular beat again, Jack took a long, slow breath and let it slide from his lungs in a quiet sigh. It pained him to see that being pregnant with his child had put her into a coma so deep she couldn't even see the dog she loved. And he wasn't quite sure what he could do to fix it.

Shoving his hands into his jeans pockets, he started across the grass, making no move to be quiet. Didn't matter, though. It was as if she were on another planet. She didn't react. To him or to Quinn.

Not a good sign.

He walked up to the bench and sat down beside her. Only then did she turn her head to look at him. Despite the dim light, he saw the tracks of tears on her cheeks and the glistening sheen of them still dazzling her whiskey-colored eyes. His heart lurched. Dammit, he'd never been any good with a crying woman. Tears made a man as useless as—well, hell.

There was *nothing* so useless as a man facing a teary woman.

"What're you doing here?"

"I was gonna ask you that." He stared at her for a long moment, then let his gaze slip past her, looking for Liz's stroller, before focusing on her eyes again. "Where's the baby?"

She snorted a laugh that sounded painful as it ripped from her throat. Reaching up, she swiped her hands over her face and blew out a shaky breath that seemed to tremble through her. "God."

She tipped her head back and stared up through the leaves at the sky above. "Do you realize how many times you've asked me that question?"

He frowned. "You're not answering it."

"No, I'm not."

That icy ball of worry formed in his gut again and sent chills leaping through his bloodstream. "What's going on, Carol?"

She finally turned her gaze from the star-scattered sky to meet his. Desolation glittered in her eyes and her mouth trembled as she said, "The baby's gone."

"What? Where?"

"Her *mother* reclaimed her."

"Her *mother*?" Jack leaned in close. "Who?"

"Lacey Reynolds," Carol said, whispering the name as though she still couldn't believe it.

Lacey? Jack's mind whipped up an image of the girl, one of his sister Peggy's best friends. A chubby kid with a nice smile and plans for the future. Plans that were now pretty much screwed. As a brother, he felt for the kid. Becoming a mother at eighteen wasn't exactly the best life plan he could think of. As the sheriff, he'd have to make a call on Lacey. Soon. "Jesus."

"That about covers it."

"How do we know the baby's Lacey's?" he asked, cop voice stern and harsh. "She could be lying."

"There would be no point in that," Carol said, her voice carrying the weight of the world. "Why would she? Anyway, Phoebe examined her. She has given birth. Phoebe's running a DNA test to be sure, but we all know the truth now."

Carol pushed up from the damp green-slatted bench

and walked toward the Nativity scene. The lights focused on the life-sized statues inside the wood-and-straw manger silhouetted her. She'd only taken a few steps before she stopped again and turned around to look at him.

Jack watched her. A tall, lean woman with long legs, she wore jeans that were worn and faded, her long-sleeved green T-shirt clinging to the curves he knew lay just beneath that soft fabric. Her sun-streaked hair lifted into the rising wind and she scooped it back from her face with an impatient hand. New tears blossomed in her eyes. "Oh, God, Jack. I feel like my heart's been torn out."

He stood up too, and faced her. "I know." He'd seen how much she loved that baby. How Liz had become the center and the focus of her life. Hell, he loved the tiny girl, too. "I know you do."

"I had to leave the apartment," she said, more to herself than to him. "Couldn't stay there. Too quiet. Too . . . empty."

She folded her arms across her chest and rubbed her hands up and down her arms briskly. Quinn walked to her and leaned his whole hundred and fifty pounds into her and Carol staggered under the comforting weight. She dropped one hand to the big dog's back, nearly at her waist, and groaned. "She took her. She just took Liz and I couldn't stop her." Carol's gaze flicked to his. "How could I stop her?"

"You couldn't," he agreed and took the few steps separating them. "I'll have to talk to her, though. She abandoned that baby, Carol."

"Don't."

"That's my job."

She laughed harshly again and this time slapped one hand to her throat as if to ease the pain. "Funny. You keep insisting you're not a cop, but your first reaction to this is *all* cop."

He didn't like the sound of that—all the more because he had to admit it was true. He felt for the girl—but even more for Carol. Although the simple truth was, what Lacey had done was a crime. He'd have to notify his sister Maggie, too, since she was the rep for Social Services. But he figured he could wait for that until tomorrow. He shifted position, tightened his jaw, and looked down into the face of pain.

"I know you feel like shit," he said, "but abandoning a baby is a crime. Even in a 'safe haven' state."

She blew out a breath. "A what?"

"Safe haven. It's a law. Most states have one of some form or another. Anyone can abandon their baby, no questions asked, no charges filed, as long as they drop the kid off at a safe place. Like a hospital. Or a church." He raked one hand through his hair and inhaled sharply. "It still goes against the grain, but it saves a lot of lives. Far fewer kids found thrown away in trash cans."

"Oh, Jesus."

"And the manger in the town square is hardly a designated safe drop-off zone."

"She said she left Liz there because she knew Quinn and I would find her."

"Doesn't matter. I've got to talk to her."

"Now?"

"No." He reached for her. "Carol, I'm sorry about the baby. I really am."

"Me, too," she whispered on a sigh that reached across the short space separating them to tug at his heart.

He closed that space with a single long stride and dropped both hands onto her shoulders. There was nothing he could do to ease the hurt she was feeling over Liz, he knew. But there was still something else to be addressed. And *that* problem, he could handle. "There's something else we have to talk about."

She laughed shortly. "I can't take much more, so tread carefully."

"Fine." He squeezed her shoulders gently and didn't know for sure if it was for her benefit or for his own. Wasn't sure if it mattered. "I've been thinking about this all afternoon, Carol." He swallowed hard, pushed the knot of doubt down his throat and blurted, "I want you to marry me."

"*What?*" Carol stared up at him and blinked frantically, trying to brush the tears aside to clear her vision. "*This* is taking it easy on me?"

"I heard," he said simply, his gaze boring into hers with the intensity of a man determined to do the right thing, no matter *how* much he didn't want to.

"You heard *what,* exactly?" she asked, voice tight as she held on to the slim thread of control that was already unraveling in her fist.

"About the baby," he said. "Not Liz," he corrected, before she could draw a breath. "*Our* baby. I heard about the pregnancy test."

"Oh, sweet God." Her chin hit her chest and a sigh of frustration and misery welled up inside her. It was all she could do to keep it from bursting out and turning into a wail that would shake the leaves off the trees. She slipped out from under his grasp and backed up a step or two. Oh, she so didn't need this right now.

"Why did I come here, again?" she muttered thickly and kicked off into a jerky pace around him that jangled her nerves and pumped her blood in fiery hot bursts. "Oh, yeah. I *wanted* small-town life. I wanted to know people. To be involved. Well, hell. I'm *involved,* all right."

"What're you—"

"It's unbelievable." She shook her head and threw her hands wide. She wanted to tear at her hair. Punch something. Scream. She did none of it. "The CIA should come here. Sign these people up."

She glared out at North Pole Avenue as if she could see everyone in town and blast them all with a steely-eyed glare that even had Jack backing up a step or two. When she shifted that glare to him personally, she watched him brace for attack.

Well, good.

She wanted to hit something.

Only the fact that she was a *lady,* dammit, kept her from hauling off and kicking him.

Gritting her teeth, she muttered, "You can relax. I'm not pregnant."

"You're—" He frowned at her.

"*Not*. That's right." She blew out a breath and didn't even try to read the expression in his eyes. She knew it would be relief and wasn't sure she wanted to see it at the moment. *Oh, that stung, didn't it?* she thought, holding that small twist of pain tight within her. She wouldn't let him see. Wouldn't let him know that after losing Liz, she'd taken that pregnancy test and *prayed* that it would be positive.

She'd never be able to replace Liz and the space the tiny girl had carved into her heart. But another child would have created its own space there and would have eased the misery swamping her.

But no.

An eighteen-year-old girl could get pregnant accidentally—but it seemed a twenty-eight-year old woman couldn't. That bitter disappointment still clung to the edges of her heart, but she knew damn well that Jack didn't share it.

"You're saved," she said sharply, giving in to the urge to snap at something. "A last-minute homer in the bottom of the ninth and all's well that ends well."

"Carol—"

Quinn whined and she stopped long enough to soothe him with a smooth stroke of her hand atop his head. The one constant in her life. Her champion. The one living soul in the world she could absolutely count on to love her no matter what.

Her dog.

Her heart would, she thought, be much better off if she'd just remember that from now on.

"You're safe, Reilly." She shook her head as she stared up at him. "Jesus, you should see your face."

He stiffened, his features turning to stone. "Look, I don't know what you're so pissed at me about. You're not pregnant. You should be glad. And if you had been . . . I was just trying to do the right thing and—"

"Oh, yeah." She stepped in close and poked him in the chest with her index finger. That solid, hard wall of muscle absorbed her small assault as if she hadn't even touched him. "The right thing," she repeated, sounding the words out slowly as if they'd been spoken in a foreign language she didn't really understand. "The right thing is *what,* exactly? Sacrificing yourself on the altar of guilt? Slapping yourself into chains and making me your jailer? No, thanks."

"That's not what I said."

"You didn't *have* to say it," she snapped and started pacing again. Needing to move. Needing the action. She'd felt all evening as if she'd been locked into a small, dark room. And now, her blood pumped hot and thick in her veins and her heart pounded erratically enough that she half-expected it to jump from her chest. "Christ, it's written all over your face, Jack."

He scowled at her, clearly not appreciating being called an open book. Of course he was relieved there wasn't a baby. Wasn't he?

"I take care of my responsibilities, Baker."

"*Oh,*" she sighed dramatically. "Be still, my heart." Then she slapped one hand to her chest, paused for a long moment, and added, "Wait a minute, it *is*."

His jaw muscle twitched and she was delighted to see it. There was nothing she'd like better than to have a fight. Fatigue dragged at her with sneaky claws. She'd cried too much. Her eyes burned and her throat was raw. She felt as though she'd been pulled through hell backward. But she was still standing, dammit.

And she'd be damned if this last, hard hit would take her down.

"God, Jack. You ought to write a book. Men all over the country would be *grateful* to get your advice on how to propose."

"You gonna keep reaming me all night? 'Cause if you are, think I'll sit down."

"Oh, then by all means," she nearly snarled, "have a seat."

He didn't move. Just stood there facing her, with legs braced wide apart in a fighting stance and his arms folded across that broad, muscled chest. In the light of the Nativity, she looked up into those blue eyes of his and saw the same shutters she'd always seen. Even proposing, he'd kept her locked out. Kept himself far away from what was happening.

She was furious all over again.

"Did you seriously think I'd snatch at that proposal?" she demanded, her voice so harsh, it startled Quinn.

"I don't—"

"You don't know?" she finished for him. "Well, le me be the first to tell you, then. *No*. I wouldn't have."

He straightened up to his full, impressive height and did a good job of looming over her. "Do I get a chance to talk here?"

"No. You've had your say." She had to tip her head back to meet his gaze. Behind his head, the nimbus of a street lamp out on the main street shone out around him like a damn halo. Right.

Saint Jack.

The Martyr.

Her eyes stung again and she wanted to sigh. No more tears, she thought. She couldn't do one more bout of crying. Her eyeballs would simply roll right out of her head. Which might take the sting out of this headache that had her wincing even as she faced him down . . . but it wouldn't be worth it.

"Dammit, Jack, I *told* you, that night. I said, if something happened, I'd take care of myself."

"I wouldn't walk away from you. From a kid I made."

"And you think that would make for a happy little scenario?" She walked in close. So close she could smell him. That blend of soap and shampoo and male that was all him. That was just . . . *Jack*. And she nearly weakened. She wanted to lean into that broad chest and have his arms come around her. She wanted to be held and to be told everything would be all right—even if it was a kind, loving lie. She wanted things to be different.

But they weren't and she told herself it was better to get used to the reality and start dealing with it. "You think I'd stand for you resenting me and poor little junior? Or is that what you really want?" The question just occurred to her and it popped out of her mouth before she could censor it. "It's not enough for you to be miserable about your life—you have to make the people around you unhappy, too?"

"Christ, Baker, I was trying to—"

"Help. Yeah, I know that's what you think. But I don't want a pity proposal, thanks. Been there, done that."

"What?" His brow furrowed, his blue eyes narrowed, and he stared at her, waiting for an explanation.

He didn't have to wait long.

Chapter 18

Jack felt like he'd been sucker punched. Didn't make a damn bit of sense, but that didn't seem to matter. For some reason, in his mind at least, he'd never put Carol together with another man. Which was stupid since she hadn't been a virgin the first time they were together. And still, the image of her standing—or worse yet, lying—beside some faceless man, smiling up at him, really bugged the hell out of Jack. "You were married?"

"Engaged," she said sharply, pushing her hair back when a stray wind sneaked through the line of trees and tossed it across her eyes. "Briefly."

His heart pounded. She'd loved someone enough to want to marry him. That's all he could think of. All he could focus on. Who was that man? How much had she loved him? And why hadn't she married him?

She looked up at him, her eyes slowly narrowing. Uh-oh. A dangerous woman, he thought, then silently admitted they were *all* dangerous. Some more so than others. In the weeks that he'd known her, Jack wouldn't have considered Carol scary. But damn if she wasn't making him reconsider his perceptions.

"It was my own fault," she said, shaking her head at

the memory of something that still irritated her. "I never should have said yes. Should have looked him in the eye and said no."

"Didn't have any trouble saying it to me," he pointed out, voice as tight as the steel vise wrapped around his chest.

"True." She gave him an abrupt nod and almost smiled, if you could call that slight twist of her lips a smile. "Maybe that's a good sign. I'm learning and growing. Yay, me."

"Carol—" He didn't know what he was going to say, all he knew for sure was that he hated seeing her so torn up. So furious. So . . . hurt. Dammit, he'd thought he was doing a good thing. The *right* thing. But she was looking at him as if he were a bug she was planning on squishing. And the gleam in her eye told him she'd enjoy it.

"When he proposed, he said he loved me," she said and her voice dropped several notches. The rustling of the leaves in the trees almost drowned her out. Almost. "A part of me didn't believe him, right from the beginning," she admitted, talking now as if Jack weren't even there. "Dammit, I knew he didn't love me, but I wanted it so badly I convinced myself to believe him. It was *so* good to hear those words."

Her head snapped up and she pinned him with a long, frosty look, and when she spoke again, that quiet, wistful quality was missing. "When you've never heard those three words—'I love you'—before, they become . . . *magic*. Like the Holy Grail or something. You spend your life looking for them. Then when you finally *do* hear them"—she wrapped her arms around her chest and held on—"you're willing to overlook a lot of pesky little details—like truth—just for the chance of hearing them again."

"Carol, those words—"

She sucked in a long breath and gave him a tight smile. "This is just perfect, you know?" she muttered darkly, and shook her head as if even *she* couldn't believe what was happening. "I love Liz and lose her—then I love *you*"—she snapped a furious look at him—"and you can see how well that's turned out."

Love?

"Oh, don't panic," she said, gritting her teeth now. "Love isn't contagious." She choked out a harsh laugh. "And it's not fatal. I'll recover."

Jesus.

She loved him.

The dark, cold places inside Jack suddenly opened, blossomed, and the opening was almost painful. A light brighter than anything he'd ever known before shone briefly into the shadows he carried and Jack took an instinctive step forward, then stopped. Even if he tried to hold her now, she wouldn't welcome it.

Three small words.

He knew what value those words held. That's why he was always so damn careful not to say them. As he watched her now though, those three words hovered on the tip of his tongue and it was all Jack could do to bite them back.

The impulse to say those words to Carol, to watch her eyes as he took the chance, wasn't new. It had been building for days now. Maybe longer. But he hadn't said anything. Hadn't even really allowed himself to think it. And if he tried now, she wouldn't believe him and he couldn't blame her.

Besides, love didn't change anything. He'd loved before and it hadn't been enough to keep his world from unraveling.

Then she was speaking again and the moment was lost, anyway.

"Robert—that was his name—said marriage was a natural progression. The next logical step in our relationship."

"And you knocked *my* proposal?" he said, irritation flickering hot and wild inside him—not just at himself, but for the long-absent Robert.

She slanted him a look that told him to back off while he still could. "Robert said that we were compatible. That we would do well together. I wanted children." She stopped, inhaled deeply, then sighed the air out again. "And oh, God, I wanted to be needed."

"Needed?"

"You don't get that, do you?" she demanded, turning on him again with a speed that made a striking rattlesnake look like a snail. "What did you say about love? That it was a *bill*?" Disgusted, she shook her head again. "So to you, being needed is just another way of being trapped, right?"

She didn't wait for him to answer. Instead, she charged on, her words picking up speed, her voice picking up an odd little hitch that made him want to hold her, soothe her, somehow erase the pain he'd brought her. The fire in her eyes kept him quiet. She was furious. Too angry to be calmed by him and too determined to have her say to be quiet now.

"You've always been loved. You had your family." She waved her arms, silently encompassing Christmas and everything in it. "This town. This place. You knew where you fit in. Where you belonged. I didn't."

"I know," he said, his voice more gentle now as he watched old pain mingle with new in the shimmer of her eyes. Everything in him wanted to offer comfort. To pull her into his arms and hold her until the ugly memories faded.

"No you don't," she said. "You couldn't possibly. You don't know what it's like to *never* have the family you always dream about." Her eyes narrowed on him. "You have no idea what it feels like to be trotted out for prospective adoptive parents. To dress up and smile and hope that maybe *these* people will choose you. You learn to slouch a little, too, so maybe people will think you're younger, because everybody knows that only the young ones get adopted. Then, when you're never chosen, you make do. You resign yourself to the state home. Not a home, really, but the closest one you've got."

"Jesus, Carol."

"You don't know what it's like," she continued, refusing to be stopped. "To not *have* a home to run back to when your world collapses around you. To know that people there will love you and welcome you no matter what and do whatever they can to help you."

He started to speak, but she held one hand up like a five-fingered stop sign.

"You don't know what it's like to make a friend and have them disappear into a different foster home." She stepped in closer. "You don't know what it's like to wish, from the bottom of your heart, to be like everybody else. To have a birthday party. Or a picnic. Or a *real* Christmas—the kind you see in movies—with snow and a tree and presents. You can't know. You never once in your life did without any of those things, did you?"

Jack took her accusations and felt each one of them hit him with the force of a slap. He looked down into those whiskey eyes of hers and found his heart aching for the child she'd been. For the pretty little girl with *no one* to call her own. And at last, he stopped feeling sorry for himself long enough to be more concerned for someone else. For Carol. She might think she'd gotten past those old hurts and disappointments, but they were all still there, curled up inside her ready to explode and knock her to her knees. As they had now.

She deserved better—from him, from everyone. She hadn't complained about the crappy hand she'd been dealt. She hadn't curled up in a damn ball and clutched her wounds and pain close, shutting out everything else. Instead, she'd beaten back early disappointments and set out to make the life she'd always wanted.

Life had never been good for Carol, but she'd survived . . . *triumphed.* Shame reached for him and grabbed hold. He'd had everything—had taken it for granted, that love, that security—and then he'd allowed one hideous night to wipe it all away. To destroy not only his past, but his future.

Now he looked into her eyes and found it hard to meet her gaze. "No," he said, "I don't know what that's like."

"Well, you were lucky." Those words came a little sharper. A little stronger, with less pain, thank God.

He'd rather face her fury than her tears.

"Yeah, I guess so." He glanced down at the dog who followed Carol's every step with a guarded gaze. Jack knew just how the animal felt. And she wasn't finished yet.

"When Robert proposed, I said yes. Because I wanted all those things," she said, staring up at him and locking her gaze with his. "I *wanted* to be loved. I wanted children. A family."

That twinge around his heart sharpened as he realized that she'd been disappointed to find out she wasn't pregnant. He tried not to hate the long-gone Robert—as well as himself. "So why didn't you get 'em?"

"A couple of reasons."

"Like . . . ?"

"Well," she said with a sigh of disgust, "there was the bimbo down the hall from him."

"Great guy."

"But the capper was, Robert went out and got a vasectomy."

Jack winced.

"Of course, he didn't bother to tell me about his decision until after it was a done deal."

"Nice."

"Oh, charming," she agreed, pacing again as if she couldn't bear to stand still. Her footsteps pounded against the damp grass and the ever-present wind tousled her hair and carried her scent to him.

Jack swiveled his head to keep up with her progress as she made a wide circle around him. Her hands flew, gesturing as she spoke, and emotions rippled across her features, changing so fast he could hardly keep up.

"He said children would be a mistake. That we got on well together. We would do better as a childless couple."

"Nice guy." Okay, Robert was an asshole. Neither one of them had done right by Carol, but so far, Robert was winning the jerk award.

"I'm not finished," Carol said quickly and he swore he saw lightning, jagged and bright, flash across her eyes as she paused long enough to shake her index finger at him with so much vigor he could only be grateful she wasn't holding a baseball bat.

"His cheating was hard to take, I admit. But the vasectomy tore at me, because he'd *known* how much I wanted children. So, I pressed him, wanting to know exactly *why* he'd had himself sterilized."

That wince again. Jack couldn't help it. Any man's nuts would squeeze up tight at the thought.

"Finally, he admitted that as I was a foster child, we couldn't be sure of my background and it was better not to take chances on procreation."

"Christ." Jack just stared at her. And because he was watching her so closely, he saw the fury pulse back into her eyes and was glad to see it. Anything was better than seeing her hurt. Even if it did mean he was about to get reamed because the weasel Robert wasn't handy.

"I handed him his ring and walked out."

"Good for you."

"It wasn't so hard," she said with a shrug that belied the expression in her eyes.

"He was an asshole."

"Yes, he was," she said, "but at least he was honest."

"Honest?" The word burst from Jack's mouth before he could hold it in. "He slept with a bimbo while engaged to you and then he sneaked off and got himself fixed without telling you and that's *honest*?"

"No, but his reasons were honest. And that at least was something."

"Meaning . . ."

"Meaning, he told me how he really felt."

"Damn if I'll be compared to that jerk and come out the loser." Jack felt his own fury rise to match the raging sea he saw in her eyes.

"You proposed—and I use the word loosely—because you thought you had to." She tipped her head even farther back and met him glare for glare. "Robert did it because he too thought he should."

"And then hacked off his nuts." He shoved both hands through his hair in frustration.

Her fists balled at her sides, and once again, Jack was struck by the urge to hunt for cover. A furious woman was nothing to be sneezed at.

"I said yes to Robert because I wanted to be loved. I wanted the fairy tale—but I realized that marriage without love would be a lot lonelier than being by myself." She pulled in a breath and held it before releasing it on a rush. "I didn't marry him because he didn't really love *me*. Who I am."

"Good call."

She ignored that. "He only wanted to do what he thought was right."

"I think I just landed back in Robert's boat."

"Damn straight. And I wouldn't have married *you* for the sake of a baby," she added quickly. "I want *love*, Jack. I want the whole package. To love and *be* loved. I want kids. I want 'permanent.' "

Jack just looked at her. His insides twisted with regret and pain and shame, dammit. Fine. He'd screwed this up royally. In trying to do the right thing, he'd only insulted her. Hurt her.

He did belong in Robert's boat.

Jack watched her, in the weird half-light thrown by the Nativity scene and then dappled by the shadows around them. He felt the tremors coursing through her body as clearly as though he were holding her to him. And suddenly, his arms ached to do just that.

A huge stab of pain sliced at his heart and he almost reached for his chest to massage it away. True, he'd been living with a throbbing ache in his heart for two long, miserable years. But this was so much more. So much deeper. This pain he'd brought on himself. And there was no one else to blame for it.

She lifted her chin and her hair, driven by the wind,

danced around her head in a blond halo. Her shoulders were squared, her eyes tear-free, and her bottom lip was firm. She faced him proudly and her strength humbled him. She wasn't going to cry again and for that he was grateful.

But she also wasn't going to waste any more time on him. And for that, he was sorry. Hell, he was even sorry there was no baby. And he hadn't expected that. He shouldn't have been anything but relieved. But there was a twist of *disappointment* squeezing his insides that told him nothing was simple.

A part of him grieved for a child who had never existed, just as he mourned the loss of what Carol might have been in his life.

"Tonight," she said, dragging his attention back to her, "when Lacey told me about the boy who'd made her pregnant, she said that he'd told her he loved her. That she was special . . ." Her voice broke on that last word and she had to pause for breath before continuing. "I understood. God help me, I knew just what she meant. Just how much those words could mean to ears hungry to hear them." Her gaze locked with his again and the raw power in those golden eyes slammed him hard. "I *need* to hear them, too, Jack. I need to hear those words said and to be meant. And I won't settle for anything less."

"I'm not asking you to," he argued, though even *he* wasn't on his side anymore. "I told you—I was just trying to do the right thing."

"You want to do what's right?" Her voice was a challenge and her eyes fired sparks at him that should have singed him. "Well, you know what's right, Jack? *Loving* when you get the chance. And *living* every minute of every day." She bit down hard on her bottom lip, then swept right on, clearly on a roll. "But you can't see that. You're too busy beating yourself up for surviving to actually live the life you *could* have. So don't tell me you know what's right, Jack." She shook her head slowly. "Because you don't have a clue."

It stung. All of it. Standing there listening when he wanted to argue but knew he didn't have any ammunition. Years of being a martyr had only brought him pain. Only alienated him from everyone he'd ever cared for. He'd locked himself into a small chamber of misery and snapped like a tiger at anyone who'd tried to free him. He'd hugged his agonies close and used them as a shield to keep the world at bay. But he'd told himself he'd been doing it to protect those around him as much as himself. That excuse didn't really fly now, though. Did it?

"Dammit, Carol," he finally said, when she paused long enough for him to jump in. "You think I *want* it to be like this?"

Impatiently, she scooped her hair back. "If you wanted it to be different," she said, "it could have been." Then she stepped in close to him, looked way up, to lock her gaze with his, and delivered that killing blow a second time. "I *love* you."

His heartbeat staggered slightly and he had to fight against every instinct that clawed at him, making him want to grab her and hold on.

"I'm not afraid to say it," she said, and her tone taunted him. "But you don't have to worry. I'm sure I'll get over it."

Moments ticked past, measured in soft breaths and Quinn's pitiful whine. The wind picked up and danced through the limbs of the trees, sounding like a whispering crowd offering comments on the scene being played out in front of them. From a block or two away came the muffled sound of a dog barking and under it all was the ever-steady rhythm of the sea, rushing in to shore.

Everything had changed for him in the last few weeks, Jack thought. He'd stumbled across Carol and she and Liz had dragged him back into the world of the living. But did he belong there? At best, he was alive only because of a whim of fate—at worst, because he'd allowed his partner—his *friend*—to die, instead.

And if Will had died because of him, did he have the *right* to live happily? He shook his head, tumbling those dark thoughts back into a corner of his mind where they'd fester a while before leaping out at him again.

"Do you want me to move out of the apartment?" he asked, steeling himself for her answer.

Now it was her turn to wince. And that slight stab of pain hit him as hard as it had hit her.

She kept her gaze locked with his. "Are you still going to be here only temporarily?"

He paused. Temporary was the only way he knew anymore. "Yeah."

Carol nodded stiffly, as if even that slight movement ached. "Then there's no point in your moving out. I think we can stay out of each other's way well enough, don't you?"

"If that's what you want."

One corner of her mouth turned up and then flattened again. "That is so very *far* from what I want, Jack." Her voice dropped to a hushed whisper of sound as she added, "But we don't always get what we want, and I should know that better than anyone."

"Carol—"

"Just," she said, lifting one hand to cut him off even

as she started past him, "don't say anything else, okay? It's been a lousy night and anything you can say won't make it better."

"Okay." He shoved both hands into his pockets to keep from reaching for her as she passed him. Her scent stayed with him even as she walked away. Her steps were slow, tired, fatigue dragging her down into the ground as if the park were sitting on quicksand. Even the bells on her shoes weren't tinkling with the same carefree joy he usually associated with her.

Quinn paused beside Jack long enough to look up at him and whine again. Maybe he was losing what was left of his mind, but Jack almost thought the dog was disgusted with him. Hell, join the club. But the moment passed and the big dog hurried to catch up to his mistress.

Jack turned to watch her leave and a tight, cold band wrapped itself around his heart and squeezed. With her hand on the big dog's back, she walked alone in the shadows, and for the first time since he'd known her, she looked . . . *fragile.*

By mid-morning, word about Liz had spread all over Christmas and Jack was standing on Lacey Reynolds's front porch, his sister Maggie at his side.

The house had seen better days. The dark green paint on the shutters was peeling, a porch rail was missing, and the doorbell hiccuped drunkenly as it rang inside the house. The grass needed mowing, the bushes needed trimming, and the screen door flapped loosely around its frame. It was a good old house, but it had been neglected too long and now, Jack thought, it would probably be easier to just raze the place and start from scratch.

"How's Carol doing?"

He shifted his gaze to Maggie, looking trim, professional, and just a little sad around the eyes. She'd seen enough misery in her time at Social Services to be as hardened as Jack. Yet Maggie, like Carol, had found a way to look at life and still smile. Usually. Today though, her empathy for Carol shone from her eyes and sounded in her voice.

"I think she's all right."

"You think?" she asked, one dark red eyebrow winging up. "I thought you and she were, uh—"

"You thought wrong," he said, cutting her off.

"Well, color me surprised."

"Give it a rest, Mag."

But she wouldn't, of course. He hadn't really expected her to.

"She needs you right now, Jack. I know what losing this baby must be doing to her and—"

Impatience leaped from him. "Look. She doesn't particularly want me around right now, so can we just do the job?"

Both eyebrows lifted now and she managed, even though she was at least eight inches shorter than he, to look down her nose at him. And damned if he didn't deserve it.

"Fine, *Sheriff*."

The front door suddenly swung open, sparing Jack the necessity of a reply. Lacey's mother stood in the doorway, blinking at the sunlight like a vampire who'd stayed up too late. "What is it?"

"Mrs. Reynolds, we're here to see Lacey."

She groaned tightly and pushed at the screen-door latch. The door popped open like a cork pushed from a bottle and Jack caught it before it could slam into the house.

"Great. The baby's been screaming all night and now that it's finally asleep, *you* come along and wake me up."

"We're very sorry to disturb you, Mrs. Reynolds," Maggie was saying in that cool, rational tone that used to drive him nuts when they were kids. "But this official visit is necessary to check on the well-being of the child in question and its"—she paused to glance around—"home situation."

Jack smelled liquor, baby formula, and just a whiff of desperation. It was dark in the living room, only the sunlight slanting in behind them to light up the corners of the room. Magazines were scattered across a table, laundry—whether clean or dirty, he wasn't sure—piled on the couch, and the television was tuned to a game show with pretty people and annoying music.

A part of him wanted to rush in, grab the baby, and take her back to Carol. He wanted to walk in her front door, holding that baby, and be the damn hero. He wanted to be *her* hero.

Hell, he *wanted,* as he hadn't wanted in years.

Scrubbing one hand across his face, he pushed that wild impulse aside and stared at the once-blond, now-brassy older woman in front of him. Her eyes were red and her hand shook as she reached for a cigarette and lit it. She sucked in the smoke like it was oxygen for a starved brain, then exhaled it reluctantly.

"Where is Lacey?"

She stared up at him and he wondered if she was just sleepy or still drunk. Then she breathed on him and he figured it was a little of both.

"Are you here to take the baby?" she demanded.

Maggie answered that one. "We're here to check on the baby and speak to your daughter."

"Stupid girl," Lacey's mother muttered as she turned

and headed down the short hall toward a closed door. She took another short drag on the cigarette, then stabbed the air with the fiery tip of it. "Didn't think she was smart enough to hide a pregnancy. Then she turns around and does something idiotic like claiming the kid. Told her she should have left that baby with the shopkeeper. What the hell is Lacey going to do with it?"

She stopped in front of a closed door, gave a brief, perfunctory knock, then opened it and walked inside. Here, Jack thought, Lacey had done all she could to combat the closed, quiet air of defeat clinging to the house. The walls were a cheerful pale yellow, and white curtains fluttered at a window that overlooked a weed-choked flower bed. Posters were tacked to the walls and framed photos cluttered every surface.

The girl herself sprang up off the bed as though she'd been shot and faced them all with a guilty, embarrassed expression.

"They're here to see about the baby," her mother announced, then stepped back, folded her arms across her chest, and tapped one bare foot against the carpet.

Jack's gaze swept the small room and landed on the baby. Asleep on Lacey's bed, Liz's tiny face was scrunched in sleep and she looked in as much distress as her mother. He recognized the blanket covering the infant. Carol had bought it that first week with the baby and had covered her with it every night. Tiny yellow ducks pranced across a soft white fabric and something inside Jack shifted and groaned.

His hands itched to hold her. His heart ached for what he'd lost. What he, Carol, and little Liz had lost.

"Hello, Lacey," Maggie said softly and eased up on the girl as though she were a wild thing poised for flight.

"Hi." She looked from Maggie to Jack to her mother

and back again. Her eyes were wide and filled with tear
she was trying not to shed.

"We've got a few questions," Maggie was saying.

Jack responded to the emotions crowding the girl'
anxious face. She was probably terrified. Wondering i
she'd be going to jail. But jail wouldn't serve anyone a
this point. Maggie had agreed to keep this private a
much as she could. "It's okay, Lacey," he said, wanting t
relieve her of at least this much. "You're not in trouble."

She breathed a sigh of relief that was short-lived a
her mother spoke up again.

"Oh, yes she is," Deb said, stabbing the air with he
cigarette again. "She's a kid. What does she know abou
babies? Nothing. She can't take care of that baby an
I'm sure as hell not going to raise it."

"Mom—"

"No way," the older woman said sharply. "I did m
time in the trenches. I raised you, didn't I? Well, I'm fin
ished. You got yourself into this mess. You can get your
self out."

Jack's teeth ground together. He was helpless. H
couldn't take Liz out of here, and return her to the warmt
and love in Carol's apartment. He couldn't help Lace
against her mother's anger. Rage coiled inside him at th
unfairness of the situation. But anger wouldn't help he
either.

"This isn't really productive," Maggie said.

Deb opened her mouth to say something else, bu
Jack stopped her with a hand on her arm. This, at least
he could give Lacey. "Mrs. Reynolds," he said, keepin
his grip gentle, since she felt like a sack of sticks. "Wh
don't we step out into the living room and let Maggi
and Lacey have a talk?"

"Talk all you want," the woman said, looking bac

over her shoulder at the daughter she'd thought was going to amount to something. "It won't change anything. You're stuck now. Stuck here. Just like me." Deb narrowed her gaze. "For all your fancy talk of college, you're no smarter than me, are you?"

That parting shot left Lacey weeping.

Chapter 19

"I can't believe you had sex and didn't tell me." Peggy glared at her best friend. "And not just sex, for crissake. You got *pregnant* and you *still* didn't tell me."

"I can't believe I didn't, either," Lacey admitted. "I wanted to . . ."

"So what stopped you?"

She shrugged, feeling the weight of guilt drop back onto her shoulders. The hardest part of keeping the secret had been not telling Peggy. Now, trying to explain why she hadn't, felt almost as hard. "It was embarrassing."

Peggy leaned in close from her perch on the end of Lacey's bed. Her red hair stood up in the tiny tufts and spikes it had been trained to adopt and her blue eyes shone with interest and hurt. But her smile was slow and wide. "Too embarrassed to tell *me*? Jesus, Lace. We got our periods together!"

"Yeah, I know." And Mrs. Reilly had explained the whole procedure—from menstruation to eggs and sperm and ovulation—until both of them had wanted to run screaming from the room. Maybe, Lacey thought now, she should have paid closer attention.

"Weren't you scared?"

"Only terrified," Lacey admitted.

"How'd you do it? How'd you have the baby all alone, Lace?"

She'd nearly managed to blank that whole night out of her mind. But still the ragged edges of her memory tugged at her. "When the pains started, I went down to the caves," she admitted, her voice soft.

"At the beach?" Incredulous, Peggy stared at her.

"Yeah." Lacey inhaled sharply. "I stored a bunch of stuff down there ahead of time. Like blankets and towels and water and stuff."

"*Jesus,*" Peggy whispered, clearly impressed. "Did it hurt? Wait. Stupid question. Of course it hurt. But Lacey, how did you do it all alone?"

Lacey's mind took her back to the shadow-filled cave. She heard the lapping of the ocean as the low-tide waves slapped against the shore. It had been cold and dark and terrifying. She could almost smell the damp air and see the pale shadows tossed from her lantern to the rock walls of the cave. The sand beneath her blanket had felt as soft and giving as asphalt and she remembered with exquisite clarity the screaming pain that had lanced through her body again and again.

She shivered slightly, swallowed hard, and said, "I had a book. A midwife book. It told me what to do."

"What if something had gone wrong, though?" Peggy asked, her voice quiet. "You could have died or something, Lace."

"I didn't, though," she said, closing a mental door on the memories. "And after Liz came out, I cleaned her up and took her to the manger and hid in the bushes until Carol and Quinn found her."

"I can't believe you didn't trust me to help you."

"I do trust you, Peg," she said quickly, fervently, needing

her very best friend to believe her. "But I just felt like I couldn't tell *anybody*. I'd been so stupid. And I was so scared."

Peggy's expressive eyes filled with sympathetic tears that she deliberately blinked back. "You weren't stupid, Lace. You just made a mistake, that's all."

"A big one," she said, glancing at the baby again.

"True. So, who's the father?"

Lacey squirmed uncomfortably. "You remember Damian?"

"That guy who worked at the garage outside of town for a while?"

"Yeah."

Peggy thought back and remembered a blond-haired guy with a vine tattooed around his bicep. "Wow. An older man."

"He was only nineteen."

"Older than us." Peggy shook her head and looked at Lacey for a long minute. "How did you hide it, Lace? You must have been so scared."

"I was." She shivered at the memory of being alone and knowing that she was going to have a baby she wouldn't be able to keep. "Only time in my life being fat paid off, though. Nobody noticed anything different about me."

"Not even me." Peggy reached out one hand and squeezed Lacey's fingers. "I'm so sorry. I should have known. Should have seen it."

Lacey squeezed back. "It's not your fault. I did it all."

A couple of minutes of pained silence ticked past until Peggy spoke up again, in an effort to make Lacey smile. "So, was it good?"

"Huh?"

"Sex," Peggy prompted. "The guy. Was it good?"

Lacey closed her eyes, trying to remember. So much had happened since then, it was like trying to imagine something that had happened to somebody else. And oh, God, sometimes she really wished it *had* happened to somebody else. "It's kind of a blur."

Peggy snorted and leaned back. "Then he wasn't any good at it."

Lacey laughed for the first time in days. "Maybe it wasn't his problem. Maybe it was just me."

"Nah." The tiny redhead pooh-poohed that notion entirely with a wave of one small hand. "My sister Eileen says, *every* woman is good at it. You just have to find a man with skill. *That's* why she told me to hold out for more than a quick roll in the back seat with a high school guy." What she said suddenly struck her and she winced and groaned. "God, I'm an idiot. I'm so sorry."

Lacey flinched and couldn't quite hide it.

"I didn't mean anything, honest—" She blew out a disgusted breath. "I just—you know how when my mouth starts moving I can't keep up."

"It's okay. You don't have to be sorry." Lacey knew Peggy wasn't trying to be mean. And hey, it was the truth, wasn't it? She *had* let a smooth-talking guy get her out of her panties. If she'd been smarter, if she'd been more careful . . . Too late to think about that now, she told herself. "Don't worry about it."

"Jesus, Lacey, I should be shot." Peggy slapped one hand across her mouth and still talked. "I should be kicked out of the Best Friends' Hall of Fame and tied up in a kennel loaded with fleas."

Lacey laughed again, and God, it felt good. She could always count on Peggy for that. No matter what, their friendship had endured. They'd always been there for each other. It was the two of them—and sometimes

Donna—against the world. *Until now,* a voice in the back of her mind whispered. *Now everything will change. Peggy's going to college and you're not. She'll make new friends. She'll do all the things you planned, but she'll be doing them without you. You'll be alone.*

A twinge of something sharp and painful sliced at her and Lacey tried desperately to ignore both it *and* that taunting voice. She'd done the right thing.

"Did he know about the baby?" Peggy asked a minute or two later, when the baby's gurgling broke the silence.

"No. I found out after he left," Lacey said, preferring to forget the whole thing. It hadn't been pleasant. It hadn't even been fun. But how could she ever forget, she wondered, when the living proof of that night was lying in a splash of sunlight, kicking her little legs?

Outside, a lawnmower growled from somewhere down the street and the McCorys' dog barked like he was being attacked by aliens. A breeze fluttered into the room beneath the partially opened window and Lacey watched the curtains dance.

"So, what're you gonna *do*?" Peggy sat at the end of Lacey's bed and stared at the baby as if waiting for her head to spin.

Lacey looked down at her daughter and sighed again. She was doing that a lot lately, she'd noticed—sighing, that is. But she was just so *tired.* It had been three days and Lacey felt as though she hadn't slept at all.

Liz cried a lot.

And then there was the whole diaper thing, which was usually pretty gross, and then there was feeding her and burping her and changing her clothes 'cause she burped up something disgusting and then the whole thing started over again and really . . . Lacey just wanted to cry.

But she couldn't.

One of them crying was enough.

"I'm gonna take care of her," she said and hoped Peggy didn't hear the tremble in her voice. Heck, she hoped *Liz* couldn't hear it. Then she remembered Carol covering the baby's ears so she wouldn't hear anything that might upset her and Lacey smiled briefly. But Carol wasn't here now. It was all up to her. She could do this. She loved Liz. She was her daughter. She was *supposed* to take care of her.

"Uh-huh," Peggy said, tearing her gaze from the baby with a tiny shudder and shifting it to her friend. "But what about school? What about the dorms?" Her voice climbed a notch as she added, "And the apartment we were gonna get? It was all gonna be so cool, Lace."

A pang of regret bounced in Lacey's chest and slammed hard against her rib cage. There was so much she had been going to do, she thought. So many things she had wanted to see.

She looked at her baby, lying wide awake and staring up at the slant of sunlight spearing through the window. Plans change, she thought grimly and tried not to feel the sharp pull of disappointment that hovered near the corners of her mind.

"I'll go to community college for a while," she said, lifting one shoulder into a shrug that belied the worry settling over her like a thundercloud. "I can still transfer later."

"How much later, Lace?" Peggy asked, folding her hands together and dangling them between her knees. "I mean, do you wait until Liz is grown up? Or in kindergarten? Or high school maybe? What?"

"I don't know," Lacey said, wishing she knew the

answers. Weren't moms supposed to know everything? If they did, she was in trouble because she didn't. She didn't even know the right questions.

"It's not too late," Peggy said, reaching out to cover Lacey's hand with hers again. "You could talk to Carol. See if she'd take Liz back and—"

Lacey pulled her hand free and shook her head. Maybe she reacted so strongly to the suggestion because she'd thought the same thing herself too many times to count in the last few days. But that would be abandoning her baby twice. And what kind of person would that make her?

"I can't," she said, her voice strong enough, she hoped, to convince not only Peggy, but herself. "I can't just give her away like she's . . . nothing. She's a person. She's my daughter."

"Whoa." Peggy leaned back against the wall. "Weird, but that's the first time I've thought about it like that. You have a *daughter*. I mean, you're a *mother*. How weird is that?"

"Yeah . . ." Pride, fear, and confusion tangled together in her chest, making it almost impossible to draw a breath. Her heart pounded like a sledgehammer against her ribs and she was almost getting used to the bass-drum sound of it in her ears. It was weird. And Lacey didn't know what the heck to do. She'd been so sure of her future, before. She'd worked so hard. So long, to get out of Christmas. To go to school. To become . . . *somebody*. And now . . .

"What's it like?"

"Huh?"

"You know, having the baby. Being the—*mom*."

Lacey looked at her friend, and just for a moment, put aside all but the one emotion that was still strong enough to swamp her when she let it. "The love is amazing, Peg. I mean, it's so *big*, you know?"

Peggy's eyes teared up with emotion and Lacey knew she was lucky to have a friend like her. Peggy hadn't made any judgments. Hadn't yelled at her for not letting her in on the secret. She'd just been there. As she'd always been.

"It must be scary, though," Peggy said quietly.

"Terrifying."

"Is your mom helping?"

Lacey laughed shortly, but felt tears spring to her eyes. She'd really hoped that her mother, once over the shock, would *care*. But Deb Reynolds had meant every word she'd said to the sheriff and Peggy's sister. She wasn't going to help. She hadn't even *held* Liz. Not once.

"No. She says the baby's my mess and I'm the one who has to clean it up."

"Wow." Peggy's eyes widened, but she didn't look surprised. Only sad. "I can't imagine my mom saying that."

"I know." For one tiny moment, Lacey wished that Mrs. Reilly was her mom. Or at least that *her* mom was more like Peggy's. But she'd wished that before and nothing had changed, so what was the point? Besides, *she* was a mom, now.

"You'll be a good mom," Peggy said as if reading Lacey's mind.

"Will I?" she asked, glancing at the baby long enough to feel the tug on her heart. "I want to be, Peggy. But I just don't know how. What does a good mom do, you know? How do I know?"

"Maybe it's something you learn."

She'd thought that once. But if you learn something by watching it, what kind of skills had she learned from her own mother? And what would she pass on to Liz? Those thoughts skittered through her mind like BBs rattling around in a pan.

What kind of life could she give the baby who was now depending on her for everything? Liz would look at her and expect to be taken care of. Loving her wasn't enough. She'd need food and clothes and later books and doctors and maybe dance lessons or gymnastics and—

Panic, pure, hot, and wild, roared through her veins, stealing her breath, tearing her eyes, strangling in her throat.

"What am I supposed to do, Peg?"

Peggy scooted off the bed and sat on the floor beside her best friend. She wanted to help. She just didn't know how. So she figured the best thing she could do was something Maggie had said. Just *listen* when Lacey felt like talking.

"I don't know, Lace," she said, folding her legs Indian style on the worn carpet. "But you love her, right?"

"Oh, yeah."

Peggy smiled. "Then I think you'll figure it out."

"I hope so," Lacey said, reaching up to stroke her daughter's tiny hand.

"The first night was the worst," Carol said firmly and pulled a clean sheet from the pile of laundry.

It felt good to be busy. When she was busy, her arms didn't ache to hold Liz. She wasn't thinking about the baby's sweet face, or the soft sighs she made when snuggling in close to Carol's chest, or the feel of tiny fingers plucking at her neck.

Carol groaned inwardly and tried to shut it all off. But it was impossible.

And it wasn't only Liz she was missing.

The hole Jack's absence had left in her heart ached continually. So staying busy was her only answer.

Her only saving grace.

In fact, she'd been so busy in the last few days, the apartment and the shop below practically gleamed. The scent of lemon oil and soap clung to every surface. The windows were squeaky clean and she could have served dinner on her kitchen floor. But she was running out of things to do and she had no idea what she'd do when she reached the end.

"Honest," she said, mentally crossing her fingers to absolve the lie. "I've been okay since that first night."

"Uh-huh." Phoebe watched her over the rim of her wineglass.

Carol shot her a quick look, then focused on the sheet as she folded it neatly, smoothing her palms along the creases. "I admit it, I did a lot of crying when Lacey took the baby back."

Oh, God, just saying the words aloud unleashed the emotions still churning inside her. Carol's heart pinged, throbbed, then eased back into the steady, constant pain she'd grown accustomed to in the last few days. She took a deep breath in an attempt to steady both the pain and her voice as she said, "It was awful. And the longest night of my life, I think. But I'm better now. It's been three days and I think I'll be okay."

"Of course you will." Phoebe set her glass onto the coffee table and leaned back into the cushions of the sofa. "Even Quinn will recover eventually."

"I hope so," Carol said, letting her glance slide to the open door of her bedroom. The big dog was there, just as he had been for days, lying beneath Liz's empty crib, waiting for her to come home. Wasn't fair, she thought. Poor dog, couldn't understand where his baby had gone to.

But Phoebe was right. Eventually, he'd forget. She'd take away the crib—as soon as she could bear to—and their lives would go back to the way they had been before this summer had happened. And that would be good, right?

They'd been happy. She and Quinn, in their nest. Just the two of them. Then Liz had come along.

And Jack.

Oh, Jack. *Why aren't you here?*

"We'll both be fine." She said it because she needed to hear it. "I've still got my shop and Quinn and—"

"Jack?" Phoebe asked quietly.

"No," she said, and a different sort of agony rippled through her. She hadn't spoken to him since that night in the square. Since she'd turned down a proposal he hadn't wanted to make. Since she'd turned her back on her dreams and lost the child she loved all in one night. "No, I don't have him, either."

And she so wanted him. She heard him moving around in his apartment and it was all she could do to keep from crossing the narrow hall and pounding on his door. She wanted to scream at him. To tell him to wake up to the possibilities. She wanted him to swing her up against him and wrap his arms around her. She wanted to hear his heartbeat beneath her ear as he cradled her to his chest. She wanted to mourn Liz's loss with him, because she knew he loved that baby, too. She wanted so damn much. And she wasn't going to get any of it.

Because he wouldn't come after her.

And she couldn't go to him.

Not again.

"I could have him killed for you."

Startled, Carol looked over at her friend. Phoebe's

eyes sparkled with sympathy, anger, and just a dash of wry humor. Phoebe knew what this was costing her. Her lies weren't clever enough to hide her pain from her friend.

"Thanks," Carol said, "but I'll pass."

"That's a good sign," Phoebe told her. "When you no longer want bloodshed, you're getting over the bastard."

"Right." But she wasn't. Carol had the distinct feeling that she'd never really be over Jack Reilly. Oh, she'd learn to live without him, as she'd learned to do without so many things in her life. But the emptiness would always be there. The wish that things had been different. The dream of what might have been would torment her when she tried to sleep.

Why hadn't he loved her enough to live?

Because he did care. She knew that. She felt it. He just didn't care *enough*.

Nodding, she set the folded sheet aside and reached for the next one in the basket. "You don't have to worry about me, Phoeb."

"I like worrying. I'm good at it."

Carol smiled and silently thanked heaven for her friend. Strong. Dependable, predictable Phoebe. It was good to have at least one person in your life you could count on.

"Did I tell you I'm thinking about volunteering for Doctors Without Borders?" Phoebe asked suddenly.

"Uh, no." Predictable, she'd just been thinking. Seems she was wrong about a lot of things. "Since when?"

"Actually," her friend said, "I've been thinking about it since before Cash left town."

"That'd be wonderful, Phoebe," Carol said, grateful for the shift in conversation. She couldn't keep talking about Jack and Liz. Couldn't keep thinking about them.

Not if she wanted to stay sane. And sanity was all she had left.

She shook another clean sheet out with a snap of both wrists. "You'd be great at—" Her words dried up. Her throat closed tight.

One of Liz's baby blankets flew free of the sheet it had clung to in the dryer. The thin yellow fabric floated on the still air for a heartbeat or two, then drifted to the floor and lay there like a banner.

Carol couldn't stop looking at it. Her eyes filled, her heart broke, and she dropped to the arm of the sofa, hand at her mouth to muffle the sobs crowding her throat. Her gaze still locked on that blanket, she muttered thickly, "Oh, God, Phoebe. I miss her so much. I miss them *both* so much."

Phoebe jumped up, came around the end of the couch and plopped down beside her. Drawing Carol close, she wrapped both arms around her and rocked, as she would have an injured child. Stroking Carol's hair back from her face, she whispered soothing nonsense and waited for her friend's heart to mend.

Journal entry

> *I don't know what to do. Liz won't stop crying. I tried to make her stop, but she doesn't want to eat. She keeps screaming and Mom's really pissed now and banging on the door. But that only makes Liz cry harder. I'm so tired, too. Feels like I haven't slept in weeks. And I think Liz knows that I don't know what's wrong. She looks at me and I think she's wishing she had a* real *mom. One who knows stuff.*

But I'm all she's got.
I just want to run away.

Jack felt like a lowlife.

"You down far enough yet?" Sean asked, sitting in the chair opposite his brother. "Or would you like me to kick you a little just for the hell of it?"

Jack shot him a look. "You'd have to crawl down pretty far to reach me."

"Might be worth the effort."

The living room at the rectory, the priests' house, was cozy. The furniture was worn just enough to be friendly and even the air in the place seemed . . . peaceful. Which was why he'd ended up here, he supposed. He needed a little peace and he sure as hell wasn't getting any at the apartment.

Not with Carol just across the hall.

Only steps away from him, and she might as well have been on the moon. As good as her word, she'd been so polite the last few days he practically had frostbite. She smiled, and nodded if she passed him in the hallway and pretty much treated him like the inconvenient tenant he was.

And everything in him ached to go back.

To turn back the clock so he could reclaim what he'd found and appreciated too late.

Jack fell back into the burgundy leather chair and the squeak of the leather was the only sound for a long minute. Finally, he shifted his gaze to his brother's patient stare. "I screwed it all up."

"Big surprise."

"Thanks for the support."

"Hey," Sean said, lifting his beer to take a drink. "I'm Father Supportive. But I've been your brother a lot longer than I've been your priest. And I'm here to tell you, Jack. You really made a hell of a mess of things."

His fingers curled around the cold bottle of beer in his hand and his thumb idly traced the damp label. Brain racing, heart pounding, he admitted, "I miss her."

"I know."

"She's like the air, Sean. I can't draw a breath without missing her."

"Jack—"

"I thought I could be with her—" He broke off, pushed himself out of the chair, and stalked across the room to the fireplace. Leaning his forearm on the oak mantel, he stared down into the cold, empty hearth and studied the remnants of ashes from long-ago fires as if looking for evidence. "*Care* for her—and not lose myself."

"You didn't lose yourself, Jack," Sean said with a grunt of disgust.

"Didn't I?" He half-turned to shoot another look at his brother, sitting on the worn, tapestry-covered sofa. "Am I the man I was when I first came home?"

"No." Sean smiled and shook his head. Standing up, he walked across the room and stood beside the brother he'd always looked up to. Admired. Loved. And for the first time in two years, he saw the man he'd always known. The man he'd been waiting impatiently to see again. "*No,* you're not that man anymore. You're the man you used to be, Jack." He reached out and clinked his beer against his brother's in a quiet toast. "And can I just say . . . it's about time."

Jack swayed as if the words had had physical impact as well as an emotional one. Simple words that struck such a note of truth inside him that he was staggered by it. That was it, he thought, his brain racing to catch up to his heart. The last few days, he'd wondered why the pain that had been such a constant companion for the last two years had suddenly shifted, taking on a new and more disturbing ache.

But the simple truth was, he wasn't in mourning for the past anymore. Now he was mourning the future he might have had. And a chance at life that had been handed to him like a gift he'd been too stupid, too wrapped up in his own misery, to appreciate.

Shadows inside him drifted to the side, parting like the Red Sea in front of Moses. And the Promised Land stretched out in front of him, if he had the strength and the will to risk it.

CHAPTER 20

Christmas came to the rescue.

The people in town were determined to surround Carol with so much love that she wouldn't miss Liz.

Oh, no one actually *said* so, but Carol knew what they were up to. Her shop had never been as crowded with people as it had in the last few days. Not just the tourists, looking to find a special slice of Christmas in the middle of summer—the locals had kept up a steady stream in and out of her shop. The bells over the doors jangled out a welcome every few seconds, it seemed, and Carol was just as busy chatting as she was ringing up sales.

It felt . . . *good.*

Her friends and neighbors, the people she'd come to love, had all gone out of their way to let her know they cared. That she was a part of them. A part of the town. That she belonged.

She wasn't alone anymore.

Not really.

Carol leaned her elbows on the shiny glass countertop and watched as Mavis Donaldson and Edna Hawkins laughed and visited in front of the candle display. The two elderly women were her latest visitors and they hadn't stopped cheerfully arguing since they'd stepped into the shop.

Her gaze warmed as she realized that these women and all the others like them had given her a gift. They'd made her realize something very important.

All her life, Carol'd wanted a family. She'd ached for the normalcy of a husband and children of her own. A place where she would be loved and needed. Then when Liz and Jack came along, she'd built a perfect little fantasy world only to have it crumble beneath her feet.

And though the pain had been staggering, in the last few days she'd discovered something along with the misery. She *was* needed. And she belonged to this place, this town.

She *had* a family.

The people here had opened their arms and welcomed her inside and now they were doing all they could to help her through a rough time. What else was that but family?

"Carol?" Edna called out. "This big red cinnamon candle? How much?"

"For you Edna, five dollars."

"Five dollars? For a candle?" Edna's pale blue eyes went wide behind her bifocals.

"For heaven's sake, woman," Mavis said with a shake of her permed, steel-gray head. "Where've you been living? Can't buy anything for less than that anymore." Shooting Carol a quick glance, Mavis assured her with a wink, "If she doesn't buy it, I will."

"Didn't say I wasn't going to buy it, you old bat," Edna countered, tightening her grip on the fat pillar candle. "Carol, don't you listen to a word my sister tells you, hear?"

"Yes, ma'am." Carol grinned and it felt good to smile again. Felt good to see the natural pattern of her days fall back into place. This summer had been a dip in an otherwise straight road. A wonderful detour—but now she was back on the highway.

She would survive.

It wouldn't be easy, but nothing in her life had been easy and she'd made it this far, hadn't she?

Quinn pushed himself to his feet and whined as he came around the counter, then stopped, staring toward the door. She stared at the dog, swallowed, then held her breath and slowly swiveled her head to follow his gaze.

Her stomach pitched, her heart lurched, and a swirl of sensations stuttered through her system.

Jack, his features carved in stone, stepped into the foyer and paused long enough to look through the glass door of the shop, directly at her.

Even from a distance, his eyes held the power to slam into her with a fierceness that weakened her knees and shattered her defenses. Her brain knew that it was over between them, but it seemed her body—and her heart—hadn't gotten the message. Gazes locked, it was as if the world had slipped away, leaving just the two of them, separated by far more than a shining pane of glass.

Quinn surged forward. The trance holding Carol in place snapped. She curled her fingers around the big dog's collar and held on when he would have rushed across the shop to either greet—or *eat*—Jack.

At that same moment, Jack nodded at her, then turned and headed for the stairs and the apartments above. He didn't glance her way again.

The dog whined and strained forward, tugging at Carol.

"No, Quinn," she murmured, "you go lay down."

Reluctantly, he turned around and took up his spot behind the counter again.

Carol drew in a long, shaky breath and held it, hoping to steady the fluttering in her heart. It didn't help. She stared at the empty foyer and told herself for the hundredth time in the last few days that she would be all right.

She'd begun to see light cresting from behind the dark cloud that had settled over her so many days ago. And she wouldn't go back into that darkness.

She still ached for Liz—and probably always would. That kind of soul-deep agony just didn't disappear. It would fold itself into the corners of her heart and throb occasionally, just to remind her she was human. And she could live with that. Especially because she knew she'd still be able to see the child. To watch Liz grow up in the town that had become home.

Jack, though, was a different story. Gaze still locked on the spot where Jack had stood only moments before. She felt the residual sizzle in her blood and the regret pooling in the pit of her stomach.

Once Jack left, it would be over and the dream would go with him. She wouldn't see him again, and though it killed her to admit it, she thought that was probably best. Seeing Liz would ease her heart. Seeing Jack and not being able to be with him would tear it apart.

Hours later, Lacey paced the length of her room, then turned around and made the same trip back again. If she'd been walking in a straight line, she thought, she might have already walked to Mexico or something.

She stopped by the window and stared out at the night beyond the glass. Lamplight shone from the windows of the other houses on the street. That idiot dog down the street was still barking at nothing and the wind slipping in under the window sash was cold and damp, sliding in right off the ocean.

Lacey shivered, but didn't close the window. That small connection to the outside was all she had to remind her that she wasn't completely alone.

She felt like a prisoner, trapped in a cage of her own design.

In her arms, Liz wailed with an ear-splitting shriek that seemed to drive into Lacey's head like little spikes. Her head pounded, her temper popped, and her heart jumped and raced nervously.

"What's *wrong*?" Lacey cried and didn't even notice that her voice was hitting the same notes as Liz's screams. She bounced the baby in herky-jerky motions, frustration bubbling through her bloodstream. "I don't know what you *want*." She stared down into the baby's features, dark red with fury and twisted in pain. "How'm I supposed to *know*? Why won't you stop crying? Please, please, *please* stop." She jiggled the baby desperately, the jerking motion soothing to neither one of them. Her arms tightened around the tiny girl and Liz squirmed, as if trying to escape.

Her little cheeks burned a bright red and her eyes looked shiny. Her forehead felt hot and she wouldn't drink her bottle. Was it from all the crying? Was she sick? Was she *dying*? "What is it, Liz?" Lacey said on a tight, desperate moan, her voice breaking along with her heart. "Why won't you stop crying? Why can't you tell me what's wrong? Why am I asking *you*?"

She walked again, with a hurried stride that fed off the frustration and desperation churning inside her. Ten quick steps to the wall, turn around, ten steps back to stop in front of the dresser. In the mirror above the dresser, Lacey caught her reflection and hardly recognized the girl in the glass.

Her blond hair was dirty, tucked behind her ears. Her eyes were swollen from crying and her lips were thinned into one grim line across her face. She reached up and rubbed her eyes while still jiggling Liz, hoping for a miracle.

But miracles didn't happen when you most needed them.

She blew out a breath and stared around her. The walls were closing in. She was pretty sure the room was shrinking because she suddenly felt like she couldn't breathe.

Liz jerked and squirmed in her grasp again, as if the infant was doing all she could to jump out of Lacey's arms and run away. Lacey knew just how the kid felt.

She wanted nothing more than to run screaming out of the house, hit the street, and keep right on running. If she ran fast enough and far enough, she might be able to forget that Liz was here—that Liz *needed* her. That she was all the baby had.

That she'd *asked* for this.

Oh, God. How had everything gotten so screwed up? How had she lost so much? How had she ever thought she'd be able to take care of a baby?

Tears stung Lacey's eyes and she blinked them back as the baby's face blurred and went out of focus. All Lacey wanted to do was crawl into her own mother's lap and be held. To be told that everything would be all right. That she'd done the right thing and that they'd get through this mess together.

A harsh jolt of laughter scraped her throat. *That* wasn't going to happen. Deb Reynolds hadn't been the cuddling kind of mother in *way* too long. And she'd already made it clear that Lacey and the baby were on their own.

On their own.

On *her* own.

Tears she couldn't stop and didn't bother to hide overflowed her eyes and rolled along her cheeks, dropping onto Liz's face like warm rain.

"I can't do this," Lacey murmured, hearing the shake and quiver in her own voice as it strained to be heard above the baby's incessant wails. "I wanted to. I really did. But I can't. I just can't. I'm sorry, I'm *sorry*." Shaking her head, she turned around, laid the baby down in the middle of her bed, then backed away, like a war-weary soldier keeping a cautious eye on a ticking bomb.

"I can't do it. I suck at the mom thing. You won't stop *crying*. You won't be quiet. God, just be *quiet*!" Her own helpless scream lifted into a horrifying harmony with the baby's. Cringing at her own blind panic, Lacey whispered, "Please. *Please* stop crying." She hiccuped and gasped in a fast breath when the baby's screams only intensified. "I can't do this, Liz. I just can't. I don't know what you want. I don't know what to do. I don't have anybody to *ask*."

She shook her head and her dirty hair slapped at her cheeks. "I thought I could do it." She backed up another step, then another. "I really tried." One more step. Her calves bumped into her desk chair and she automatically stepped around it, never taking her gaze from the screaming baby. "I did try. I wanted to. I can't."

The baby's screams got louder. As if Liz knew she

were being abandoned again and was determined not to be forgotten so easily.

Lacey clapped both hands to her ears as hot tears of misery streaked her face. "Stop. Just stop crying! Stopit-stopitstopitstopit . . ."

Liz flailed her arms and legs, tossed her little head back and forth, and screeched like a tiny demon.

Lacey gasped for air to draw into her heaving lungs, then hit the doorway, turned around, and ran. Liz's screams followed her. Chasing her down the hall, through the living room and kitchen and right out the back door. Like a howling ghost, those cries swirled around her in the darkness, grabbing at her, no matter how far she ran.

In the middle of the yard, Lacey stood barefoot on the grass, feeling the dew, cool on her feet while the cold ocean wind slapped at her, as if trying to push her back into the house. To deal with the mess she'd created. To take care of the child she'd claimed to want so desperately.

"I can't go back," she whispered brokenly, staring up into the night sky. Her gaze fixed on just one of the thousands of twinkling lights and she talked directly to it, as though it were a hole in Heaven's floor and her voice was headed directly to God.

"I can't. I know I should. I know she's mine. But I *can't*." She shook her head, pushed her hair back from her face, and let the tears fall. "I feel like I'm all twisted up inside. Like I can't breathe. If I stay, I might get mad at her. And I can't get mad at her, she's just a baby. Oh, please . . . tell me what to do. *Help me*."

But Heaven must have been closed for the night, because no thunderous voice echoed out of the sky.

There was no band of angels flying to the rescue. There was only the wind. And the baby's screaming. And her own pounding heart.

The baby's cries echoed on and on around her, drifting through the house and out the open door to lie like a smothering blanket atop her. Lacey dropped to her knees as the tears raged and fought inside her.

Misery, anger, frustration, pooled together, whipping through her system until she shook with the force of the emotions. Her head pounded in time with the racing beat of her heart and Lacey felt as though her brain was about to dribble out her ears.

Covering her face with her hands, she listened to the wind rustle the leaves of the trees. She listened to the distant sound of a train traveling along the coast. She listened to the throbbing punch of her own heartbeat.

And she listened to the baby scream.

On and on and on.

She wanted to run.

She wanted to get away.

She was a terrible person.

A worse mother.

God.

She had to get out.

Carol propped her feet up on the coffee table, picked up the bowl of popcorn, and settled back into the sofa cushions. Quinn lay on the floor right in front of her, his head tipped up, resting on her leg.

"Don't worry," she said, catching the big-eyed look her dog was sending her way. "There's enough popcorn for you, too."

He woofed his thanks, then snapped the kernels she tossed him out of the air.

"Okay, tonight it's a *Stargate* marathon, so no talking, right?" Carol reached over, rubbed Quinn's head, and told herself she was glad to have everything back to normal. She'd taken the crib down an hour ago and had only paused a time or two to cry a little at the sad emptiness of it. Tomorrow, she'd return it to Maggie and move on, as she'd moved on so often in her life.

Quinn nudged her knee again, looking for more popcorn, and she obliged him, filling her palm. Delicately, he nibbled at them, brushing her hand with his warm breath.

Without the crib to remind him of what he'd lost, Quinn had begun to act like his old self. And so, Carol thought, was *she*. Picking up the remote, she punched in the right channel and focused on fiction rather than reality.

The knock at her door had her grumbling even as she tripped over Quinn on the way around the sofa. "Do you have thumbs?" she asked. "Can you open the door? No, I don't think so. So why not let me go first?"

He waited by the door, a friendly sentinel, ready to welcome or defend.

Carol turned the knob, pulled the door open, and met Lacey's tear-filled gaze.

"Oh, God, Carol, the baby won't stop crying. Maybe she's sick or something."

Carol's stomach pitched, and when Jack's door opened across the hall, she didn't even glance at him. All she could see was the tear-streaked face of the girl in front of her and Lizardbaby, lying in the crook of her arm. Everything inside Carol leaped up in joy and she tried hard to get a rein on her heart's instinctive reaction. But how could she when the child she loved so much was there, within reach again?

As if demanding the attention that was her due, little Liz screwed up her tiny features and let loose with a howl that snapped everyone into action.

In response to the baby, Quinn moaned and sounded like a freight train as he pushed past Carol and moved to stand beneath his baby. Lacey jiggled the infant in a frantic, herky-jerky motion that told Carol the girl was walking the fine edge of control.

Jack stepped out of his apartment and Carol moved at the same time, edging closer to Lacey and the baby.

"Everything okay?" he asked.

"Fine," she said, not trusting her voice to work on more than a one-word answer.

His features tightened, but he didn't go back into his own apartment. Instead, he turned away from Carol and expertly scooped Liz out of Lacey's arms. Instantly, the baby quieted. Silence dropped over the three people clustered together in the tiny hallway lit only by the Christmas-tree sconce. Lacey stared at the baby, hurt confusion dazzling her eyes. "How did you . . ."

"She probably sensed how tense you were, that's all," Carol said quietly, trying to quell the urge to grab the baby from him. She remembered just how good he was with Liz. How the baby had settled for him and no one else and she wondered why it was he couldn't see it. Couldn't see how much he had inside him to give.

And she wondered how she would ever live without him.

"She's going to sleep," Jack said and swayed gently from side to side, easing the baby's tiny hiccups of distress. Quinn moved in close, nudging his nose up against the child, leaning into Jack and whining in sympathy.

"I couldn't make her stop," Lacey said, her face crumpling. Fresh tears streamed from her eyes and ran unchecked down her cheeks. "She's been crying forever and she wouldn't stop." The girl's voice rose and fell like waves on a choppy sea. She looked from Carol to Jack and back again, carefully keeping her gaze from landing on the now-sleeping baby.

"Nobody has all the answers," Carol said, stepping close enough to rub Lacey's back with long, gentle strokes. "You're doing the best you can."

"It's not enough," Lacey said, and at last looked at her daughter. Shaking her head fiercely, she repeated, "It's not enough for her. She deserves better than me. Better than what I can give her."

"It's okay. Liz is all right now. Everything will be all right." Carol wrapped her arms around the girl and held on, sensing that Lacey was hanging on tight to the unraveling threads of control. The girl curled into her, laying her head on Carol's shoulder and sobbing as though her heart were being ripped out of her chest.

"You did the right thing coming here, Lacey," Jack said softly.

"I needed help," she said.

"And you were smart enough to get it," Jack told her.

The girl sent him a grateful, tear-filled look, then inhaled sharply and turned back around. "Nothing's all right, Carol. Nothing is." She wrapped her arms around Carol's waist and clung to her as a drowning man would grab at a lifeline. "I can't do it. I tried. I really did. But I can't do it."

Carol's heart lurched painfully in her chest. Hope was a desperate cry through her brain. Her blood roared through her veins and her stomach did a quick spin. Her emotions churned and charged through her mind, one after the other in a crazy parade of color and sound. She didn't know what to think. What to dream.

Lacey pulled her head back to look at Carol. Ignoring the man and baby behind her, she met Carol's gaze squarely, and in a voice that dripped with shame and regret, she said, "Would I be a terrible person—a terrible mother—if I asked you to take Liz?"

Carol's knees went weak at the same time that yearning rushed in to fill her heart so completely, it ached in response. "Lacey . . ."

"You love her," the girl said, her words tumbling from her mouth in a torrent that wasn't slowed down by little things like commas or periods. "I know you do because of how you treated her before you knew about me and I know I really hurt you when I took her away and I know I don't have the right to ask you to be my baby's mother, but I can't do it, Carol. I tried and I just can't do it because moms are supposed to *know* stuff and all I know is how much I *don't* know. And if I keep her"—she tossed a glance at the sleeping baby lying in the sheriff's arms—"I'll mess it up and I'll ruin things for her when she doesn't deserve that, you know?"

At last, she ran out of breath and steam. It was as if all the air left her body at once and she slumped, from the top of her head right down to the toes of her sandals.

Stunned and too overcome to speak, Carol felt the sting of tears fill her eyes. Her vision blurred as she watched a girl become an adult before her eyes. And pride rippled through her.

She risked a glance at Jack and saw naked emotion in his eyes. Pleasure for her, and sympathy for Lacey. If there was another, deeper emotion there as well, she didn't identify it. Because what would have been the point?

She drew in a breath, then reached up to cup Lacey's face in her hands. This girl, suffering the pangs of guilt and defeat, was the one important thing right now. The one person she had to reach. Had to convince. Staring into those blue eyes so filled with despair and shame, Carol felt another solid tug on her heart.

"I'm proud of you, Lacey," she said, speaking slowly, clearly, willing the girl to believe her.

Lacey's bottom lip trembled and she blinked at the tears crowding her eyes. Soul-deep confusion glittered in those watery blue eyes, but along with that emotion was another. Hope. "*Proud* of me? But I messed up everything."

"No." Carol spoke quickly, shaking her head for emphasis. "No, you didn't." Smoothing the girl's tangled hair back from her face with a gentle touch, she smiled through the tears clouding her own vision. "You wanted to love Liz, there's nothing wrong with that. You wanted to take care of your baby, that's good, too."

"But I failed."

"This isn't failure," Carol said, and dipped her head to make sure Lacey was looking directly into her eyes as she said, "This is growing up. This is realizing that what you *want* to do isn't always what you *should* do."

She thought about that for a long minute, never looking away from Carol's steady gaze. Breathing slowly, deeply, easing back from the brink of despair.

"You think?" A world of longing colored those two words.

"Oh, yeah." Carol pulled Lacey in close for another tight, brief hug. "I *know*."

The girl nodded and swiped away her tears before glancing at her daughter again while speaking to Carol. "Would you want to, you know, *adopt* her, so you could be her real mom?"

Carol's heart squeezed tight in her chest and she had to fight to speak past the huge knot lodged in her throat. "I love Liz, Lacey. I always will. And I'd love to be her mom."

"Good." Lacey nodded, then for the first time since arriving at Carol's door, she smiled. Faintly at first, but it was at least a smile. "And I can still see her, too, when I come home from school and stuff?"

"Anytime you want," Carol assured her.

A soul-deep yearning careened through her system as Carol watched Lacey gently take Liz from Jack's arms. Once his hands were empty, he shoved them into his jeans pockets as if he didn't know what to do with them anymore.

Liz squirmed, screwed up her little face, then settled uneasily into sleep again, her soft breaths huffing into the stillness. Lacey ran one finger over the baby's cheek. "I really do love her."

"I know," Carol said, her voice pitched low enough to be a lullaby. "Me, too."

Nodding again as if reassuring herself that she was doing the right thing, Lacey handed the baby over and Carol cradled Liz close, feeling the slight weight in her arms slide right down into her heart.

Where she belonged.

"Why don't we go inside, Lacey?" Carol said, barely able to tear her gaze away from the child she held so closely.

"Okay." The girl blew out a breath that seemed to

shudder right through her, then she turned and went into the apartment.

Left alone in the hallway, Carol and Jack stood separated by no more than a foot of empty space. The indistinct light threw shadows across his features and made his expression that much harder to read. In her arms, Carol held the baby she loved—and within reach was the man who could make the dream complete.

Within reach and yet so far away.

"I'm glad for you," he said, his voice rumbling along her nerve endings to sizzle and pop in the pit of her stomach.

"Thanks, Jack." Throat tight, her heart ached now only for him. For the other missing piece of the whole.

Jack stepped in closer. She could smell him. That faint, indefinable scent that screamed inside her and made her think of long, dark nights spent wrapped in his arms. His gaze moved over her hungrily, burning her flesh as surely as though he'd touched her.

"Carol, I—"

"Carol?" Lacey's tremulous voice wobbled from inside the apartment. "Can I have a Coke?"

"Sure."

Whatever he might have said was lost in the shattered spell lying between them. And maybe it was just as well, Carol thought as she took a single step back. She couldn't bear to hear another apology. Couldn't watch him turn his back on what might have been, one more time.

"I've gotta go," she said, eager now to have Liz back home. To savor the richness of having a child to love. To protect. To help her forget the wildness she saw in Jack's eyes and the craving for more that rippled through her.

Giving Jack one last look—because really, how could she help herself?—she closed the door, leaving him where he'd wanted to be.

On the outside.

CHAPTER 21

Jack slammed his fist into the wall and hardly felt the pain. Impossible to worry about that simple discomfort when his heart—his soul—was torn with grief and misery.

His arms felt empty, now that the feather-light weight of the baby was gone from them. His heart was even emptier because he'd lost Carol. Again. And the only person he had to blame was himself.

Shaking his aching fist, he whirled around to face the silent apartment. Shadows darted around the edges of the room, taunting him, reminding him that *he* was the one who'd stepped away from the light. He was the one who'd walked willingly back into the heart of the darkness that had been his home for two years.

His conversation with Sean still ringing in his ears, Jack knew exactly what he had to do. His gaze shifted to the far corner of the room. To the cardboard box his lieutenant had sent from LA.

"If you want a damn future—and you *do*," he said aloud, mainly because the silence was devastating, "then first you have to bury your past."

He stalked across the room, grabbed up the heavy box, and carried it to the sofa. He dropped it onto the cushions,

then before he could lose his nerve, ripped at the strap
ping tape holding the box closed. His heart slamme
against his rib cage, his breath caught in straining lung
that felt like balloons filled to near bursting.

Jack swallowed back the tide of emotions raging insid
him. He'd avoided this box for days. Never considere
opening it until recently. Never *would* have considered i
if not for Carol.

Longings, cravings, rose up in him and nearly stran
gled him. He wanted to live again. Wanted to be the ma
he'd once been. The man Carol and Liz deserved.

With the cardboard flaps thrown open wide, he stare
down into the remnants of his past as the chains holdin
him to it tightened around his throat. Crap from his desk,
photo of his ex-wife, a snapshot of him and Will togethe
at a softball game. The commendation he'd received fo
killing that boy in the alley.

Memories, good and bad, charged through his brain
one after the other, until they were nothing more than
blur of color and sound. He inhaled deeply and smelle
the past as it reached out for him.

Steeling himself, Jack reached into the box, and almos
instantly, his fingers curled around a videotape. The tap
of the shooting. The piece of evidence that had saved hi
ass. Taken at the scene by an interested bystander at a
upstairs window, the tape had upheld the story he'd tol
IAD. Internal Affairs had then cleared him of any wrong
doing. But Jack hadn't been able to accept that. His frien
dead, his wife's accusations ringing in his ears, Jack ha
picked up the burden of blame and strapped it to his back

Carol was right.

He had been a martyr.

But Judgment Day was finally here. Fist closed ove

the videotape, he walked to the television, slapped the tape into the VCR, and pushed PLAY.

The screen jumped to life and the tape flickered, rolled, then settled again. The film, taken by a local man hoping to catch footage of stray lightning, started out focused on the rain-choked sky. The camera jumped, the cameraman cursed, then, at the sound of a racing engine, swung the lens down to focus on the alley two stories below.

Jack watched as his squad car roared into the darkness, headlights slicing through the curtain of rain, illuminating every drop until they glittered like diamonds. A torrent of water poured along the alleyway, plastic bags and crumpled papers sailing on the current, looking like a poor man's boat parade. Videotape couldn't recapture the stench of that damned alley, but it seemed to Jack that the smells oozed from the television, reaching for him, trying to drag him back.

The sounds rushed at him with eagerness. The car engine, the pounding of the rain, the car door opening as Will stepped out before the car had stopped rolling.

Jack saw himself climb out of the car, squinting into the rain, just a step or two behind Will as they headed into the inky darkness, looking for a killer.

The first shot erupted and Jack jolted in the comfort of his living room. He saw the flash, watched himself instinctively duck as the bullet pinged into the wall behind him. He saw Will turn and stare at him blankly as if trying to figure out what had happened. Jack's hands fisted on his knees, his gut twisted, as he heard his voice shout from the past, "*Get down!*"

But it was too late. The second shot came too fast. Too accurately. Jack watched the look of stunned surprise etch itself onto Will's face just before he staggered backward, collapsing into an overfull Dumpster and splashing down face up, into the dirty river at his feet. Trash spilled over the edge of the dirty brown Dumpster, falling into Will's face with the same steadiness as the raindrops pelting him.

Jack groaned, old pain new again, tearing at him with claws of memory and talons of regret.

It all seemed to move so slowly, he thought now, watching the scene play out like a badly written movie. But that night, seconds had become hours, minutes were days. The shooter kept firing. One shot after another, wild, crazy shots. Hitting Will had been some terrible stroke of luck—or fate. Jack couldn't get to his partner. His friend. He saw himself trapped behind the car, saw the fury, the pain on his own face, and remembered the sense of helplessness. Of inevitability.

He knew what was coming next and braced himself to relive it. At the next muzzle flash, Jack took a chance. He stood up and fired three rounds in quick succession.

A scream knifed through him, echoing from the television, pulling him back into the nightmare, back into that stinking alley. He watched himself run first to the shooter, making sure the gun was out of play. He felt again the hideous shock of finding a child bleeding to death in the rain.

But even through the ache of memory, he watched himself go by the book. Secure the gun. Then check on Will, calling for an ambulance as he ran, footsteps sliding and sloshing through the muck.

Jack's stomach did a hard lurch, then settled as he watched himself bend over Will. And as he hadn't been able to do then . . . he mourned the friend he'd lost that night.

The ambulance had been too late, of course. Will was gone. The boy died not long after.

The videotape recorded the wail of the ambulance, then the screen went dark and the VCR went into automatic rewind mode. He hardly noticed the hum of the machine as it reset the past to play again.

Jack's hands slowly unfisted. His stomach stopped churning. He'd finally faced the past—and in the truth, he'd found a hard-won peace.

Two days later, Carol slept late.

Sunlight streamed through her bedroom window and lay across the foot of the mattress in a dazzling slice of golden light. Outside the window, birds sang and children were laughing and squealing.

Exhaustion tugged at her and Carol smiled. Getting back into "mommy" routine was tough. But it was all worth it. Every tear, every ache, every joy, tangled up together in her heart, and they each centered on one tiny girl.

Lacey was packing for college, making plans with Peggy Reilly for a future that once again looked bright and full of promise. Adoption proceedings were already in the works and Lizardbaby was home, where she belonged.

"Speaking of whom," she said on a chuckle as she rolled off the bed. "I'm guessing you're pretty hungry by now, aren't you, Liz?" And Quinn's kidneys were probably ready to explode.

Carol leaned over the crib.

Empty.

She frowned, picked up the discarded baby blanket, the

one with the ducks, and ridiculously, looked under it. As if the baby were only playing hide-and-seek and would soon pop out and yell, "Surprise!"

"Okay, let's not get crazy," she whispered, trying to ignore the sudden shift in her heart rate from slow and lazy to a frantic bass drumbeat.

Mouth dry, Carol felt fear blossom in the pit of her stomach and reach out with long tentacles to every corner of her body.

Outside, children were playing, laughter sweetening the air. But inside, a child was missing and Carol heard only her own panic climbing up her throat. But she didn't surrender to it. Not yet. Instead, she kept looking in the crib, telling herself she must be dreaming. She'd put the baby to bed last night—with Quinn curled up right beneath the crib in his usual position.

Quinn.

Carol shot a glance and saw the dog was gone, too. She dropped to her knees, looked all the way under the crib, then under her own bed for good measure.

Nothing.

"I don't believe this," she muttered thickly, fear quickening inside her now and dancing to the frantic rhythm of her heart. "How do you lose a dog and a baby?"

She asked herself the question, but didn't have an answer. All she knew was the baby wasn't here. Her dog was gone. And the sunlight spearing through the bedroom window looked like the accusatory finger of fate reaching down from heaven to point at her.

"Jack," she told herself, grabbing up her short dark blue terry-cloth robe and yanking it on over her boxer shorts and tank top pajamas. "I'll get Jack. He's still the sheriff. He can help. God, what's going on? What's happening?"

She wheeled through the room, slamming her shin into the bed frame as she took the corner too sharply. Stars burst behind her eyes and she winced, but it wasn't that temporary pain that had tears filling her eyes again. Grabbing the doorknob, she rushed out through the hall and, barefoot, skidded to a stop in the living room.

It was freezing in there.

The air-conditioner was on full blast.

A roaring fire snapped and crackled in the hearth and the scent of cinnamon candles drifted through the room like a spicy cloud. Nat King Cole crooned from the stereo and in the far corner of the room stood a straggly pine tree adorned with strings of lights and shiny bulbs. Quinn, wearing a bright red ribbon tied to his collar, lay on the floor in front of the tree and looked, she thought, a little embarrassed.

Confusion rattled around inside her, leaving her knees weak and her spine tingling. Every nerve in her body sat straight up as Jack stepped out from behind the tree, Liz cradled in his arms.

Okay, the panic was gone. Even from across the room, she could see that Liz was fine, cooing happily in Jack's embrace. So . . . fear gone. Replaced by *confusion.*

"What's going on here?" she asked, tugging the edges of her robe closer together and tying the cloth belt tight at her waist.

"It's Christmas," he said, one corner of his mouth tilting into the half-smile that never failed to strike something warm and soft and delicious inside her.

Christmas. In August. "I don't understand." She shook her head, trying to take it all in, but failing. Her brain felt a little fuzzy from too much sleep and no caffeine.

Liz squirmed and twitched in Jack's grasp, her tiny fists batting at the air, her little legs kicking as though trying to ride a small, invisible bike. Carol, though, watched Jack, trying to read the expression in his eyes. Trying to figure out just what the heck he was up to.

"I told you," he said as he stepped to the window and swept the curtains aside. "It's Christmas. A real, old-fashioned, 'like an old movie' Christmas."

Her own words. She recognized them. She'd thrown them at him that night in the park. And now . . . *what?* She frowned, then shifted her gaze to the windows. It was snowing. Beyond the glass, dazzled by sunlight, snowflakes fell gently against the windowpane, collecting on the frame, building and then melting in the California summer sun.

"Snow?" Carol felt a rush of wonder as she hurried across the room. Standing beside Jack, she looked up at him for a long minute, and saw that his blue eyes were clear and focused and . . . *open.* There were no closed shutters, keeping his pain in and her out. There were no shadows in those shining blue eyes. No old pain haunting him. No secrets lurking.

Her heart tripped a little and she swallowed hard, not yet willing to believe the fluttery sense of expectation building inside her.

Shaking her head, Carol threw the window open, reached one hand outside and let the cold, delicate snowflakes dance on her open palm. Summer sunlight washed over her from a clear, crisp blue sky. Beneath her, her front yard was filled with snow and the kids from the neighborhood were making good use of it. A snowball war was in full force and a snow family stood proudly near the porch.

Summer and snow.

It was only then that she caught the underlying roar

of an engine at work. She leaned out and saw the snow-making machine parked in her driveway and watched as snow rocketed from the funnel and spilled into the hot, still air.

Her breath caught.

"You did this," she said, drawing back inside to stare up at him. His eyes danced with pleasure and that half-smile was still in place. He'd done all of this. For her. "Why?"

Liz gurgled and swung her fists again and Jack smiled down at her for a moment before lifting his gaze to Carol's again.

"For you," he said, reaching out one hand to stroke her cheek. "You said you'd always dreamed of a real Christmas. Well, here it is."

Soul-deep pleasure rocked Carol, weakening her knees and stirring her blood. She sucked in a gulp of air and briefly closed her eyes, savoring the sensation of being *this important* to someone. To *Jack*.

Yet, she needed to hear him say the words. To give voice to the promises she could nearly *see* in the air around them. "Why are you doing this?"

"Carol," he said, wondering now where his great speech had gone to. He'd been working on it for the last two days. He'd wanted everything to be perfect. He'd found the snowmaker and become a B and E man to get into her apartment and set things up. He'd kept Quinn quiet and endangered his life by tying that damn bow on the big dog's neck. He'd sneaked Liz out of her crib while Carol slept and then waited what seemed forever for her to wake up.

And now that she was here, in front of him, all he could do was look at her.

Her honey-blond hair was ruffled from bed and her big amber eyes shone with expectation. God, he prayed silently, don't let me screw this up this time.

"Yes?" she prompted, bringing him back to the matter of the now-missing speech.

"Right." Jack swallowed, then handed the baby to Carol. "Take Liz for a minute, will you?"

"Sure, but . . ."

"Just let me say this, okay?"

Outside, the kids were laughing, their high-pitched voices sailing through the room and rocketing around it like bullets ricocheting off cave walls. He didn't need the distraction. Slamming the window shut, he started talking, with Nat King Cole singing backup.

"You were right."

"Good start to any conversation." She smiled and tucked Liz's blanket a little more tightly around her thrashing legs.

He smiled quickly at the smart-ass remark, then realized she was just protecting herself. From him. He had to earn her trust. Earn the right to make promises to her. "When you said I'd been too busy punishing myself to actually *live,* you were right. I've been a pain in the ass for two solid years, Carol. I got used to it."

"Jack—"

She reached out one hand to him, but he shook his head, determined to say it all. To get it all out into the open where they could look at it, together.

"When you're an ass for that stretch of time, it gets to be second nature," he said and stalked past Quinn, ignoring the dog's curious whine. "You don't remember being any other way and maybe you don't *want* to remember." He whirled around and looked at her. "I didn't. It was easier to just crawl into that black hole and stay there narling and growling at anyone who got too close."

Carol inhaled slowly, deeply, then let the air slide rom her lungs. But she didn't interrupt and he was grate- ul. Damn, he wished he could remember the speech.

"When I came back here, to Christmas, I figured I'd e here a few weeks, then leave again. Hadn't planned n staying. Didn't figure I deserved to be here anymore."

"That's so dumb—"

He held up one hand and gave her a tight smile. "I elieve I already covered the 'pain in the ass' thing."

"Right." She sat down on the arm of the chair and ently rocked Liz. "Go on."

"Then I met you." He smiled again and shrugged elplessly. "It was over for me the minute I saw you."

"You hid it well."

"Yeah. I did." He stalked across the room and stopped n front of her. Taking hold of her upper arms, he drew her o her feet and looked down into her eyes, losing himself n the golden shine of them. "I didn't want to love you, arol. Thought I could get away clean and retreat to the hadows again."

"Love?" She squeezed that one word out, but it cost er. Tears she'd been holding inside escaped the corners f her eyes and trailed along her cheeks. "You *love* me?"

"I do. Jesus, I really do." He lifted one hand to skim he backs of his fingers across her cheek. "I love you so nuch it rattles me. You turned me inside out and side- vays, Carol. Made me want things I'd told myself I'd ever have again. Made me want *you* so bad I could ardly see straight. And you made me question every- hing I'd been telling myself for two years. You forced ne to remember what it was like to be really *alive* and to vant to feel that way again."

Carol's legs buckled, so she locked her knees to stay

upright. The scent of cinnamon was rich and full and she sucked it down deep inside her and stored it as a memory. Snow and Christmas trees and music and . . . Jack. Always, Jack. She kept her gaze locked with his and let herself believe.

"I watched the tape."

She frowned, confused. "What tape?"

"The tape of the shooting," he said. "It was in that box that was delivered to me."

"Oh, God, Jack . . ."

"It's okay," he said quickly, with a shake of his head. "I had to see the past, come to terms with it, before I could see a future."

"What did you see?" she asked, trying to keep a tight rein on the wild surge of hope and expectation that built steadily inside her.

"That it wasn't my fault," he said simply. "It just happened. It was a tragedy, but it wasn't my fault."

"I'm so glad, Jack." She stared up into his eyes and felt a jolt of surprise as she read peace in those shady blue depths. He wasn't haunted anymore. He'd found his way out of the darkness and then he'd come to her.

"I straightened out a few other things, too," he was saying, and Carol told herself to pay attention. "Went to see Ed Thompson."

"The sheriff?"

"Not anymore," Jack said and lifted one shoulder in a shrug. "I'm the new sheriff. Recommended by Ed and duly appointed by the city council."

"Permanently?"

"Well, until the next election," he admitted. "I hear Ken Slater's thinking about running for sheriff next time."

"He'll never beat you."

"That's what I think."

He grinned at her and the full power of that smile slammed into her with the force of a line drive hardball to the stomach.

"There's more," he added while Carol's head was still spinning.

"What's left?" It was all so good. So wonderful. Her heartbeat was doing a fast two-step and even her blood felt as though it was dancing through her veins.

"I went and talked to Lacey."

She took a breath and held it. "About what?"

"She handpicked you to be her daughter's mother," Jack said, his voice a low rumble of sound that sidled up and down her spine like goose bumps. "I wanted to see if she had a problem with me being Lizardbaby's father."

"Oh, Jack." Carol lifted one hand to her mouth and stared at him. He was all blurry, though, so she blinked and cleared the tears away to see him better.

"I want us to be a family, Carol. The four of us. And however many more we have."

"I—"

"Before you say anything—I'm not saying I'll never be a pain in the ass again," he warned her, "but I figure you know how to handle that."

She laughed. "I do."

"Remember those words," he said, grinning now. "Mostly though, I want you to know that I will love you forever. And I'll spend the rest of my life making sure you're not sorry about loving me."

"Oh, God." Carol stood up, suddenly unable to sit still. She clutched Liz to her like a life preserver and looked up at the man who had changed so much in her life.

He dipped into his jeans pocket and drew out a small red velvet box.

"Jack—" Carol held her breath and looked from the closed box to his gaze.

"Marry me, Carol," he said and opened the box to display an antique ring—a ruby center with a spray of diamonds surrounding it. "Build a family with me. Build a future—for all of us."

Staring up into those blue eyes that had devastated her from the very first, she knew she'd finally found the love, the life, the home she'd always dreamed of. She swallowed hard and said, "You know, when I first brought Liz home—when I first rented the apartment to you . . . I was sure it was all some kind of mistake."

"And now?"

"Now . . ." Carol smiled and felt her heart actually lift in her chest. "Now, I'm sure it's all some kind of wonderful."

He blew out a breath. "So that's a yes?"

"I do love you," she said, hearing her voice break slightly with the weight of emotion pressing down on her. "And I will marry you—"

He grinned and reached for her.

She held up one hand.

"On one condition."

"Name it."

"We go downstairs and you build Liz and me a snowman."

"You've got a deal, lady." He grabbed her close, wrapped his arms around both her and Lizardbaby, and then dipped his head for a kiss that tasted of promises.

And that year, for Carol, Christmas came in August.